00 400 943 746

The Battered Body

A SUPPER CLUB MYSTERY

The Battered Body

J. B. Stanley

WHEELER
CHIVERS

This Large Print edition is published by Wheeler Publishing, Waterville, Maine, USA and by BBC Audiobooks Ltd, Bath, England.
Wheeler Publishing, a part of Gale, Cengage Learning.

The text of this Large Print edition is unabridged.
Other aspects of the book may vary from the original edition.
Set in 16 pt. Plantin.
Printed on permanent paper.

LIBRARY OF CONGRESS CATALOGING-IN-PUBLICATION DATA

Stanley, J. B.
The battered body : a supper club mystery / by J. B. Stanley.
p. cm. — (Wheeler Publishing large print cozy mystery)
ISBN-13: 978-1-59722-997-5 (pbk. : alk. paper)
ISBN-10: 1-59722-997-0 (pbk. : alk. paper)
1. Cookery—Fiction. 2. Large type books. I. Title.
PS3619.T3655B38 2009b
813'.6—dc22 2009010059

BRITISH LIBRARY CATALOGUING-IN-PUBLICATION DATA AVAILABLE

Published in 2009 in the U.S. by arrangement with Midnight Ink, an imprint of Llewellyn Publications, Woodbury, MN 55125, USA.
Published in 2009 in the U.K. by arrangement with Llewellyn Worldwide Ltd.

U.K. Hardcover: 978 1 408 45656 9 (Chivers Large Print)
U.K. Softcover: 978 1 408 45657 6 (Camden Large Print)

Printed in the United States of America
1 2 3 4 5 6 7 13 12 11 10 09

To Owen and Sophie
I love you more than cupcakes

“The most dangerous food is wedding cake.”

— James Thurber

One: Chocolate Angel Food Cake

"It's how much?" Librarian James Henry turned pale as he glanced back at the real estate listing on his lap.

The real estate agent, a prim blonde with purple-tinted lipstick and calculating blue eyes, reached over her polished mahogany desk and removed the listing from her client's soft lap. "I'm sorry," she smiled icily. "I'm sure we can find you something in your price range that would suit you just perfectly." She uncapped a ballpoint pen and held it poised over a blank sheet of paper. "What would you say your price range *is*, Mr. Henry?"

"About half of that one." James gestured at the listing that his Realtor was tucking into a blue folder, and his eyes slid toward the shiny brass plaque on her desk. Apparently, Joan Beechnut had been the area's leader in home sales for the last three years.

Seeing that her client had noticed her laurels, Joan smiled proudly, revealing small, ferretlike teeth coated by a thin line of purple.

"I'm planning to win again this year," she stated haughtily, and then she began flipping through her binder of house listings. "It's too bad you didn't call me earlier in the fall," she chided him as her fingers raked through listing after listing. "If you had, you would have had so much more to choose from. As it stands, well, *most* folks don't put their houses up for sale right after Thanksgiving. They've got Christmas shopping on their minds and no one likes to move over the holidays."

"Well, *I* have to," James replied rather testily. "My father is getting married on Christmas Eve, and I'm sure Pa would rather not carry his new bride over the threshold only to remember that his adult son is sleeping in the bedroom down the hall."

Joan's brown eyes, hidden beneath an expensive pair of aquamarine contacts, twinkled at the thought of some interesting gossip. "A second marriage, eh? Did your parents get divorced?"

"My mother died a few years ago," James stated flatly. "That's how I ended up as Shenandoah's head librarian. I used to be a professor at William & Mary. That's why lots of folks in Quincy's Gap call me Professor," he added with pride.

Blue Ridge Realty wasn't in James's hometown of Quincy's Gap, however, and Joan was unimpressed by James's title. "And what about you?" She gestured at his left hand. "No wedding ring, I see? Will you be living all alone in the three-bedroom, two-bathroom house you'd like to purchase?"

James squirmed in his chair. He didn't appreciate the "all" Joan had placed before the "alone" for emphasis. "Yes, it'll just be me."

Joan flipped through more listings. "No pets?"

"No."

"Hmm, then you don't need a big yard." She turned back several pages.

"But I like to garden," James piped up before the Realtor restricted him to a yard that could be mowed with a pair of barber's clippers. "In fact, I'd like an excuse to buy a riding mower, and if the house had a deck or a patio, that would be great too. Decks are perfect for growing tomatoes."

"Tomatoes, huh?" Joan stared at James for a moment and then removed a listing from the binder and placed it in front of him with a flourish.

James gazed at the image of a sad-looking ranch with a flat and treeless expanse of front lawn. Even though the photo was black and white, James could see that the roof was stained, the front stoop appeared to be sagging, and chips of paint the size of dinner plates were missing from the wooden siding.

"It's a perfect fixer-upper for a handy guy," Joan said enthusiastically, as though the house were a valuable gemstone that only required some simple polishing in order to make it sparkle. "A new coat of paint, a bush planted here and there, and you're good to go."

"And a new roof, replaced stoop, and who knows what else inside." James handed the listing back to her. "And I'm rather a novice with power tools, so I'd prefer not to buy something that needs this kind of overhaul."

Shoving the rejected home back into the binder, Joan laced her fingers together and leaned forward on her desk. "You know, I have some lovely apartment rentals over at Mountain Valley Woods. They're just starting to lease Building F. Why don't I take you to view a few of them? You could move into a brand new two-bedroom apartment and relax while waiting for the perfect house to come onto the market."

James thought about the idea of living in Building F of Mountain Valley Woods. He could easily visualize the crisp, white walls, pristine carpeting, and sparkling kitchen. He could also imagine the lifelessness of such a dwelling. Even if he filled it with his books and bought some prints to hang on the unscathed walls, he knew that an apartment would never feel like home. Even the decrepit ranch Joan had shown him had more character than four square rooms that had never witnessed a moment of human history. Besides, how could he possibly live in a place with the ridiculous title of Mountain Valley Woods? It was as if the developers strung together every geographic noun they could think of to use as the complex's name.

All they needed was to add River, Brook, or Stream and they'd have listed all the things on a Shenandoah County map, James thought with a wry grin, and he stood. "I've got some time, Ms. Beechnut, so I'd rather keep looking at houses, if that's okay. But right now, I've got to get back to work."

Doing her best to disguise her frown, Joan rose as well and vigorously pumped James's hand in farewell. "Don't worry, we'll find you something. But even if the perfect house just fell into my lap today, it would take at least thirty days to close, so you may want to go ahead and make plans to stay someplace *else* on your father's wedding night."

Ruffled by the smirk in her voice, James pivoted. "I've got friends who will put me up as long as I need," he declared with feeling.

"Well, those must be some nice friends," Joan replied and closed the door to her office.

"They're the best," James mumbled happily to himself as he got into his old Bronco and headed back to work.

At the library, James realized that he had used his entire lunch hour at the Realtor's and hadn't had the chance to eat anything. He dug through the staff fridge for any enticing leftovers, but was disappointed to find only an assortment of condiments and a piece of string cheese that had turned hard enough to double as a cudgel.

"I come bearing dessert." Scott Fitzgerald, one of the twenty-four-year-old twin brothers who formed James's full-time staff, breezed into the kitchen. He dumped a covered cake plate onto the counter, shoved a wave of his unkempt hair behind his ear, and removed the Tupperware lid with a flourish. "Yum, yum! It's Mrs. Hurley's famous chocolate angel food cake. She brought it in 'cause Francis and I helped her design and print out her own Christmas cards using our computers. She told us we were magicians and that she was going to make us a dessert every week 'til Christmas." He smiled. "We've got the best job, Professor."

"Yes, we do, Scott." Saliva leapt into James's mouth as he inhaled the rich scent of buttery chocolate. "Oh my, I think it's still warm."

"Yep." Scott reached for a knife and two paper plates. "She said she just took it out of the oven, strapped it to the back of her bike, and headed over here. That's the kind of woman I'd like to marry someday, Professor." He cut an enormous slice of cake, slapped it onto his plate, and handed the knife to his boss. "Of course, the future Mrs. Fitzgerald also has to have a fine appreciation of sci-fi and fantasy, video games, and the Discovery Channel." Scott's front teeth sunk into the moist cake. He chewed and swallowed as rapidly as a rabbit munching on a lettuce leaf.

Eyeing Scott's lanky frame, James cut a marginally smaller piece of cake for himself. "What I'd give for your metabolism," he muttered to Scott. "Enjoy it while you can."

"No problem, Professor," Scott said dutifully as he washed down his cake with a swig of Mountain Dew. "I ate a double-decker bacon-ranch cheeseburger for lunch, and it barely made a dent. I totally should have super-sized the whole meal." He glanced toward the door of the break room. "Uh-oh, Francis isn't looking happy out there. I'd better see what's up." Scott hurriedly wiped his mouth with a paper towel and dashed out of the break room and around the circulation desk.

James cut himself another piece of cake as he watched Francis grab his brother's slim arm and gesticulate toward the Children's Corner. Assuming that Francis had merely found a glitch involving the craft he had planned for the kindergarten class that was scheduled to arrive any moment, James finished the cake in a leisurely fashion. The twins were more than capable of handling twenty-four energetic five-year-olds.

Licking the last crumbs from his plastic fork, he washed the cake knife and pondered over whether to brew a fresh pot of coffee.

At that moment, however, a patron approached the circulation desk with a tower of hardcover romance novels, and James hustled from the break room to check out her books and pack them neatly in her deep-red *Friends of the Shenandoah County Library* tote bag.

"I gotta do *somethin'* to keep warm over the winter months," the elderly woman told him with a sly grin. "Some steamy books, a plate of cookies, and a tumbler of whiskey. That's the trick to survivin' the long, cold nights when you live by yourself."

Watching the old woman shuffle away, James wondered about his own plans for the winter months. First and foremost, he wanted to buy a house. Secondly, he had to figure out the details of Jackson and Milla's wedding gift. He knew that he wanted to treat them to a wonderful honeymoon, and since they didn't want to leave until after the New Year, James had four weeks to come up with the perfect trip. And just as soon as his father's wedding was over and the newlyweds were out of town, James wanted nothing more than to focus his attention on rekindling a romantic relationship with

Sheriff's Deputy Lucy Hanover.

"Professor!" Francis approached the desk wearing a worried frown and carrying a basket brimming with cotton balls. "He's gone! Glowstar's gone!"

Searching his memory bank for the name Glowstar, James came up blank. "Who?"

"Our elf," Francis answered impatiently. "The Elf on the Shelf? You know, the stuffed elf we take out every year who *magically moves around the library and watches the kids to make sure they're good.*"

"Right!" James remembered and grinned. "And he reports their behavior to Santa Claus after every library visit. I hadn't realized his name was Glowstar."

Francis's frown deepened. "This is serious, Professor. The younger kids always get pretty wild this close to Christmas vacation, and Glowstar's the only way we've been able to keep them in line. The whole 'You better watch out' chorus Scott and I like to sing has lost its power without that elf." Francis cast a frantic look over his shoulder. "For example, I've got twenty-four kindergartners back there that are supposed to be gluing cotton balls together to make Santa's beard. Instead, they're gluing them to their fingers, the chairs, the carpet, their friends' hair . . ."

"Oh." James could see that this was no laughing matter. He hated when the library became untidy. "You're not using glitter with this project, I hope."

Francis glanced away. "Um, it's supposed to create 'the twinkle' in Santa's eye."

James walked around the circulation desk. "And what is it being used for in lieu of an eye twinkle, may I ask?"

"Uh," Francis removed his glasses and began rubbing them vigorously on his plaid shirt. "Well, one kid has doused his side of the table with a magical silver snowfall, and now there's glitter everywhere *but* on Santa's face."

"We need to distract them before things get any worse." James took Francis by the elbow. "Announce a reward. The first kid to clean up his or her space will be given the opportunity to find Glowstar and win a prize for spotting his whereabouts. I'm sure the elf's just hiding in the stacks somewhere."

"And their reward?" Francis inquired. "They're going to need motivation, Professor. These twenty-first-century kids don't lift a finger without the promise of instant gratification, so I'll need to tell them ahead of time what to expect."

James's gaze swept around the library. All

he had were bookmarks and tote bags. He doubted the average five-year-old would work too hard for literary paraphernalia. "I bought a box of candy canes at Food Lion," he mused aloud. "I was going to put them out on the circulation desk for our patrons to take as they exited. Do you think that'll work as a motivator?"

"Absolutely!" Francis quickly nodded. "I think our entire educational system would grind to a halt without candy, Professor. Kids will do anything for sugar. I'll go make the announcement before all the picture books are covered with glue and glitter."

As Francis jogged back to the chaotic Children's Corner, James decided to empty the reshelving cart while conducting his own search for Glowstar. By the time the cart was empty, a gang of mischievous kindergartners had pulled books from a dozen lower shelves. The kids discovered dust bunnies, old Band-Aids, and a few pieces of hardened chewing gum, but there was no trace of a six-inch elf dressed in red and green felt.

An hour later, the twins had finally finished picking up the trails of sticky cotton balls and vacuuming up most of the silver glitter from the carpet. James was just replacing the last stray — a picture book entitled *Everybody Poops,* which was one of the library's most popular titles and *not* just with the juvenile crowd — when Bennett Marshall walked in.

"What are you doing here?" James asked his friend. "This isn't your regular route."

Bennett reached into his mail satchel and withdrew a thick pile of letters and catalogues held together by a rubber band. "Larry got bit by a dog this morning. I'm helpin' out with his route, because the United States Postal Service doesn't care what kind of evil canines are runnin' loose in this world. The mail must be delivered, come rain, snow, hurricane-force winds, or rabid, wild-eyed, furry hounds of hell."

"Larry's never mentioned any threatening dogs on his route," James said, gesturing for Bennett to follow him into the break room.

"That's 'cause there aren't any. He's got the cushiest route in the whole valley. At least as far as dogs go. Nah, he was bit takin' his cat to the vet this mornin'. Apparently that crazy feline decided to try to ride a pit bull like it was in some kind of kitty rodeo. Larry was attacked while pryin' his cat off the back of one mighty irritated young dog. That pup had just gotten a whole mess of shots and was in a foul mood before Larry's cat treated him like a pincushion." Bennett smirked. "Guess animals get just as agitated as we do about visitin' the doctor."

James laughed. "And they don't get lollipops either. Doc Spratt has given me a green lollipop ever since I can remember. Would you like some chocolate angel food cake while you're here? It's homemade."

Bennett cast a longing glance at the cake and then shook his head. "Can't do it, man. I got some bad news when I was at the doc's office last week. Shoot, *I* felt like bitin' somebody on my way out of there."

Concerned, James closed the break room door and motioned at the table. "Sit down and tell me what's going on."

"Nothin' major, my man. I don't have cancer or anythin' that should be puttin' that long look on your face." Bennett pointed at the cake. "I just gotta keep an eye on my sugars. Seems like bein' over forty comes with a whole mess of possible ails, and it would appear as though I've got one of them."

"Which one?"

Bennett formed quotation marks with the first two fingers of his hands. "Mature onset diabetes." He dropped his hands. "But I don't need any pills or anything yet. I can control this thing by gettin' back into the gym and watchin' what I eat. And truth be told, James, I've only been *watchin'* the food as it leaves my plate and is shoveled into my mouth. Ever since we got back from the barbecue contest this summer, I've been indulgin' way too much."

Relieved to hear that his friend wasn't seriously ill, James scooped some grounds into the coffee machine and pushed the brew button. "I know what you mean. I tried on the suit I'm planning to wear to my father's wedding, and I look like a big, gray whale. I'd better hope there's no fog out that night or someone might harpoon me."

Bennett threw his head back and laughed. "My friend, you always know how to cheer me up." He shifted to one hip and removed his wallet from his back pocket. "Take this," he said, handing James a business card. "She's my nutritionist. I'm meetin' with her once a week until I get on track. My doc recommended her, and man, I did not want to go see her one bit, but she's just as nice as she can be."

"Ruth Wilkins, huh?" James put down the card and poured coffees for them both. "And what does she advise you to do?"

"Keep a journal of everythin' I'm eatin' and what kind of exercise I'm doin'." Bennett took a sip of coffee. "See? I'm gonna have to write this down now."

James grimaced. "Sounds like a hassle."

"Maybe." Bennett shrugged. "But I've only got one body. I gotta start takin' care of it."

"Well, I'm good at making lists, so I guess keeping a food log isn't too different. Though my to-do list is getting as long as Santa's these days."

Bennett took his coffee cup to the sink and began to rinse it out. "What's on it?"

James ticked the items off on his fingers. "Find an amazing honeymoon trip for Milla and my father, buy a house, locate Glowstar — our Christmas elf who's gone missing — and make an appointment with your nutritionist so I can fit into my suit."

Chuckling, Bennett began digging around in his mailbag. "Oh, you've got one more thing to put on that list, my friend."

"That's true," James answered, surprised that Bennett was aware that the most important item hadn't been mentioned aloud. "I want to take Lucy out for a truly memorable date. I want to prove to her that I never stopped caring about her, even though I was dating Murphy over the summer."

"Murphy is the other item *I* was going to add to your list," Bennett grunted unhappily. "Murphy Alistair. Editor of the *Shenandoah Star Ledger* and soon-to-be the destroyer of life as we know it." He unfolded a glossy postcard and held it out to James with a flourish. "Read it and weep, my friend. Then go to your calendar and circle January first, because that's the day your ex-girlfriend's *fictional* account about *our* lives hits the shelves. Put that on your list so you can flee town with the rest of us."

James paled. "It wasn't supposed to be released until February." He unfolded the postcard and gazed at the colorful graphics with horror. "Oh, Lord," he muttered miserably.

"Yessir. Unhappy New Year to us all. At least you've got that chocolate cake to comfort you." Bennett clapped him on the back and then slipped on his coat. "You'd better take Lucy out on that date before Murphy's book comes out. After all, now that she carries a service revolver *and* a nightstick, I'd be mighty nervous about bein' near her when she gets her hands on a copy of that novel." Bennett zipped his coat. "Shoot, we may just have another murder on our hands."

"Don't even joke about that!" James called out as Bennett disappeared through the break room door. Returning his attention to the postcard, his eyes soaked in the image of Murphy's book cover and he shook his head in disgust. It showed the interior of a bakery, with shelf after shelf overflowing with plump croissants, golden loaves of bread, and delectable pies, tarts, and cakes. Splayed out on the black and white tiled floor was the body of a man wearing a varsity letter jacket. The man was facedown and his features were disguised by locks of curly golden hair, but a pool of blood had spread out beneath his head and shoulders and had formed a small stream that ran to the very edge of the postcard.

"Oh, brother," James mumbled crossly as his eyes traveled away from the dead man to the pair of women standing above him. They both wore tight, starched, white aprons bearing the word *Cravings* in crimson cursive across the chest and were clutching one another in fear. One of the women was older and James assumed that she was meant to represent Megan Flowers, the owner of the Sweet Tooth, the bakery beloved by all in Quincy's Gap. The younger woman with the inflated bosom and shapely legs was undoubtedly meant to be Megan's teenage daughter, Amelia.

"I don't think Megan's going to like that image of Amelia," James said aloud. "And they're wearing an awful lot of makeup for two people who got up at three a.m. and spent the morning covered in flour and sugar."

Flipping over the card in annoyance, James read the blurb on the back.

Small towns are full of secrets, and Quimby's Pass is no exception. It seems that the isolated highlands of Virginia are not as bucolic as its residents believe, and when a former high school football hero is fatally poisoned, neighbor will turn against neighbor in search of justice. When the authorities are stumped by the killer's cold trail, the true heroes of the *The Body in the Bakery* arise. These average citizens — a librarian, a teacher, a mailman, a secretary, and a dog groomer — join together in an attempt to solve the murder. Can they stop the ruthless killer in time, or will another corpse show up somewhere on Main Street? Based on an astonishing true story.

Publishers Weekly calls *The Body in the Bakery* "the first must-read book of the New Year," and Kirkus hails it as "a fast-paced thriller that unveils the chilly truth not only about Quimby's Pass, but about the deceptions lurking beneath the surface in small towns throughout

America. A fantastic read."

The Body in the Bakery by Murphy Alistair. **Pre-order your copy today!**

James reread the blurb and then examined the graphic on the front one more time before tossing the postcard in the garbage.

He stomped into his office and gathered his briefcase and coat. He bid a terse farewell to the twins and paused in the lobby to slip into his wool coat. As he was fastening the buttons, Bennett reappeared from inside the library, brandishing two audio books.

"Uh-oh. You're wearin' a scowl deep as a dried river bed," Bennett remarked.

"You can't be surprised," James replied curtly, jerking his gloves onto his fingers. "Where did you get that postcard anyway?"

"A man on my route tossed it into his recycling basket and the picture caught my eye. That card went to everyone in town, James. You've probably got one in your mailbox right this very minute."

"And that means Lindy and Gillian and Lucy do too."

Bennett nodded unhappily. "I'm afraid so."

James wound his plaid scarf around his neck three times and then squared his shoulders. "I'm just not ready for this book to come out, Bennett. I have so many other things on my plate right now."

"Well, you'd better move that date with Lucy to the top of your list. In fact, I think you should run right over to the Sheriff's Department, pick her up, and take her out for some fancy, candlelit dinner. Maybe you can get that postcard outta her mailbox on the sly."

Taking his keys from his right coat pocket, James looked at Bennett in confusion. "How much harm could a postcard do? It's not like it says anything about us. I'm more concerned about what's in the actual book."

"It's your call," Bennett said, opening the door. A blast of December air caused them both to hesitate before stepping outside. "But I'm tellin' you, man. Lucy is going to be mighty sore that Murphy called her a secretary."

James groaned. "You're right, she's going to hate that. And somehow, I feel like she's going to blame me for everything."

"Well, you did get in bed with the enemy." Bennett nudged James with his elbow. "No pun intended."

"Thanks a lot, Bennett." James gave his friend a harmless shove. "You go on ahead. I forgot something inside."

"A book?" Bennett asked as he opened the door to his mail truck, revealing plastic bins filled with tidy rows of letters and catalogues.

"No," James answered. "I'm going back in for the rest of that cake." As he turned toward the library's familiar warmth, James eyed the Santa cutout Francis had taped to the front door. He studied the cheery man's soft paunch and round cheeks. Seeing that his own reflection in the glass door bore a resemblance to St. Nick's physique, James frowned and grumbled, "Bah, humbug."

Two: Blueberry Candy Cane

James entered through the back door of his childhood home and, as he closed the door behind him, felt a whoosh of air next to his left ear as a magazine smacked against the wall.

"Watch it, Pop!" James instinctively ducked in case his father was prepared to lodge another missile his way.

"Sorry 'bout that. Didn't realize it was near time for you to be comin' through that door," Jackson muttered darkly from his seat at the kitchen table. "But if I gotta look at one more flower arrangement or answer one more question about menus, tablecloths, dance music, or church programs, then Milla's just gonna have to get married all by herself!"

After picking up the magazine from the floor, James set it on the table, smoothed the wrinkled cover, and sat down across from his father. "You don't mean that, Pop. You love Milla." He offered Jackson a sympathetic smile. "But I can see why you'd rather not spend your time reading this stuff."

Jackson grunted and gestured at piles of colorful clippings illustrating wedding cakes, floral centerpieces, tuxedos, stationery, and limousines. "When your mama and I got married, we met some folks down at the church, said a word or two, and then had a little lunch back here at the house. Sandwiches and tea and beer. I wore my best suit and your mama wore a dress she borrowed from her best friend. Whole thing cost us about three hundred dollars." He pushed the clippings away. "I still remember every second of that day. It didn't cost much but it was real nice. It was simple and to the point and, well, pretty damned perfect."

James nodded. "I can imagine how overwhelming all of these choices must be. Have you talked to Milla about why she wants so many . . . trimmings?"

"Guess her first wedding was one of those courthouse deals. Her man was being sent overseas for some kind of military training and it's all they had time for. So now she wants the church, the party, a fancy white dress. All of it."

"Are you worried about the cost?" James asked gently.

"Pffft, no!" Jackson waved off the suggestion. "I'd buy that woman whatever she wanted, but I think it's right foolish to spend such a pile one day outta our lives. At our age and all — to be gettin' trussed up like a pair of Thanksgivin' turkeys. Never mind dancin' or ridin' in cars that can seat twenty and have television sets inside. It feels downright ridiculous."

Part of James agreed with his father, but he knew better than to take sides between a couple planning their wedding.

At that moment, the bride-to-be walked through the door, her arms laden with grocery bags. James rushed forward to relieve Milla of two of the four paper sacks she carried.

"Hello, boys!" she trilled merrily. Her cheeks were flushed with the cold and her eyes glittered with their customary animation. "I am *so* delighted. I found the most beautiful lamb chops when I was Christmas shopping in Harrisonburg today. You two are going to eat like kings this evening!" She plopped the bags on the granite countertop, placed some milk and eggs in the fridge, and then swung around. Observing the downcast eyes of her fiancé and the manner in which James averted his glance, she asked, "Why the long faces?"

Jackson turned to his son with a rare look of appeal. James mouthed a silent "no way," but Milla was too sharp not to notice. Pointing at the magazine photos, she took a step toward Jackson. "All right, now. 'Fess up. You're squirmin' like a mouse in a python's grip with all these wedding decisions, aren't you?"

"Well . . . ," Jackson began and then trailed off.

"Pop's not stressed about the actual ceremony, Milla," James said, still hesitant to intervene. "I think all the choices and, I don't know, modern wedding *extras* are making him feel a tad overwhelmed."

"Thank you, James," Milla replied kindly, and then she picked up Jackson's hand. "Darling, we don't need to have anything fancy. I just want our wedding to be beautiful. I'd like some greenery in the church and a nice dinner with champagne for our friends afterwards. And I'd like to have you hold me in your arms for one slow dance. That's all."

The couple exchanged affectionate smiles. "When you put it like that, it seems an easier beast to tame. But Milla, I gotta take a break from lookin' at these crazy bride magazines." Jackson stood and placed the entire pile into one of the emptied food bags. "It feels downright girlie for a grown man to be readin' about fluff and frills. Besides, I can't even remember the last time I read the paper from end to end or watched a solid hour of game shows on TV."

"Oh, my." Milla's shoulders shook with laughter. "I vow to never keep you from *The Price is Right* again, my love." She began to put away the rest of the groceries. "And we don't need to worry about the cake anymore anyway. My little sister is coming into town this weekend and she's going to bake it for us. She also offered to bake the dinner rolls for our main meal and create a gorgeous dessert bar for our friends. Isn't that good news?"

"Your sister? The famous one?" Jackson was clearly surprised. "I thought you two got along 'bout as well as wolves and sheep."

"We're not *that* bad!" Milla chuckled as

she pulled a large mixing bowl from inside one of the lower cabinets. "I just don't get her and she doesn't get me, but we don't hate each other. We're different creatures, that's all. Now, Wheezie, my older sister, can't even breathe the same air as Patty. I don't think those two have spoken a civil word in twenty years, but that's not a tale to be told when I need to busy myself makin' my men some succulent chops." She added a few pinches of herbs to the heaping tablespoons of Dijon mustard settled at the bottom of the mixing bowl.

"Wheezie's an interesting name," James remarked.

"It's really Louisa, but I called her Wheezie when I was a toddler and it just stuck. Oh! And speaking of names, I've got to remember that I'm not supposed to call my baby sister Patty anymore. It's Paulette Martine now. The Diva of Dough."

"Seriously?" James asked incredulously. "Even *I* know who that is." He poured himself a glass of water and studied Milla's familiar features. "We don't have a single culinary magazine in the library that hasn't run an article on her this year. And she wrote that cake book too, right? The one all the moms and church ladies check out so they can out-bake their friends?"

Milla spread the mustard mixture onto the surface of the lamb chops. "*The Diva of All Cake Books.* I believe it's sold a million copies by now. Patty's been quite successful," she added, but James thought he caught a trace of ire in Milla's voice. "And you can stop studying me, James. I don't look a lick like her. Never did. Wheezie and I take after our mama, but the 'Diva' always favored Daddy's side of the family."

Jackson looked troubled. Without a word, he set off for the den and James suspected he was in search of a bottle of Cutty Sark. A few minutes later, he could see that his assumption was correct. Jackson set a tumbler on the kitchen table and resumed his seat.

"Oh boy." Milla set the oven to heat and then put her hands on her hips. "*Now* what's eating at you, Jackson? Is it Patty?"

"Call me a fool if you want, but ain't your famous, jet-settin' sister gonna find our little country town mighty dull?" And beneath his breath his muttered, "And the man you're gonna get hitched to?"

"But Quincy's Gap is absolutely charming!" Milla declared defensively. "And Pat-Paulette said she's looking forward to some time away from her busy celebrity life. She says she gets no privacy and is looking forward to slowin' down some." Milla retrieved a plump tomato and a small cucumber from the fridge, wiped her hands on the dishtowel, and then knelt down beside Jackson. Taking his hands in hers, she looked up at him with one of her illuminating smiles. "This is my chance to reconnect with my sister, dear, and that means so much to me. We're not getting any younger and our time on this earth is best spent with those we love. If you and James and I all welcome my sister with open arms, I know she'll come to adore our town and the man I chose to marry." She turned moist eyes upon James. "Will you both help me to make her feel at home?"

"Of course," James responded on behalf of himself and his father.

Satisfied, Milla commenced chopping the cucumber at breakneck speed into paper-thin slices. James never grew tired of watching her work her magic in the kitchen. He had first met her when he and the other supper club members had enrolled in one of her cooking classes and had been impressed with her ability to teach others some of the tricks of her trade, but he never imagined that Jackson would fall in love with her. James was thrilled that his father had someone in his life, for Jackson had inched out of his shell more and more with each day spent in Milla's company. The only negative about his father's engagement was that Milla cooked for the Henry men every night and James had had a difficult time exercising away the results of Milla's rich meals. Rubbing a hand across his soft belly, he resolved to be stricter with his diet once he lived on his own.

"James?" Milla glanced up briefly as she made a quick salad dressing using tomato juice, balsamic vinegar, an envelope of Italian salad dressing mix, and a spoonful of sugar. "I wanted to ask you for a big favor."

"There's no sayin' no to a bride-to-be." Jackson smirked and took a sip of Cutty Sark.

James ignored his father. "Sure, Milla. What is it?"

"Would you mind picking up Paulette from the airport this Saturday? Jackson and I have some wedding errands to run, and we've got to buy more canvases too. His paintings are simply *flying* out of that D.C. gallery." She rubbed Jackson affectionately on the shoulder.

"I'm happy to help," James answered.

Milla rubbed a cucumber slice between her fingertips. "There's just one catch about this favor. Actually, two catches."

James raised his eyebrows. "And they are?"

"My sister would only fly to Dulles so your trip is going to take half the day, what with going there and back. The other issue is that . . ." Milla wound the dishtowel around her hand as she tried to find the right words. "Paulette can be a tad prickly, especially around strangers."

"Imagine that, bein' that she calls herself a diva and all," Jackson grumbled.

"She could always rent a car if you're busy," Milla hurriedly backtracked. "It's just that it would be awfully expensive from Dulles to my house and she's already incurring enough expense to fly here and make all this food for us. I'd at least like her to be driven by a friendly, trustworthy, and kind-hearted person. No one fits that description better than you, my dear."

As Milla spoke, Jackson began to sort through the mail. James could see the familiar graphics of the postcard announcing Murphy's book peeking out from beneath Jackson's *Reader's Digest.*

Lunging forward, James snatched up the postcard, stuffed it into the pocket of his pants, and, imbalanced, fell against Milla with his arms outstretched. He turned the awkward movement into a hug and announced, "I'd do anything for you, Milla."

"Thank you, James." She squeezed him gratefully. "Her flight comes in at ten, so running to the airport won't interfere with the Christmas Cavalcade. I know you and your friends have plans to watch it Saturday night. I've gotten too old to stand out in the cold, even though I love all those lights and how excited the kids get." Milla pushed gently on James's arms. "Now let go of me, honey, so I can get those chops into the oven."

As he climbed the stairs to change from his work khakis into jeans, James heard Milla say, "Jackson, I just love that boy of yours."

"He's all right most of the time," Jackson huffed. "But now he's gone and crumpled both my *Reader's Digest* and my *Star Ledger.*"

Shaking his head at his father's customary gruffness, James continued down the hall to the room he had occupied since the day his parents had brought him home from the hospital. Kicking his shoes off, he laid back on his bed and picked up *Pillars of the Earth,* a book he made a point of rereading every five years or so. Before he could get too absorbed in Follett's prose, he heard Jackson roughly shake a newspaper page and exclaim, "Look here, Milla! If my eyes are workin' right, James's ole girlfriend has gone and written a book about our town. And it's one of them murder mysteries. Look at this mess of blood on the cover."

James covered his face with Follett's novel, hoping to block the image of Murphy's book cover.

"Oh, dear!" Milla stated woefully after a few moments of silence. "It says in this article that one of the characters is an intelligent, overweight librarian. I sure hope that librarian isn't our own sweet James."

"I bet it is. That boy attracts trouble like a bear to a honeycomb." Jackson shook his head. "Too bad *he* can't sleep away the winter. He might have finally found a book that he'll wanna ban from his library."

James woke up at seven o'clock Saturday morning and stumbled downstairs for some coffee. Jackson had already consumed half the pot and was most likely out in his shed, working on a new painting. He would expect breakfast before James departed for the airport, but luckily Milla had a sausage and cheese casserole in the freezer that only required defrosting. After turning the oven on, James finished his first cup of coffee, took a warm shower, and dressed in a gray wool sweater and a pair of jeans. He then threw on his coat and walked out to the shed, his breath puffing from his mouth like smoke from a steam engine.

"I'm coming in!" James shouted as he knocked twice on the shed door. He opened it just in time to see Jackson throw a drop cloth over his latest work.

"Isn't that going to smudge the paint?" James asked in concern.

Jackson waved a dry brush near James's face. "Ain't no paint on there yet."

"Well, come on in and get some breakfast casserole. That'll get your creative juices flowing."

Jackson frowned. "My juices are just fine. I decided that I'm gonna paint Milla's sister. Only problem is I don't know what a diva's hands look like close up, so I gotta wait to see her in the flesh, while she's makin' one of her famous cakes."

James checked his watch. "Well, shortly after lunchtime you'll have a celebrity in your life."

"That'll make two of them, then, if I'm includin' you," Jackson murmured as he closed the shed door.

"What's that, Pop?" James asked.

"Nothin'. You'd best get goin'. There's gonna be a snow today, and them mountain roads are gonna be a mess. The state's not prepared for an early snow. I know that for a fact 'cause the mayor said they weren't loadin' the trucks up with sand 'til after Christmas."

Glancing up at the scattering of thin clouds in an otherwise blue sky, James eyed his father in disbelief. "You think we're getting snow today?"

"*I* don't need to think. I know 'cause that hound down the road hollered at the moon all night long. That mutt's been alive for twenty years, and every time he sets up that kinda racket durin' a cold night, we get snow the next day. And not some dustin' either. We'll get 'least an inch." Jackson shook his head, his mouth forming a fractional grin. "Damn dog's never been wrong once."

"Amazing." James decided to humor his father. "I'd better hit the road then, Pop. I just hope Paulette's flight beats out the storm."

After filling a travel mug with coffee, James headed north toward Washington-Dulles. Milla had left her sister's flight information on the kitchen table along with a note warning that Paulette might not be traveling alone. James tossed the paper on the Bronco's passenger seat, cranked up the heat, popped in the latest Clive Cussler audio book, and spent the next two hours contentedly lost in one of Dirk Pitt's grandiose adventures.

Five miles away from the airport, James began to wish he possessed even the smallest amount of Pitt's inventiveness and daring. If so, he might have discovered a way to circumvent the stand-still traffic looming ahead. After spending ten agonizing minutes bathed in the spotlight of a blinking arrow sign set up by the Virginia Department of Transportation, James knew that he was going to be late fetching Paulette.

Over the next thirty minutes, the traffic inched forward as three lanes were forced to converge into one. James tried to ignore the forward progression of his clock radio as he craned his neck to see if there was any end to the clogged roadway.

"This is where a high-tech guy would be searching for alternative routes on his GPS system," he muttered and switched off the audio book. He couldn't concentrate on Dirk's romantic interlude and was suddenly irritated by the fact that Cussler's hero had been shot three times but still had no difficulty in scaling a cliff or scooping a hundred-and-twenty-pound woman into his arms and carrying her up seven flights of stairs.

As James's anxiety mounted, he longed for something to chew on, but all he had stored within the center console was a blue and purple candy cane presented to him by the Salvation Army volunteer outside of the grocery store. Peeling back the wrapper, James sniffed the candy cane suspiciously.

"What happened to red and white?" he demanded of the confection, and then he took a small bite. He tasted sugared blueberries and tart raspberries coated beneath of smooth layer of cream. The sweetness immediately alleviated some of his tension, but when he pulled up to the curb outside of the Continental Airlines gate and saw a woman in her late sixties with a blunt cut of snow-white hair pacing angrily back and forth while hollering into her cell phone, his agitation was renewed.

James slammed the Bronco into park, leapt from the car, and waved at Paulette. He recognized her immediately because Milla had informed him that Paulette closely resembled Meryl Streep's character in the movie *The Devil Wears Prada.* The displeased woman surrounded by a small mountain of Louis Vuitton luggage had a slim figure, well-tailored clothing, and a pair of narrowed, angry eyes.

"Paulette?" James extended his hand as

the older woman snapped her phone closed and bared a row of white but rather pointy teeth.

"Where the *hell* have you been?" she snarled at James. "I have been standing outside for *fifteen* minutes." She gestured at her shoes. "Do these heels look *comfortable* to you?"

James didn't know whether he was more surprised by her hostile tone or the fact that Milla's sister wore black stiletto boots and was enveloped in what appeared to be a fox-hair fur coat. As she swiveled to bark orders at a pale, reed-thin young woman with slumped shoulders and white-blonde hair, James noticed a rather flattened fox head on Paulette's left shoulder and a bushy tail draped across her right.

"Willow!" Paulette shouted. "Get the luggage into this heap with wheels and let's get going! The pollution from the jet fuel is going to clog my pores! My hair is already a wreck from standing out here. I hope no one of *significance* recognizes me!" And with that, the Diva of Dough wrenched open the Bronco's rear door and settled herself inside.

James turned to the young woman, his mouth agape. "Is she for real?"

" 'Fraid so. I'm Willow Singletary, Ms.

Martine's assistant." She smiled weakly. "Don't take her personally. She always gets strung out when she travels. She thinks New York City is the center of the world, and that the second she leaves it, she'll be forced to live in a mud hut and scavenge for her own food." She picked up two suitcases and shuffled toward the truck. With a lowered voice, she added, "She doesn't get much better than this though. It's why I go through two packs of cigarettes a day."

Relieved that there would be at least one friendly passenger in his truck, James helped Willow load the enormous suitcases into his Bronco. From her position in the back seat, Paulette directed the stacking of her luggage and then, apparently satisfied that everything had been stowed to her specifications, opened her cell phone and began to discuss future television show ideas with her producer. Her loud and animated chatter lasted for over an hour and a half. Unused to such a consistent barrage of noise, James stole glances at Paulette in the rearview mirror and longed to drown out her nasal voice with a dose of Clive Cussler.

Eventually, James began to make quiet small-talk with Willow and learned that she had been Paulette's assistant for the past three years and that her job requirements included, but were not limited to, seeing to the Diva's travel arrangements, answering fan mail, editing her cookbooks, handling all the personal phone calls Paulette deemed unimportant, and fetching her non-fat, no foam vanilla lattes from Starbucks whenever the Diva required a caffeine fix.

Willow leaned toward James and muttered softly, "Though these days she prefers the eggnog lattes. The Diva's a *total* eggnog junkie."

"Wow," James whispered and said a silent prayer of gratitude for the wonderful job he held. "I hope you get paid a lot for all you do."

"For being a slave, you mean?" Willow murmured lowly and then uttered a humorless laugh. "I haven't had a raise since I started, but I'm planning to ask for one on this trip. After all, weddings are supposed to bring out the best in people."

James had no idea whether Willow was being sarcastic or not, but he didn't have the opportunity to ask her as a few miles north of the town of Battle Creek, Paulette shoved her phone into a purse large enough to contain a small goat and inquired sharply, "Is there some logical explanation for your indigo tongue?"

"I ate a blue candy cane on the way to the

airport," James answered somewhat sheepishly, and then, as he met Paulette's judgmental stare in the rearview mirror, his embarrassment quickly morphed into irritation. "The Charlottesville airport is much closer than Dulles. You could have saved a lot of time by flying in there."

"And subject myself to one of those tin cans with wings the airlines call 'sky buses'? Never! Those things are death traps!" The Diva removed a compact from her purse and touched up her flawless makeup. "Are we almost there? This *vehicle* is most uncomfortable."

James rubbed his steering wheel with tenderness as though to ward off Paulette's last remark.

As the Bronco climbed a steep hill, Willow whistled at the sight of a dramatic slope covered in green-topped pine trees and leafless hardwoods. "I bet this looks lovely in the snow," she said.

"The Shenandoah Valley is the most beautiful place on earth," James bragged. "I'd rather be here than on a beach in Hawaii or some café in Paris."

Paulette snorted. "As if *you'd* know what a Parisian café is like. *I* went to culinary school there and the dirtiest alley in France has more grandeur than these puny, blue hills. Oh, how I detest the country! How on earth could my sister be living in such a state of crudeness?"

Annoyed beyond measure, James switched on the radio. "Jingle Bells" played merrily through the speakers as the Bronco moved rapidly through the town of Grove Hill. Most of the towns along the highway could be driven through in the time it took one to sing the chorus from "Jingle Bells," but James was tempted to pick up speed in order to shorten the amount of time he was forced to spend with the Diva.

"Is your town like all these others?" Paulette inquired with a trace of anxiety. "I haven't seen a single Starbucks, let alone a decent hotel or restaurant." She leaned forward and poked Willow in the shoulder. "I told you we should have had cooking supplies FedExed down here. How am I supposed to make my sister's wedding cake using materials from a store called *Food Lion?*"

James couldn't take it any longer. "We're actually still usin' the barter system 'round these parts," he drawled. "But I'm right sure you could find something to trade for a dozen eggs and some fresh-milled flour. Someone might fancy that fur coat of yours. Now, sugar's mighty dear, what with the war and all. And I sure hope you brought your own toilet paper for the outhouse."

"Very droll, young man," Paulette replied acerbically, but James thought he caught a glimmer of amusement in her cool, gray eyes.

Having been instructed to take Paulette directly to the only inn near Quincy's Gap, a quaint bed-and-breakfast called the Widow's Peak, James was greatly relieved when he turned off the main road and made the steady but gentle climb up the winding driveway to the front of the restored 1800s farmhouse.

"Oh my," Paulette muttered as James turned off the engine. "Willow, you'd better have bought out all the rooms for the next two weeks. I don't want to have our work interrupted by couples on romantic getaways or those bed-and-breakfast junkies that actually seek out these sorts of establishments. Also, I was assured that we could have full use of the kitchen. Make sure they're aware that I will not stand for any interruptions when I'm baking, no matter what time it is." After a moment's pause, the Diva of Dough sharply chided, "Why are you still standing there, you fool of a girl! No wonder you can't find yourself a husband. You're as slow and stupid as a particular member of the bovine kingdom. Get going!"

After Willow scurried away, James marched to the rear of the Bronco, opened the door with an angry jerk, and blocked Paulette's exit from his truck. "Ms. Martine, your sister is about to marry my father and for that reason, and that reason alone, I'm going to be as cordial to you as possible, no matter how you act in return. However, people in this part of the country are polite to one another as a rule, and no one's going to be willing to accept the kind of treatment your assistant does."

Paulette smiled a slow, deliberate smile. "But that's exactly why I employ Willow. *She'll* put up with anything, especially since I caught her . . ." She trailed off, straightened the fox head on her shoulder, and then said, "I'm weary, so *do* excuse me . . ." And without a thank-you or goodbye, the Diva of Dough strode into the inn as though she were the Queen of England.

From the safety of his Bronco, James frowned as he watched her walk away. It was going to be a long two weeks with Paulette Martine in residence only a few scant miles down the road from the Henry home. Sighing over the certain loss of the harmonious existence he had enjoyed prior to the disappearance of Glowstar, the news of Murphy's book release, and the arrival of the Diva of Dough, he turned the key in the ignition. As the Bronco eased back down the driveway, James glanced at the sky, which was thick with heavy pewter-colored clouds. The bank of clouds seemed to close in around the surrounding mountains and James was seized by an uneasy, claustrophobic feeling.

"Pop was right. It *is* going to snow. This sky does not bode well for the Christmas Cavalcade tonight," he murmured to himself as he headed north toward home.

But if it snows really hard, he thought with a sudden surge of hopefulness, *Paulette might be forced to stay inside the inn for a few days.*

"In that case," he said with a sympathetic chuckle, "God help those innkeepers."

Three: Hot Buttered Rum

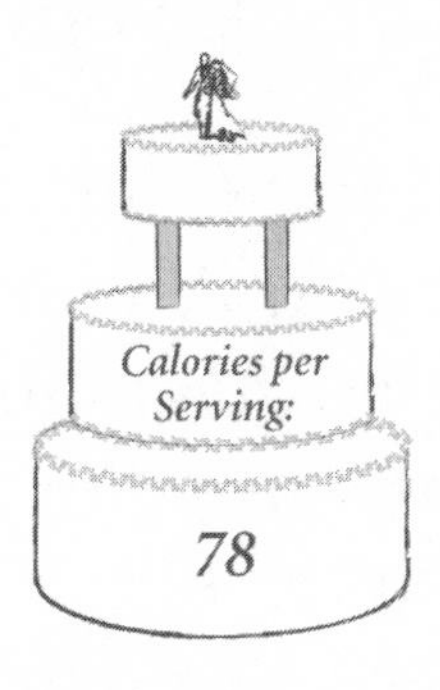

At five o'clock that same Saturday, the supper club members gathered on the front porch of Gillian's house. Every one of them was bundled up beneath layers of shirts, sweaters, and outerwear. An unpleasant wind had developed over the course of the afternoon, which seemed intent on forcing goose bumps to erupt on the back of everyone's neck.

"This is the bad part about living between two mountain chains," James said with a shiver. "The wind just attacks you."

"I know. My lips are peeling off like pieces of old wallpaper. Still, I do hope we get some snow!" Lindy Perez, the cheerful high school art teacher, declared. "Everything's so beautiful when it's covered by a fresh layer of pure white." She stretched her short arms out in front of her. "Reminds me of the feeling I get whenever I stare at a new canvas or a block of fresh clay. I get all tingly all over just thinking about the possibilities."

Gillian opened the front door of her large Victorian house and emerged onto the porch carrying a silver-plate tray loaded with a teapot and five pottery mugs. "Oh, it's so dark already. The winter solstice is almost upon us, so I've made us some soul-warming herbal tea," she announced, setting the heavy tray down on one of the wicker side tables. "Gather around and inhale this fragrance. While you sip, be grateful that we're not looking at the winter as the *famine* months as our ancestors would have done."

"When it comes to your teas, I might prefer goin' without." Bennett took the top off the teapot and sniffed. "Lord help us! What are you tryin' to sneak down our throats, woman? Fresh mulch tea? Ugh!" He grunted as Gillian lifted the teapot and placed it directly beneath his nose. "This stuff smells like my backyard."

"Excellent olfactory observation. I am *so* proud of you for activating your other senses!" Gillian replied. "This is pine needle tea. It's very high in vitamin C and helps relieve congestion. *You* sound a bit stuffed up to me, Bennett. If you lack the confidence to experiment with a new taste, then I'll give you some leaves to take home. You can take a *nice* pine needle tea bath and all your aching joints will be soothed. Isn't nature *incredible?*"

"How'd you know my joints were sore?" Bennett looked at Gillian in surprise.

"You know how intuitive I am," Gillian stated. "When I was in my mid-twenties, I took yoga classes from a very spiritual woman. She told me that I was deeply in tune with my inner —"

"I brought something to warm us up too," Lucy interrupted, gesturing at a large metal thermos resting on the porch floor. "Hot buttered rum. It's a recipe my folks have used for years to make it through the cavalcade without turning into human ice sculptures. It'll send a shot of heat right down your gullet and straight to your toes."

"Now that's more like it. Hit me with a cup of *that* brew." Bennett pointed at the thermos. "Look there! I think our first vehicle is comin' down the road."

The five friends moved to the edge of Gillian's porch and cheered at the sight of a Shenandoah County recycling truck.

The Christmas Cavalcade was established fifteen years prior in order to encourage hometown pride. Each of the Quincy's Gap municipal departments decorated a vehicle of their choice with Christmas lights, garlands, ornaments, plastic statues, stuffed animals, and anything else they felt would spread holiday cheer. Members of each department hung out windows, sat inside trunks, or perched on top of the roof of their cars, trucks, vans, or buses in order to distribute goodies to the multitude of children who flocked to Quincy's Gap in hopes of filling paper lunch bags with free holiday treats.

Gillian's house was perfectly situated for viewing the cavalcade. She lived in the heart of the downtown historic area, and all the parade vehicles would begin their journey at the old courthouse, which was two blocks north of her three-story, pink and green home.

As usual, dozens of bystanders had set up folding chairs and portable heaters on the sidewalk in front of the house, for Gillian had always been gracious about allowing the spectators the use of both her lawn and her bathroom. One year, she had even baked Christmas cookies for the cavalcade observers, but most of her organic, gluten-free goodies had found their way into the storm drain at the corner. Out of kindness, one woman had told Gillian that the children got enough treats during the event and didn't need any more sugar.

"We don't want 'em to be spoiled," she had said tactfully. "You don't need to bake them anything when they're gettin' all this candy already. But thank you so much for bein' so kind."

Gillian restricted her cookie making to an even dozen, which she now shared among her friends. They all hated the cookies, but were unwilling to offend their hostess by leaving them uneaten. This year, however, James had a plan in place in order to avoid having to chew on a baked good that tasted remarkably like chalk. He took two cookies from Gillian's multicultural holiday platter, which showed a rainbow of children's faces around the border and a dove carrying a holly branch in the center, and stuffed them into a snack-sized plastic bag that he had placed in his coat pocket earlier that evening.

James thought that he had slipped the cookies into his jacket undetected, but Lucy sidled up to him and said, "Smooth move. Got room for mine?" She unfolded her fist in order to reveal a pair of crumbling cookies resembling a blend of Milkbone biscuits and cow dung.

"Sure. Come closer and drop them into my pocket. I'll throw them out at home later on."

"Like I said. Smooth move. This is just your way of getting me near you," Lucy teased. "But I'm glad you came prepared. You ever heard the term 'meadow muffins'? That's what Gillian's cookies taste like."

James laughed and then, as Lucy placed her hand in his coat pocket, grew serious. "Actually," he whispered, "I did want to talk to you about, ah, the two of us starting over." He leaned his head closer to hers as the garbage truck roared in front of the house. "I'd like to take you out on a date. Not like the dates we had before, ah, before . . ." he trailed off.

"Before I got crazy obsessed with Sullie and drove you into the arms of Murphy Alistair?" Lucy asked, her cornflower blue eyes glinting.

"Exactly." James exhaled. "I know we've been taking it slow — that we've been working our way into trusting one another, et cetera. But I'm ready, Lucy, and I want to prove it to you." He turned to her, blocking her view of the green pickup truck from the Shenandoah Parks Department, which carried an enormous fir tree decorated with garlands of red berries and strings of glowing pinecones.

"That's wonderful to hear, James." There was a smile in Lucy's voice. "We should find a way to celebrate, because you *know* that I've been ready since this summer!"

"A celebration." James repeated the word, reveling in the positive images it evoked. "That's exactly what I want to talk to you about. I'd like to do something especially romantic. Not a simple dinner and a movie or watching TV at your house like we used to do. Something memorable, so that we'll always remember how we began our fresh start." He lowered his voice even further. "Lucy, I'd really like to take you on —"

"Hey!" Gillian exclaimed and poked James in the back. "They're throwing seedlings strapped to teddy bears! I didn't get one last year and I *so* wanted to plant a tree near the corner of my front porch." She set down her teacup and, seeing that James didn't share her enthusiasm, grabbed Bennett's arm instead. "*Please,* Bennett, can you catch me one? Hurry!" When Bennett nodded his agreement, she yelled, "The truck is going to pass us by!"

James turned away from Lucy in order to watch his friend sprint down the sidewalk as quickly as he could in a pair of heavy black boots. He shoved his way through the crowd and chased after the departing pickup, determined to get the attention of one of the men riding in the pickup's bed.

"Yo!" Bennett waved his arms and hollered at one of the Parks Department's employees. "Hit me with a teddy bear, man! The lady in the pink house has gotta have one!"

A brown Smoky the Bear was hurtled through space too far to Bennett's right. James watched as Bennett dove for the bear, stretching out his arms as far as he could. Unfortunately, he landed with a thud on the cold asphalt and the bear fell onto the sidewalk several feet away. The crowd cheered at Bennett as he leapt to his feet and shoved the plush animal inside his parka.

"Woman!" Bennett growled, stomping onto the porch and presenting Gillian with her prize. "Gimme a little more notice next time you want me to beat my way through a crowd of women and kids and try to catch somethin' that my grandma could have thrown with better aim."

"You're my *hero!*" Gillian hugged Bennett and then pointed at the bear. "Look! There's a blue spruce sapling tied to this Smoky. I can plant it and we can all sit out here, spring after spring, sipping on a lovely cup of vanilla lavender tea, and watch it stretch its branches skyward."

"Who is 'all of us'?" Bennett scowled. "Does your *boyfriend* like vanilla lavender tea?" He made a big show of dusting off his coat sleeve, his pride clearly wounded as a result of making a dramatic but ineffective diving catch in front of his closest friends and about two hundred parade bystanders.

"As a matter of fact, *Detective* Harding does like tea," Gillian replied smugly. "He's very *open* to new experiences." She refilled her cup. "And he's *not* my boyfriend. We haven't pigeonholed our relationship by trying to *define* it using conventional terms. We're merely enjoying one another's company by living in the *now*."

"I'm surprised he has time to drink tea," Bennett persisted. "*Sheriff* Jones tells me that she's keeping him pretty busy."

Gillian frowned. "I don't think the detective is kept occupied by your *girlfriend's* insistence, but because he's passionately devoted to protecting the good citizens of Abington County."

Bennett poured himself another tumbler of hot buttered rum. "Ms. Jade Jones is *not* my girlfriend. She and I . . . we're . . ." He pulled at his toothbrush mustache and intently searched his mind for the correct term.

Lindy held out her hands. "Enough! You two can tease one another about the romantic partners you collected at the Hudsonville barbecue festival this summer all you want *after* the cavalcade is over, okay? Besides, all this talk about boyfriends and girlfriends makes me miss Luis."

"Where is the dashing Principal of Blue Ridge High again?" James inquired.

"He went to Mexico because his mama's really sick," Lindy answered sadly. "He's her only son and he's devoted to her. I hope she gets better soon, because I really miss him. He's promised to bring our relationship out into the open at school. I can't wait to see the looks on certain fellow teachers' faces when they realize he's now off the market." She drained her glass and looked at the empty contents with a smirk. "Lucy, can you pour me another? These rum things are so delicious that I can almost forget about Luis bein' gone and that my feet are too numb to be cold." She smiled crookedly and touched the tip of her nose. "Shoot. I'm not cold anywhere. I'm feelin' good *all* over! How much rum is in here, Lucy?"

Lucy laughed. "Enough to make me wanna run out to the street and see what the convicts are tossing from that bus!"

The white bus in question was crammed with jail inmates. The group of men, who wore orange jumpsuits and red Santa hats, waved and blew kisses to the crowd as they threw penguin finger puppets from the windows and into the hands of eager children.

"You're probably responsible for several of those incarcerations," James cautioned Lucy. "They might throw something at you besides a penguin."

"They got *themselves* into those jumpsuits," Lucy retorted firmly. "And only those who committed minor offenses get to ride in the parade bus. All the same, I think I'll wait for the firemen. They're a lot better looking than those jailbirds, and I hear they've made frosted gingerbread cookies shaped like dalmatians. One of those would go nicely with my hot buttered rum." She grabbed Lindy's hand. "Come on, Gillian. Let's go ogle some of the men in yellow."

The three women joined the crowd in

order to whistle and coo at the burly, handsome men poised on top of their newly washed fire truck. On the roof were two wooden cutouts. One was of Santa. His rear end was on fire and his mouth formed a pink *o* of surprise and dismay. Standing alongside Santa's burning bum was Rudolph the Reindeer, who held a bright red fire extinguisher between his two front hooves but seemed unable to use the device. The Quincy's Gap Volunteer Fire & Rescue had used the same cutouts for years, yet they never failed to make the children laugh.

In addition to Santa and Rudolph, the fire truck was decorated with blinking chili pepper lights and was towing a small trailer bearing a burning Christmas tree and a pile of smoking presents. A lone fireman sat on the edge of the trailer and held up a sign reading *Don't Forget to Unplug Your Tree!*

The fire truck was followed by the county's only street cleaner. It moved at a snail's pace while the driver tossed out small bags of coal (which were really black gumdrops) and cheerfully admonished the throng to clean up after themselves. "I'm goin' on vacation!" He yelled over the roar of his machine. "And I don't wanna be cleanin' up after y'all at five in the mornin'!" He punctuated his message by stepping on the street cleaner's accelerator, creating a puff of foul-smelling black smoke.

The children were delighted. They begged for a repeat performance while simultaneously stuffing their mouths with black gumdrops. When the voter registration vehicle came along, sending out voter application registrations in the form of paper airplanes, the children stuck out their black tongues until the woman in the passenger seat, who appeared harried by the entire experience, frantically flung out a large portion of her supply of candy canes in lieu of voting paraphernalia.

"Too much candy will rot your teeth!" she shouted as she hurled candy canes at a row of preteens.

"They're too young to vote anyhow!" Bennett shouted in the children's defense.

After three glasses of hot buttered rum, James found himself laughing at everything the cavalcade had to offer. He even managed to choke down one of the three cookies left on Gillian's platter — a feat so impressive that Bennett offered to eat the remaining two. He had just swallowed the second when the snow began to fall. What began as a few flakes blown lazily around the porch by the wind quickly morphed into a genuine snowfall. Within minutes, the flakes seemed to grow smaller and multiply in a steady march toward the ground.

"Oh!" Lindy clapped her mittened hands. "It's beautiful!"

Everyone agreed. The first snow of the season, illuminated by the twinkling colored lights entwined around Gillian's railings, seemed magical. For the spectators gathered on the sidewalk, however, the precipitation became unpleasant in a hurry. The wind whipped cold snowflakes against their cheeks and noses, making them red and chapped. Moist bits of snow sneaked under scarves and wriggled down the front of jackets and planted wet kisses on exposed wrists.

"Good thing we've almost reached the finale," Gillian said as she pointed at the crowd. "I believe those children by my front gate are turning blue."

"Nah," Bennett argued. "They've just got cotton candy all over their faces."

"I feel sorry for their parents. How are they ever going to get those kids to sleep? They're totally hopped up on sugar," Lindy remarked with ill-disguised glee.

"Speaking of sweet," Lucy gestured across the street, where a minivan had come to a stop in a parking spot reserved for event volunteers. "Isn't that Milla?"

Beneath the sheen of a streetlamp, it was easy to recognize the lavender hue of Milla's van as well as her vanity plate, which read *LV2COOK.* James groaned. "Oh no. She's brought her sister, the harpy, with her. Brace yourselves, my friends. This woman is as fork-tongued as a serpent."

"Oh come on." Lindy swatted James with the end of her crimson scarf. "How can anyone related to Milla be mean? You must be exaggerating."

"Trust me. Paulette Martine is Queen of the Shrews," James answered nervously as Milla, Paulette, and Willow crossed the street and headed toward Gillian's house.

Lucy, who had been watching the newcomers' arrival with interest, gripped James by the hand when he mentioned Paulette's name. "You didn't tell us Milla's sister was the Diva of Dough! Oh, James! Do you think she'll be baking cakes while she's here? I watch her TV show all the time. Man, oh man . . ." She paused to lick her lips. "You know frosted cakes are my big weakness, and this woman makes them like nobody's business. How lucky for you that she's related to your daddy's future wife!"

"Yes, I'm feeling *really* lucky about having her join the family," James mumbled caustically as Milla stepped onto the porch.

"Hello, my dears!" she shouted merrily, but James sensed that her smile was partially forced. "I'm so sorry to barge in on your fun like this. Normally, I'd be all snuggled in my nightgown with my darling Sir Charles the Corgi at my feet and a Nora Roberts novel in my hand, but my sister was just dying to witness our little event, so here we are. Did we miss the whole thing?" she asked anxiously.

"It's just about done," Lindy answered regretfully. "That's the Department of Finance limo," she explained to Paulette and Willow, who had yet to speak. "They toss chocolate coins to the kids along with little slips of paper telling them that it's never too early to open a bank account."

"How quaint," Paulette responded flatly, and then pursed her lips. "And this 'assemblage' is what passes for entertainment around here? You voluntarily stand out in the frigid cold while vehicles decorated with as much *kitsch* as can be found in your 'dollar' stores pass by distributing stale, tasteless confections."

Bennett leaned over to Lucy and whispered, "Does she talk like that on her show? All highfalutin and frostier than a snowman?"

Lucy nodded, surprisingly unruffled by

Paulette's criticism of their holiday event. "The Christmas Cavalcade is pretty creative," she explained to their guest and gestured at the street. "Here comes the Sanitation Department. They're one of the crowd pleasers because they throw out these little rubber frogs called *Mistle Toads.* They're stuffed with gooey chocolate and when you squeeze their bellies, it oozes out of a tiny hole in their mouths. No one knows how the garbage men manage to get the chocolate inside the frogs."

"How fascinatingly repulsive," Paulette replied with a frown. "All I really wanted was a cup of hot tea with my sister, but the establishment masquerading as my hotel is only stocked with Lipton. No Ashby, no Mariage Frères, no Tazo — not even a packet of humble Twinings. There's simply nothing suitable for me to drink in that hovel and I didn't even *ask* for coffee." Paulette indicated Willow with a nod of her chin. "And my assistant was incapable of procuring us a suitable rental car for this evening so that she could track down some essentials, so Milla agreed to pick us up in her uniquely colored van and take us to the home of someone who purportedly had good taste in tea." She scanned her audience. "Is it possible that one of you has a sophisticated palate?"

Gillian perked up immediately. "That must certainly be me! I have an entire *spectrum* of organic herbal teas. Would you care to come inside and peruse my pantry?"

Paulette nodded. "You can stay out here, Willow. Perhaps one of the rubber frogs from the garbage truck will turn into your prince if you kiss it with enough desperation. Come along, Milla. No sense you catching a cold with your 'big day' coming up."

As soon as the Diva of Dough, followed by a subdued Milla, entered Gillian's house, Willow breathed a sigh of relief. James quickly introduced her to his friends and then offered her the last of the hot buttered rum. "I think you may need this more than anyone here."

"Thanks." Willow accepted the tumbler. "I used to carry a flask of vodka with me everywhere. Paulette likes freshly squeezed orange juice in the morning before her five or six daily lattes from Starbucks, so I'd just make myself an OJ and add a little splash of survival vodka. It got me through 'til lunchtime, anyway."

"I'd need more than a flask if I were workin' with that she-devil." Bennett pulled on his mustache.

"Well, I don't even have *that* now." Willow looked at the floor, shamefaced. "Paulette smelled the vodka on my breath one day and that was that. I guess it was good because only alcoholics drink at work like I was doing. So now I smoke instead." She dug a pack of cigarettes out of her coat pocket and grinned abashedly. "I'll just go out to the street for a minute." She eyed Gillian's front door nervously. "If *she* comes out, just tell her I went to catch one of those frogs. She'd love to think I was obeying her orders to the letter."

The four friends watched the young woman scuttle down to the sidewalk, where she bent her head down and cupped her cigarette with her left hand, clearly determined to get it lit despite the swirling wind and snow.

"Poor thing," Lindy said, and then she clucked her tongue. "No one should be treated like that."

"I told you what Paulette was like." James lowered his voice. "And I tried to talk to her about being nice because this was her sister's community and people are kind to strangers in these parts, but I guess she's not called a diva for nothing."

"Well, the *Diva's* going to miss the finale." Lucy looked pleased by the idea. "Here comes Santa!"

An old yellow school bus corroded by rust lumbered down the street. The spectators in front of Gillian's house gave their heartiest cheers and the children began to shriek at the top of their vocal ranges as they hopped up and down in excitement. The bus, which was driven by a very authentic-looking Santa Claus in denim overalls and a red flannel shirt, was occupied by the mayor and her staff. Each adult wore a green elf hat, pointy ears, and a red clown nose. The elves hung out the open bus windows, jingling hand bells and smiling widely in order to display their fake "redneck" teeth, which protruded from their mouths in crooked rows of brown and yellow.

Just below the line of windows, the bus had been spray-painted with the words *Hillbilly School Bus.* A chicken coop had been erected on the roof and several agitated chickens, ducks, and white geese strutted about on a pile of straw. A shotgun rack had been built behind Santa's back and he waved at the crowd with a hand brandishing an empty whiskey bottle. Plush raccoons, squirrels, and rabbits hung from hooks inside the open passenger door while the mayor's four basset hounds occupied the rear bucket seat. Every inch of the bus's exterior was covered in a mismatched hodgepodge of Christmas lights.

Santa and the elves sang "All I Want for Christmas Is My Two Front Teeth," paying no mind to pitch, tempo, or any other musical element that might produce a harmonious sound. In fact, each time the group hit a high note, the mayor's dogs began to howl, which the bystanders found incredibly funny.

"What's the big prize this year?" Lindy asked.

James laughed as the elves began to shower the crowd with red, green, and silver Hershey's kisses.

"The kid's prize is a new mountain bike, complete with helmet and knee pads," Lucy answered. "And boy, would I love to win the adult prize. It's a thousand-dollar Christmas shopping spree. Vendors from all over the county donated gift certificates good in their stores for the next two weeks only. How much fun would it be to spend all that much money at once?" She rubbed her hands together excitedly.

"But you're a county employee, just like the rest of us." Bennett gave Lucy a perplexed look. "We're excluded from winning the shoppin' spree, so why get all worked up?"

"A girl can dream, can't she?" Lucy demanded crossly. "Anyway, if Gillian gets out to the street in time, she might catch the Hershey's Kiss with the winning message on its tag." She glanced through Gillian's living room window. "How long can it take to make a pot of tea anyway?"

"That crazy redhead's probably whispering some Buddhist chant as the water boils," Bennett said with a snort.

The hillbilly bus slugged past Gillian's house. Its exhaust issued a series of loud reports that caused the youngest children to scream in mock fear and the mayor's bloodhounds to increase their frenzied keening. Amid the raucousness, Willow made her way back onto the porch. Her pale face was illuminated by Gillian's lights and her white-blonde hair was nearly obscured by snow. She seemed immune to the cold, and James thought that she looked quite pretty with her cheeks tinged pink by the chilly air.

"This parade is so cool!" she exclaimed. "Do you see how psyched all those kids are? Staying up late and being given all this free loot? And are those *real* chickens on the roof of that ancient school bus? You'd never see anything like this in New York. It's all so . . . I don't know . . ."

"Fun?" James suggested.

"Yes, but without the glitz and glam of a Macy's parade." Willow unwrapped a chocolate kiss and popped it in her mouth. "Take the candy, for example. In the city, we'd be looking inside this chocolate for razor blades or white powder. But here, you feel safe. Everything seems more genuine. More pure. I feel like I'd be welcome here no matter how much money I made or what I wore."

"That part's true, but we've got plenty of crime here too. Trust me," Lucy countered, and then quickly softened her tone. "But you're right about the sincerity. I'm glad you were able to see our hillbilly Santa at any rate. After all the years I've seen this parade, I still don't know who he really is."

"Maybe it's not a costume." Bennett winked and nudged Lucy.

At that moment, raised voices could be heard emanating from within Gillian's house. The supper club members exchanged worried glances, for one of the voices was clearly Gillian's and she rarely shouted. James could also discern that Milla was yelling at both Paulette and Gillian and wondered whether he should go inside or let the women sort things out for themselves.

Willow must have sensed that James was

torn over what course of action to take. She touched his arm lightly and timidly said, "I wouldn't go in there if I were you. She'll just turn on you if you're in her line of fire."

"But Gillian's my friend and Milla's my . . ." He paused. "Well, Milla is Paulette's sister. I guess she knows better than anyone how to handle the Diva of Dough."

Suddenly, Gillian's screen door was flung open and Paulette strode outside, clinging to the fox-fur collar of her coat. James couldn't help but notice that the blouse she wore underneath seemed to be covered by some kind of wet stain.

"I'm soaked to the bone!" Paulette raged and turned a pair of angry gray eyes on Willow. "Get my umbrella open, you dolt. I'm already in danger of coming down with pneumonia, no thanks to the liberal, tree-hugging lunatic that owns this house. Milla! I mean it! I'm leaving this minute!"

Without a word to anyone else, Paulette stomped down the stairs. Willow followed a half-step behind, holding a black umbrella covered by gold interlocked Chanel Cs over the Diva's head.

"I apologize for my sister's behavior," Milla said as she and Gillian stepped onto the porch. "I know how much you love animals. I do too, and I had no idea she could be so cruel about them."

Gillian was dabbing at her eyes with a tissue. "I'm sorry too. I should never have asked her if that fox fur on her coat was real. If only she hadn't gone into all that detail about the fur farms and . . ." She choked back a sob.

Milla squeezed Gillian's shoulder and then shot an embarrassed glance James's way. "It was a mistake to come over here — I just wanted Paulette's first evening to be a positive one, and I knew there'd be good tea and wonderful company here. Oh dear, I hope we didn't completely tarnish your time together."

James enveloped his future stepmother in a tight hug. "Don't worry about it, Milla. You just added more color to a colorful night."

Milla smiled at him in gratitude and then trotted after her sister.

"What happened in there?" Bennett asked Gillian.

"That *woman* said such horrible things about the mink and fox fur farms where they get fur coats like hers. She told me how the animals . . . how they gnaw at their own limbs because they're so upset to be in such tiny cages." Gillian sniffed as another tear rolled down her cheek. "She told me she was proud that the fox cub used on *her* coat had obviously been electrocuted before he could cause any damage to his pelt." After blowing her nose, Gillian balled the tissue into a tight wad inside her fist.

"Don't think about it any more," Lindy stopped Gillian from dwelling on the morbid subject by putting her arm around her sniffling friend and pivoting her toward the front door. "Let's all go inside for a bit and talk about something else, okay?"

Gillian nodded and allowed Lucy to pick up the tray bearing the teapot and cups.

"Well, you must have done somethin' to fight back against the Wicked Witch of the North," Bennett said, searching Gillian's face. "She left here pretty steamed, so I'd say she didn't get the last word anyhow."

"Steamed is right," Gillian replied and blew her nose with finality. "I poured an entire cup of jasmine pearl oolong tea on her. I thought she might be able to sympathize over the plight of an electrocuted animal if *she* felt a little heat herself. I knew it wouldn't burn her. The water hadn't boiled yet. Still, now I've wasted a particularly delicate handful of tea leaves on that fur-wearing *monster!* And I cannot *stand* waste!"

"I just can't believe that someone who

makes such tantalizingly sweet and beautiful cakes can be so, well, sour." Lucy closed her thermos and went inside.

James was the last one on the porch. He took a brief look down the street, where the school bus had already turned the corner and was heading down Main Street at a steady crawl, and then blinked. For a moment, he was positive that he had seen a small, red elf duct taped to the yellow vehicle's rear emergency exit door.

"Glowstar?" James called in confusion, and then he shook his head. How could the library's elf have found his way onto the hillbilly school bus? Who would kidnap their elf and then tape him onto the last vehicle of the Christmas Cavalcade?

"Nah," he muttered with a shake of his head. "It couldn't be Glowstar. Must be some other elf." Still, he couldn't help watching the small red form as it disappeared into the distance. Its plastic face looked very familiar. James knew that come Monday, he'd have to at least mention the sighting to the Fitzgerald brothers. He also knew that they wouldn't rest until the mystery of the missing elf had been solved.

Lucy's Hot Buttered Rum

1 pound butter
1 pound brown sugar
1 pound powdered sugar
1 quart vanilla ice cream, softened
1 tablespoon cinnamon
1 tablespoon nutmeg
1 bottle dark rum
6 ounces boiling water per serving (approximately)

To prepare batter: Melt the butter in a large saucepan over medium heat. Stir in the sugars until they dissolve. Remove from heat and blend in the ice cream, cinnamon, and nutmeg. Pour the mixture into a container and freeze.

To serve: Remove the batter from the freezer. Allow it to soften. Place 2 rounded tablespoons of batter in a coffee mug. Add 1 to 2 tablespoons dark rum. Add approximately 6 ounces of boiling water (more or less depending on the size of the mug) and stir until the batter is melted. Sprinkle with cinnamon, nutmeg, or both. Prepare to feel warm and fuzzy all over.

FOUR:
THE DIVA'S BEEF WELLINGTON

"I've never been thin, Dr. Ruth," James admitted as he stared at the kind face of Ruth Wilkins, Bennett's nutritionist. "And I don't need to look like Brad Pitt. I just want to feel comfortable in the tuxedo I'm wearing to my father's wedding — in all my clothes, actually. I'd like to be healthy, but not in exchange for eating a bunch of tasteless food for the rest of my life."

The nutritionist nodded and uncapped her pen, keeping it poised above a yellow legal pad. "You can just call me Ruth, Mr.

Henry. 'Dr. Ruth' always makes people think of the famous sex therapist, and that's not *quite* my area of expertise." She shrugged self-effacingly, laced her fingers together, and smiled encouragingly. "Why don't you start off by telling me what kinds of foods you like? And you can be honest with me. I'm not going to pass judgment on what you enjoy eating. I'm not here to ask you to change your tastes in food, but to help you achieve your goals."

James released the tight grip he'd been applying to his leather armchair, which faced Dr. Ruth's desk and was adjacent to a coffee table filled with synthetic food. Bennett had called the nutritionist "doctor," so James had also come to think of her as Dr. Ruth. He picked up a piece of fake food from the table next to him — a plastic chicken drumstick — and examined it curiously.

"I like meat and potatoes," he answered as he replaced the chicken leg and scooped up a pile of peas, which had the consistency of hardened Play-Doh. "I'm not a big seafood fan, but I do like a lot of green vegetables as well as all kinds of fruit." He paused. "I love salty stuff like cheese puffs, peanuts, buttered popcorn, and Doritos. And I've got a sweet tooth as well. I feel like my meal isn't really done until I've had something sugary, especially after supper."

"That's not uncommon. Many people need dessert to provide a sense of closure to their meal." Dr. Ruth took a few notes. "It sounds like you eat a nice variety of healthy foods. That makes my job easier." She gave him an approving smile. "It's also encouraging that you have a specific aim, such as wanting to fit more comfortably into your clothes. When is your father's wedding?"

"In less than two weeks. On Christmas Eve," James said.

Dr. Ruth tapped her pen thoughtfully against her notepad. "Healthy weight loss is gradual, Mr. Henry. You might lose four or five pounds by the wedding, but not fifteen or twenty. I don't want you to go into this with unrealistic expectations."

James nodded. "Oh, I know. The wedding just gave me the motivation I needed to make an appointment with you. I probably won't lose *any* weight now that my father's future wife's sister is in town. She's a famous baker, and she's going to be making the wedding cake. Somehow or other, I promised to taste a sample of all of her favorite recipes and pronounce which cake I think should be served at the wedding."

"That's quite an honor," Dr. Ruth said with an amused grin. "And actually, you could still lose weight while being the official cake taster. Two or three bites are not going to make a difference as long as you're not combining those high-calorie samples with other unhealthy treats in the course of one day." She turned to a wooden letter tray near her right elbow and pulled out a sheet of computer paper. Sliding on a pair of reading glasses, she looked up at James over the lenses and asked, "The baker's name wouldn't happen to be Paulette Martine, would it?"

"That's her. The Diva of Dough," James replied, unable to keep a hint of bitterness from his tone.

"I'm doing a television show with her this Thursday. The crew from the CBS affiliate in Charlottesville is driving up here to interview us about how we approach holiday feasts. I'm supposed to talk about practicing moderation in order to avoid weight gain, and Paulette is going to illustrate examples of decadent foods that are worth blowing a diet for. Of course, I don't support diets, but a change of lifestyle. Still, it should be an interesting show." She picked up a framed photograph on her desk and showed it to James. "Channel 19 plans to run clips from the show on their evening news program as well. I'm hoping to gain a few more clients from the deal so that I can keep up with the cost of tuition."

As James examined the photograph of Dr. Ruth's three sons, who all resembled NFL linebackers, he wondered whether he should warn Dr. Ruth about Paulette's waspish manner. The nutritionist, a petite brunette with lovely skin and glistening blue-green eyes, was markedly gentle and soft-spoken in comparison to Paulette Martine. James hated the idea that Paulette might browbeat Dr. Ruth in front of thousands of television viewers. "Well, I'll definitely tune in," he said. "But look out for Paulette. She's got a rather venomous tongue."

Dr. Ruth returned her family photo to the corner of her desk and nodded. "I've watched Madame Martine's Diva of Dough show several times. I'll be focusing on the nutritional content of her beautiful cakes, but like I told you, I don't recommend depriving oneself of desserts or food treats, so Paulette and I shouldn't find ourselves at odds. After all, life isn't about eating broccoli. Healthy eating entails choosing a wide variety of foods, including an occasional Twinkie or a bag of salt and vinegar chips."

Confident that Dr. Ruth could hold her

own against Paulette, James asked, "So what do I do now?"

"I'd like you to start a food log. You should write down everything you eat over the course of the day and the calorie amount in each food. Then, write a total for all the calories at the bottom of each day. I've written down a couple websites to help you find out how many calories are in the most common foods." She handed him a piece of paper showing a sample food log and a listing of three website URLs. "I'd also like you to add any exercise you've done per day, including walking, weight training, or other cardiac activities. You can deduct those calories from your food total."

"What about drinks?" James inquired as he glanced at the paper. "I have a bunch of coffee every day."

"Do you add cream or sugar?"

James nodded. "Yes. Both."

"Then you need to add that on, because there are calories in your coffee." Dr. Ruth touched James's hand. "This is just for me to see what your eating preferences are. Just be as thorough and honest as you can. Remember, I'm not here to judge you."

"Can I try to lose some weight while I'm working on this log?"

"That would be great!" Dr. Ruth declared.

"If you'd like to try to restrict your daily caloric intake to around twenty-two to twenty-five hundred calories, then go for it!"

"Maybe Bennett and I can hype each other up," James murmured as he wondered how much he could eat on a two-thousand-calorie-a-day plan. "It'll be nice to talk this over with him. And if I get stressed about the wedding or he gets stressed about his upcoming taping for *Jeopardy!* then we've got one another for support."

"Having a friend with similar goals is certainly a plus," Dr. Ruth said as she glanced at her watch. "Unfortunately, our time is up. Let's make an appointment for next week. We'll start our session by getting your weight and see what your body fat number is, and then we'll look over your food log and see where to go from there. Sound good?" She smiled warmly.

In spite of the mention of the words "body fat," James felt a tingle of excitement. He felt absolutely sure that he could work with this woman to improve his eating habits. Dr. Ruth wasn't going to lecture him or guilt him into changing his eating habits. Instead, she would act as a guide on his journey to a healthier future. The nutritionist seemed so sincerely optimistic and encouraging that James found himself wanting to please her.

"Thank you." He stood and shook her outstretched hand. "I'm really glad I came today," James said as he moved toward the door. "I really didn't want to, to tell you the truth, but I feel like this is exactly what I need."

"I've heard that a time or two." Dr. Ruth laughed. "But you did walk through that door and now you've got a plan in addition to a refreshingly positive attitude. I think you're going to be one of my success stories, Mr. Henry."

James whistled as he walked down the hallway of the medical office building housing Dr. Ruth and a dozen other professionals. As he passed a vending machine stuffed with Fritos, Hostess Cup Cakes, and candy bars illuminated by soft lights and humming enticingly, his stomach issued a loud rumble. "It's almost suppertime," he said to himself. "I'd better have a big one too, since this is the last meal I'll be eating that Dr. Ruth doesn't need to know about."

"Something smells delicious," James remarked as he entered his house through the back door leading into the kitchen. He stopped short when he saw Paulette bent over the kitchen counter, working a rolling pin over a layer of dough dusted with flour. Jackson sat silently at the kitchen table, studying Paulette's every move.

James looked around in confusion. "Where's Milla, Pop?"

"She drove to Harrisonburg to get us a hunk of meat, but she should be walkin' through that door any second now," Jackson answered. "Paulette here is gonna fix us a dinner that'll make our bellies stick out for miles."

"I think I've got that down pat." James turned to Paulette. "What are you treating us to, if you don't mind me asking?"

"A *divine* beef Wellington, made with succulent filet mignon, liver pâté, portobello mushrooms, and my homemade puff pastry."

James was impressed. "Wow. Here I thought your specialty was cakes."

"It is," Paulette replied. "But I'm quite adept in all areas of the culinary arts." She paused in her work and turned to Jackson. "Can you see me well enough?"

"Sure can. I'm sketchin' in my mind." Jackson tapped a gnarled finger against his wrinkled temple. "Don't need no paper. By the end of the evenin', I'll know your hands as well as you do."

Paulette looked quite pleased by this declaration. She gave Jackson an indulgent smile and then gestured at the plastic tumbler sitting next to a frying pan filled with sautéed onions and mushrooms. "I'm ready for a refill, brother-in-law."

"Yes ma'am! Three fingers comin' right up." Jackson jumped out of his chair and poured some of his favorite Cutty Sark into her glass. "I didn't reckon you for a gal who could knock back the sauce. Figured you'd be one of those fruity rum and umbrella kind of drinkers."

"I'm tougher than I look," Paulette replied with a sly grin. "Besides, Milla and I grew up in Mississippi, remember? We practically bleed scotch whiskey. And I was quite relieved to discover that you're not a beer drinker. Such a crude beverage." She gave a little sniff to underscore her disapproval.

James couldn't believe his ears. Paulette and his father were actually getting along. Not only that, but they were apparently intent on getting drunk together. As he headed upstairs to change clothes, he heard the sound of Milla's van crunching up the gravel driveway.

Thank goodness — another sane person has arrived. I wonder if Milla and her sister have patched things up since Saturday, James thought, recalling Paulette's scurrilous behavior at Gillian's. When he reentered the kitchen a few minutes later, the room was filled with Milla's tinkling laughter and the bass rumble of Jackson's more reserved chuckle. Paulette placed each portion of the pastry-wrapped meat into a casserole dish while doing a perfect imitation of Martha Stewart.

"*Everyone* thinks I'm jealous of her because she's got her own exclusive cookware and bedding line with Macy's, but *please.*" She rubbed her hands vigorously with a red and green plaid dishtowel. "Macy's is *so* colloquial. *I've* been approached by Nordstrom's to come up with the desserts for their café menu. Clearly they recognize *real* talent, wouldn't you agree?"

Milla slid the baking dish into the oven. "How lovely, dear. And Willow tells me that you're going to be on one of our local shows on Thursday. That's very exciting."

Paulette took a slug of her drink and shrugged. "It's only a Virginia morning show with a few thousand viewers, but I've got a new cake recipe I'd like to try out before I film it for *my* show. I was going to make it anyway for you and Jackson to sample, so why not prepare it on air?"

"Yummy." Milla poured herself a glass of

merlot and then filled a second glass and handed it to James. "You're still going to help us taste all the wedding cake candidates, aren't you, dear?" She clinked the rim of her glass against his and sighed contentedly. "I'm so glad to have y'all gathered here together. My old family and my new family. Perfect."

Settling regally into one of the kitchen chairs, Paulette picked up the knife and fork laid out on the table and began cleaning spots from their surfaces with a paper napkin covered with rotund snowmen. "You were always disgustingly sentimental, Milla. I'm surprised you managed to muster up enough gumption to run your own business."

"You're not the only one who knows their way 'round pots and pans," Milla retorted sharply. "And my classes have been quite successful, thank you kindly." She sat down opposite her sister, but her posture was much less rigid than Paulette's stiff-backed carriage. "I gotta say, though, I'm getting a bit tired of teaching all those classes up in New Market and then driving down here to be with my future spouse. Jackson and I have decided to live in this house after we're married. My place is too small for the both of us, and I know Sir Charles will be tickled to death to run footloose and free around this yard."

"I still cannot believe you named a dog after that two-timing future king of England." Paulette eyed her sister curiously. "So what *are* you going to do? Please tell me that you're not going to revert to being a cloistered housewife." Paulette cast a judgmental stare at Jackson.

"Don't give *me* the hairy eyeball, woman," Jackson grumbled at Paulette. "Milla's the boss of her own mind."

Milla reached over and covered her fiancé's weathered hand with her own. "Jackson is always supportive of everything I do, and I've decided to open a gourmet gift shop right here in Quincy's Gap. We get a lot of tourists passing through, and the local folks are always complaining about having to drive to the big malls to buy anything unique, so I figure I'll get plenty of business."

James leaned over Milla's shoulder and refilled her wine glass. "That sounds great. What kind of things will you carry?"

"*Quincy's Whimsies* will be filled with all kinds of gourmet food. I plan to make things that neither the bakery nor our grocery stores carry." Milla pointed at Paulette. "And I'll stock all of your cookbooks, of course. Plus, I thought I'd feature products by some of our area craftsmen and women. I've already talked to a woman who makes the most gorgeous pottery, a gentleman who can fix me up with beeswax candles and fresh jars of honey, and a young man who makes goat's milk soaps and lotions. I took a goat's milk bubble bath the other night, and my skin felt *just* like a twenty-year-old's! Lord, the stuff is pure magic, I tell you!"

Paulette perked up fractionally at this pronouncement. "Really? I'd like to sample some of this *person's* products."

"We can visit his farm tomorrow. I'm thinking of using this young man's products for wedding favors." Milla got up, reduced the temperature of the oven, and turned on the front stove burner. She poured beef stock and some red wine into the meat drippings collected in a frying pan and began to stir the concoction.

"I doubt I have the appropriate attire for mucking through fields of goat droppings." Paulette's expression quickly turned sour.

"Relax, sister." Milla giggled. "You won't be forced to rough it too much. The boy's got a shed next to the house where he sells his wares."

"Just don't go displayin' that fur coat of

yours 'round this town anymore," Jackson ordered. "If James's redhead friend doesn't spray it with red paint, then you might just get attacked by a huntin' dog."

Paulette paled. "Oh, my. I guess I'll have to settle for my cashmere overcoat. Your hunting dogs won't go after that, will they? I could spray it with my Chanel Number Five. My *parfum* costs two hundred and sixty dollars an ounce, but I brought two bottles along, as I fully expected to encounter foul odors here in the *country*."

"The dogs'll only jump up on you if you've got dead animals draped across your collar or raw liver stuffed in your pockets. No need to go wastin' your fancy scent on our local mongrels," Jackson answered with a twinkle in his eye.

James couldn't help but smile over how much Jackson seemed to be enjoying Paulette's company. It was as if having someone around with a similar acerbic personality influenced the old man to adopt an attitude of playfulness and good humor. "Just keep things simple while you're here, Diva. It'll ease your way. Folks are friendly as church mice 'til you get their backs up. Then they're slow to forgive," he added, gesturing at James. "There's no call for you to be pickin' fights with my boy's friends. They're good people. All of 'em. Ya hear?" He turned to Milla and winked. "I'm done speech-makin'. We 'bout ready to eat?"

"Yes, dear heart. I just had to reduce this sauce until it was ready to pour over the beef. And now it is. Voilà!" Milla set a plate filled with a serving of Paulette's beef Wellington in front of Jackson. "See? I know French too."

James eyed the golden-brown pastry and inhaled the scents of wine, meat, mushrooms, onion, and cooked butter. He spread his snowman napkin onto his lap in anticipation. "This entrée isn't low-calorie is it?" he asked Milla as she handed him his plate.

"Not even the teeniest bit," she answered happily, placing a dish of steamed asparagus in the center of the table.

"*None* of the world's finest prepared foods are completely low-calorie," Paulette added, and she opened her napkin with a flourish as she stared at James's paunch. "Are you concerned about the caloric content for a specific reason?"

Nodding, James speared a piece of succulent meat with his fork and admired its pink center as he swirled it around in the fragrant drippings coating the bottom of his plate. "Starting tomorrow, I'm going to be keeping track of everything I eat, so tonight,

I feel a bit like a man going to the gallows. This is the last meal I can eat without paying attention to the food's nutritional content." He put the meat in his mouth, reveling in its flavor.

"Well, if this is your final supper," Milla paused to pour James more wine, "then it's mighty lucky my sister's made the dessert."

The next morning, James turned on the shower and, while waiting the three full minutes it took for the water to turn from piercingly cold to marginally hot, he reluctantly took off his flannel pajamas, tube socks, and leather slippers and prepared to weigh himself. Shivering, he paused for a second to consider how much he had eaten the night before.

Three glasses of wine, a serving of beef Wellington, steamed asparagus, and two pieces of Paulette's Ten-Layer Fudge Cake. I wonder if the scale can even compute all this poundage, he thought anxiously and then stepped onto the chilly surface of the metal scale.

When the numbers surfaced in their silver window, James groaned. His weight was higher than he had expected by a whopping eleven pounds.

"I probably gained five of these last night."

He got off the scale and then, after waiting for the screen to return to zero, stepped back on, hoping that there might have been an error in the previous reading. The scale added another three tenths of a pound for his efforts.

"Damn it," he muttered, snatching the shower curtain aside and hustling into the stream of hot water. The heat immediately eased some of his tension, and as he lathered his hair with shampoo, he gave himself a pep talk. "It's okay. Today is a fresh start." After rinsing his head, he opened his eyes and stuck his tongue out at the scale, which seemed to be mocking him on the other side of the clear shower curtain. "This isn't over, buddy."

After getting dressed, James packed his lunch, poured coffee into a travel mug, and tried to ignore the covered cake plate resting in the middle of the kitchen table.

"I don't see you. I do not see you," James spoke to the white ceramic dome that seemed to call to him from across the room. "I'm not even thinking of all those layers of sweet, buttery, and incredibly smooth chocolate icing or about how moist and springy the cake —" he cut himself off. "Nope. Not interested."

After shoving an apple into his lunch bag,

James shrugged his coat on and cast a second glance at the cake plate. *I wonder how much is left,* he thought.

Unable to stop himself, he lifted up the cover several inches, revealing the remaining wedge of fudge layer cake. A whiff of chocolate scent floated beneath his eager nostrils.

"I'm not even going to eat one of the chocolate curls sitting there in that bed of chocolate frosting. That's how much willpower I've got." He inhaled deeply, and his mouth filled with saliva in anticipation of receiving an exquisite morsel of Paulette's dessert. "Well, maybe just a few crumbs . . ." James heard the weakness in his voice, but could not tear his eyes away from the hunk of cake.

"Who you talkin' to, boy?" Jackson asked gruffly as he entered the kitchen in an old bathrobe.

James slammed the lid back on the cake plate and stood up guiltily. "No one. I'm . . . I'm off to the library. Are you planning to work on a painting of Paulette's hands today?"

"Yep. Soon as I polish off that leftover cake for breakfast." He patted his flat stomach as James watched on with envy. "I reckon it'll help inspire me, 'cause I'm gonna show her frostin' this very cake in the paintin'. I liked how she angled her wrist just so to get it on there all nice and smooth."

James wished his father luck, and after gazing longingly once more at the cake plate, he headed off to work. Instead of driving to the library, however, he swung into a parking spot in front of the Sweet Tooth, the town's bakery.

Megan and Amelia Flowers, the mother/daughter team who kept the townsfolks' bellies filled with homemade breads, cookies, and pastries, were bent over the display window, smoothing a sheet of red velvet fabric across the bottom ledge.

"Good morning, Professor," Megan greeted James briefly, and then she stood erect and put her hands on her narrow hips. "I had the *pleasure* of meeting your newest family member yesterday."

"Uh-oh," James moaned softly, and then he frowned. "Why would Paulette come in here? She does her own baking."

"For a croissant to go with her *latte,*" Amelia answered, her full lips turning into a practiced pout. "But she told my mom that our croissant wasn't flaky enough and bought a baguette instead. She didn't like that much either. Said it was only supposed to be crusty on the *outside,* not inside *and* out."

"I'm sorry." James tugged on his scarf, which suddenly felt too tight. "Paulette can be really impolite, and she seems determined to offend everyone in Quincy's Gap."

Megan picked up a large box wrapped in red and green foil and stuffed with wax paper, and she began to fill it with candy-cane-shaped loaves of egg bread. Megan had ingeniously dyed half of the dough red and left the other its natural shade of whitish-yellow, so that when braided, the bread looked striped, just like the sugary version of a candy cane.

"She didn't stop her criticism with my breads either." Megan continued crossly. "She made her shrinking violet of an assistant buy three of my cakes — whole ones, mind you — and then they left, no doubt so that our visiting *celebrity* could hold that girl down and force-feed her slices of my cake. I thought I was rid of them, but twenty minutes later they were back! That *TV* cake baker was chock full of *suggestions* on how to improve my recipes!" Megan furiously sifted powdered sugar over the candy-cane bread.

"They weren't suggestions." Amelia placed another gift box filled with iced gingerbread animals in the window. "That witch came in here lookin' to pick a fight. She told my mom that her cakes were dry and her icing was crunchy as kitty litter! I'd have liked to pull her white hair out strand by strand when she said that."

Megan shot a proud look at her daughter, and her tone immediately softened. "Honey, you go on and get to your studying now. I know you've got exams tomorrow, and I can handle things for the rest of the day." She watched her daughter leave. "I can't believe she'll be done with college soon. Where does the time go? She's dying to move to New York, but how could I let her go there if the city is populated by people like Paulette Martine?"

"Oh, I wouldn't judge all of Manhattan based on her," James cautioned. "In fact, I hear New Yorkers are pretty friendly. They just seem intimidating because they wear black so much."

Megan looked unconvinced. "I'll really miss Amelia's artistic touch when she leaves me to pursue her fashion design career. I mean, look at this candy house she made for the window." The baker gestured at an enormous gingerbread house built in the style of a southern plantation.

"It looks like Tara from *Gone with the*

Wind." James marveled at the immense, two-story structure. It had a roof created from vanilla wafers, two chimneys crafted of colored sugar cubes, graham cracker shutters, icing railings complete with green gumdrop garlands, flowers and shrubs made of marzipan, and a split-rail fence built using chocolate-covered pretzel sticks. It even had wreaths on the double front doors, made of mini red and green M&Ms and a marshmallow snowman with a black licorice hat in front of the veranda.

"Can you help me carry this masterpiece to the window?" Megan asked James. As they lifted the house, which would form the centerpiece of the window display, Megan's mouth deepened into a frown. "That woman actually had the nerve to tell me that I should run right out and buy the book she wrote about baking cakes. I was so mad I could have shoved her into the oven! She's mighty lucky it was turned off."

"For what it's worth, *I* love your cakes." James eyed one of his favorites: Megan's butterscotch cake.

Dusting off her hands, Megan touched James on the sleeve. "It wasn't my intention to take my ire out on you, Professor. You know you're one of my best customers and I'll never stop being grateful to you for sticking up for Amelia and me when our reputation was on the line." Looking at her colorful window display, Megan's frown dissipated. "Enough of my yammering. What can I get for you today?"

"I think I'll take my employees some hot cross buns. Scott and Francis are still up in arms over our missing library elf." The bells hanging from the front door tinkled as another customer walked in. James continued speaking without turning around. "I might have to take out an ad in the *Star,* imploring the thief to bring it back before those two conduct a house-to-house search."

"It so happens we're offering a holiday discount to all our advertisers," a familiar voice said.

James pivoted slowly on his heel, reluctant to meet the hazel eyes of Murphy Alistair, editor of the *Star,* author of the soon-to-be-released novel about the death that had occurred inches from where he now stood, and his girlfriend of almost half a year.

Ex-girlfriend, he reminded himself, noting how attractive Murphy looked in a black turtleneck, jeans, and a red toggle coat.

Murphy gave James a thin smile. "How are you?"

"Fine," he answered tersely, and then

couldn't help but add, "I saw the postcard promoting your book."

"Cool cover, don't you think?" Her face glowed. "Advance sales are great too. My agent says there are actually two movie studios that want the rights as well. Can you believe it?"

Megan silently placed a white bakery box tied with green-striped string onto the counter. Along with most people in Quincy's Gap, she knew that James had broken up with Murphy because the good-looking reporter had neglected to tell him that she had written and then sold a novel featuring James and his supper club friends as bumbling amateur sleuths.

"Anything else, Professor?" Megan queried with a false cheerfulness, hoping that her two customers wouldn't get into a heated argument. Having had a corpse in her bakery a few years ago and her daughter briefly viewed as a murder suspect was more than enough excitement for the single mom.

"No, thank you." James paid for his buns and then brushed past Murphy. "Have a nice holiday," he told her with a polite formality he normally reserved for strangers.

Murphy's enthusiasm was instantly quelled. "You too," she replied, and then, as

James opened the door, she called out, "You're going to need to face the fact that this book is coming out! Try to consider that it might do some good for the town. Tourism will increase if people come here to see where the novel's events took place. Especially if it gets made into a movie." She glanced at Megan. "Your business might triple! Same with Dolly's Diner! Couldn't everybody use a bit more money in the bank?"

"So that's why you wrote it?" James asked in a dangerously soft voice. "Out of altruism?"

Squirming, Murphy focused on an arrangement of custard-filled donuts covered with white icing and red and green sprinkles. "No. I wrote it because it was a good story. But it could also be a boon for Quincy's Gap."

"Maybe," James opened the door and the silver bells jingled with a tinny, merry sound completely incongruent to what he was feeling. "But I can think of five of your neighbors who are seeing this book as a bane, not a boon."

Megan broke the tension by laughing. "If y'all use words like that, there isn't a soul in this town who's going to be able to understand that book!"

Murphy's mouth curved into an amused grin and James suddenly felt petty. After all, he hadn't even read the novel yet. Perhaps he and his friends had been portrayed as wise and generous servants of their community, though in truth, he doubted Murphy's book would appeal to Hollywood unless it was riddled with colorful content. He knew that part of his anger stemmed from the fear that he might be humiliated in print by someone he had trusted with his most intimate thoughts.

"Have a Merry Christmas, Murphy," he said with as much sincerity as he could muster and left the bakery. As the door closed, he thought he heard her whisper, "It won't be merry without you."

Murphy then turned to Megan Flowers and declared, "I'm going to take every single one of your donuts. A girl's gotta have *something* sweet in her life, and if it isn't going to be a man, then it may as well be a donut."

"Amen, sister," Megan agreed as she began to fill Murphy's order.

FIVE: BENNETT'S BREAKFAST CASSEROLE

"I love this. Our havin' breakfast for supper!" Lindy exclaimed as she settled on the floor in front of Bennett's leather couch and kicked off her fleece-lined boots. She wiggled her toes, which were encased in black socks stitched with poinsettias, and issued a contented sigh. "I feel like I'm gettin' ready for a sleepover party."

Bennett gestured at his red cotton sweatpants. "I feel like I'm nearly wearin' pajamas. You can go on home and change into a flannel nightgown if you want."

Lindy pretended to be insulted. "Now why are you assumin' that I wear some kind of grandma gown? I happen to sleep in pink satin pajamas from Victoria's Secret, thank you very much."

"I bet those look *lovely* with your skin tone and black hair," Gillian complimented her friend. "No satin for me, of course. *I* wear an organic cotton/bamboo blend nightgown. It's a planet-friendly fabric. As you might expect, there are no dyes, so the gown's natural beige. Still, I feel much *closer* to Mother Earth during sleep." She took a spoonful of apples from a Pyrex baking dish. "Are these baked, Lucy?"

Following Lindy's example, Lucy had removed her boots and was warming her feet in front of the fire, her dinner plate balanced on her lap. "No, they're raw Gala apples, but I soaked them overnight in a marinade of orange juice and cinnamon. I figured they'd offset the salty taste of Bennett's breakfast casserole."

"And my cucumber and red onion vinegar salad," James added. "I'm relieved to discover that it's actually possible to have a healthy meal that doesn't taste like cardboard. I've got a full plate here containing less than five hundred calories. Amazing." He took a bite of Bennett's casserole.

"Hmm," he said, toasting his friend with his empty fork. "Well done."

"Thank you, my man. And now, before we watch Dr. Ruth and the Diva of Dough go at it, let's get the *Jeopardy!* board game fired up. I've only got a few weeks before the real show tapes, folks, and I wanna be one of the few African American men to win a big ole pile of money from those rich TV folks."

Bennett placed the game board on the floor and the supper club members gathered around it, enjoying the crackling fire, the delicious food, and one another's company. As usual, Bennett answered question after question correctly.

"I think this one might actually stump you." Lucy held up a card with a triumphant flourish. "Here it is: after June, this month is the most popular for wedding ceremonies."

"Pffah! Easy!" Bennett snorted. "What is August. And Las Vegas is the top destination for weddings, followed by Hawaii and then the Bahamas. The average honeymoon lasts for one week. Wanna hear some more?"

"Have you memorized all these questions?" Lucy accused playfully.

"Not yet," Bennett replied. "But I got all the answers from the DVD version in the ole noggin, as well as a bunch from the Trivial Pursuit games. Personally, I think they exaggerated the title of that *Genius* edition." He looked at James. "I could tell you a whole mess of weddin' statistics in case you wanna pass them on to your daddy."

"Sure. Maybe it'll make him feel better to know that weddings make *all* women go completely crazy," James answered, and he received scowls from the three females in the room.

"The average wedding ring costs around two grand," Bennett said hurriedly to deflect attention from James's comment. "Most couples invite about one hundred and seventy-five people to their wedding."

"I don't even know that many people, and half my family is Catholic!" Lindy joked.

"Well, we've all messed up the averages for the ages of your run-of-the-mill bride and groom. According to the facts, I should've been married at least twice by now," Lucy remarked sourly.

"Statistics can be misleading. *I* believe that it's never too late to find your soul mate. The *yin* to your *yang.* Our kindred spirit, finally guided home," Gillian gushed. "Look at Jackson and Milla." She reached over the game board and gave Bennett's hand a warm squeeze. "Perhaps you and Jade are meant to entwine your lives together like two vines of climbing roses stretching toward the sun." Reaching her arms into the air above her head, Gillian exhaled loudly as Bennett cocked his head to one side in bewilderment.

"Speakin' of roses." He cleared his throat and continued to watch Gillian out of the corner of his eye. "I can tell you the names of a dozen climbing roses from Baltimore Belle to Dublin Bay to Silver Moon, but if I don't get a handle on more pop-culture facts, I'll be toast. Without a doubt, it's my Achilles' heel." His expression turned grim. "How am I supposed to know the name of Paris Hilton's dog for cryin' out loud? I think it's already pretty damned impressive that I know she lugs around a Chihuahua like it was a handbag."

"She's got two, actually," Lindy answered hastily. "The first one, Tinkerbell, got too large to be a fashion accessory. I believe Paris's latest Chihuahua is named Bambi."

"How do you know this stuff, woman?" Bennett looked impressed. "Are you some kind of *Entertainment Tonight* junkie? 'Cause I do *not* have time for that."

"No, Mr. Mailman. I read *People.* If you wanna be up on all that's goin' on in the world of celebrity gossip, pick one up at the gym and start studyin' up. You need to know who's goin' out with who, who's pregnant, who's lost twenty pounds on the leek soup diet, who's won an Oscar, an Emmy, a Grammy."

"You could come to the library if you need a copy," James suggested. "Though you can't get near it when Mrs. Turner and her Mom's Morning Out girlfriends are in the building. And come to think of it, once school lets out, the junior high and high school girls hog all those kinds of magazines." He frowned. "If only my patrons got that excited about literature." He picked up a question card and turned to Gillian. "This environmental group was founded in Vancouver in 1971 and was originally known as the Don't Make a Wave Committee."

"That's an easy one." Gillian fluffed her cloud of red and blonde-streaked hair. "What is Greenpeace."

Bennett clapped her on the shoulder. "Well done, woman."

As they played on, James told his friends about his visit to Dr. Ruth. "She is the epitome of kindness. Even though it's a hassle keeping this food log, I already feel more optimistic about getting fit since I saw her on Monday." He pointed at the television. "I just hope she got a word in edgewise on *Good Morning Virginia* since she had to share the spotlight with Paulette."

"The Diva's been quite busy making enemies since she got to town, hasn't she?" Lindy said, packing up the game pieces. "I hear she raised quite a ruckus at Food Lion because they don't carry super-fine sugar."

James nodded. "You can add Megan and Amelia Flowers to the growing list of folks who will be happy to see her go back to New York. And I can't say that I'm one of her fans either. I'll be quite relieved to drop her off at the curb at Dulles after the wedding."

"Okay, folks, it's time for the news." Bennett clapped his hands, returned his playing piece to the game box, and turned on his small television set with the rather grainy screen. "We've got sugar-free caramel pudding and Cool Whip for dessert. So grab a spoon and eat up. By the time you've heard Dr. Ruth speak, you'll all want to become her clients."

The image on the television screen morphed from an orange tabby cat gulping down a bowl of Meow Mix to an image of a somber-faced anchorman. The news anchor, who had shellacked hair and a subtle tan, related the details of a convenience store robbery that had occurred shortly after dark that same day in the outskirts of Charlottesville.

"Tony Kim, the clerk on duty this evening," the anchorman intoned, "did not possess keys to the safe and could only offer the assailant the cash from his register. Apparently, two hundred dollars was not enough to appease the armed robber, and he demanded wallets and jewelry from each one of the store's customers."

The camera switched from the anchorman's face to a scene of police cars with flashing lights parked helter-skelter around the perimeter of the small gas station. Members of Charlottesville's police force gesticulated and conversed with deputies from the local Sheriff's Department. James felt that their behavior seemed a bit theatrical due to the presence of the television crews and decided to ask Lucy if she agreed, but when he glanced over at her and noted the rapt attention she was giving to the broadcast, he decided to keep quiet.

After providing a teaser on the weekend weather as well as the outcome of the men's basketball game between rivals Virginia and Virginia Tech, the camera zoomed out in order to show a wide-angle view of the entire news desk. At this point, the anchorwoman arched her eyebrows and said, "And things heated up in the town of New Market today. The life of a well-known chef, television star, and author was threatened after she appeared on our own CBS morning show. Stay tuned for the surprising events that were captured on film by one of our crew members."

As James and his friends sat in stunned silence, the Aflac duck flew on screen and jumped in the driver's seat of a taxi cab, planning to take over the injured driver's fares and save his family from certain starvation.

"I can't stand it!" Lucy grabbed James's arm, causing him to overturn his spoonful of caramel pudding onto the front of his sweater. "What happened this morning? Don't leave us hanging like this!"

James shook his head dumbly. "Honestly, I have no idea." He protested. "No one called me at work and the house was empty when I got done with lifting weights, so I'm as mystified as you are." He flexed his arm and poked his sore bicep, hoping Lucy would be impressed, but she had already returned her attention to the TV.

The Aflac commercial was followed by a lengthy ad expounding the myriad virtues of Chrysler's new minivan. A pair of shiny-haired, white-toothed children sat in the back seat, laughing as they watched the Cartoon Network on their Sirius satellite television system while an unusually happy-looking teenage boy played video games using the screen above the third row of seats. In the front, the smug, slim, and casually dressed parents gazed proudly at their progeny in the rearview mirror and exchanged deeply contented grins. At the end of the ad, the family disembarked from their cool car and prepared to share a picnic lunch on a scenic overlook near the ocean.

"Those parents are gonna shove all three kids off that cliff," Lindy declared. "That's why they're smiling."

"I thought it was because all of their cup holders were filled with little bottles of whiskey," Bennett remarked, and then groaned as a weight loss commercial featuring Special K cereal droned on and on. "If that woman in the red dress pivots in front of that mirror one more time, I'm gonna bludgeon her with the cereal box. I'm tired of all these damn ads!"

"Me too," Gillian agreed. "Our culture is simply *barraged* with capitalistic messages. That's why I prefer to record all of my favorite shows from the National Geographic Channel and fast forward the steady stream of 'buy-me's'! It's *very* empowering."

"Shhhh," Lucy hissed. "They're finally coming back on!"

"Earlier today on CBS's *Good Morning Virginia* show there was a face-off between area nutritionist Ruth Wilkins and celebrity chef Madame Paulette Martine, also known as the Diva of Dough." The anchorwoman began her story by facing the camera with a stoic expression. "The focus of this morning's show was on opposing positions regarding Americans' tendency to overindulge on rich foods between Thanksgiving and New Year's.

"Ms. Wilkins began the *Good Morning* segment by providing pointers on how to avoid the curse of holiday weight gain. Then Madame Martine allowed several members of our studio audience to sample her famous cakes. Here's a taste of what those lucky few experienced."

The screen switched to a setting familiar to all of the supper club members. The segment had been filmed at Milla's culinary school. Paulette, wearing an apron covered with forest green fleurs-de-lis, stood proudly behind three gorgeous cakes resting upon glass pedestals. She swept her hand over Milla's butcher block as though trace particles of sugar or flour lingered on the polished surface.

"These cakes are the *perfect* accompaniments for the season," Paulette began, her voice clear and authoritative, yet strangely soft and melodic as well. "The first is a praline pecan bundt cake. This is an easy cake to create, and it's a wonderful gift to take to a neighbor who's feeling unwell, to a holiday potluck party, or even to the school bake sale. The cake's buttery center is delectably moist and the praline icing simply cascades over the hills and ridges created by the mold. Lastly, the rim is covered by toasted and candied pecans. The result is that this dessert is just as easy on the eye as it is to eat!"

The host, a tall woman wearing a red suit, took a small bite of the praline pecan cake. "Delicious!" she exclaimed, and then she asked Ruth, "In your opinion, how many calories are in a single slice?"

"About one thousand," Ruth answered calmly.

"One thousand? That's nothing!" Paulette flicked a dishtowel in dismissal. "A slice of this cake is worth every calorie! Remember, my fellow food lovers, real food *tastes* like real food. It might contain fat and calories and butter and cream, but you shouldn't put anything less onto your tongue!" Paulette theatrically threw her arms out wide.

"This is a season of celebration! We should be *enjoying* this special time with our loved ones, and part of that tradition is sharing *homemade* foods. I ask *you!*" She pointed a spatula at the men and women seated on the other side of the counter. "Would you rather eat this lemon meringue layer cake with a filling of cream and strawberries or a rubber chicken from Lean Cuisine? Would you rather count calories or gather around the table, slice this cake, pour some coffee, and make some Christmas memories?"

Someone in the audience shouted, "I'd like some of that there cake right this minute!" and more requests followed.

Paulette issued a tinkling laugh that sounded extremely false to James's ear and pointed at the lemon meringue cake. "People often reserve meringue cakes for the warmer months, but I love this cake in the winter because the stiff peaks of meringue remind me of miniature mountains covered with a layer of fresh snow." She pivoted the cake so that the camera could focus on the slice she was cutting. "Look at the interior of this gorgeous confection. The lemon cake is so moist that it will feel like a cloud inside of your mouth. Next, the tart sweetness of the strawberries will make you close your eyes and moan. This cake is like mistletoe. The object of your desire *cannot* resist you if you offer them a slice of this heaven." She handed the cake wedge to the show's host. "You find me a person who would rather eat a bran muffin, and I'll show you someone who is, quite simply, afraid of experiencing pleasure."

Ruth shook her head in vigorous disagreement. "That's an unfair —"

"And if you'd rather your sweet packed a little punch, then might I suggest my Eggnog Cake with Butter Rum Frosting?" Paulette completely ignored the nutritionist's protest and, unfortunately, so did the show's host. "And *I* don't use rum extract. I use the rum that comes from a large bottle with a handle! Yes, *mes chéries,* dark rum and plenty of it, so if you're on the wagon, stay away from this cake!"

The audience tittered appreciatively. Paulette began to cut slices of the eggnog cake while emphasizing that it could be made at any time of the year, as the batter didn't actually contain an ounce of eggnog.

"Though eggnog happens to be my secret vice," Paulette whispered into the microphone attached to her apron. "I can drink gallons of the stuff. Especially when I'm whipping up one of my triple-tiered chocolate mousse cakes. If I'm drinking eggnog, then I can't drink the cake batter!" The audience laughed harder and issued a hearty round of applause.

"She really knows how to work a crowd." James couldn't help but be impressed.

Lucy nodded. "That's why I was excited to meet her. She's totally charismatic on her television show, and just *look* at those cakes! I'd love to get my hands on all three of them."

James eyed his pudding cup. "I know this is a healthy dessert, but I'd much rather have a slice of that ten-layer chocolate fudge cake Paulette made for us a few nights ago. She's a nasty piece of work, but she's *almost* tolerable when she's baking."

Paulette described the smooth, buttery frosting while deftly stepping directly in front of Ruth's more diminutive figure. As she watched the camera zoom in toward the nutmeg-flecked icing, Gillian asked, "How *does* one create ten layers? They must be thin as a fingernail; *delicate* as a butterfly wing."

"It's pretty incredible, actually," James said. "I saw her remove three cake pans from the oven. After they had cooled, she overturned the cakes from the pans and stacked all three layers on top of one another other. She then started measuring from the bottom to the top with a ruler. She'd stick a toothpick into the cooked cake every half inch or so and then swivel it around and repeat the process." He gestured at the screen. "The cake was about the same height as that eggnog cake on TV, but it looked like a porcupine with all the toothpicks sticking out of it."

"Let me guess," Lindy said. "The Diva then cut the cake layers using a serrated knife, right?"

James shook his head. "Incorrect. She used dental floss. It slid right through the cake and each layer looked absolutely even."

"Mighty clever." Bennett cast an admiring glance at the television.

As the five friends watched, the camera focused on Paulette's head and shoulders as she took a bite of her cake and smiled in satisfaction. "Scrumptious! Now, why would you want to live a life that doesn't include cakes such as these? Forget spending your money on diet food or weight loss centers. They're just going to suffocate you with rules and restrictions. Enjoy life. Instead, run out to the bookstore, buy my latest release, *Holidays with the Diva of Dough,* and forget about the gym and the nutritionist. Do you want to be skinny and miserable or do you want to be *happy* and eat cake?"

The audience burst into spontaneous applause and the camera returned to the studio anchor desk. "Following the conclusion of the *Good Morning* segment," the anchorwoman stated mechanically, "Madame Martine signed copies of her new cookbook and then left the studio. In the parking lot adjacent to the Fix 'n Freeze location where the show had taken place, Ms. Martine was cornered and, according to witnesses, harassed by Ruth Wilkins's three sons."

The camera switched to a street scene and James recognized the lavender front door belonging to Milla's cooking school. A woman clutching two of Paulette's books against her ample chest stood on the threshold, doing her best to look appropriately shocked and outraged.

"They blocked her path!" The woman declared as though a grievous crime had been committed. "Those three boys! And they were yellin' all sorts of off-color stuff at Madame Martine. I'm a God-fearin' woman, so I won't repeat any of the ugly words they said, but one of them told the Diva she should get out of town. They were definitely threatenin' her!"

"She ain't lyin' either," a man standing nearby raised his voice in agreement. "The biggest one, the Wilkins boy who plays nose tackle for the Hokies, he told Miss Paulette that she was gonna pay for messin' with his mama's business. Said it'd be her fault if they couldn't finish up at school 'cause no one was gonna wanna make appointments after the word got 'round that it's okay to eat cake." The man shrugged. "Shoot, that Paulette woman just said what we all wanna hear anyhow."

"Poor Dr. Ruth," James murmured as photographs of her three sons wearing football pads, numbered jerseys, and fierce scowls were displayed for the viewing audience.

"Those pictures made them look like thugs!" Lindy exclaimed. "This is silly. Boys always try to look all sorts of tough for their sports photos. The media is trying to influence public opinion against the Wilkins family!"

"Welcome to the twenty-first century," Bennett muttered darkly.

The final video clip showed two of the Wilkins brothers pounding on the passenger window of Paulette's rental car. The third had his arm around his mother as she shouted at her other sons to stop, Ruth's normally radiant face eclipsed with anxiety.

The members of the supper club watched with growing dismay as the largest brother abruptly shoved his handsome face, twisted by anger and humiliation, against the glass separating him from Paulette. As the footage had been captured from behind the car, it was impossible to see what the Diva of Dough's reaction was to the young man's wrath, but when he dragged his index finger slowly against the exposed skin of his throat, all of the supper club members gasped aloud.

"Oh my," Gillian breathed. "That young man needs to learn how to control his *baser* emotions."

"Too late for that." Bennett reached for a second helping of pudding. "Those boys are already in a whole heap of trouble."

Six: Grilled Chicken and Portobello Sandwich

"I have a surprise for you," Milla told Paulette over breakfast. "Well, two surprises, actually. The first is this." She handed her sister a tumbler of eggnog. "I made it myself. I know it's your favorite durin' the holidays."

James poured himself some coffee and watched Paulette as she raised the glass up to her face and sniffed. "You remembered the nutmeg."

" 'Course I did." Milla handed James the creamer. "I figured since you had a bit of a shock yesterday you could use a treat."

"Nonsense. I couldn't have *paid* for better publicity." Paulette took a delicate sip of eggnog and then took another, rather unladylike slurp, and replaced the tumbler on the table with a thud. "That story will be picked up on the national level by tonight. I'm quite pleased." She looked at James appraisingly. "You're out and about rather early for a weekend. Don't librarians lounge around reading or organizing their spice cabinets during their free time?"

Milla answered before James had the chance. "Our spices are already in alphabetical order, and James is gonna see a house that's just come on the market. His Realtor lady called last night all excited."

"Foaming at the mouth, most likely," James mumbled.

"We are headin' over to the Holiday Inn to visit with some special guests. And then we're all goin' out to lunch."

Paulette's eyes narrowed. "I've barely recovered from our midweek foray to that disgusting goat farm. Who would these *special* people be?"

"Oh, just your children," Milla replied casually.

"Truly? Chase is here?"

"*And* Chloe." Milla chided with a smile.

"I thought it would be nice if we could all spend some time together before the weddin'." Folding her napkin into a neat square, she hastily added, "Wheezie's here too."

Her face instantly darkening, Paulette scraped back her chair and placed her hands on her hips. "You invited Louise! How could you do that to me?" She pulled her cell phone from her purse. "You should have known better. I'm calling Willow and telling her to book us on the next flight home. I did *not* agree to be a participant in one of your Hallmark moments."

Milla reached over and gently clasped her sister's hand. "In case you didn't notice — we're getting *old,* my dear. Do you want to go to the end of your days without seeing your own sister again? She's your flesh and blood, Patty. She looked out for you when we were little — keeping the Howell boys from picking on you, baking you special treats, sewing your dresses after you tore them climbing trees . . ."

"And what?" Paulette was angry. "I ruined her life in return? Is *that* what you're going to say next? That I rewarded all those kindnesses by destroying her dreams?"

Grabbing Paulette's other hand, Milla pushed the cell phone aside and stared fixedly into her eyes. "It is time for guilt and pride and blame to be set aside. What happened was a long time ago. If Wheezie was willing to come, to make peace with *you,* than you should be willing to hold your arms out to your eldest sister and embrace her." James had never seen such a fierce determination animate Milla's features. "You owe her that much, Patty."

Paulette pulled away and fell silent. James hurriedly finished his breakfast of low-sugar oatmeal and loaded his bowl, spoon, and coffee cup into the dishwasher. He could feel both women watching him as he wrapped a scarf around his neck and zipped up his parka.

"You've always been such a sentimental fool," Paulette finally said, her voice tinged with annoyance. "So after this charming family reunion, I suppose I'll be allowed some time alone in order to bake *your* wedding cake samples."

"Certainly." Milla cleared the breakfast dishes. "And James will be ready and willing to taste them all this evening. Right, my dear?"

James paused. "Just a bite of each." He then opened his pocket journal and recorded the calories he had just consumed.

Cinnamon & Spice Oatmeal	120 calories
Banana	110 calories
Coffee w/cream	40 calories

Not bad, James thought to himself. Though usually reluctant to leave the warm and cozy kitchen, he was more than happy to step out into the morning's sharp cold in order to escape Paulette's discontented stares.

Joan had offered to pick him up at her office so that they could drive to the house in one vehicle, but he had politely declined. James knew that she would use that opportunity to influence his opinion on the property by touting its fine qualities while de-emphasizing its flaws. She had already mentioned the fact that the owner was being relocated and was therefore very motivated to sell.

"It was a promotion, you see," Joan's voice was airy as she relayed this bit of gossip to James over the phone the night before. "So he doesn't need to focus too much on profit. Apparently, his new house in Nashville is on a two-acre lot and has twice the square footage of the one they're selling. It's a good thing too because his wife is expecting twins, and though this house might be perfect for *you,* a bachelor, or for a couple with *only one* child, it's rather tight for a family of four. Do you need directions?"

James had already driven by the house twice, so he knew exactly where it was. He desperately hoped the interior was in good repair, because he had liked the house occupying 27 Hickory Hill Lane upon first glance. A two-story cottage with a front porch and a fenced-in yard, the little yellow house seemed tidy and welcoming.

Even in winter, when the trees and shrubs in the yard were bare and the lawn was brown-tinged in its dormancy, the white icicle lights dripping from the porch eaves illuminated the entire façade of the home. The buttery paint color, the curls of white smoke emanating from the chimney, and the well-groomed appearance of the yard were very attractive to James, and he was anxious over the thought that someone else would snap up this gem before he had the chance to get inside.

"I hope you haven't been waiting long!" Joan chirped loudly as she rattled a fistful of keys. She hesitated at the end of the front path, clasping her hands together theatrically. "Isn't this a charmer?"

"I like it," James admitted cautiously.

"Wait until you see how darling it is

inside!" Joan unlocked the front door and asked James to wait on the threshold, and she breezed around turning on lights, her spiked boot heels clicking across the hardwood floors.

He then followed her mutely through a spacious living room, a brightly lit kitchen, and three small but comfortable bedrooms.

"The baths have both been redone and the appliances in the kitchen are new as of this year," Joan trilled. "You'll have to buy your own washer and dryer, but aside from that, you could practically move right in." She frowned as they stood in the center of the third bedroom, which obviously belonged to a young boy. "I guess you'd have to remove all those glow-in-the-dark stickers on the ceiling and repaint that. Hopefully it won't require sanding. I really wish people wouldn't use those things! Too, too tacky!" She looked at James. "Do you want me to ask the seller to deal with that repair? It could be one of the terms of your offer."

James was surprised. Had his immediate affinity regarding the house been that transparent? "That's okay." They returned to the kitchen and gazed out over the deck. "I'd like to walk around the backyard really quickly," James said.

"Of course. I'll stay right here and give

you a moment to think." The real estate agent pointed at a copse of trees lining the right-hand corner of the property. "And don't worry about that swing set or the tree house back there. You could always get rid of those by putting an ad in the *Star.* People love getting something for free, whether it's a swing set or lumber."

"I'm sure you're right," James agreed just to get Joan to stop talking.

Exiting through the one-car garage, he was again impressed by the tidiness of the house. There wasn't so much as an oil spot in the garage, and the flower beds in the backyard had been cleared of leaves and the spent stalks of perennials, and they were redolent with the fragrance of fresh mulch. James read the carefully written signs identifying which blooms he could expect to appear in the spring and early summer. He was also delighted to see a raised square of earth surrounded by wire mesh fence at the rear of the property.

"A vegetable garden!" James exclaimed in delight, and he walked around the perimeter of vacant soil. Glancing upward at the group of trees, he couldn't help but draw in a breath as he took in the sturdy tree fort, which had been built to resemble a little castle, complete with turrets and a trap door. A stout rope ladder offered access to the aerial kingdom and a toy telescope had been attached to one of the walls to allow for the scouting of enemies.

I couldn't tear that down! James thought, wishing that he was still small or agile enough to scamper up the ladder and spend a future summer afternoon reading inside the leafy escape.

When he returned through the garage into the house, he found Joan examining the contents of the refrigerator.

"Looks like they're having chicken for dinner," she remarked, as though it were perfectly acceptable to scrutinize a seller's fridge. "So . . . should we go back to the office and draw up an offer?"

"Yes." James's heart tripped in excitement as he gazed around the room. "I love this house. This is where I'd like to live. It already feels . . ."

"Like home?" Joan smiled with sincerity. "I recognize the look on your face. I've seen it a thousand times before, and I never get tired of it."

James spent the next hour signing documents and rereading the legalese written in a minute font on a stack of preapproval papers drawn up by Shenandoah Savings & Loan.

"I commend you for having your financial ducks in a row," Joan said. "If only *all* of my clients were this prepared. I can't tell you how many times I've worked my tail off to get to the offer stage only to discover they don't have enough money in the bank to pay for a single mortgage payment!"

"It's not easy to come up with the down payment most banks require these days." James felt he needed to defend those struggling to become homeowners for the first time. "In my parents' day, it was easier to purchase a house. Now, people have to wait longer and longer until they have enough money."

"Which they can save by not maxing out their credit cards. Or by living with their parents." Joan shot James a meaningful glance. "But I fear this trend only helps to foster dependency in our children. My own sons, for example, will find their bedrooms transformed into exercise and craft rooms as soon as they graduate college. They're welcome to come home for visits, but that is it!" She stacked a sheaf of papers with violent decisiveness.

"You might find that you need them around more than you'd originally planned," James commented argumentatively. "That's why I moved in with my father. I wasn't trying to leech off him, but to care for him. My financial situation wasn't part of the equation. I quit my job in Williamsburg to be with him."

Joan blinked and then made a quick recovery. "That's so devoted of you! But now he has a new wife to coddle him and *you* can get busy finding one of your own, right? Maybe you won't need to take down that tree house after all."

Fighting an urge to tell the Realtor that she didn't possess an ounce of tact, James requested that she call him as soon as the owners responded to the offer and marched out of the office. Even though it was only eleven, his stomach was rumbling in hunger. He dialed Lucy's number on his cell phone.

"Are you free for lunch?" he asked her. "I'm craving a diner meal."

"Sure am," she answered. "I've got one of those awful split shifts this weekend and am on the clock at one, so I'll have to meet you at Dolly's armed and dangerous."

James visualized how Lucy's toned yet feminine body filled out her brown and beige uniform. "That's just how I like you. You know where to find me."

"Yeah, yeah. Your island booth. Why do you always sit there, James?"

Reflecting on the vacation poster with its

pristine white sand and cerulean ocean, he replied, "Because I dream of going to a place like that someday. I'd like to put a lounge chair in the shade and just read. For once, I'd catch up on all those books piled up on my nightstand that I never seem to have time for."

"Seems pretty antisocial," Lucy remarked.

"Oh, it'd be great if you were there with me. I'd rather talk to you than read a book anyway." He sighed as he pictured them sharing a giant cocktail served in a hulled-out pineapple as an ocean breeze fluttered through the palms above their double hammock. "Hopefully, I'll be too short on cash to go this year, but I'll tell you all about *that* over lunch."

Dolly welcomed James as though he had been away at sea for six months. "Where have you been?" the red-cheeked proprietor demanded as she pulled him into her cushioned bosom. "You're not goin' into hidin' already 'cause of Murphy's book, are you?"

Several diners instantly stopped eating in order to listen to his response. James glanced at a couple to his left and eyed their fried chicken and mashed potato platters with longing. "I've been working and helping Milla out with wedding preparations.

I'm not going to allow *The Body in the Bakery* to change my life. My only hope is that the book is good for the town."

"Oh, it's gonna be!" Dolly declared happily. "I've already got calls from newspapers, magazines, and even the TV people about doin' a story on our diner. If they're houndin' me, they must be nearly breakin' down the door of the Sweet Tooth to see if it looks like a place where somebody might've been murdered."

James frowned. "Someone *did* die there, remember?"

"How could I forget?" Clamping her hand over her mouth, Dolly led him to his usual booth. "You want sweet tea, hon?"

"Unsweetened, please." James removed his food diary from his coat pocket. "I'm keeping a food log," he explained before Dolly could ask. "Even with artificial sweetener, tea costs me no calories, but I've got to write everything down in order to show the nutritionist what I like to eat. But I'll wait to order lunch. Lucy's joining me."

Dolly's eyes glimmered with interest. There was nothing she enjoyed more than a fresh piece of gossip. "You two gonna rekindle the ole fire?" She reached over and gave his arm a playful pinch. "And what nutritionist? Not the lady whose sons went after the Diva of Dough!"

"One and the same." James spoke loud enough for the eager ears of his fellow diners to hear him defend Dr. Ruth. "Dr. Wilkins is a lovely and gentle person. Her sons were only standing up for her because Paulette Martine made a fool of their mother. Could you imagine having to pay for three college tuitions at once? Dr. Ruth can't afford to lose clients because that woman from New York chose to mock one of our own."

He knew that his last statement would resonate with most of the diners. He heard a man seated nearby whisper, "Damn right. That Yankee's gonna make our local gal go broke," while a woman said, "Poor Dr. Ruth. Her boys were raised proper. See how they did their best to look after their mama?"

Dolly's Diner was the epicenter of Quincy's Gap. James was confident that within the hour, public opinion on Dr. Ruth Wilkins would change dramatically and Dolly would do her best to see that her customers viewed the nutritionist with sympathy. To reward her for her loyalty, James told her about the offer he'd made on the house and then asked her for advice on where to send Milla and his father on their honeymoon.

"You're kinda waitin' 'til the last second, ain't ya? Their weddin's next Wednesday. On Christmas Eve?"

James nodded.

"And your daddy's not likely to wanna fly in an airplane, bein' that he's so shy and all. And no offense, James, but they're a bit too old to be drivin' one of those big campers, so you've gotta find someplace they can get to in their own car." Sensing that a customer behind her needed something, she turned away. "Lemme ask Clint what he thinks. That man of mine never seems to be able to put his socks in the hamper, but he knows how to surprise me with a romantic getaway now and again when he sets his mind to it."

As Dolly bustled off, Lucy walked in, her hips swaying attractively as she held on to her jiggling nightstick with her right hand and her overloaded purse with the other.

"That uniform certainly shows off how fit you are," James complimented her.

Lucy gestured toward the hostess station and looked displeased. "Peggy says you bought a house today. Why didn't you tell me?"

"That Dolly is something else . . ." James quickly explained that, at this point, he had only made an offer. "I *hope* to be buying a house today and if the sellers accept the offer, you'll be the first person inside after the closing, I promise."

Mollified, Lucy perused the six page menu and decided on the grilled chicken and portobello sandwich with a side of fruit salad. When Dolly arrived to take their orders, James reluctantly asked for the same meal. "But can you make mine on a whole wheat bun instead of the sourdough? And may I have mustard on the side?" he asked, hoping that a good dose of spicy brown mustard would liven up his potentially dull entrée.

"It's too bad you have to work tonight," he told Lucy once Dolly headed for the kitchen. "Paulette is coming over with cake samples. I could save you some if you'd like."

Her blue eyes wistful, Lucy waited a moment before shaking her head no. "I'd better not. Can't chase after the bad guys if my thighs chafe from rubbing together. And now that I've been partnered with Donovan, I've got to prove myself as fast and tough as he is. Last time we had to chase some teenagers vandalizing the walls of the Laundromat, I was left in the dust while he chased two of them down. Not a day goes by that he doesn't remind me of how I couldn't keep up."

"Well, even if you're not as fleet of foot, you're a hell of a lot smarter." James tried to assure her. He knew that working alongside the close-minded, obnoxious, redheaded deputy was bound to be a challenge for any man, but as Donovan was also incredibly chauvinistic, Lucy faced an even greater struggle having him as her partner.

As Lucy relayed a series of anecdotes featuring Donovan's attempts to make her look foolish in front of Sheriff Huckabee, Dolly appeared with their grilled chicken sandwiches.

"James, I've got your problem all worked out," she informed him cheerfully. "Clint reckons you should give your folks a weekend at a cottage near Asheville. It's a fun city to walk around and has a lot of art to see. He thought your daddy might like that." Dolly removed a plastic bottle of mustard from her apron pocket and placed it on the table. "He knows about a real nice hotel that has cottages for folks to stay in so they can be alone, but don't have to worry about fixin' meals or makin' the bed."

James was touched that Clint had come up with such an appropriate locale for his reclusive father. "Tell your husband that he's brilliant. It sounds like the ideal gift."

Dolly beamed and gave his shoulder a maternal pat. "I took the liberty of meltin' a slice of mozzarella on your sandwich." She pointed at the tomato slices next to his sandwich. "Slip a few of those sweet, juicy tomatoes under your bun and you won't even think you're eatin' healthy." She smiled at Lucy. "You're lookin' right good, Deputy Hanover. Guess keepin' the peace 'round here has made you trim, but don't go gettin' too skinny. A man likes somethin' to hold on to."

With a wink, Dolly nudged James with her fleshy hip and then moved on to cajole, tease, and gossip with her other customers.

After gazing after the proprietress with affection, Lucy raised her glass of iced tea in a toast. "Here's to your offer getting accepted."

"And to going out to celebrate tomorrow night if it does." James clinked her glass and the two smiled at one another over their rims. "This might be one of the most exciting weekends of my life, Lucy. If only I could find that damned elf, then all would be well."

Lucy frowned. "His name wouldn't be Glowstar, would it?"

"How'd you know?" He nearly choked on

a bite of chicken.

Smiling, she said, "Because we received a ransom note about a certain 'part-time, green-skinned employee of the Shenandoah County Library.' I know the twins love sci-fi, but they don't usually paint their faces until Halloween, so I figured the letter was a joke."

"A ransom note!"

"Yeah, it's actually pieced together using sentences from the *Star.* The ransomer wants a million dollars in unmarked bills to be placed next to the library's book drop bin at midnight on Christmas Eve."

"The night of the wedding," James mused. "I wonder if the timing is deliberate."

"Come on, James, it's not like this is for real. Donovan put the note in the shredder." Lucy didn't seem perturbed by James's irritated frown. "It's obviously some kids messing around. The whole thing's a harmless joke."

"Not to Scott and Francis, it isn't," he replied seriously and spent the rest of his meal in relative silence, pondering over what sort of person would take the time to create an untraceable ransom note for a stuffed elf.

That evening, as James, Milla, and Jackson

awaited the arrival of Willow and Paulette with the cake samples, Joan phoned to tell James that his offer had been accepted. After allowing him to absorb the wonderful news, she asked him to look over his calendar and together, they scheduled a closing date for the third week of January. By three o'clock on January 23, the yellow house on Hickory Hill Lane would be his.

The joy in James's voice as he effusively thanked Joan alerted Milla and Jackson as to the result of his offer. Before he had even hung up the phone, Milla had pulled a bottle of champagne from the fridge and was enthusiastically tearing the plastic sleeve from its neck.

"So we're finally gettin' rid of you?" Jackson smirked as he popped the cork. Holding the bottle in one hand, he placed his free one on his son's arm. "You coulda stayed, son. We wouldn't have minded . . . much."

"I'll only be ten minutes away, Pop." James was moved by the rare demonstration of affection. "We'll see one another all the time."

Jackson seemed pleased about the proximity of James's new house. "Good. That's far enough to keep you outta my shed and close enough to get you over here for chores."

Milla snatched the champagne from her fiancé's hand. "You're going to talk until all the bubbles go flat." She poured out three glasses, paying no attention to the stray splashes peppering the countertop. "To your first home, my dear. May you fill each room with many happy memories!"

"Look out, boy. She's gonna want grandkids now for sure." Jackson drained his glass in a single gulp. "You'd best be walkin' down the aisle after we're done with our march next week. Though no bride could ever be as purty as mine."

James busied himself refilling their glasses as Milla gave Jackson a grateful kiss.

"Where's your sister?" Jackson barked, embarrassed into gruffness by the public display of love. "The woman's always late."

"No need to lose hair over a few minutes," Milla scolded and then took a large swallow of champagne. "After all the arrows slung today, I sure needed a drink."

"I take it the family reunion didn't go so well?" James inquired, noting the pinched look of Milla's face.

Milla shook her head but clearly didn't feel like elaborating any further. The trio drank champagne and waited, exchanging small-talk about the wedding, James's house, the bitterness of the December wind,

Glowstar, Dr. Ruth, and Bennett's *Jeopardy!* preparations.

After Jackson tapped on his wristwatch for the third time, Milla picked up the phone and called over to the Widow's Peak.

"Willow? Have you seen my sister?" she asked lightly. As she listened to Paulette's assistant, Milla began to frown. Finally, she said, "I understand, and no, I don't want you to get into any hot water. We'll see her when we see her, and you as well, my dear."

Jackson waited until Milla had replaced the phone in its cradle before declaring, "She's not comin', right? What are we supposed to have for dessert without her damned cake?"

Milla opened the freezer door and began to push around packages of frozen waffles and bags of vegetables. "We'll have to settle for ice cream. Willow says my sister is locked in the kitchen and is never to be bothered when she's baking. Apparently, Paulette told her that if that ever happened Willow would be fired on the spot. The innkeepers have had to give my sister the key to the kitchen door so she can lock herself in for as many hours as she wants."

"That's not too strange to me," Jackson remarked. "I don't like folks bargin' in when I'm paintin'." He gave James a pointed look.

"Sorry, James." Milla sighed as she placed a half gallon of Edy's Mocha Almond Fudge on the counter. "It seems we wasted your Friday night for nothing. If Paulette's still cooking, then we're not going to taste her cakes 'til morning. I could never have imagined she'd turn out to be quite this self-absorbed."

"That's okay, Milla." James gave his future stepmother a one-handed hug before turning resolutely away from the tempting carton of ice cream. "Having cake for breakfast sure beats the Fiber One I was planning on eating before church."

However, there was no cake for breakfast either. In fact, the phone rang shortly after six a.m., shattering the silence in the house. Milla had taken to spending the night whenever she didn't have classes to teach the following day, and when her shriek resonated throughout the early morning's darkness, James raced downstairs without slippers or robe, fearful that his father's fiancée had sustained a terrible injury.

"What is it?" he asked her as he bolted into the kitchen, quickly noting that though she seemed unharmed, her face was like a pale moon in lightless gloom.

Wordlessly, Milla handed him the telephone receiver as though it were a lethal object and then moved over to the sink. She turned on the faucet and watched blankly as the water streamed between the divides of her trembling fingers.

"Hello?" James's voice was filled with trepidation.

"James?"

It was Lucy. He relaxed a fraction and then suddenly recalled that she was a sheriff's deputy scheduled to be on duty that day.

"What's happened?" he asked her over the sound of the running water.

"It's Paulette," she answered evenly. "She's dead. I'm here at the Widow's Peak."

"I'll be right over."

"No, James." Lucy's tone was firm. "We haven't determined if the death is accidental or not. I'll call you as soon as we know something."

"Lucy, I'll be there in ten minutes," he stated as though she hadn't spoken, and then he hung up the phone. Drawing Milla toward him, he gently pushed down on the faucet until the harsh stream of water ceased and then whispered, "I'll find out what happened. I promise."

He then eased Milla into his father's arms and the two men exchanged imperceptible nods. "Make her some coffee," James whispered as he headed upstairs to pull on some clothes. “Pour in a shot of Cutty Sark. Make yourself one too. I have a feeling it’s going to be a long day.”

Seven: Sweet Potato Pecan Pie

When the Bronco crested the top of the hill leading to the entrance of the Widow's Peak Inn, James expected to see Sheriff's Department cruisers with their light bars flashing, but there was only one sedan present parked neatly off to the side. The porch lights flanking the double front doors still burned, providing meager competition with the waking sun.

Mr. Mintzer, the owner of the inn, sat on one of the wicker rockers with a coffee mug cradled in his hands. He gazed at James dully and did not rise to greet him.

Noting that the older man wore no coat and that his sockless feet were encased in a pair of unlined slippers, James speculated that the innkeeper was in shock. Touching him lightly on the arm, James squatted next to the silent man. "You must be cold, sir," he spoke softly. "Could I get you a coat from inside?"

After a long pause, Mr. Mintzer answered mechanically. "You can hang your coat in the hall closet. It's just past the stairs."

Since Paulette had booked every room, James felt it safe to assume that the red barn coat, gray wool hat, and thick leather gloves belonged to the gentleman out on the porch. Without pausing to announce his presence to Lucy, James returned outside and made sure that the innkeeper was appropriately attired.

"Can I get you anything else?"

James handed Mr. Mintzer his gloves, growing more and more concerned at the vacant look in his eyes. Without warning, the man blinked and grabbed him by the hand. "She was an awful woman, but we'd never wish this on her." He shook his head. "That picture'll be burned in my mind for the rest of my days. Her on the floor — her face covered like she was wearin' a mask made of mud. It's a good thing Hattie wasn't up when I forced my way in. Ever since that first mornin', when that woman told my wife her eggs were runny and her fruit salad wasn't ripe, Hattie's given up cookin' for her." He shrugged and stared off into the distance again. "It feels awful odd to take it so slow in the mornin' when you've got guests, but there's been no need for us to stir until we were sure she didn't need the kitchen. Looks like we won't be goin' in there for a spell anyhow."

"So you found Paulette?" James couldn't help asking.

"I like to have coffee about six," Mr. Mintzer explained. "When you get older, you just can't sleep late anymore, even if you want to. It's like your body's tryin' to tell you that time is runnin' out and you'd best get up and live a full day. Anyhow, I collected the paper and went to fix the coffee but the kitchen door was locked. I'd given that baker lady a spare key but I still had mine and I knew she didn't wanna be bothered when she was makin' cakes, but a man's gotta have his coffee! Isn't that so?"

"Absolutely," James agreed, wishing he had a cup that very moment.

"She was in the kitchen when we went to bed last night." He creased his brow in thought. "That musta been a bit before ten. I couldn't believe she was still in there all those hours later. Never heard of somebody cookin' all night, but then again, I've never met someone like her." He raised his eyebrows quizzically. "When she didn't answer my knock this mornin', I felt in my bones that somethin' wasn't right, so I unlocked the door and there she was." The man huddled forward in the chair and took a sip of coffee that had surely lost all trace of heat. "Looks like her heart just gave out and she toppled over. What a shame. And what a mess too."

Wondering whether Donovan or Lucy had questioned Mr. Mintzer yet, James decided to satisfy his own curiosity. "Did you hear any strange noises over the course of the night?"

"Nope, but I sleep like a stuffed bear. Harriet's the one who'll wake up if the wind changes direction, but I don't know if she heard anything 'cause I sent her straight upstairs. I didn't want her to see the kitchen like, well, you know."

James felt that he had to view the scene of Paulette's death, but he wasn't sure how to gain access to the kitchen. He was determined to do so, however, as he had promised Milla that he would return with a full explanation of how her sister had died.

As he stepped from the center hallway in search of Lucy, he ran into Deputy Keith Donovan pacing around the dining room while barking orders into his walkie-talkie.

"You!" Donovan's freckled face immediately turned ruddy in anger and he lowered his radio to his hip. "Isn't it a little early for you to be sniffing around for your girlfriend? Or are you on the hunt for a nice, big, free breakfast? 'Cause if you are, the kitchen's closed. No cake for you, my friend."

Fighting back the urge to respond to yet another of Donovan's barbs, James pointed toward the porch instead. "I think Mr. Mintzer's in shock. If you don't convince him to come inside, he could require medical attention."

"He's a grown man," Donovan replied caustically.

"But it's *your* scene, right? If something happens to him, you'll be held responsible. What if the press hears about such neglect?"

After sending him a look that could freeze water, Donovan pushed open the swing door separating the dining room from the butler's pantry. "Hanover! Get outside and see to Mr. Mintzer. He's freezing his ass off out there on the porch. Bring him in here and question him before he turns into a human Popsicle."

"Where's Willow?" James inquired casually.

"I sent her to her room." Donovan smoothed his red hair and gave James a superior smirk.

"Mr. Mintzer told me that his wife is a really light sleeper." James sat down in a nearby chair as though awaiting orders from the deputy. "If there was any foul play last night, she'd be the one to know. I'm sure the press and Sheriff Huckabee will be pretty impressed that you figured everything out within an hour of being called to the scene. You might even get a commendation."

Though Donovan wasn't exactly wise, he was smart enough to be suspicious of James's motives. "Don't you have some books to shelve? Go on, get outta here."

"I'm just trying to help Lucy out," James lied. "She's your partner, so if you tidy this up quickly, then she looks good de facto. I mean, the deceased is a *celebrity.* This case could make you famous."

The deputy spent a moment pondering the meaning of *de facto* and then pointed at James. "You stay right here. If you move from that chair, I'll find somethin' to charge you with. Go ahead and try me if you think

I'm kiddin'." He made a V with his fingers and directed them at his eyes. "I'll be watchin' you even when you don't know it. Are we clear?"

"Yessir." James did his best to act submissive, but as soon as he heard the heavy tread of Donovan's boots clomping up the wooden staircase, he eased open the swing door and entered the butler's pantry.

The narrow, closetlike room, which had been painted a robin's-egg blue with white trim, housed stacks of cream-colored dinnerware, glass tumblers, a variety of ceramic platters, soup tureens, and casserole dishes, as well as wine goblets and a crystal punch bowl set. The plates were so clean that they gleamed beneath the light cast by a single overheard fixture. The wooden door leading into the kitchen was slightly ajar, as though someone had meant to close it behind them but had been too hurried to pull it completely shut. Using his sleeve, James pushed on it gently, and it swung inward with a minimal creak of hinges.

The sight before him was confusing at first, probably because the room seemed like it had been the center of a flurry of activity that had instantly paused and had never been resumed.

James's eyes fell upon the body on the

floor. His reaction to its presence was suspended by the fact that the face he knew belonged to Paulette Martine was, in fact, so completely camouflaged that it could have been any woman in black pants, black boots, and an apron splayed on the cold tile.

His gaze traveled upward from her figure to the countertop above. There, a commercial-sized KitchenAid mixer had been overturned and its contents had streamed onto Paulette's face and hair, covering her with a thick layer of batter. Droplets of liquid batter had splattered in an outward radius from her visage and had then hardened into a firm crust. Taking a hesitant step forward, James leaned toward Milla's sister and then hastily drew back.

Paulette's mouth was ajar and obviously filled with batter. That was disconcerting enough, but it was the anguished tilt of her chin and the scratch marks left in the wood above her right arm that proved that she had not experienced a peaceful death. The fingers that had reached out, smearing batter onto the shellacked wood and digging into its surface deeply enough to remove strips of stain, were now fixed into an inert claw, and James had a hard time tearing his eyes from Paulette's thin, vulnerable fingers.

"What happened to you?" he whispered,

letting precious minutes tick by as he fixated on the obscured face.

A knocking sound from above his head drew him back to reality and reminded him that he had no time to waste. Frantically, James scanned the room, trying to absorb the cooking paraphernalia scattered about the kitchen. Cake pans, measuring cups and spoons, spice jars, egg cartons, a butter tray, potholders . . . it all looked as it should, except for the unsettled mixer and the dead body.

The muffled sounds of voices emanating from the downstairs hallway forced James to retreat to his chair in the dining room. He quickly took his gloves out of his pocket and pretended to be tapping the chair's arm with them. Lucy walked in alone and frowned at him. "I know you went into the kitchen, so you can stop acting like you've been in that seat all along."

"I had to come." James picked at a loose thread on his right glove. "It's Milla's sister."

Lucy's face was unreadable. "And what's your impression of the scene?"

Gathering his thoughts for a moment, he looked around the sage-colored walls at the watercolor scenes of wildflowers and birds, framed pieces of lace, and colorful plates from Blue Ridge pottery. Gentle winter sunlight flowed through the large bay windows and fell in wide panels across the floor. James thought it must be a lovely room to sit in, sip coffee, and dine upon a hearty breakfast. One could hardly start the day off unpleasantly when it had begun with such warmth, he imagined.

"It seems like she was using the mixer and then something caused her to grab onto the counter, like she was having an attack of some kind." He spoke quietly, as though they were not in the appropriate place to discuss an unexpected death. "She knocked the machine over and then fell down where she's now lying. The batter poured over the counter and onto her face, but she didn't have the strength to get out of the way." The image of her open mouth appeared in his mind's eye. "Did she choke on the batter, do you think?"

Lucy spent a moment in thought. "Maybe, but I think something else killed her. Something quick, but painful. Those scratches on the wood, did you see them?"

He nodded. "They make me believe she was in incredible pain. Agony even. And the way her neck is arched and her chin lifted . . . she reminds me of one of those casts of the people who died when Mount Vesuvius erupted. They were frozen in postures of that kind of agony. Haunting."

"I'm not familiar with that, but I'll Google it back at the station." Lucy made a brief note on a small pad. "You didn't touch anything did you?"

"Of course not."

"Good, because we're waiting for someone to bring us another camera. Mine's busted." She listened as footsteps trod on the floorboards above them. "Donovan thinks she had a heart attack or brain aneurism or something. He's planning to rule it an accidental death."

James heard the doubt in her voice. "But you don't agree?"

"If there were no motives to hurt her, then I might share Donovan's opinion, but I'm going to ask Huckabee for an autopsy with all the works. It'll take awhile, and if everything comes out clean, then I'll look like an idiot. But think about it, James. She made a lot of people angry."

"No matter what the results are, Milla and the rest of us will be grateful that you followed your instincts and asked for a second opinion." James stood up and reached for her hand. "Your senses are more fine-tuned than most people's are, Lucy. Listen to what your gut is telling you. It's never been wrong."

Lucy smiled with gratitude and then immediately resumed her professional expression. "You've got to leave now, James. You're going to compromise my authority here and I've already got an uphill battle ahead of me."

"Understood. I'll tell Milla that this was an accidental death. At least for now."

"Skip the 'for now' part," Lucy ordered. "Over the next few days I'm going to be interviewing her and Willow and anybody else who spent time with Paulette, and no one needs to know about my personal suspicions."

James was stunned. "You don't believe that Milla could actually hurt her own sister, do you?"

But Lucy had turned her back on James as though he hadn't spoken. He watched her disappear through the swing door into the butler's pantry. The door flapped several times behind her, as though mocking him, and then fell still.

After zipping up his coat, James pulled his scarf tight around his neck and walked out of the inn. As he drove slowly down the steep driveway, he passed another brown cruiser, driven by Deputy Glenn Truett. A man with a round face, thick neck, and curling gray mustache sat regally in the passenger seat. James glanced at the figure, which strongly reminded him of a walrus, and hoped he wouldn't be recognized. Sheriff Huckabee wouldn't be pleased to know that James had been allowed into the inn.

With a sudden jolt of clarity, he realized that Lucy might not be forthcoming with her friends regarding information on Paulette's death. In fact, it seemed as though she'd be visiting the Henry home in the imminent future not as a friend and potential girlfriend, but in an official capacity as a member of the Shenandoah County Sheriff's Department.

"We're not on the same side anymore," James murmured unhappily.

Driving home he reflected on the number of times he and Lucy and the rest of the supper club members had joined forces in the name of justice. They were a good team — each person possessing unique gifts and abilities. But now, their group seemed to be splintering. Bennett was busy with Jade and *Jeopardy!*, Gillian was running two businesses and spending time with Officer Harding, Lindy was pining for the absent Luis, Lucy was acutely focused on her career, and what about himself?

Just yesterday he was in a celebratory

mood. He was soon to be a homeowner, was taking steps to live a healthier lifestyle, and would witness his father's nuptials.

"The wedding!" he exclaimed as he parked alongside Milla's lavender minivan. "I wonder if they'll still get married on Christmas Eve."

Once again, to his dismay, life had thrown James and his loved ones off course. With weighted steps he walked toward the house he had lived in for the majority of his years. He had never been so reluctant to go inside, for he knew that his words of comfort would be insufficient. The cold wind seemed to follow him through the door, diminishing the warmth within.

The remainder of Saturday crawled by and the Henry house was markedly silent. Shortly after James's return, Milla had driven off to the Holiday Inn to break the news to Paulette's children, and Jackson had pulled on his painter's overalls and locked himself in the shed. James phoned his friends in order to tell them what had happened, and within two hours of his calls, the women of Quincy's Gap began to appear on his doorstop bearing casseroles, pies, and bottles of whiskey.

"Is the weddin' still on?" Dolly inquired

as she popped a chicken and sausage casserole in the oven.

James shrugged. "I don't know."

"Word's going 'round that Paulette Martine's family's in town." Mrs. Emerson, the minister's wife, chimed in as she put the kettle on for tea. "An older sister and her two children. You all might be gatherin' for a different type of service."

Mrs. Waxman, James's part-time library employee and his one-time junior high school teacher, shook her head as she unwrapped her famous sweet potato pecan pie and began to cut it into thick wedges. "A funeral instead of a wedding. Now there's a shame."

"Maybe not," Gillian countered as she hung up her coat on a hook near the back door. "Saying a loving farewell to someone whose spirit has moved on to a place of peace shouldn't be an occasion of *sorrow.* There's no reason why Milla and Jackson shouldn't hold their commitment ceremony afterwards. After all, both services are just the congregating of friends and family in order to pay homage to *love,* the *highest* power of all!"

Mrs. Emerson issued Gillian a disapproving frown. "But the tone of each service is quite different."

Slipping from the room before the two women could embark on one of their regular theological debates, James felt rather envious of his father. Safe within his shed, Jackson was probably painting to the soft strains of the light jazz station. With the space heater churning full force and a thermos of coffee and one of Milla's cinnamon scones close at hand, Jackson would emerge from the unsettling day with more fortitude and calm than Milla or his son.

James tried to seek a few moments of solitude in his room, but Lindy and Bennett tracked him down as soon as they arrived, just as he was leaving his second message on Lucy's voicemail.

"Poor Milla," Lindy said sympathetically as she perched on the end of James's bed. "So Paulette just collapsed in the middle of baking a cake?"

Replacing the phone on the cradle, James said, "Where did you hear that?"

Bennett jerked his thumb toward the stairs. "The entire Quincy's Gap gossip network is downstairs, my man, including Mrs. Mintzer's cousin. By the time they leave, they'll know what kind of cereal you eat, whether you're taking any prescriptions, your waist size — you name it!"

"With all that food down there, *everyone's*

going to know my waist size because my pants will have to be sewn by hand," James mumbled gloomily.

"They mean well," Lindy insisted. "And women comfort one another by talking. It's what we do. Milla's down there now, just wrapped up in a cocoon of prattle and laughter and tears. After she and the gals get it all out of their systems, they'll sleep for fourteen hours and wake up, ready to take life by the horns all over again."

James took Lindy's hand in his. "I hope you're right." He sighed. "But I wish Lucy would call. I keep expecting her to show up with her little notebook and interrogate us all. And that would still be better than not hearing from her."

Bennett gazed at James intently. "Why would she come over to question you and yours? It was an accidental death."

"Lucy's got one of her feelings," James confessed.

Lindy and Bennett exchanged anxious looks.

"Good thing the women down there brought plenty of liquor," Bennett said as he rose to leave. "Call us if you need to bust outta here. I'll be home studying."

"And I've got a phone date with Luis tonight, but I can put it off 'til tomorrow if you need to talk."

James smiled at his friends. "Thanks to both of you. And thank Gillian too. But right now, I'm warming to that idea of a fourteen-hour nap."

Lindy kissed him on the cheek and then eased his door closed. However, the wood wasn't thick enough to keep her hushed words from reaching James's ears. "I wouldn't be surprised if it turns out the Diva was murdered, would you?" she asked Bennett. "She brought out the worst in folks."

"For Milla and the Henry men's sake, I sure hope that's not the case," he answered. "And for mine too. How the hell could I concentrate on trivia if there's a killer loose in Quincy's Gap?"

James had never felt such a pull to attend Sunday service at the Methodist church as he did the day after seeing Paulette's body. He, Milla, and Jackson all awoke early and gathered in the kitchen for morning coffee and stilted conversation.

Sitting across the table from Jackson, Milla appeared sad, tired, and confused, but there was something else to her demeanor that James couldn't quite comprehend. She seemed nervous, almost frightened, as though she expected more bad news to arrive any moment. Jackson threw her uncertain looks every now and then, and James sympathized with his father's discomfort. After all, what could be said to console Milla when she had lost the sister she had just begun to reconnect with after years of a relationship sustained by birthday and Christmas cards?

When James suggested they go to church, Milla issued the first genuine smile he'd seen since Friday evening. Ignoring Jackson's eye rolling and a few grumbles about having to wear a suit, Milla covered James's hand with her own. "That would be lovely."

Now, as he stood beside her in the pew, his arm protectively about her shoulder, he tried not to focus on how diminished she looked. He thought back to when his mother had died — at how shrunken Jackson had appeared for many months afterward.

Death lessens us, he thought, and then he tried to empty his mind. Eventually, the simple beauty of the church was able to distract him from his sorrowful musings. He drew in a deep breath, inhaling the fresh pine scent from the garlands draping the ends of the pews and resting against each windowsill. Brilliant red poinsettias flamed across the length of the altar, softened by the glow of candlelight from the Advent wreath on the plain wooden table above. Silk banners — handmade by the women of the congregation and depicting scenes of trumpeting angels, a manger sheltering the Holy Family, and the word JOY — were positioned in between the stained-glass windows. The chapel fairly shimmered with color and the sound of joyful singing.

Milla's soprano, which was light and pure as birdsong, moved everyone seated around her. It was as if she recognized the mixture of blessing and anguish that defined her life and accepted her reality with faith and grace. Tears rolled down her cheeks, and other women smiled at her through wet eyes of their own. To James, this expression of empathy was another example of the kindness and compassion that formed the heart of the community he had come to love with all his being.

The congregation sang on and James let his gaze drift around at the familiar faces. He smiled at children hiding beneath the pews, elderly couples leaning into one another as they shared a hymnal, a husband's hand resting on the swell of his wife's belly. He saw the heartfelt jubilation in Reverend Emerson's flushed cheeks, watched Clint squeeze Dolly in a brief embrace, and heard the intertwining of Megan and Amelia Flowers's alto voices.

Milla looked up at him and smiled, and James knew that she too felt flooded by peace. Lindy had been right about the resiliency of women. The neighborhood ladies had invaded their home, stuffed the fridge, freezer, and cupboards with food, talked up a storm, and then vanished like a thunderstorm sent scuttling onward by an easterly wind. The members of the household had slept then, but had woken to a morning of fresh uncertainty and grief, which the prayers, music, and fellowship of the Advent service had gently washed away.

After church let out, Milla told Dolly and several other women that the wedding would be postponed until Paulette could be laid to rest. If Jackson was surprised or disappointed by the news, he showed no sign, but bid the women a brusque good morning and hustled off to turn on Milla's minivan so that he could enjoy the luxurious comfort of its heated seats.

James was just losing the feeling in his toes when he noticed Lucy's Jeep entering the church parking lot. He told Milla he'd meet her at the van in a few moments and moved off to intercept his friend.

"Why haven't you called me?" he inquired

sharply as soon as she alighted from her car.

She scowled in return. "I've been working non-stop. No one wants to dig deeper into Paulette's death, but I fought tooth and nail to get a second opinion from the ME in Albemarle County, and I'm glad I did. This guy's the best, and he was just about to close up shop for the holidays but as a favor, he agreed to examine the victim."

Mind reeling, James asked two questions at once. "A favor to whom? And why are you calling her a victim?"

Lucy kicked at a loose stone in the asphalt. "The ME's a friend of Sullie's. We still chat over e-mail every now and then. Just about work stuff."

James wasn't pleased by this news. "So you're communicating with the guy who came between us the first time?" He held up his hand. "Forget I said that. I'm sure it's all work related." He jerked his head toward the van. "Milla's getting ready to leave. Are you planning on questioning her? Why did you say 'victim' instead of 'deceased'?"

"Paulette was probably poisoned. When the ME cleaned her face off . . . and her eyes . . ." Lucy looked uncomfortable, but she took a deep breath and continued. "Her eyes were open and the pupils were really small, like little pinpoints. Her throat was really swollen and there was a funny smell inside her mouth. It wasn't just the batter, which smelled kind of sweet. Something sour. Kind of rotten."

James leaned against the Jeep as Lucy's words sank in. "Poison?"

"It'll take some time to get the lab results back. With Christmas coming this week, we're not going to know anything soon. Maybe not until after New Year's."

"What will you do until then?"

Lucy's eyes hardened. "I won't be sitting around twiddling my thumbs. I'm going to look for the killer. Her family, her assistant, Dr. Ruth Wilkins. There are plenty of people with motive, so I need to move fast before alibis get created and people practice their stories on each other."

"Well, we're heading home right now, so you'd better come over before we start collaborating over our false testimonies," James joked, but in truth, he was worried Lucy might view Milla as a genuine suspect.

"That's not funny, James." A flicker of sadness appeared in Lucy's blue eyes. "I'm just doing my job. Someone hurt Milla's sister. The best way for us to discover who did this is for me to get to know her. That means getting to know her friends *and* her enemies."

"Sometimes it's hard to tell who's who," James muttered.

She touched him briefly on the arm. "Truth has a way of removing people's masks, James. I won't give up until everything's laid bare. Sooner or later, the facts will point to Paulette's greatest enemy, and then that person will have to face judgment."

Once Lucy had driven away, James returned to Milla's side and offered her his arm. As they made their way to her van, the church bells began to toll. James opened Milla's door and settled her inside, then paused in the open air, clinging to the remnant of hope delivered to his weary spirit through the ringing bells.

He then went home to dine on casseroles and a wedge of sweet potato pecan pie that was bound to put him over his daily caloric limit by a count of 531.

Mrs. Waxman's Sweet Potato Pecan Pie

2/3 pound sweet potatoes (enough to make 2 cups mashed)
2 eggs
3/4 cup white sugar
1/2 teaspoon salt
1 teaspoon cinnamon
1/2 teaspoon ginger
1/4 teaspoon cloves
1 2/3 cups cream
1 (9-inch) unbaked pie crust
3 tablespoons butter, softened
2/3 cup packed brown sugar
2/3 cup chopped pecans

Preheat the oven to 350 degrees. Peel the sweet potatoes and cut them into chunks. Place them on a baking sheet and bake until tender (about 20 to 30 minutes). Mash the potatoes and take care to remove all the lumps.

Beat the eggs lightly. Mix together the eggs and sweet potatoes. Stir in the white sugar, salt, cinnamon, ginger, and cloves.

Finally, blend in the cream. Pour the mixture into the pie shell. Bake at 350 degrees for 55 to 60 minutes or until a knife inserted into the center of the pie comes out clean. Allow the pie to cool.

To make the pecan topping: Combine the butter, brown sugar, and pecans. Carefully drop spoonfuls over the top of the cooled pie. Broil the pie until the mixture begins to bubble — about 2 to 3 minutes depending on the oven. Don't overbroil, or you'll end up with syrup! Cool again.

Serve with homemade whipped cream or a cup of coffee.

EIGHT: LEMON STRAWBERRY LAYER CAKE

Jackson stood in front of the open refrigerator in a state of befuddlement.

"There's so much Tupperware in here I can't tell if I'm lookin' at green-bean casserole, lasagna, or a fruit cobbler."

In normal circumstances, Milla would have leapt up to assist her fiancé, but she was out of earshot. In the den, she sat in front of the blank gray television screen, knitting an unidentifiable object made of navy blue yarn. The nervous clicking of her needles transmitted her state of mind more than any words could have, and neither of the Henry men had any idea how to console her.

"I'll fix you both a plate, Pop." James shooed his father out of the kitchen and managed to microwave a turkey tetrazzini casserole with a side of green beans mixed with butter and pecans. Carrying two plates into the den, he motioned for Jackson to erect a pair of TV trays while he returned to the kitchen for glasses of water.

Worriedly, he watched as Milla pushed the food around on her plate. Jackson ate hungrily, of course, asking for seconds by holding his empty plate directly under his son's nose so that James had to interrupt his own lunch in order to fetch another helping.

"I just wish those deputies would get here so we could get this over with!" Milla exclaimed suddenly.

James put his fork down and studied her. "Are you nervous about being interviewed, Milla, or about what you might have to tell them?"

When she didn't answer, even Jackson stopped chewing and looked at his fiancée with mild surprise. "It's those kids of hers, ain't it? You were actin' funny after you saw them. I reckon things got nasty."

"Have you met them yet?" James asked his father.

Jackson shook his head. "Nope. Thought I'd let them do their family thing alone, seein' it's been awhile since they've gathered together. I was paintin' most of the day. Those baker hands . . ." He seemed to become lost in the image he held in his thoughts.

Milla's expression was pained as she glanced at James. "You'll see them all this afternoon. We're meeting Chase, Chloe, and Wheezie for dinner at Dolly's."

The doorbell rang and Milla started in her chair, causing her ball of yarn to fall onto the floor and unravel across the braided rug. James rose, rewound the ball, and then placed it on Milla's clammy palm. "Just tell the truth, even if it makes someone look bad," he cautioned. "They'll find out about Paulette's children anyway. You know Lucy won't rest until she discovers what happened to your sister."

Both Lucy and Donovan were at the door, dressed in uniform and their espresso brown Sheriff's Department parkas. After exchanging terse, polite greetings, James led them into the den. He carried in two chairs from the kitchen table and positioned them on either side of Milla. Jackson quickly left his recliner in order to seat himself to her right. With James on her left, the Henry men had created bookends of love and protection for a woman who suddenly seemed so fragile.

Lucy removed a mini recorder from her pocket and explained to Milla that she and her partner were simply gathering information. "Can you tell me what Paulette did yesterday, Friday, December nineteenth?"

Milla seemed relieved by the simplicity of the first question. "I don't know when she got up or anything, but she was here for breakfast by eight thirty."

"What did you eat?" Donovan demanded.

"Scrambled eggs and fried tomatoes."

"You sure that's all?" he prompted.

Milla shrugged. "Coffee and eggnog. Nothing else."

Lucy nodded encouragingly and wrote something in her notebook. "What did you do after breakfast?"

"We went over the menu for the wedding supper. My sister is, *was* . . ." She got up and retrieved the tissue dispenser and quickly blew her nose. "Sorry. Paulette planned to make onion rolls and the wedding cake for us. I'd hired Dolly's Clint to fix us his chicken in a cognac cream sauce with garlic mashed potatoes and mixed green salads too." Realizing that last bit was unnecessary, she returned to the point at hand. "After breakfast, we picked up my sister's assistant, Willow, ran a few errands, and then met our family at the Apple Orchard truck stop for lunch."

"State their names please," Donovan directed.

"Chase Martin is Paulette's son, Chloe Martin-Hicks is her daughter, and Louise Rowe is the eldest of us three sisters. My maiden name is Rowe."

Donovan narrowed his eyes and leaned forward. "But Paulette's last name is *Martine.* Why are her kids *Martins?*"

Milla issued a derisive snort. "It's all about marketing. First of all, her real name was Patricia Rowe. Growing up, everybody called her Patty. She married Chase Martin Senior but kept his name after their divorce. She just Frenchified herself is all. Probably 'cause she went to cooking school in Paris before she was married."

"Any idea where the ex-husband is at the moment?" Donovan's eyes gleamed.

"Across the planet in Hong Kong. He's a chef there. They've been divorced since the kids were in grade school, and Chase Senior has lived in Asia ever since." Milla pointed the sharp end of her needle at Donovan. "Can I ask a question now, or is this a one-sided conversation?" James smiled to see that she was recovering some of her pluck.

Lucy looked apologetic. "In a minute, if that's okay. Could you tell us about your family lunch?"

Stroking the length of knitted yarn, Milla was quiet for a moment. When Donovan opened his mouth to prod her into speech, Lucy placed a restraining hand on his arm and held her fingers to her lips. James felt a rush of gratitude for the gentleness and consideration Lucy was showing Milla.

"It wasn't the warm and fuzzy reunion I was dreaming of," Milla admitted with reluctance. "Paulette was delighted to see Chase. Even though they live in the same city they're both so busy that they rarely sit down face-to-face. They get along well, though, and they're very similar. Chase is a wealthy and successful lawyer, and Paulette is real proud of him. She heaped praises on his handsome head the moment we sat down." She sighed. "I only wish she'd been half as kind to Chloe."

"The daughter," Donovan stated unnecessarily. "So they don't get along, huh? What's her story?"

"Chloe saves manatees in Florida. She's a widow. Her husband died in a boating accident five years ago." Milla picked at the yarn. "She and my sister are, were, total opposites. Chloe's a bit of a hippie. She likes baggy T-shirts, living on the beach, wears her hair long and loose, and is passionate about animal rights."

"Bet she wasn't happy to see her mama's fur coat," Jackson murmured lowly, but Donovan obviously heard and exchanged a quick, predatory glance with Lucy.

"Lucky for us she wasn't wearing it," Milla grinned briefly at her fiancé and then continued. "Louise, Wheezie, is our oldest sister. She lives in Natchez, Mississippi. That's our home town. She and Paulette haven't seen each other for a really long time, so things were a little strained between them." Milla held out her hands plaintively. "You know how that can be."

"It sounds like things were a little uncomfortable," Lucy suggested.

Milla nodded in agreement. "Paulette started nagging Chloe about spending all her money on useless sea cows, and the poor girl started crying. Wheezie tried to stick up for Chloe, and Chase told her to mind her own business. Considering Wheezie's his aunt, he should have shown her more respect." She shook her head. "I'm afraid that's why *I* joined the ruckus. Wheezie deserves better than to hear fresh talk from that spoiled, arrogant boy."

"Were any threats made at this time?" Donovan inquired hopefully. "You might as well tell me now, because we're headin' right over to the Holiday Inn after we're done here."

Milla's face grew stormy. "There were arguments and that's all. The kind that happen between related folks all the time. I doubt anyone went back to their hotel room after lunch and started building a bomb or loadin' a gun!" She threw her yarn forcefully into a basket near her feet. "Now I want to know what killed my sister and I'm not going to say another word until you answer me in plain talk."

"We don't know," Lucy replied softly. "The test results won't be —"

"Don't you give me the run around, Lucy Hanover!" Milla pointed an angry finger at the deputies. "I can tell Patty didn't just lie down, close her eyes, and die — not with the questions you've been asking. You wouldn't be sniffing for a trail if there wasn't somethin' wrong with how she passed. So what was wrong with how y'all found her? Tell me please. She was my sister!" Milla's voice broke and she pressed a tissue over her eyes.

It pained James to hear her plead this way.

He stared at Lucy, willing her to respond to Milla, but she avoided eye contact while Donovan studied the three of them with the smug posture of someone reveling in his position of authority.

"You're not going to answer me, are you? In that case, I guess I need to call Chase and tell him to get a hotshot lawyer from his firm to fly down here." Milla rose to her feet. "I don't see why we should spill our guts and get nothing in return." She directed her anger at Donovan.

"It's possible that we're dealing with a case of poisoning," Lucy said in a nearly inaudible voice.

As Milla sank back into the chair Donovan hissed, "Shut your mouth, Hanover," through clenched teeth.

"But that's all the information we have until the medical examiner's report is complete. Even then, we need to wait for the lab results," Lucy continued as if she hadn't heard her partner speak. "And I have to ask for your word that you won't mention that fact to anyone outside this room." She looked at each of them in turn. As Donovan spluttered in indignation, James, Jackson, and Milla all promised to keep the information to themselves. And despite the red-headed deputy's attempt to bully more detail from Milla, she refused to talk to him anymore.

"I guess I can't lay her to rest then," was her only remark, and this was confirmed by Lucy's regretful frown.

James walked the deputies to the door, noting that the sky had turned an ominous gray and a strong wind was battering the barren trees. Dried leaves skipped across the lawn and as Lucy pulled on her leather gloves, it began to rain. She gestured for Donovan to go on ahead and then said, "Maybe we shouldn't think about dating until this case is done."

"Or at all," James whispered, stung by her suggestion. "I remember how you acted when Gillian was under suspicion at the barbecue festival. You were loyal to your job first and your friends second. Is this going to be a repeat of that experience? Now that Milla and her family are on your radar, all your other relationships are insignificant?"

"I'm not trying to hurt you." Lucy reached out for his arm, but James yanked it out of her reach. "But I swore an oath to uphold the law, James. Would you respect me if I wasn't true to my word?"

"No," he admitted, his tone softening. "But I'll always come second with you. The law will be the forefront of your life. Before your husband or children. Isn't that right?"

"Who said anything about children?" Lucy folded her arms across her chest, squinting as rain ricocheted off the open screen door and onto the exposed skin of her cheeks. "Can we talk about this later? It's cold and Donovan's going to filet me when I get in the car."

Feeling that there wasn't much else to say, James nodded anyway. "Sure. After the case."

Crossing through the inside of the house, James walked into the dining room, parted the curtains, and watched as the cruiser disappeared down the gravel drive. He stood there for a long time, a familiar ache of loss blooming within his chest. Finally, when the rain eased into a downpour, obscuring his view of the ridged pine trunks surrounding their house, he turned away and headed upstairs. As he had done so often throughout his lifetime, he searched for solace in the one place he knew it awaited him: within the pages of a book.

The rain persisted overnight and then ceased as if a spigot had been abruptly turned off, leaving a wake of sodden, frost-tipped ground and a cold mist that seeped into every porous surface.

The weather befit James's mood. He had fallen asleep reading the day before, to wake to yet another casserole. Milla and Jackson were feigning an interest in a wildlife program on turtles. During a particularly long commercial break, Milla informed him that the rest of her family had been interviewed all afternoon and instead of going out for dinner, each one of them escaped to their individual hotel rooms with cartons of takeout from a nearby Chinese restaurant.

Even his supper club friends were of no comfort. Bennett spent the evening with Jade Jones, who had driven up from southern Virginia in order to eat at Dolly's Diner and play the role of Alex Trebek while her dinner companion answered dozens of trivia questions correctly. Gillian was having her business partners Beau Livingstone and Willy Kendrick over for a meal, and Lindy didn't answer her phone at all, which meant she was probably having a long-distance date with Luis.

Scott and Francis, bundled up against the cold in bright orange ski parkas, barely acknowledged James's presence when he arrived at the library that morning.

"Is that today's *Star*?" he asked them.

Francis nodded. "I guess you already know about the Diva of Dough. Sorry to hear about her passing, Professor."

Glancing at the cover story, it didn't take James long to figure out that Murphy was unaware that Paulette's death was being viewed as suspicious by the Sheriff's Department. The article focused on the Diva's celebrity status and hinted that the deputies interviewed had been less than forthcoming, but promised to deliver more information after the late cake maker's family members and New York staff were interviewed.

"Thank you, Francis." James returned the paper to his employee.

"I hope Milla's holding up okay. She's one of the nicest people we know. If Scott and I . . ." He trailed off and then began again, "I couldn't imagine not having my brother around." Embarrassed, he tapped on the newspaper with his right finger. "Ms. Alistair's dropped the ball with this edition. I'm sure she was busy covering her lead story, but there's nothing in here about Glowstar's ransom note."

James froze in the act of unlocking the front door. "How did you know about that? Lucy told me they thought it was a hoax and had shredded it right after it was read."

"Lottie told me," Scott replied proudly. "I think Deputy Truett has a crush on her. He tells her everything they've got going on at the Sheriff's Department. Guess he doesn't know she's *my* girlfriend."

"You use any excuse you can to say that word, do you realize that? And a lot of good *she's* done us. She didn't consider the note newsworthy either!" Francis scowled, folded the paper, and stormed inside. He flicked the lights on with violent motions and then rounded on his brother. "Do you even care about Glowstar or this job or anything besides your *girlfriend?* You've totally left me hanging on *Age of Conan,* and you don't even read anymore!"

"What's *Age of Conan?*" James looked at Scott. "Is that true? About not reading?"

Scott looked glum. "It's a video game. We used to play online as a team. I was an assassin and Francis was a necromancer. His character got killed last night because he didn't have me to protect him." He slowly unzipped his jacket. "And I still love books, Professor. I just don't have as much free time as I used to." He lowered his voice. "If Francis had a girlfriend, this wouldn't be so hard. I know he wants me to be happy, but he's feeling left out."

"You could always stake out the book return bin on Christmas Eve," James joked. "Bring some of your high-tech gear and trap

Glowstar's kidnapper."

Scott's eyes widened. "Awesome idea, Professor! The note said midnight, right?" He balled up his coat and ran toward the break room. "Hey bro! Let's powwow!"

The morning passed quietly. Since school was out until after New Year's, several mothers towed grade school children into the library in order to check out books and videos to serve as entertainment over the holidays, but other than the Children's Corner, the shelves remained untouched. There were very few hold or transfer requests, and since the Fitzgerald brothers had already repaired three broken hardcover spines, emptied the shelving cart, cleaned the computer screens, and dusted the shelves, James had no qualms about leaving them in charge of the floor while he answered e-mails.

Shortly before three o'clock, when he was about to interrupt the brothers' animated plotting concerning the recovery of Glowstar in order to suggest a coffee break, Willow entered the library carrying a covered cake plate.

"I baked you something," she whispered almost guiltily.

James took the cake from her hands and said, "There's no one here. You don't have to whisper." Smiling, he jerked his head toward the break room. "Come on back. Would you like some coffee?"

Nodding, Willow followed him into the room behind the circulation desk and seated herself at the round table. "I made this cake for you. I didn't know what to do today, so I baked. It's one of Paulette's recipes. I think she was planning to make it on Friday, actually. Lots of people have served it at their wedding, but it's a bit too sweet for me."

"You look tired," James said gently. "I think you and I could both use a caffeine boost." He opened a tin and began to scoop ground coffee into a paper filter. "How are you holding up?"

"As well as can be expected, considering I'm out of a job and will probably be arrested any second now."

James's hand jerked, sending coffee grounds across the counter. "What makes you say that?"

Willow sighed lugubriously. "I hated her, for starters. And I was at the inn most of the day. I'm not an idiot," she said more forcefully. "The cops wouldn't have questioned us like they did unless there's foul play involved."

After setting the pot to brew, James studied Willow carefully. "Well then. *Did* you kill her?"

Instead of a passionate refusal, Willow simply shook her head. "I've been tempted to more times than I can count, but I wouldn't gain anything by it. I can hardly be an assistant to a dead woman."

"True," James agreed. "But weren't you going to ask her for a raise this week?"

"You've got a good memory," she said with a thin smile. "And I asked on Thursday and was told to forget it."

Above the gurgles of the percolating coffee, James scrutinized Willow carefully. "Weren't you angry?"

"Of course! I smoked six packs of cigarettes between then and Saturday night!" she exclaimed. "I'm *still* mad. In fact, I hope the bitch suffered." Willow's hand flew over her mouth. "I'm so sorry. I know she was about to join your family."

Poor girl, thought James and smiled at her kindly. "Don't worry about it." He pointed at the cake plate. "I want to show you a magic trick. I'm going to lift the top off this cake and within one minute, twin twenty-four-year-old men, who also happen to be first-rate librarians, will appear in this room."

Easing the lid straight up in order to keep

the creamy lemon frosting from smudging, James took a whiff of the heavenly scent of sugar-laden sweetness and then glanced at his watch. "Fifty-five seconds remain. What is this marvel, anyway?"

"Lemon-strawberry layer cake," Willow answered, visibly relaxing. "I made the jam in New York and brought a few jars with us."

"So you're an accomplished cook as well?" James positioned his body so that it blocked the beautiful, pale yellow confection.

Flushing attractively, Willow nodded. "I grew up in Vermont. My mom was an excellent cook, and she taught me a lot about preserving the taste of fresh foods. Every summer, we made tons of jams, pies, fruit tarts. Even homemade ice cream. That's why Paulette hired me. Frankly, I can make anything she can. But the food I love to create is candy. Truffles, caramels, chocolates filled with fruit purées."

"Did someone say chocolate?" Scott poked his head into the break room. "I only smell coffee."

Francis pushed his brother forward and then lifted his nose and inhaled, his eyes narrowing. "No, not chocolate. It's something else."

"And with six seconds remaining, may I

present Scott and Francis Fitzgerald?" James pointed at his employees with paternal pride.

"Did you know your boss was a magician?" Willow directed her question at Francis, who stared at their visitor with undisguised interest.

James stepped to the side in order to retrieve a few paper plates and a knife and thus, the cake was revealed. Scott nudged his brother in the side until Francis noticed the unexpected treat.

"Did you make that?" he asked Willow. When she bowed slightly in assent, he took the knife from James's hand, quickly cut himself a slice, and stuffed a bite into his mouth. "*You're* the magical one!" he pronounced enthusiastically. "A cake enchantress!"

Scott rolled his eyes in mock disgust, but Willow's face gleamed with pleasure.

"This is delicious." Francis edged around his brother and sat down at the table. "You should move down here and open a candy shop. If your chocolates are anything like this cake, you'd be a big hit."

"It's true." Scott pushed his heavy glasses back onto the bridge of his nose. "There's not much to do during the winter except read and eat. You'd be an instant success."

"That's really sweet," Willow replied, her bright smile directed solely at Francis. "And I'm going to have to move, all right, since I can hardly afford the rent on my studio apartment in Brooklyn without a job, but I may go back to Vermont." She caressed the mountain ridge on her Shenandoah County Library cup. "Though I really love it here. It reminds me so much of home, but I bet it's a lot warmer in Quincy's Gap during the winter."

As James watched Willow chat with the twins, the young woman seemed to cast off her downtrodden air. The more she talked and smiled, the more he felt that this quiet, eclipsed person could truly bloom in a town like Quincy's Gap. She and Francis obviously felt an immediate attraction, and James wondered if there were an occupation she might be able to take up somewhere in the Shenandoah Valley. After all, most jobs throughout the region were likely to promise a kinder boss than Willow had found in Paulette Martine.

This girl's no murderer, James thought as he listened to Willow laugh at one of Scott's jokes. And he was suddenly struck by an idea.

"Willow? Are you planning to go home to Vermont for Christmas?"

"No." Willow's smile evaporated. "Paulette insisted that I stay to help her make the wedding cake and rolls for your parents' reception, so I don't have a flight. Even if I could get one, I get the impression that I'm supposed to stick around."

"In that case," James clapped his hand on her shoulder. "How would you like to spend Christmas with my family? I may have thought of the perfect job for you."

By five thirty that afternoon, it was already dark. James hated the winter solstice. The short-lived periods of December daylight were tinged with a grayness that eventually gave way to a deep, charcoal-colored sky and the horizon felt heavy, as though it were hanging too near to the ground. Food log in hand, James walked reluctantly up the flight of stairs leading to Ruth Wilkins's office.

If I didn't have this appointment, he thought, smiling at the irony of the situation, *I'd be sitting on the sofa in front of the fire with a book and a bag of cheese puffs on my lap.*

Dr. Ruth had a scented candle burning in her office and had strung glitter-covered snowflake garlands across her window. Dozens of holiday cards were tacked onto her bulletin board and the screen saver on her computer showed a man raising up a little boy so he could place the star on top of the Christmas tree.

"That's a nice smell." James gestured at the candle. "Orange and cloves?"

"Very good." Dr. Ruth swiveled the candle and read the label. "As well as sandalwood, lemon, and bergamot. It's supposed to be a type of aromatherapy appetite suppressor. It was a gift from a client."

"I'm already thinking about what to have for dinner, so maybe it takes awhile to work." James handed her his food log and then sat down in the chair across from her desk. "I was doing fine until this weekend."

"That happens a lot. There's a routine about the workweek that makes it easier to stay on track." She fell silent and examined his log. "You did really well for the most part. I think I could offer you some substitutions for a few of these high-calorie casseroles and I'd like you to try to limit your dessert calories to one hundred and fifty per day."

"We've still got about a dozen casseroles left," James commented.

"Except for today, I don't see any cakes listed here." Dr. Ruth looked at him expectantly. "What happened to your role as official cake taster?"

James stared at her. Was it possible she didn't know about Paulette's death? "Do you read the *Star,* Dr. Ruth?"

"I'm not much of a newspaper person. I read the news online each morning, but I've been too busy getting ready for Christmas to even play games on Pogo. That's my guilty pleasure." She caught the worried expression on her client's face. "Is there something I should know?"

"Paulette Martine is dead," James said. "It happened Friday night."

"Oh my goodness." Dr. Ruth folded her hands together as though in prayer and turned her face toward the window. "We must have seen her just hours before she passed."

James hadn't anticipated this remark. Instead of asking her for any details, he decided to remain quiet and wait to see what Dr. Ruth would tell him.

"I was really mortified over how my boys behaved at the television station. Hank, my oldest, told me that Ms. Martine taunted him once the cameras stopped rolling. Apparently she said that I might need to pick up a McDonald's application, since my clients were sure to desert me after they heard about how I'd floundered on the show."

"That certainly sounds like her."

Dr. Ruth smiled wanly. "No matter what she may have said about me, my boys were raised better than that. I'm afraid being at college, playing football, and spending all their free time hanging out in a fraternity house has allowed them to forget how to control their emotions and behave like Southern gentlemen." She pointed at the photograph of her sons. "The younger ones were given their own penance, but since Hank behaved the worst, I wanted him to apologize to Ms. Martine in person."

"When did you go?" James asked.

"Mid-afternoon. I had a client at two, so it was some time after that." Dr. Ruth gazed at her desk calendar. "Ms. Martine's assistant told us that her employer was in the kitchen and couldn't be disturbed. I went ahead and knocked, and Hank and I were allowed in."

James tried to imagine Paulette's irritation at being disturbed. He was confident that she didn't receive Hank Wilkins's apology with the grace and courtesy Dr. Ruth would have hoped for. "How'd it go?"

"She listened to Hank, but wouldn't look at him, because she was too busy cracking eggs into a bowl. When my son finished speaking, she dismissed us. That's really the best way to describe it. And so we left."

"Did Willow come into the kitchen with you?"

Dr. Ruth cocked her head. "That's an odd question, but no, she didn't. No one was around when we left." She handed James his food log. "You must have had a very trying few days. If you feel like you need comfort foods this week, that's completely understandable. However, you may find that other things can relax you just as well. A long, hot bath, for example." She placed a blank sheet of paper in front of him. "And I've got more homework for you. I want you to pay attention to how hungry you are when you eat." She drew the number five in the center of the paper. "This is your number when you're satisfied. Anything above that means that you're full. An eight, for example, means that you've stuffed yourself."

"So what does a one mean? I'm about to die of starvation?"

"Pretty much," Dr. Ruth replied seriously. "Most of us have never experienced the intense hunger at that end of the scale. When we're really hungry, we're more at a three. Four is the beginnings of hunger."

James laughed. "I think I'm at a four right now."

Dr. Ruth checked her watch. "It's getting to be dinner time, so that makes sense. Do your best with your food log and remember to record any exercise you've done as well. Those are negative calories for your chart. I'll see you next week, after you don your tuxedo for the wed—" She cut herself off. "I'm so sorry — I'm talking about things I don't know a thing about."

"That's okay," James assured her. "The wedding's been postponed for now. We're having a Christmas Eve memorial for Paulette, since her family's in town." Seeing the sympathy in Dr. Ruth's eyes, he longed to have her return to her more optimistic self. "On the bright side, this'll give me more time to fit into my tuxedo."

His words resonated with callousness, and he quickly felt ashamed. "Have a lovely Christmas," he told Dr. Ruth, and then slunk from the office. As he walked out to his car, he realized that he was now in possession of information that Lucy would need to know.

"It's time for an emergency supper club meeting," he declared to himself as he flipped open his cell phone.

Nine: Salmon with Herbs

"There's only one thing for us to do," Bennett stated as he set aside his copy of *The Encyclopedia on World History* and brought his mug of frothy cappuccino to his lips. "We're gonna have to crash your Martine family dinner party tonight — get a firsthand look at these suspects ourselves."

"What dinner party?" Gillian asked.

"Milla and the rest of the clan are getting together at Mamma Mia's in New Market," James answered. "I'm driving her there so I can check out the suspects myself."

"I'm not on the same *plane* with you, James." Gillian frowned in disapproval, her silver eye shadow winking as she did so. "It seems rather judgmental to call these out-of-towners suspects. The *Star* indicated that Paulette's death was *natural.* Her body and spirit have simply been returned to the ever-welcoming arms of our Mother Earth."

After sending a perplexed look Gillian's way, James recklessly forged ahead with his plan to include the supper club members in the Sheriff's Department's investigation. "I don't know about the redistribution part, but ask Lucy whether it was *natural* or someone helped her reach Elysian Fields or what have you."

"Are you holding out on us?" Lindy tugged on Lucy's sleeve, threatening to spill her mocha latte.

Lucy freed herself from her friend's grasp and stirred a pink packet of artificial sweetener into her latte. "Way to put me on the spot, James," she muttered crossly.

Willy, the owner of the Custard Cottage, forestalled her from continuing by arriving at their table with a tray bearing five small cups of custard. "I've made up a new flavor, folks," he said while passing out the plastic spoons and paper napkins he had stored in the front pocket of his pin-striped apron.

"Give this a taste and tell me what you think. I'm not sure if it's ready to be added as a flavor-of-the-week, and since y'all have experience bein' food judges, I'm gonna leave the decision to the experts."

Relieved to be out of the spotlight, Lucy spooned an oversized bite of custard into her mouth and then winced as the coldness coated her latte-warmed mouth. Her friends followed suit, taking more reserved bites.

"I taste chocolate, and that's always a good thing," Lindy stated.

Bennett wiped some custard from his toothbrush mustache. "Yeah, but marshmallow's the main attraction in this one."

Gillian closed her eyes and hummed for a long moment, her hoop earrings bobbing against the skin of her neck. "There's a very *subtle* integration of a cakelike cookie. It tastes so familiar, like something from childhood. Nostalgically delicious."

Willy beamed. "Yes ma'am! All three of you are right, but our Gillian gave me the answer my ears were searchin' for. I may now introduce y'all to my newest flavor: *Memories of MoonPie.*"

The dozen or so patrons in Willy's cozy eatery burst into spontaneous applause. Smiling like a proud parent, he passed out rounds of samples to everyone and listened to their feedback with careful consideration. Willy was a relative newcomer to Quincy's Gap, but one would never know it by watching him work. Not only did he know the name of each of his patrons, but he knew their favorite flavors and toppings as well. He was aware of their current dieting goals, their occasions for celebration, and when they just needed to be cheered up. Most of the townsfolk viewed him as some sort of magician and paid him weekly visits, no matter how cold it was outside, because Willy was filled with enough warmth and good cheer to change a person's outlook in the twinkle of an eye and a carefully selected dish of frozen custard.

Because of the enchanted setting, James had thought that the Custard Cottage would be the perfect place for the supper club members to put their heads together and form a plan to identify Paulette's murderer, but everything depended on Lucy's willingness to share information with her friends.

"All right." Lindy put her spoon down, crushed her empty custard cup with the flat of her hand, and stared daggers at Lucy. "Time to level with us. We've helped out *your department* before, remember? We can help again. Or are we unnecessary now that you're a deputy, even though we helped get you in that uniform you're so proud of?"

Lucy glanced at Lindy in surprise. "Sheath your claws. I'm not your enemy."

Lindy was instantly contrite. "Sorry, sorry. I'm such a grump today. See, when I finally talked to Luis this weekend, he told me that his mama's fadin' fast and that her last wish is for him to marry the daughter of her closest friend."

"Ouch!" Bennett exclaimed. "The dyin' wish of a boy's mother. Man, that's heavy. He can't ignore that one too easy."

"Thanks, Bennett." Lindy was clearly crestfallen.

Gillian nudged Bennett's arm so that the spoonful of custard he was about eat ended up smeared across his cheek. "Luis loves *you,* Lindy. He might be tormented by his mother's wishes for a space of time, but eventually the *true* feelings of his heart will *shine* through. He'll acknowledge the fact that his sweet mother was simply trying to be the vehicle of his happiness by pushing him to marry."

Lindy brightened immediately. "You mean his mama's pushing this other woman at him so that he'll make a commitment to me?"

Gillian shrugged. "Destiny moves in *mys-*

tifying ways. Who can tell what chain of events will draw one soul to another?"

The rhetorical question hung in the air as each supper club member fell silent, thinking of the person who caused their heart to beat faster. James flicked his eyes at Lucy and found that she was staring at him intently, her gaze tender and somewhat sad.

"Why are you doing this?" she demanded, a glimmer of anger crossing her features. "Splitting me between my friends and my job."

"I'm forcing your hand for Milla's sake," James answered. "And because it's the right thing to do. The five of us make a great team. You know that, Lucy. If justice is what you seek, then we're on the job beside you. Just like we've always been."

She studied him for another moment and then searched the curious faces of her friends. Nodding, she seemed to come to a decision. "Paulette was poisoned," Lucy whispered softly. "At least that's what the medical examiner believes." She held up a finger and pointed it around the table. "And that fact doesn't go further than this table."

"Maybe she killed herself," Bennett suggested flatly. "She didn't seem too happy."

Lucy shook her head. "That's pretty unlikely. Unless we count her family reunion, there's no evidence to suggest she was disturbed to the point of wanting to end it all. Plus, most folks don't like to suffer when they make a deliberate choice to check out. Paulette definitely felt a lot of pain." She glanced at James. "The way we found her body made that clear." Lucy succinctly described the scene in the kitchen.

Gillian fanned herself with her hand. "How terrible! Such a cruel death. Someone must have *truly* wanted her to suffer. Perhaps the way they felt *they* had suffered."

James frowned. "I think she enjoyed issuing a little verbal torture to everyone she met. The only person I ever saw her be civil to was my father, and *he* was plying her with whiskey."

"I suppose Willow must be at the top of your suspect list," Lindy said to Lucy. "That girl took more than her fair share of abuse."

"She was at the bed-and-breakfast too," Lucy agreed. "But why travel to Quincy's Gap and then kill Paulette? That would be downright stupid. With her boss a stranger in town, Willow would be elected Most-Likely-to-Kill-the-Diva right off the bat."

Lindy scooted back her chair and approached the glass case filled with assorted custard flavors. She pointed at one and then gestured at a candy jar filled with peanut-butter cups. A few moments later, she returned with one of Willy's famous "concretes," in which he combined the custard and candy toppings — and in this case a few ribbons of hot fudge — using a pair of spackling knives. James loved to watch him blend the sweet ingredients. Willy's hands were quick and deft, much like the hibachi chefs juggling spatulas or pepper mills at a Japanese restaurant.

"Sorry for the interruption. I just think more clearly when I've got a little chocolate running through my system." Lindy sighed in contentment as she swallowed of bite of chocolate mixed with fudge and peanut-butter cup. "We should consider that Willow may have intentionally waited until Paulette's family was in town to act. She probably knew more things about the Diva's life than anyone else, so if there was any family conflict, she could use that to her advantage."

"Clever," James said in admiration. "Though I wouldn't wait around to see if the poison worked if *I* were a murderer. On the other hand, there was definitely tension between Paulette and her daughter as well as her older sister, Wheezie. Apparently the son could do no wrong."

"That's how my mama feels about me!"

Bennett thumped his chest and grinned.

As the friends sipped coffee and watched Lindy devour her frozen custard, Lucy created character sketches of Paulette's family. She shared details from her interviews with the three relatives, stating that each of them had seemed genuinely shocked but not overly distraught by the news of Paulette's death.

"Frankly, Chloe seemed relieved, as though she had no one to criticize her anymore. Chase got a greedy gleam in his eye, and Wheezie was, I don't know, resigned. Though I swear she smiled once and then tried to hide it by coughing. All of the family members gave brief and careful answers to our questions — never saying more than necessary. I got the feeling that each one of them was hiding something."

"How do you *sense* something like that?" Gillian asked, fascinated.

Lucy pondered her friend's question for a moment. "When someone's keeping something from me, it's like a curtain drops over their eyes. It's invisible, but I still see it. I can't explain it better than that."

James studied her for a moment, wondering if he'd be attracted to Lucy's cornflower blue eyes, luminescent skin, and lustrous cinnamon-hued hair for the rest of his days.

She always looked especially appealing when they were involved in a case together. He was suddenly struck with the realization that they got along best when they were investigating a murder. The rest of the time they seemed at a loss over how to take the relationship to a romantic level and keep it there.

James also saw, in this oddly timed moment of self-reflection, that for years he had been at the mercy of Lucy's whims. He had wanted to claim Lucy as his own from the day they met, and since that time, only his relationship with Murphy had interfered with those feelings. Lucy, however, seemed only interested in behaving like a couple when he was already dating someone else. Clenching his fists, James looked away from her animated face. His emotions were warring within him as he thought about never kissing her again for the rest of their lives.

Why does everything have to be so complicated? He thought crossly. *Am I ever going to find the right person to spend my life with? Because apparently, it's not going to be Lucy Hanover!*

Gillian observed James's hangdog look and covered his hand with hers. "Poor Milla. What did she and your father decide to do about their wedding?"

"It's postponed. There's going to be a memorial service for Paulette on Christmas Eve instead." James scowled. "Unfortunately, it's bound to turn into a media feeding frenzy. Newspaper reporters and TV crews should be descending on us any second now."

"You hear that, Willy?" Bennett called out to the proprietor. "The press is coming to Quincy's Gap. Better stock up."

Willy scrutinized the contents of his cooler and smiled. "I'd best make lots of extra coffee-flavored custard. Those journalist types go nuts for anythin' that has so much as a whiff of caffeine."

James was highly tempted to ask for one of Willy's cinnamon cappuccino custards, but he was determined to restrict his caloric intake that day and feared that having dinner at the family-style Italian restaurant in New Market would be enough of a challenge to his resolve.

"So tell me, Bennett," Lindy raised a dark eyebrow, "how exactly can five people crash a dinner party at Mamma Mia's?"

"Easy." Bennett wiped a trace of whipped cream from the rim of his wide-mouthed cup and sucked it from his finger with a smile. "We act like we just happened to have run into our old friend James. Because the man is so polite, he'll introduce us to Milla's kin and then he'll feel like he's gotta ask us to join the party. We protest at first, but then we sit down and order a few rounds of booze. *We* only pretend to drink, while encouraging the rest of them to get soused, and then we sit back and listen."

"Do you think they'll be *completely* honest and open with you there?" Gillian asked Lucy.

"No," she answered truthfully. "I'll dress in plain clothes and hang out at the bar, but I can't sit with the rest of you. I can't even come in at the same time. Maybe I can still eavesdrop from the bar." She looked keenly disappointed.

The group fell silent, recognizing that their crime-solving methods were now firmly and truly altered since Lucy had become a deputy.

"It doesn't matter," Lindy said after a moment, and slung her arm around Lucy's shoulder. "As long as we're together, we can do some good." She put her free hand in the center of the table. "The Flab Five is back at it! Who's with me?"

Grinning like children, the friends piled their hands on top of hers and James felt, at least for the moment, that equilibrium had been restored.

■ ■ ■ ■

James had never been to Mamma Mia's before as it had only been open for a little over a month. The restaurant's décor was a strange blend of luxury and outright tackiness. The walls were wood-paneled and the tablecloths were a pristine white and had been ironed and starched to crispness. Despite these elegant details, there were also dozens of Italian flag garlands criss-crossing the ceiling and trellises of silk bougainvillea in a very unnatural shade of electric pink obscured the walls. The centerpieces on the tables were comprised of dyed-green carnations and miniature Italian flags. The music was at odds too, alternating between Frank Sinatra, Pavarotti, and the soundtrack from *Moonstruck*.

Upon entering the quirky restaurant, Milla quickly took care of the seating arrangements and, after introducing James to her family, placed him between Willow and Chloe.

Paulette's daughter was the absolute opposite of her mother. Where Paulette had been all thinness and sharp edges, Chloe was soft everywhere. With a round body, wide eyes, and unfashionably long hair, which she wore in a thick ponytail straight down her back, Chloe wore a loose T-shirt, a flowing denim skirt, and Birkenstock sandals. She greeted James with the open kindness and warmth that James had come to associate with Milla, and he found himself immediately hoping that the young woman had nothing to do with her mother's sudden death.

Her younger brother, Chase, gripped James's hand with unnecessary firmness and then, ending the contact with abruptness, fussed over the crimson silk handkerchief poking from the front pocket of his Brooks Brothers suit. He was clearly Paulette's son, having the same angular jaw, dark eyes, and trim figure. Like his mother, it seemed physically impossible for Chase's mouth to turn upwards in a smile and, after seating himself with regal grace, the New York lawyer gazed upon the present company with a mixture of boredom and disdain.

Aunt Wheezie was a sweet old lady. She embraced James, calling him a handsome boy, and then hung on to Milla's arm, her expression affectionate. For someone in her late seventies, Wheezie was startlingly childlike and innocent. She glanced around Mamma Mia's with the wide-eyed wonder of a young girl being offered her first carousel ride. When the waiter appeared, she giggled and ordered a Shirley Temple as though she were requesting a double shot of tequila.

"I'll handle the wine," Chase announced. "I'm sure to have the most qualified palate."

He's a male version of his mother, James thought and then smiled as Gillian breezed through the restaurant's front door wearing a purple poncho over a tangerine colored sheath and enormous drop earrings that fell like silver waterfalls to her shoulders. Lindy was right on her heels, looking attractively chic and exotic in a red wool coat, slimming black pantsuit, and chunky necklace made of asymmetrical, multicolored beads. Bennett wore a blue button-down and a mustard-colored tie, but had replaced his sports coat in favor of his favorite bomber jacket. Lucy was nowhere in sight.

"James! And Milla too!" Lindy trilled upon pretending to notice their large party. "What a surprise!"

She quickly walked over to Milla and gave her a warm kiss on the cheek. Shortly afterward, she was kissing everyone in welcome. Even Chase seemed to warm to her effusive charm.

"You *must* join us," Milla insisted before

James had the opportunity.

Gillian waved off the invitation. "Oh, we could *never* intrude on an *intimate* family gathering."

Aunt Wheezie stroked her purple poncho with delight. "Are we having a party? You can sit next to me, sweetie. I like your pretty red hair."

Gillian beamed. "You have such a *youthful* aura about you. I believe I might be rejuvenated just by being in your presence."

Milla looked to James for help. "Would you ask the waiter to slide another table over here? It's almost Christmas and your friends have become like family to me. I'd so love to have them eat with us."

James bowed, feeling a prick of guilt for enacting such a deception upon a woman who had always been the epitome of sincerity and kindness. "Anything for you, milady," he told her.

Once everyone was settled, the waiter bustled off toward the kitchen and returned with a bottle of wine. As he poured the burgundy-colored liquid into her glass, Lindy pointed at the bottle and said, "I think we're gonna need at least two more of those." She turned to Chloe and clinked glasses with her. "Y'all need some cheerin' up, right?"

While Lindy regaled Chloe with details of her relationship troubles, Gillian asked Wheezie and Milla about their childhoods in Natchez. Chase, who guzzled down his first glass of wine as though it were Gatorade, seemed grudgingly impressed to learn that Bennett was to be a *Jeopardy!* contestant in a few weeks and proceeded to toss out question after question of legal trivia. Bennett refilled Chase's glass and pretended to ponder each question as though he had never been so challenged by another person's wisdom before.

Each of the supper club members had previously chosen a member of the party to get to know, and James had volunteered to focus his attention on Willow. He had a difficult time concentrating on small talk, however, once the waiter appeared with their appetizers. They were served on enormous porcelain platters meant to be passed around the table so that everyone could sample each dish. There were stuffed mushrooms bathed in a four-cheese sauce, fried zucchini sticks with marinara dip, lamb ravioli in a creamy pesto sauce, and spicy bruschetta covered by a thin layer of parmesan, sun-dried tomatoes, and fresh basil.

"Do you remember when I came to the library? You said that you might have an idea about a job for me?" Willow gently reminded James as he accepted a mushroom from the platter she held out to him.

"Indeed I do. Excuse me, Milla." James interrupted a conversation between Gillian and his future stepmother. "Would you mind telling Willow about *Quincy's Whimsies*?"

For the first time since receiving the news that her sister was dead, Milla's face lit up and her eyes sparkled with animation. "I'm planning on opening a gourmet gift store in the spring. I'm going to carry handmade gifts, made by craftsmen right in our own Shenandoah Valley, and eatable gifts as well. Nothing that would compete with the Sweet Tooth or the Custard Cottage, of course. I was thinking of offering some pre-made dinners and a line of jams, sauces, purees — that sort of thing."

"How about handmade chocolates and candies?" Willow asked eagerly.

Milla nodded with a smile. "Those would be an excellent addition to our inventory, my dear. I was also thinking of carrying specialized kitchen tools and cookbooks. Pretty tea towels and potholders and aprons. Oh! I can see it all already!"

"You could make culinary gift baskets too," Willow suggested, caught up in Milla's vision. "Instead of sending people a bouquet of flowers for Valentine's Day or Mother's Day or whatever, a customer could create a personalized gift basket stuffed with the recipient's favorite candy, jam flavor, scented candle — that kind of thing."

"That's brilliant!" Milla declared. "And we could make baskets of local products to sell to the tourists. I love it!" She clapped her hands. "How would you like to be the manager of *Quincy's Whimsies,* my girl?"

"Me? Really?" Willow blushed and put her hand to her chest, clearly stunned. "But you barely know me."

James refilled both of their wine glasses, reveling in the glow on Milla's cheeks and the spark of hope in Willow's pale blue eyes.

"I know enough," Milla declared forcefully. "You're a hard worker, a creative thinker, and you can cook. James brought me home a fat slice of that lemon-strawberry layer cake, and I was licking my fingers for hours afterward." She studied Willow over the rim of her wine glass. "I assume you could bake every one of Paulette's cakes, couldn't you?"

"Yes. I've even helped her improve her recipes." Willow looked both proud and embarrassed of her skills. "I could take over her show if I had any personality, but I don't, and I'd hate to be on TV anyway. I really love to make things from scratch though. Fresh foods are so fulfilling, and I love the look on people's faces when they taste something really delicious that I've made."

"I enjoy that too." Milla smiled at Willow fondly. "That's why I started my cooking school, so that my students could learn to put that look on those gathered around their tables. But now I'd like to surround myself with a shop stuffed to the brim with pretty things, gossiping with my customers while I sit on a stool, drinking a cup of tea, listening to the cash register ring and ring."

Willow sighed euphorically. "That sounds so lovely. I'd be thrilled to be a part of your enterprise. I'll need to wrap up my life in New York and find an apartment to rent down here first." She looked at James from beneath her lashes. "Does Francis live in an apartment? Maybe he knows of a vacancy in his building."

"No. He and Scott live in an apartment in a converted garage, but there's a brand new complex not too far from town you could check out. For the price of your Manhattan studio you could probably get a three-bedroom palace in Quincy's Gap."

Willow and Milla continued to brainstorm

about their future endeavor while two waiters arrived bearing their entrées. James watched with delight as the heavy platters were placed on the table.

"Beautiful!" Aunt Wheezie shouted with glee and James felt like doing the same. Before him was an Italian feast featuring slices of veal saltimbocca slathered in brown sauce and melted mozzarella, thin pieces of chicken piccata embellished with paper-thin slivers of lemon, mounds of fettuccini Alfredo mixed with prosciutto and peas, salmon filets flavored with lemon and herbs, and lobster tortellini in a creamy tomato basil sauce.

Having already consumed a large serving of spinach salad, James was determined to make good choices during this part of the meal, so he helped himself to a salmon filet and half a chicken cutlet. Every bite of the rich fare was delicious, and it took an iron will to steer clear of the enticing but undoubtedly fattening noodle dishes. No one else was skimping on samples, however, and James couldn't believe how much food the party was able to consume.

With two glasses of wine and excellent food in his belly, James was having a hard time viewing his tablemates with a suspicious eye. Even Chase, who had warmed up conspicuously due to the entire bottle of wine he drank, was joking around with Bennett as though they were old friends.

Everyone was laughing and rosy-cheeked, and it wasn't until James left to use the restroom that he became aware of a familiar figure sitting at the bar. Lucy was wearing a baggy gray wool coat over jeans and a black turtleneck. Her head was slightly bent and her hair partially obscured her face. A half-filled cup of coffee sat between her hands and James realized she had been watching them in the mirror behind the bar.

"How long have you been here?" he asked without looking directly at her.

"Since your appetizer course."

James felt a pang of pity for Lucy. She was utterly outside the circle of camaraderie and, instead, sat at the bar like a brooding P.I. from a vintage detective story. "Did you have anything to eat?"

Lucy nodded. Through clenched teeth, she whispered. "Go away, James. I've heard a lot sitting here, and I can't listen if you're talking to me. Besides, someone might notice."

Thus dismissed, James remained in the bathroom until his countenance, flushed with injured pride, returned to a relatively normal hue. By the time he resumed his seat, the dinner party was busy sampling squares of tiramisu, miniature chocolate-covered cannoli, and slices of triple-berry cheesecake. James noticed that in his absence, fatigue and stuffed bellies had forced the assemblage to grow more taciturn, and he was relieved when the waiter finally presented the check to Chase.

"Just tell us what we owe you, my dear." Milla fished her wallet out of her purse. "I'm helpless with dividing up checks after only one glass of wine."

"There's no need," Chase replied magnanimously. "I'll take care of it." He slid a gold card on top of the check and handed the server book to the waiter.

As the rest of the party thanked Chase effusively, aware that their meal had cost hundreds of dollars, Chloe began to sulk unattractively.

"He can afford to be generous," she whined as Chase's attention was diverted when his Waterman pen rolled under the next table.

Willow gazed at Chloe in sympathy. "I know. It's a messed-up world when lawyers make more than teachers or firemen or animal rescuers, right?"

Chloe nodded but was determined to be petulant. "It's not just the huge salary he collects by ruining the lives of those wronged by drug companies. Mother's left him all *her* money too. I'm totally broke, but I won't get a dime because I didn't follow the *recipe* she laid out for my life. *Chase* did everything she wanted, and that's why he gets the big payoff."

"I guess that's going to be a fair amount of money," James mused aloud.

"Royalties from her cookbooks and product endorsements alone will allow him to buy that house in the Hamptons. Now he can set up his *latest* mistress in style. I wonder how his *wife* would feel about that!" Chloe seethed, and James was taken aback by what now appeared to be a rather mercurial personality.

Chase had overheard that last bit and colored angrily. "You and your sea cows. If you hadn't pissed mother off at every turn and then married a loser who got so drunk that he fell off his own boat and drowned, then you'd be sitting pretty too." He signed his credit card receipt with a violent scrawl. "Let's go, Wheezie. We'd better take you back to the roach motel before you fall face-first into the tiramisu. Willow? I'm assuming you need a ride," he added ungraciously, all traces of his alcohol-induced gaiety gone.

"We'll take her back to the Widow's Peak,"

James answered on Willow's behalf, and Milla gave him a grateful smile.

Straightening his tie, Chase pushed back his chair, threw his napkin on the seat, and strode from the room without waiting to see whether his aunt and sister were ready to leave.

"Party's over!" Wheezie declared with less energy than before, and she seemed to shrink into herself. Chloe mutely helped her aunt into her coat and then left, her eyes shining with unshed tears.

Willow and the supper club members stood up and gathered their coats and purses. James turned around to examine the bar area and saw that Lucy was already gone.

"Yes, the party's over," he said to Lindy as he helped her with her coat. "But now we've got *a lot* to talk about at the memorial service."

TEN: EGGNOG CAKE WITH BUTTER RUM FROSTING

James woke on December twenty-fourth to the sound of Milla's hand blender. He only had a half-day of work ahead of him, but with Paulette's funeral services scheduled for that evening, he'd been hoping to eat a peaceful breakfast while finishing the last chapter of *The Thirteenth Tale.* From then, he planned to move sedately through a quiet day. After showering and dressing for work, he arrived in the kitchen to find Milla baking, Jackson repairing the garbage disposal under the sink, and the coffee pot empty.

"I like your Santa tie," Milla shouted over the whir of the mixer.

So much for quiet, he thought.

Smoothing a small crinkle in his holiday tie, which featured Santa and several reindeer reading a book in front of a fireplace, James held out his clean coffee cup in accusation. "You've been up a while."

"Dear oh dear," Milla clucked. "We've gone and left you high and dry. Let me just get these in the oven, and I'll brew you a fresh pot. Can I fix you breakfast?"

James eyed the array of dirty bowls, wooden spoons, cake pans, and deflated bags of flour and sugar. "No thanks. I'm just going to toast a Kashi waffle and have some fruit. I think you've got enough going on here already. Are you planning to feed cake to the entire town today?"

"Just those who show up to my sister's memorial service," Milla answered as she slipped two filled cake pans into the oven. "I want everyone who is kind enough to express their sympathy to have a slice of Paulette's favorite cake."

"Which one would that be?" James asked as he sniffed one of the batter bowls.

Gloomily, Milla cradled an egg in her palm. "She was my own sister and I didn't even know. Willow had to tell me, but it's the eggnog cake she made for the TV show last week. That woman and her eggnog."

Stepping forward to wipe away the lone tear cascading down the curve of her cheek, James said, "I bet the time Paulette spent with you last week made a real difference to her, Milla. Look at things this way: She flew down to Quincy's Gap to celebrate your wedding, she was over here in the morning chatting and having breakfast, and she cooked us dinner and laughed it up with Pop. I think it's safe to say that her last days were some of her better ones."

Milla stood on her tiptoes and kissed James on the cheek. "You are a darling boy, James Henry. I'm going to come over and cook three times a week when you move down the road."

"I'm counting on it!" James declared, gave his soft paunch a pat, and carried his breakfast into the den. He finished the last page of Diane Setterfield's excellent novel to the sound of Jackson releasing a torrent of expletives. Even from the safety of the den, James was able to discern that Milla dumped a bowl of refuse down the garbage disposal, having forgotten that there was no longer a canister attached to the sink. The entire contents, including raw egg spittle and clumps of cake dough, had ended up on Jackson's face.

"I am *not* a trash can!" he heard his father splutter indignantly.

"You sure you don't want a crepe, James?" Milla called from the kitchen. "I could scrape enough dough off your daddy's forehead to make you one!" She chuckled. "Jackson, honey. You just got a free sugar facial."

James made a hasty escape while his father was in the bathroom cleaning the muck off his face, knowing that Jackson would grow even more inflamed if there were another witness to his humiliation.

"Don't expect to see him until it's time to go to church," Milla whispered and handed James his lunch sack and a thermos of coffee. "He's determined to finish that painting of my sister's hands before the service. I'll be cooking him steak every night as punishment for making him fix this dumb disposal when all he wanted to do was sneak out to his shed."

"That's why you're so good for him, Milla. You drag him out of that shed from time to time. Call me if you need me to buy out the rest of Food Lion's supply of flour, sugar, and eggs on my way home."

"I just might." Milla's eyes twinkled as she pushed him out the back door.

■ ■ ■ ■

"Merry Christmas, Professor!" The twins exclaimed as he alighted from his truck in the library parking lot.

Scott held out a narrow strip of black cloth. "We're going to have to open five minutes late, boss. We want to show you what we made you for Christmas first."

James pointed at the fabric. "Well, if that's meant to be a belt I'm very flattered, but I think it'll take a few more meetings with Dr. Ruth before that's going to fit around *this* waist."

"This is a blindfold," Francis declared with a boyish grin. "Your gift was too big to wrap, so we've got it leaning against the book return bin. May I?"

Leaning his head forward, James allowed Francis to fasten the blindfold. Each twin took hold of one of his arms and they led him over the curb, around a curve of sidewalk, and pivoted him so that he faced the book bin. With a flourish, Scott removed the blindfold and James sucked in his breath in amazement.

The twins had built him a custom mailbox. The box was wood and had been carved to resemble a shelf of books. Each book had been painted a different color and the titles of authors had been carefully engraved on the spines. Labels representing the library's filing protocol had also been painted on each tome. Upon closer inspection, James was delighted to note that the books were in proper order according to the Dewey decimal system. Even the red flag was a miniature book, which the twins had cleverly entitled *The Scarlet Letter.* The post of the mailbox, which was a stake of plain wood, bore Cicero's famous quote on books: *"A room without books is like a body without a soul."*

"We burned the letters into the wood instead of carving them," Scott explained as James touched the black script. "It saves time and it'll last forever because we covered that post with about forty thousand layers of polyurethane."

Francis noticed that their boss seemed to have gotten something in his eye. "You okay, Professor?"

James nodded, too choked up to speak. Finally, after running both hands lovingly over the carved books on the mailbox, he turned and smiled at his employees, no longer caring that his eyes were glistening with tears. "This is a marvelous, excellent gift. You found out that my new house was number twenty-seven. I can't imagine how much time went into this . . ." He hugged each twin and sniffed. "Bennett Marshall won't believe his eyes when he puts my first letter in here. I'll be on his route when I move, and there's no doubt in my mind that this will be the finest mailbox he, or anyone else, has ever seen."

Francis blushed and made a big show of tying his boot lace.

"He made one for that Willow girl too," Scott whispered. "Looks like a box of chocolates. It's a wall mount in case she ends up moving here and renting an apartment." He nudged his brother so that Francis lost his balance and sprawled on the grass. "I think he's in *love*."

"Then he won't have to ship that mailbox to New York, because Willow's moving here after the holidays," James informed the twins. Francis gaped at his boss in happy surprise. "And what about you, Scott? Did you make a newspaper column mailbox for Lottie?" James teased, allowing Francis a moment to recover his poise.

Scott's face darkened. "That girlfriend of mine's been acting weird lately, Professor. She wants me to stop playing video games and reading graphic novels for good! She even thinks I should . . ." he trailed off and looked to Francis to finish for him.

"Lottie wants him to get a different job," Francis muttered. "A *career,* she calls it."

James felt as though a cold wind had pierced his heart. "But you're happy here, aren't you?"

"Yes!" Scott answered hurriedly. "I'd never leave the library! I'm happy here, and I'm happy about who I am. I know I'm a geek who could use contact lenses and a car made in this decade, but I'm fine with riding a bike and living in Widow Lamb's garage. My job is perfect, my boss is the greatest, and I'm the luckiest guy in the world to be able to work with my brother, my best friend, every day."

"Stop it or I'll cry again!" James clutched Scott on the shoulder. "And you *are* lucky. Some people spend their whole lives trying to figure out what makes them happy and you're aware — in your mid-twenties no less — of exactly what you want and who you are."

"So what do I tell Lottie?" Scott was clearly distressed. "Love me or leave me? That's not how I talk, and I don't want to lose her."

In that moment, James had an epiphany. Lucy was basically telling him the same thing Scott longed to tell Lottie. She had made it clear that she would be devoted to upholding the law above all else and that was simply who she was. She had left it up to James to decide whether he could accept her and love her for who she was or sever their romantic ties once and for all.

But she didn't *let me decide,* he thought ruefully. *She just assumed that I wouldn't want a life with her under those conditions. And maybe she was right. Maybe I want to be first in a woman's heart. Maybe second place isn't good enough for me anymore.*

"Professor?" Scott's voice brought James back to reality and he became aware that not only were they late opening the library but they were all shivering. The three of them had been standing on the grass, idly chatting in forty-degree weather as several patrons gazed at them with a perplexity that would shortly mutate into irritation.

Handing Francis the keys to the front door, James shouldered his beautiful new mailbox and looked at Scott with sympathy. "We can't change people, Scott, no matter how much we'd like to. We must love them as they are or let them go so they'll have the chance to be loved by someone else."

Scott scratched his tousled hair in confusion. "Professor? Are we still talking about *my* situation?"

"What I'm saying is that you should be loved by someone who appreciates you *as is,* not as you *could be.* If Lottie doesn't love you now, then she's not looking for a smart, caring, loyal guy named Scott Fitzgerald and that's *her* loss." James smiled fondly at the young man. "It doesn't mean you guys are done for as a couple, but you've got to be honest with her by telling her that you don't want to change and see how she handles that declaration."

"Great. I *do* have to give Lottie the love-me-or-leave-me speech, and I've got to do it before we go undercover tonight." Scott sighed. "Poor Francis. He might be on a stakeout with the Grinch."

"That's right!" James had completely forgotten about Glowstar's kidnapping. "The ransom handoff is at midnight. I hope your abductor actually shows up, or we'll have to buy a new elf on eBay. I won't let you and Francis face another holiday season without one." With his left hand, he pulled envelopes containing generous gift cards to Best Buy from his coat pocket and held them out to Scott. "And I hope these will help take the *bah humbug* out of your day."

As James headed toward the Bronco with his treasure, Scott tore open his gift card and his eyes widened in delight. He then read the inscription in his Christmas card. It said:

> To Scott, fellow bibliophile, skilled librarian, and loyal friend. May your holiday be filled with barbarians wielding longswords and lovely maidens held captive by all-powerful warlocks. Merry Christmas. James Henry.

"Damn." Scott shut the card and blinked several times. "Now *I'm* going to cry."

The supper club members were waiting for James when he, along with Milla, Willow, and Jackson, entered the church chapel that evening. James and his companions were still reeling from the shouts of reporters and the blinding flashbulbs that had assaulted them in the parking lot.

Inside the warm sanctuary, the pews were stuffed. The townsfolk seemed to have congregated in the front while members of the media kept a respectful distance in the back of the chapel. A horde of strangers, who James feared were there in hopes of gaining a few minutes of fame by casting poignantly sorrowful glances at the television cameras, filed into the center rows.

Paulette's children and sister Wheezie

were in the first row. The pew behind them had been reserved for the supper club members and Willow. James was pleasantly surprised to observe Dr. Ruth and all three of her sons seated in respectful silence toward the middle of the crowd. He issued them a subtle wave and smiled at Dolly, who was likely to have a sore neck come Christmas Day from twisting this way and that in order to observe the demeanor of every person in the sanctuary.

"This is quite a showing," Milla murmured to James as Reverend Emerson walked to the pulpit in order to greet the congregation and then ask them to rise and join with him in the singing of "Abide With Me."

As James had spent the Sundays of his childhood at the very same church, he knew the hymn well enough to sing along while casting covert glances at the profiles of those lined up in front of him. Chase, who chose not to sing, was staring into the distance with a blank expression, while Chloe was concentrating on the words in her hymnal and appeared pale and overwhelmed. Wheezie was bobbing her head in time to the music, and James wondered if she weren't more than a little unbalanced or even afflicted by dementia. Her childish innocence seemed less like a quirky personality and more like the sign of a mental illness, but since he knew nothing about the latter, he hesitated to form judgment over Milla's sweet older sister.

Peering down his own row, James couldn't help but notice the new spark of vitality in Willow's eyes. Her face was shining with all the optimistic hopefulness of youth. She wore an attractive black dress with a cobalt blue scarf that brought color to her pale eyes. Her blonde hair shone with good health and was fastened into a chic knot at the base of her neck. Pink pearl earrings glowed softly against her cheeks, which were flushed by the cold air and by the proximity of Francis Fitzgerald (who was singing in a slightly sharp baritone two pews behind her).

At the conclusion of the hymn, Reverend Emerson led them in prayer and then invited Milla forward for the scripture reading. Her voice was clear throughout the entire recitation of Ecclesiastes 3, but when she reached verse twelve she paused. Wiping her eyes and nose with a tissue, she spoke with a tremor while reading, "That everyone may eat and drink, and find satisfaction in all his toil — this is the gift of God."

Gillian, whose hair had taken on a shade akin to paprika since their dinner at Mamma Mia's, sniffed loudly and then covered her entire face with a filmy handkerchief.

"Everything all right?" he whispered.

"Do you think Paulette was satisfied in *her* work, like that verse says? Do you think she realized what gifts *she* was given?" Gillian whimpered tearfully while Lucy patted her on the arm.

Milla finished her reading and then waited as Reverend Emerson offered Paulette's family members the opportunity to speak words of remembrance. Since Milla was already standing close to the pulpit's microphone, she introduced herself as "the middle sister" and then proceeded to tell an amusing childhood anecdote.

"As a young girl, Patty spent more time down the street than at our house. Our neighbor, Mrs. D., as we called her, loved to cook with Patty. Most girls my age were happy to set up lemonade stands or sell Girl Scout cookies for their first ventures into the business world, but not Patty. She wanted out of Natchez and while we were all spending our dimes at the movies or buying sodas and banana splits at the drug store, Patty was selling fancy cupcakes and tea cakes to all the neighborhood ladies."

Milla was lost in her memories, her gaze reaching over the heads of the congregation as she spoke of her sister with pride and a trace of awe. "She did exactly what she said she was going to do. Was in Paris by her eighteenth birthday. Some folks said she made a useful connection with one of the riverboat cooks, but however she got there, she never looked back. Even Mrs. D. never heard from her again, and that woman taught her everything she knew about baking. I do wonder what became of that sweet woman . . ."

Someone coughed discreetly in one of the pews in front, and Milla snapped out of her reverie and concluded her monologue by assuring those gathered there that Paulette had died doing the thing she was most passionate about. Then, her speech interrupted by a catch in her voice, she thanked everyone for coming and returned to her seat.

Chase was the next person to take the microphone. He too extolled his mother's entrepreneurial success, but he made no references to her *tendresse* as a mother. In fact, his eulogy lacked any indication of intimacy. His voice was flat and expressionless, and his speech reminded James of a professor giving a lackluster lecture on twenty-first-century economics.

"Sounds like he's givin' a fiscal report to a board of directors," Bennett whispered through a yawn.

"I think it shows poor taste to talk about how much money his mother's last book made at a memorial service," Lindy stated in disgust. "For crying out loud! Didn't she bake him special cookies for his birthday or build magical gingerbread castles at Christmas? He must have *one* childhood memory when she did something special for him!"

Apparently not, for Chase sat down while the congregation exchanged befuddled glances. Chloe refused to speak, which she made clear by shaking her head and crossing her arms like a willful child, but when the minister focused his querying gaze on Wheezie, she hobbled up the carpeted steps to the pulpit unaided.

"From the moment she entered this world, Patty was a bossy one," Wheezie said and pointed her finger at the bouquet of flowers that had been positioned where the coffin would have normally been situated. "That girl thought she was smarter than our whole town put together. Even Mama and Daddy were dumb hillbillies in her mind. Every day, she told me and Milla how she prayed to be told she was adopted. She hated us all and that ain't no lie."

Chase began to rise to his feet, but Chloe restrained him with both arms as the church audience sat up en masse with sudden interest. The members of the media who had been fortunate enough to find seating before the service began became instantly alert, mini recorders and small pads of paper held at the ready.

"And though she hated her family, the folks Patty hated even more were the mulattos. I know that's not what you're supposed to call them now, but that's what we called them then, and there were plenty of mulattos in Natchez. I loved one of them. A man named Alberto Marcos. I would have married him and been happy for the rest of my days, but Patty ruined it. She made Al out to Mama and Daddy like he was the worst kind of scoundrel, but the only *truly* wicked person I ever knew was my own sister."

Several members of the congregation gasped.

"I know it ain't right to speak ill of the dead, but I've been holdin' this in for too many years, and I want to tell you all that I ended up happy anyhow. Patty went to Paris as some man's floozy, and then she came back and got famous right quick. Reckon she became a richer man's kept woman."

The reporters were scribbling furiously.

James noticed Murphy and Lottie sitting side by side, listening with expressions bordering on rapture. James could practically sense Murphy spinning titles and headlines in her mind as Wheezie ruthlessly continued.

"I thought I could marry Al after we buried Mama and Daddy, but his heart turned hard toward our family and he married somebody else. He's a widower now and I'm still sweet on him, even after all these years. I came to this town to offer Patty a chance to make things right, to tell Al she was wrong to judge him and lie about him, but she laughed in my face at the notion. I hope the good Lord forgives her, or I reckon she's bakin' cakes of hot coals for the devil right about now. 'Preciate y'all comin' out. Thank you."

Wheezie returned to her seat, her head held high and a grim smile on her face. James closed his gaping mouth and turned to Milla, who was staring at her older sister with horrified astonishment. Jackson covered his fiancée's hand with his own and stared fixedly at the tops of his shoes.

Reverend Emerson was at a loss. James was certain that the minister had never presided over a eulogy speech such as Wheezie's. His eyes raked the pew of family members with a searching look until his wife, who was seated near the organist, poked the woman in the side and the first few strains of "Amazing Grace" burst into the still air. The hymn was played in double-time, followed by a rather mechanical recitation of the Lord's Prayer and a hasty benediction. Before James knew it, he found himself in the fellowship hall passing out slices of eggnog cake.

"Do you need help?" Lucy asked in a soft, concerned voice as she appeared at his side.

James nodded gratefully. "I don't know what to say to people after a service like that."

"I'll chase away anyone from the media, if you'd like." Lucy fixed a hostile glare in Murphy's direction.

"That would be a relief, thank you. And I wanted to tell you that I appreciate your coming today. If I didn't have the four of you behind me in moments like these . . ."

Lucy brushed his cheek with her fingers. The moment was fleeting, but filled with tenderness. "I'll always care about you, James. No matter what else happens in our lives, you can depend on my friendship. That's a promise."

James placed a piece of cake in her hands. "And you can depend on mine too."

Tears pooled in Lucy's blue eyes, but she blinked them away and concentrated on spearing a triangle of cake onto her fork. Slipping the morsel between her lips, she inadvertently groaned, "*This* is so good!"

Echoes of similar declarations emitted from mouths across the hall. As coffee cups were refilled and people accepted seconds on cake, Milla unveiled Jackson's painting of Paulette's hands to *oohhs* and *ahhhs* from the crowd.

James edged others aside in order to view the work of art. Once again, he was amazed by his father's ability to capture an individual's complete persona by fashioning a pair of hands through deft brushstrokes and a unique blend of hues. Paulette's were strong, determined, and graceful as they gripped the handles of a wooden rolling pin. The left-hand side of the canvas portrayed several petits fours decorated with prim and perfectly formed icing rosebuds, showcasing Paulette's love of precision. Edging off the right side was a bowl of raw eggs with a collection of fractured shells that had been scattered into the deepest corner of the canvas where Jackson's signature normally appeared. The jagged points and splintered bits of shell reminded the viewer of the Diva's sharp tongue and harsh words.

And yet, Jackson had also illustrated a fragility in Paulette's wrists — the blue and green veins traveling beneath the thin skin were a reminder of the woman's mortality. He had not spared the viewer her wrinkled knuckles or the ugly mole on the back of her palm, but the dough was clearly subservient to Paulette's will. Yet, the overall feeling James experienced while staring at the picture was that even though Paulette Martine was a woman of determination, her strength and intensity had rendered her unavoidably bitter and lonely.

"How does your daddy do it?" Lindy whispered to James. "It's so *her.* A more fitting memorial than any words."

"He truly has a *gift,*" Gillian agreed. "It's like he paints *souls* through a pair of hands. And the energy that *radiates* from every work is different, as unique as the subjects themselves. *Spectacular!* No wonder Lindy's mother can't keep them in stock in her gallery."

Scott and Francis plucked James on the sleeve and told them they were leaving in order to prepare for their midnight stakeout. After giving Milla sympathetic hugs, the pair headed for the door. However, Francis stopped short when he crossed Willow's path and the two of them exchanged shy smiles and hushed conversation as if they were the only people in the room. On the other hand, James was sorry to watch Lottie wag an accusatory finger at Scott while adopting a very harpylike snarl. Murphy stood alongside her protégée, glancing at her with maternal pride, and James instantly pushed through the throng in order to show solidarity to his employee, but by the time he got there the Fitzgerald twins had gone.

"You're turning that girl into a shrew," James growled at Murphy as Lottie threaded her way back to the buffet table. "Don't you have a book to promote? Some slander to spread? An ambulance to chase?"

Putting on a wounded expression, Murphy gesticulated around the church. "This is *my* community too, and I'm here to report on its news. Besides, I saw Paulette on TV and I wasn't going to miss a chance to sample one of her cakes. I guess baking unbelievable desserts runs in the family." She accepted a wedge from Lottie. "This is my third sample, mind you. And speaking of promotion, you'll be happy to hear that I'll be in New York for the release of *The Body in the Bakery.* From there I'm going on a twelve-city tour, so you won't have to watch me *chase ambulances* for months."

"I'm taking over as the *Star*'s editor in her

absence," Lottie added with a smug smile.

"Congratulations," James replied politely. "But keep in mind that the people of Quincy's Gap are more likely to share their stories with someone who is earnest, approachable, and modest. Kind of like Scott Fitzgerald. He's only in his mid-twenties and the entire town loves and admires him. At least anyone with a lick of sense, that is." He tried to give Lottie his sternest look. "Thank you for coming, ladies." And with that, he turned his back on the two speechless journalists.

Despite his determination not to succumb to the temptation of seeing plate upon plate of sweet-smelling cake everywhere he turned, conversing with Murphy and Lottie had put James on edge. Before he knew it, he had inhaled one slice and was carving away at a second, savoring the creamy butter-rum frosting and the spongelike moistness of the cake.

"Everything Paulette said about this cake when she was on TV was true," he said to Bennett. "Food like this is just too good to give up."

Bennett shrugged. "I'm not a big fan of eggnog."

"It doesn't actually have any in the batter," James explained. "Milla showed me the recipe. It's the nutmeg that makes people think of eggnog."

Eyeing the few remaining pieces on the table, Bennett shot off like a cannon to claim one as his own. Within minutes, all the slices were gone, the coffee urns were nearly drained, and the gathering had been reduced from well over one hundred people to less than twenty.

James washed down his last bite of cake with tepid coffee, threw away his trash, helped to clear away any signs of debris in the hall, and then slipped his arm around Milla. "Are you ready to go home?"

"Am I ever! I can't believe Wheezie! She's not even sorry about what she said. Here, *in church,* she told me that she's glad that Paulette's dead! That the only shadow over her life had been wiped away! She said our sister's only joy was in seeing others miserable and poor so she could gloat over being rich and famous and that people like that bring darkness to the world."

"Whoa." James knew he'd have to share that statement with the supper club members. With Wheezie so plainly satisfied by Paulette's death, she was a prime suspect. Assuming she had found transportation to the Widow's Peak, she could have poisoned her sister, seeking a painful death as revenge for the hurt she had suffered by being denied a life with the man she loved. Looking at Jackson and Milla standing shoulder to shoulder, James said, "Pop, I'd say you picked the finest of the Rowe sisters."

Jackson snorted. "I'm glad the whole lot of them are leavin' town. I don't want to share my Christmas roast with those miserable people." Looking at Milla's weary face, Jackson took her hand in his. "I'm sorry. I know they're your family and we don't choose our kin, but not one of them has a drop of goodness in them."

"Oh, I think there's good and bad in all of us, dear, but I'm ready for a break from them too." She sighed heavily. "I wish we really could have laid my sister to rest today. Who knows what we're going to have to deal with when those lab results come back."

"Don't think about that now," James advised as he covered Jackson's painting with a sheet and slipped it under his arm. "Let's just go home and watch *The Christmas Carol* and eat ourselves sick."

"And instead of going to bed and dreaming of sugarplums, I can dream about my new shop and *you* can dream about your darling house," Milla smiled at James.

"*I'm* stickin' to sugarplums!" Jackson

declared sulkily and the trio left the church, their arms linked, their voices lifted in laughter.

The Diva's Eggnog Cake

2 cups cake flour
2 1/2 teaspoons baking powder
1 teaspoon salt
1 teaspoon ground nutmeg
1 1/3 cups brown sugar, firmly packed
2 eggs plus enough whole milk to make 3/4 cup
1/2 cup butter, softened
2/3 cup whole milk
1 teaspoon pure vanilla extract

Preheat the oven to 350 degrees. Sift the cake flour into a large bowl. Add the baking powder, salt, nutmeg, and brown sugar. Crack the eggs directly into a measuring cup, and then add enough milk to total 3/4 cup of liquid. Beat the egg/milk mixture into the dry ingredients. Blend in the butter, and stir slightly until the mixture is smooth. Beat in the remaining 2/3 cup of milk and the vanilla. Pour the batter into three greased and floured 8-inch baking pans (or use cooking spray with flour, such as PAM baking spray). Bake for 20 to 25 minutes, or until a knife or wooden toothpick inserted in the center comes out clean. Cool in the pan for 5 minutes, and then remove the cake from the pan to cool completely. Frost with the Diva's Butter Rum Frosting, and garnish with a light sprinkle of nutmeg if desired.

The Diva's Butter Rum Frosting

3/4 cup butter
1 cup plus 2 1/2 cups confectioners' sugar, sifted
1/4 teaspoon salt
5 tablespoons heavy whipping cream
1 teaspoon vanilla extract
1 1/2–2 tablespoons dark rum (depending on taste) or 2 1/2 teaspoons rum extract
1 teaspoon pumpkin pie spice

Melt the butter in a large bowl. Gradually add 1 cup of the sifted confectioners' sugar and beat well. Slowly beat in the salt and cream. Beat in the remaining 2 1/2 cups of the confectioners' sugar 1/2 cup at a time. Continue to beat until the frosting begins to thicken, then whisk in the vanilla, rum or rum extract, and the pumpkin pie spice. Allow the mixture to sit for a few minutes. Frost the cake using this prepared frosting.

ELEVEN: JEOPARDY! JAMBALAYA

Life in Quincy's Gap was remarkably uneventful once the holiday season was through. Slowly, life began to resume its normal rhythm of five-day workweeks and fleeting, two-day weekends.

Children of all ages finally returned to school, having spent over two weeks indoors playing video games, watching movies, and sending instant messages to their friends. Their parents, finally relieved of hours of endless whining, bickering, and professed boredom from their progeny, welcomed the sight of the yellow school buses with great joy.

James usually disliked the departure of the festive holiday season and the arrival of the cold, gray days of January, but as the first week of the new year flew by, he began to grow more and more excited about his little yellow house. He had driven by it several times since his bid had been accepted, visualizing how it would look in springtime with the dogwoods in the front yard showing off their soft, creamy blossoms and the redbud trees on the sides of the property displaying cheerful clusters of hot-pink petals.

He happily imagined himself pushing a lawnmower across emerald grass, pruning the azalea bushes nestled against the house, and sweeping the dust and cobwebs from the porch. After tidying the yard, he'd sit on the back deck watching purple martins flitter in and out of the multilevel birdhouse Gillian had given him for Christmas and dream about the seedlings he'd buy for his vegetable garden.

Everyone seemed to share in his excitement over 27 Hickory Hill Lane. All of the Christmas presents he received were for his new home. Milla and Jackson had showered him with goodies to outfit his bachelor's kitchen, Bennett had bought him a fiber doormat decorated with the letter *H,* and Lindy and Lucy had pooled their money and bought him a pair of rocking chairs with padded seats for the front porch. Supplied with these treasures and his prized custom mailbox, James was itching to get the legal paperwork out of the way, but nothing he could do would speed up time, so he spent his spare moments quizzing Bennett and consoling the Fitzgerald brothers over their failure to apprehend Glowstar's kidnapper.

"Don't buy another elf," Francis had pleaded the day after Christmas. "Even though the kidnapper didn't show, we're not giving up on our little green assistant."

"The abductor came early, which is totally against the rules!" Scott had spluttered when James asked what had happened on Christmas Eve. "We were there just after eleven, but there was a note attached to the book drop and some footprints in that muddy patch near the bin. Now we know we're dealing with a female. The boots had pointy heels."

Somehow, this revelation had surprised James. He'd expected a teenage boy to be the perpetrator. "What did the note say?"

" 'Grow up,' " Scott had answered sulkily. "That's it. Don't know what they meant by saying that, but it made us pretty mad."

"Yeah!" Francis had nodded in agitation. "We had to go home and fight a bunch of virtual bad guys just so we could get back in the holiday spirit."

"Thank goodness for *Age of Conan.*" James had clapped them fondly on the back. "And I don't think this mystery girl is done toying with you, so stay sharp and focused. Don't let her get the better of you two. You're better than that."

Their confidence buoyed, the twins spent the majority of their lunch break printing off pages of trivia questions for James to ask Bennett.

Now, the day before Bennett was to leave for Philadelphia, he and James sat at the dining room table of Bennett's tidy house and reviewed the cards from the Trivial Pursuit Greatest Hits board game.

"I'll be glad when this is over," Bennett said after replying that Florida was the U.S. state at 345 feet above sea level. "I used to like facts and statistics and all that, but now I think my brain is finally full." He waved at a wall calendar. "All I've done for half a year is read and study. What am I trying to prove anyhow?"

"Bennett, it's natural to be freaking out the night before you appear on *Jeopardy!*

Especially since this is one of their rare live shows and you're about to be on television in front of millions of people, trying to answer question after question of random trivia faster than your two competitors." James dipped a carrot from the crudités he had made into a small bowl of fat-free onion dip. He waved the vegetable at his friend. "You should have let us drive up with you."

"Not a chance," Bennett replied as the doorbell chimed. "I believe I can run off with a jackpot if I'm as focused as an air-traffic controller. So no distractions allowed!" He flung open his door.

"The distractions have arrived!" Lindy called out gaily, carrying a Crock-Pot in her mittened hands. "And I've made my special *Jeopardy!* jambalaya just for you. Whoa! Try saying *that* three times fast."

Stepping inside behind Lindy, Gillian attempted the tongue twister. Then she said, "I've brought you some tea to drink tonight. Your mind is going to be spinning like a pinwheel when what it needs is to be *serenaded* and led to a place of peaceful *stillness.*" She handed Bennett a purple box covered with stars.

"Not more pine bark!" Bennett exclaimed.

Gillian smiled and patted his cheek. "No bark this time. Just some valerian, chamomile, St. John's Wort, rose hips, lavender, raspberry, orange, spearmint, licorice, and skullcap. All organic and completely decaffeinated."

"St. John's Wort? Skullcap? Are those herbs or rat poisons? Couldn't I drink a six-pack instead?" Bennett muttered. "I'd sleep like a baby, and it would taste a hell of a lot better."

"By Buddha's belly, you'd sleep terribly!" Gillian looked alarmed. "Alcohol *interrupts* sleep. It makes people have fitful dreams and actually *decreases* effectual rest. You might wake up at two in the morning and not be able to go back to sleep!"

Now it was Bennett's turn to be concerned. He pried open the purple box of tea and sniffed its contents suspiciously. "Smells kinda nice," he admitted grudgingly.

"It will serve you well," Gillian promised, and then she handed him a yellow box of tea covered by silver lightning bolts. "Drink *this* blend before the show starts. It's for mental alertness and has *stimulating* and *energizing* herbs such as ginger and a mixture of powerful antioxidants."

"Jeez. All *I* gave him was a purple rabbit's foot." James read the tea ingredients with interest.

"Well, my jambalaya is lucky," Lindy added. "It's what I made for Luis on our first real date."

"Is everything back to snuggle, snuggle, kiss, kiss with you two then?" Bennett inquired.

Without answering, Lindy walked into the kitchen and plugged the Crock-Pot into an outlet. She removed the lid, inhaled deeply, and then stirred the contents with one of the wooden spoons jutting out from a pottery canister on Bennett's countertop.

"He's been wonderful when we're alone together, but he still doesn't want to go public with our relationship at school. That bothers me!" Lindy's round face grew flush with anger. "Is he ashamed of me? Am I some fling he's having on the side? Some bimbo?"

"I doubt that's it," Gillian cooed. "Luis is no doubt wrestling with conflicting emotions. On one hand, he wants to celebrate having his mother's miraculous return to health, and on the other hand, he's struggling with that final wish she'd made."

"Marry her friend's daughter! Over my dead body! That man is mine!" Lindy's Brazilian temper flared, and her dark eyes were fiery. "He doesn't even know that girl, and he says he's in love with *me!* Then why doesn't he prove it by telling the other teachers?"

Bennett and James exchanged worried glances. Neither man had any idea how to pacify Lindy when she was gearing up for one of her rare tirades. Luckily for them and for the jambalaya, which was being stirred, mashed, and nearly pulverized by the hostile jabs delivered by the spoon held in Lindy's fist, someone knocked on the front door.

"It's me!" Lucy announced herself and entered the dining room. She placed a square baking dish covered by a checkered dishtowel in the center of the table. "I made cornbread." Draping her coat on the back of a chair, Lucy sat down and then opened her large purse. "I've got something for you in here, Bennett."

Grinning mischievously, Bennett said, "It's not a little green elf is it?"

James poked him in the side with a celery stick. "Not funny. The twins are *still* hunting for that thing."

"Hey, keep your celery to yourself, man."

Lucy's hand was sweeping around the interior of her bag. Exasperated, she pulled out balled up receipts, gum wrappers, and tissues until she could see more clearly.

"I'd suggest you just dump the whole

thing out onto the table, but I'm afraid of what might come outta there," Bennett teased.

"Like the rest of Peter Cottontail?" James playfully brandished the faux-fur rabbit's foot.

Gillian took a seat next to Lucy. "Or perhaps a few weapons?"

Ignoring her friends, Lucy scowled as she rummaged through side pockets. "Here it is!" She handed Bennett a pencil. "Keep this in your pocket. It's the luckiest thing I own."

Bennett grunted. "Thanks, friend, but this is an oral quiz. We only write somethin' for the final question and I think they've got special pens for that. I don't want to mess up their blue boards and *owe* them money, you know?"

Pointing at the pencil, Lucy scowled. "*That* is the pencil I used on the written test I needed to pass to leave my life as an administrative assistant behind. It was the most important test I've ever taken and *that* was what I used to get a nearly perfect score." She smiled at him affectionately. "Now it's going to help *you* get all the answers right."

Eyeing the pencil with newfound respect, Bennett grinned. "It'll be in the shirt pocket right over my heart." He gazed at his friends and held out his hands, palms up. "How could a man lose with so much luck on his side? Shoot, I feel downright sorry for the other contestants. No way they could be gettin' the send-off I'm gettin'. I practically feel like royalty."

"Half the town is gathering at Dolly's to watch you," Lindy said as she placed several heaping bowls of fragrant jambalaya on the table. Returning to the kitchen for more, she called back over her shoulder, "Clint's been looking for an excuse to buy one of those gigantic flat-screen TVs for his house and now he's got one. Even if you come in last place tomorrow night, you should be satisfied by the fact that you've made at least one member of your town mighty happy."

As soon as Lindy set a bowl in front of James he turned the hot rice over with his fork to allow some of the steam to escape. The spicy grains, coupled with delectable pieces of shrimp and sausage, had his mouth watering, and he was almost hungry enough to shovel a scorching spoonful into his mouth. Yet despite his eagerness to satisfy his appetite, James politely refused a piece of Lucy's cornbread.

"It looks really good," he quickly placated her before she could assume that he didn't enjoy her cooking. "But I'm trying to maintain a better balance these days."

"Balance is the key to happiness," Gillian chirped. "But I'll be glad to take James's piece and unbalance my own meal. Bennett, would you like extra sausage? Lindy was kind enough to serve me a meatless bowl of this savory fare."

"Speaking of balance." Lindy put her spoon down on a red paper napkin. "How in the world are you juggling your job, all this studying, and a relationship with Jade Jones?"

Bennett seemed to spend an inordinately long time chewing a mouthful of cornbread. He then took a deep swig of Bud Light and loaded his spoon with jambalaya. "I don't think Jade was havin' much fun sharing her time with my *Jeopardy!* prep. She told me back in December that she wasn't gonna be driving up here anymore unless I proved to her that I wanted something serious, and I guess I didn't. It was all friendly though. No yelling or throwing dishes." He popped his spoon in his mouth.

"So you're not upset?" Lucy asked.

Shaking his head, Bennett reached for another piece of cornbread. James watched him carefully, but his friend truly appeared to be undisturbed by the declaration that he was single once again. Glancing around the table, he noticed that Lindy had now turned her curious gaze upon Gillian.

"As a group our dating track record isn't too great these days. What about you and Detective Harding, Gillian? Did you spend Christmas together?"

"No." Gillian pushed her bowl away. "We're sharing a friendship, Lindy, not a romance. We like to talk about tea and yoga and *spiritual* matters. Detective Harding is very self-reflective, and I enjoy his company." She toyed with an orange curl, looking uncomfortable. "Nothing *magnetic* was ever awakened in my heart when we were together, however, and he accepts that."

"Just friends then?" James inquired, putting a wry emphasis on the phrase as he darted an accusatory glance at Lucy.

"Friends can fill a lot of voids," Gillian replied solemnly. "But not all."

An awkward silence fell upon the table. James was sorry that he had so effectively tainted the tone of conversation and wished he could take back his last statement, or at least the negative inflection. Searching for a new topic, he asked Lucy, "Any new developments regarding Paulette's death?"

"The lab results came back today," she answered. "Do you want me to talk about this, Bennett? *Jeopardy!* is about to start . . ."

Bennett waved at the television set. "We've got ten minutes. Time enough for your news *and* dessert. I can't focus on anything until I sink my teeth into one of the carrot-cake sandwich cookies Milla made."

Taking the hint, James retrieved a platter of cookies from the kitchen and removed the plastic wrap from the dish. As soon as he exposed the cookies to the air, an aroma of cinnamon and baked oats wafted into the room.

"What have we here?" Gillian asked as she helped herself to a thick cookie. "Are these slivers of carrots?"

"Yes, but don't be fooled into thinking these treats will taste like health food. There's an inch of cream cheese frosting between two carrot-cake cookies. Milla claims that they'll sharpen your senses. She even packed you a tin to take on the train tomorrow."

Bennett ate his first cookie in three quick, appreciative bites. "God bless that woman!"

With a giggle, Lindy placed a carafe of decaf coffee on the table. "I believe you like Milla's gift better than the rest of ours put together. Okay, Lucy. Fill us in."

"For starters, you can give Milla good news when you see her," Lucy told James.

"The ruling that Paulette's death was accidental still stands. The lab results indicate that she suffered from a fatal dose of salmonella poisoning."

James was stunned. "As in, the stomach bug you get from undercooked chicken or bad eggs? That killed her?"

Lucy nodded. "It can be fatal, especially to people with weakened immune systems, like folks who are battling cancer or have HIV."

"Did Paulette have cancer?" Lindy's eyes were round. "She seemed awfully healthy to me."

Looking grave, Lucy said, "She had cervical cancer. I looked up facts about the disease on the Internet, and in a lot of cases, women don't know they have cervical cancer until it's pretty advanced. Unless they get regular checkups, that is, but with Paulette's schedule, who knows if she saw a gynecologist annually."

"Understandable. It's not like anyone *enjoys* having a pap smear," Lindy muttered.

Bennett covered his ears with his hands. "Woman! This is *not* the beauty parlor!"

"Then I won't mention that the signs of cervical cancer are vaginal bleeding, discharge, and pain during and/or after intercourse either." Lucy was clearly amused by

Bennett's discomfort.

James studied the cookie on his plate, recalling how robust Paulette had seemed. "I still don't understand how eating some cake batter could have proved to be fatal. Was her immune system that weak?"

"It wasn't the cake batter," Lucy responded solemnly. "It was all the eggnog she drank over the course of the day. Willow told us that Paulette never bought pre-made eggnog. She mixed her own from an old family recipe. Milla probably has it in her recipe box; it calls for half a dozen raw eggs per quart. Having made a gallon, Paulette ingested at least a dozen tainted eggs."

"Wow," Gillian breathed. "I wonder what brand they were. They simply could *not* have been organic. Must have been grocery-store eggs well past their expiration date. Our local farmers keep *very* hygienic chicken coops. I know, because I've toured their farms."

Lucy shifted in her seat. "Wherever they came from, the ruling is still accidental death. Paulette can be buried now, and the Martin family can move on with their lives." She smiled at James. "Jackson and Milla can have closure on this tragedy and finally reschedule their wedding. Isn't that great?" As the supper club members smiled in relief on Milla's behalf, Lucy collected several plates and carried them into the kitchen with James trailing on her heels.

"Are you really satisfied with those findings?" he whispered to her as she began to wash dishes.

Lucy handed him a towel and a dripping dish, indicating that he should make himself useful as they talked. "I don't know, James. The factors involved seem so bizarre that it makes me suspicious. If someone knew Paulette loved eggnog, they could have deliberately poisoned her."

"But that's assuming the killer also knew she had cancer. It's unusual for people to die from salmonella, right? And where would a person get infected eggs?"

Instead of answering, Lucy frowned and began to attack a layer of hardened jambalaya residue clinging to the rim of one of Bennett's bowls. "I guess I just don't like to be proved wrong," she finally murmured. "But for Milla's sake, and yours, I'm glad the facts have made it clear that this isn't a murder investigation after all." Passing him the clean bowl, her sudsy fingertips lingered on his dry ones. "Tell Milla to call me if she has any unanswered questions. I'm always available," she added with a smile.

"Thank you," James returned the smile.

"I'm glad we can put this whole thing behind us and focus on more positive things. Now let's leave these dishes for one of those long commercial breaks. I want to watch Bennett answer every question one last time before he does it on live television tomorrow night and comes back to Quincy's Gap a very rich man." He pulled Lucy into the living room and sat down on the couch next to Bennett. Giving his friend an affectionate squeeze on the shoulder, James said, "The whole town will come together to watch their favorite postal carrier on TV, I'm closing on my house in a few days, and my parents can finally tie the knot. And here I thought January was a dreary month!"

When James and Milla arrived at Dolly's Diner the next evening, they were alarmed to see that there were only a handful of cars in the parking lot. It was a miserably cold evening, and one of the Valley's sharp winds was doing its best to keep everyone indoors. Once the sun had set, the thick darkness had amplified the chill in the air. By suppertime, the thermometer had dropped below the freezing mark.

James gazed up at the clear, high stars and exhaled in angry surprise. Surveying the parking lot once more, he kicked at a loose stone. "How could people be so fickle?"

"It *is* horrible out tonight," Milla said with a shiver, her breath fogging around her face. She then pointed at the front door of the diner. "What does that bright orange sign say?"

Huddling against the wind, James walked rapidly up to the sign, scanned it quickly, and beamed. "They've relocated to the firehouse! They must be expecting a bigger crowd than I'd imagined!"

Excitedly, James helped Milla back into the Bronco and, after cranking the heater to full blast, pulled out of the parking lot and headed north.

Glancing over at Milla, James realized that he was delighted to have her with him. He knew that she'd have preferred to be watching Bennett from the comfort of their den, decked out in flannel pajamas and a warm cotton robe. Instead, she had chosen to accompany James and show her love and support for one of his closest friends. He suddenly felt guilty for encouraging Milla to come. After all, she had spent the day listening to Lucy explain the details of Paulette's death, placing phone calls to members of her family, and making funeral arrangements. None of those events were easily dealt with, and James could only imagine how worn out his future stepmother must be.

"I meant to call from work and ask you how your conversations with Chase, Chloe, and Aunt Wheezie went," James said as he stopped for a red light.

Milla looked pained. "Chase was less than helpful about the funeral. He said Paulette left no instructions in her will except that she wanted to be cremated. But I already knew that. I wanted to find out where to lay her to rest, but Chase told me he was too busy to talk about the topic and he didn't offer to share in a cent of the expenses either!"

"What a jackass," James muttered darkly. "And Chloe?"

"Whined about the cost of airfare until I told her I'd take care of it. Wheezie was the worst, I'm afraid. Claimed she'd love to dance on Patty's grave." Milla sighed heavily. "Some family I've got. Without you and Jackson, I'd surely go crazy!" She shook her head. "Patty and her eggnog. She's loved the stuff since we were little girls. Mrs. D. gave her that recipe when Patty first started visiting her house. She had shoeboxes stuffed full of recipes, Patty said. Enough to fill a hundred cookbooks. I wonder what she thought about Patty becoming a famous baker."

"Do you know if Mrs. D. is still in Natchez?" James asked as he parked on the side of the firehouse. "Maybe you could tell her about Paulette. It might help you let go of some of your grief."

Milla grew thoughtful. "I'll ask Wheezie to look her up. The whole clan will be back this weekend, Lord help us. But I don't want to think about such an unpleasant subject. Let's go in and watch your friend show the world that country folk's wits can be sharp as sickles!"

James was shocked at the number of people already gathered within the fire station's garage. The engines had been parked outside and the volunteer firemen were scurrying around the large space, erecting folding tables and chairs as Dolly and Clint set out enormous platters of sandwiches, condiments, a bowl of pickle spears, and snack-sized bags of potato chips.

"Come on over and help yourselves!" Dolly called out to them and then paused to mop her pink cheeks with a napkin. "Clint's too busy messin' with that fancy TV to even say howdy."

Plucking a chicken salad sandwich from the platter, James ignored the chips and selected two pickle spears instead. "Did you make all of these sandwiches, Dolly?"

Dolly nodded and put her hands on her wide hips, glancing at the buffet with pride. "There wasn't a soul I talked to over the last few days that didn't mention comin' to watch our boy win this game show. By today, Clint and I reckoned we couldn't fit that kind of crowd in our place, so we called the Chief and he told us to move the whole circus over here. This is simple fare, I know, and I'll just pass a hat once everybody's settled in chairs with their supper to cover our food costs."

As James and Milla ate, Gillian, Lindy, and Lucy arrived. They took seats next to James, carrying pimento cheese, tuna salad, and ham and cheddar sandwiches. The firemen passed out cups of sweet tea and coffee as Clint wheeled out his new flat-screen television on a rolling cart. Passing an extension cord to one of the firemen, Clint directed the remote control at the screen and gave his wife a flirtatious wink. The townsfolk cheered and clapped as the screen sprang to life. Clint immediately muted the volume of a commercial touting the effectiveness of a male enhancement drug, but not before several of the older women let loose one or two harmless remarks at Clint's expense.

"Stop cackling at the man and give him your money instead!" The chief roared happily and handed the person at the end of the row an empty boot. "Enjoy your supper, but don't forget to fill the boot! Any *extra* money and *we* can get one of these fine TV sets for the station. We'd get a dozen new volunteers durin' baseball season alone," he joked, and he took a satisfactory bite from his roast beef and swiss cheese sandwich.

"Oh, I'm getting nervous!" Lindy exclaimed as she dropped a ten dollar bill into the boot.

"That's a generous contribution for a sandwich," Lucy remarked, adding half that amount.

Lindy pointed at a smaller table, which seemed to have appeared from thin air near the firehouse kitchen. "I'm paying extra because I plan on having more than one dessert. Dolly's made those mini apple crisp tarts you can wolf down in two bites. And if that wasn't tempting enough, she also baked a tower of chocolate and peanut-butter brownies."

"You don't say!" Lucy ripped the boot back from Gillian's hand and stuffed two additional dollars inside. "Sorry, Gillian, but I'm with Lindy. I need some sugar to take my mind off the time. I've never checked my watch so many times as I have in the last five minutes!"

"What we need is to allow our thoughts to *drift* for a moment," Gillian counseled and turned to James. "What is the first thing you're going to plan when you occupy your new home? What will make it essentially *yours?*"

James described the few decorating plans he and Milla had come up with together. By the time he received advice from the other three women on what colors to use in each room and where to shop for furniture and accessories, and listened to Gillian's insistence that he follow the basic tenets of feng shui when arranging each room, it was time for *Jeopardy!* to begin.

No one needed to yell for quiet in the garage. Even though the slightest sound echoed easily in a space with such a high ceiling and a concrete floor, only the strains of the game show's theme music could be heard until the camera's lens panned across the anxious smiles of the three contestants. Upon seeing their hometown mail carrier, the crowd hooted and hollered with such gusto that James felt as though he were attending a sold-out sporting event.

"There have got to be over two hundred people in here!" James exclaimed to Lucy.

"Isn't it wonderful?" she replied, her shining eyes never leaving the television screen.

Alex Trebek introduced the contestants, beginning with a female physician from Akron, Ohio. Bennett was next, and when the famous host uttered Bennett's name and town, the room erupted in proud whoops and applause. The last contestant, a Harvard law professor, was the reigning champion. When the camera zoomed in on his self-satisfied countenance, the townsfolk booed and hissed. The minister's wife was giving the academic a thumbs-down gesture and James was amused to note that even the mayor had joined in on the censure by sticking her tongue out at the television.

Wasting no more than a minute on introductions, Alex reviewed the categories and the contest was afoot. The law professor, whose name was Harold, quickly took charge. After getting the first five questions right, someone from the firehouse shouted, "Wake up, Bennett! You can take this guy!"

As though he had heard the comment, Bennett seemed to jerk awake. He pushed his buzzer faster than Harold and swept the entire category on *Official State Things.* Barbara, the physician, rallied slightly when Bennett chose the category *Bird Talk,* but by the time the first round was finished, Harold and Bennett were tied and, unless Barbara really came alive in the second half, the game would be won by one of the men.

During the next commercial break, the townsfolk darted to the dessert table where they hoarded brownies and tarts and armed themselves with coffee.

"He's gonna do it, by golly!" The mayor declared to her constituents as she poured milk into her coffee.

The crowd ate their treats hastily and chattered with their mouths full, too excited to pay attention to good manners. James found their boisterousness contagious.

"I haven't had this much fun in ages!" Lindy exclaimed, and James nodded in agreement.

"Christmas wasn't exactly a time of cheer for all of us," he said. "It feels like we're having a delayed holiday tonight."

With a smile, Milla hushed them and pointed at the television. The quiz show had returned and Alex briskly turned away from the camera in order to direct the viewer's attention to the next set of categories. Seeing nothing relating to popular culture, James whispered, "He can definitely win this thing."

Indeed, Bennett whipped through the categories on *Inventors & Inventions* and *The*

1920s without interruption. In fact, the second question of *Inventors & Inventions* was "In 1858, Hymen Lipman was granted a patent to attach an eraser to this."

Bennett's contestant box lit up. "What is a pencil," he responded and briefly patted his sports coat.

"I bet my pencil's in his pocket!" Lucy blurted happily. "I *knew* it would bring him luck!"

As the minutes ticked by and Bennett's score increased, Harold reinserted some of his previous acuity in the *Children's Stories* category. Indeed, it seemed as though he'd answered every question until Alex read, "This character's sisters are Flopsy, Mopsy, and Cottontail."

"Who is Peter Rabbit," Bennett instantly replied as his free hand brushed his pant pocket.

"That rabbit's foot you gave him is lucky too!" Lindy whispered to James in awe.

Barbara answered a few questions in the *Lighthouse* category, but Bennett and Harold took over on *Government Agencies* and *Holistic Healing.* By the time Bennett had answered the last Daily Double, which featured a question on herbal tea, correctly, he was leading his competition by three thousand dollars.

When the last series of commercials appeared onscreen, several members of the fire station's audience began to pace back and forth in anxiety. James also felt seized by nervous energy. Deciding to replace the cup of coffee he had allowed to grow cold, he offered to fetch desserts for the women seated around him. He moved rapidly, fearing that the show would resume, but his haste made him clumsy and he spilled sugar all over the floor and nearly overturned the coffee urn.

Armed with a fresh cup of coffee and several brownies, James returned to the table just in time for Final Jeopardy.

"I missed the category!" He slapped his forehead in disgust and looked at Lucy in appeal. "What was it?"

"Sitcoms," she replied, accepted a brownie, and stuffed half of it in her mouth.

"I can't stand the suspense!" Lindy twirled her black hair around her finger. "Hurry, Lucy! Pass me one of those apple tarts!"

Gillian stopped nibbling at her fingernail. "Me too, please!"

Milla tugged on James's sleeve. "Can you read the last question out loud? I can't read those words fast enough."

" 'The primary sponsor of this popular sitcom was Philip Morris tobacco,' " James read, and he exchanged befuddled glances with his neighbors. "Anybody know the answer?"

The camera portrayed the three contestants scribbling on their blue boards. The crowd held their collective breaths as Bennett frowned, crossed something out, and then hastily scrawled a different answer.

"Oh dear. One should always *trust* one's first instincts," Gillian murmured and began to worriedly rub her palms together.

Everyone looked concerned, but no one else made a sound. When Barbara's answer was revealed as "What is *Happy Days,*" and Alex sorrowfully informed her that she was incorrect, the throng in the firehouse breathed a small sigh of relief. Barbara had risked half of her earnings, so she was still in the running if both male contestants had bet every cent yet had written the wrong answer.

Harold's smug expression had returned. Alex informed the viewers that Harold's "What is *I Love Lucy,*" answer was correct and noted that Harold had risked enough to assume the lead over Barbara. Finally, it was time to reveal Bennett's answer.

Alex frowned as he tried to decipher the squiggles on Bennett's screen. The first four words were clear. Most of the audience members followed along as he read, "What is *I Love . . .*" The word *Lucy* had then been struck through two times and replaced by another word. James squinted at the screen, but could not make out what letters his friend had written.

"I'm afraid our leader has crossed out the word Lucy, but I'm having some trouble figuring out what he wrote instead," Alex began and squinted. "Not *I Love Lucy* but —"

"I love *Gillian!*" Bennett stated passionately and looked straight at the camera, his dark eyes reflecting the surprise every person watching him was also registering. "Not Lucy, not Jade. Gillian," he muttered as though he was alone and not speaking to an audience of hundreds of thousands. "Son of a gun," he chuckled. "I love Gillian."

And with that, Alex hurriedly explained that Bennett's wager had landed him in second place. He then hustled over to shake Harold's hand, the theme music cranked up, and the credits rolled. The last glimpse James had of Bennett showed his friend pulling furiously at his mustache as he stared dumbly into space.

A woman at the next table whispered, "Now *that* is some good television."

Twelve: Key to the Town Cookies

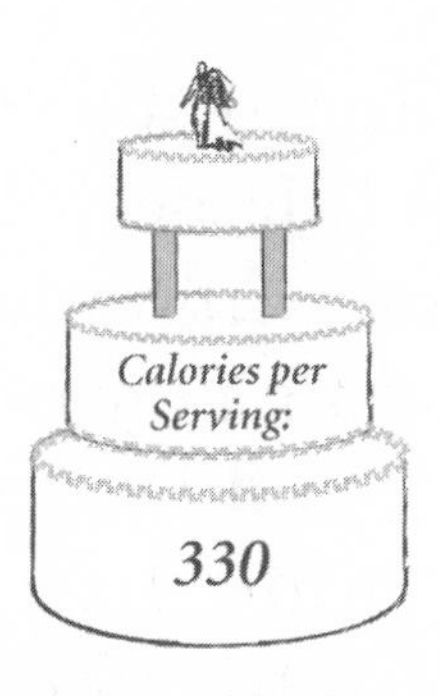

By the time Clint had switched off the television, two hundred pairs of eyes were fastened on Gillian. James, Lindy, and Lucy were also staring at their friend when she suddenly jumped out of her seat and scurried from the room, her bright red hair whirling around her head like an orange cyclone as she ran.

The sound of the door clicking shut following her abrupt departure spurred the room into life again. Tongues were soon wagging at a rapid fire, and Dolly was practically swooning in ecstasy at being present for one of the most dramatic events in the town's history.

"Goodness gracious!" Milla exhaled. "Talk about being put in the spotlight. Should you go after her, James?"

"Knowing Gillian, she's going to need some time alone. She's probably heading straight for her meditation space or whatever she calls it."

Lindy looked impressed. "You've got the name exactly right, James. She's got a small room in her house with only a few pieces of white furniture and a pair of gauzy curtains. She lights candles and listens to a CD that's supposed to remind her of the earth's natural music — birds chirping and waves crashing. That kind of stuff."

"We can leave her be for tonight," Lucy said. "But I'm going over there in the morning. I don't want to find her in her meditation room three days from now half-starved and dehydrated to the point of death." She shook her head and then eyeballed James intently. "Did Bennett ever tell you how he felt about Gillian?"

"No. He never said a word. In fact, I don't think *he* knew exactly how he felt until that question came up. You saw him. He was as shocked as the rest of us!"

Lindy giggled. "That man won't be able to go anywhere in this town without someone asking him about his love life."

"That's true, poor guy. And Dolly's going to rehash this story until no one can bear to hear it," James added, gesturing at the gleeful diner proprietor who was no doubt putting forth a host of possible outcomes regarding Bennett's declaration to a group of a chattering women.

The three friends took reflective sips of their coffee as they wondered the same thing. James noticed that no one was in any hurry to leave the firehouse, which, despite having a cement floor and an old furnace, seemed incredibly warm. Even Milla, who had seemed so tired earlier in the day, showed no inclination to depart. Her cheeks were flushed with excitement, and her eyes glimmered as she pointed to the front of the room. "Here comes the mayor. And she's got a bullhorn."

"Testing, testing." The mayor's voice burst out in a loud gargle through the mechanism.

James recognized the lanky, tousled-haired figure of Scott Fitzgerald when the young man sprang to the front of the room, made a quick adjustment to the bullhorn, and then whispered some directions to the mayor.

"Your sweet boys are here," Milla said with a smile and James felt a customary swell of pride as he saluted the Fitzgerald twins, who had been sitting just out of his visual range behind his right shoulder. Willow and Lottie were also there, but while Willow gave him a friendly wave, Lottie didn't acknowledge him at all.

Scanning the other tables, James saw Murphy seated with a group of handsome young firemen, her head bent over a pad of paper as her pen whipped across the paper.

Groaning, James pointed her out to his friends. "Guess what tomorrow's headline will read?"

"That witch," Lucy mumbled. "She can never leave well enough alone."

Lindy gave Lucy's hand a light slap. "Shame on you! She's just doing her job. You two are not that different, you know. You're both very devoted to your careers."

Squirming at the thought that his former girlfriends shared similar personality traits, James was relieved when the mayor finished her brief conference with the fire chief and once again brought the bullhorn to her lips.

"Bennett Marshall has done us proud, wouldn't you agree?" She paused and received only a smattering of applause. "Now, I know he didn't win. We all saw that he *could* easily have won, but something interfered with his claiming that cash jackpot. That *thing* was love. Right there on national television he gave up on a heck of a lot of prize money and a chance to return for another night so he could become a quiz show champion. Everybody knows he could've done it in his sleep." She surveyed her constituents. "He's probably back in some strange hotel hanging his head in shame, but I say Bennett Marshall has shown the world what the true nature of a man from Quincy's Gap is all about!" The mayor's voice grew louder and more passion ate.

"He's our local hero!" A woman shouted.

The mayor smiled at her. "A man of integrity and courage, surely. A man who knows what's important in life. And we're going to show him our love and support and hometown pride by welcoming him back to his town in *style!*"

This time the crowd's applause was resounding.

"Let's give him a parade!" A man in the front row suggested.

An elderly lady near James stood up and shook her cane at the previous speaker. "It's too damn cold to stand around outside."

"That's a good point, Mrs. Chambers."

The mayor nodded at the old woman. "What we need to do is gather together like we did this evening, but with a bit more pomp and circumstance. We need decorations, food, and an honorary item to present to Mr. Marshall."

"If it's gonna be a party, we need some liquor!" A man suggested heartily.

"And music! Maybe dancing!" Someone else added with enthusiasm.

The mayor hushed the crowd by waving her pointer finger over their heads. "Anyone who would care to volunteer, come to the front of the room. We'll divide into committee groups. I've got to see what kind of budget we can come up with. Mr. Treasurer, would you be so kind as to join me on the stage? And bring your laptop. I know you've got a bottom line of what we can spend on that thing. The rest of you should head on home. I'm sure we can convince Ms. Alistair to print off some sticky notes to slap on tomorrow's *Star* announcing the time of our little event. And if you've got a friend that didn't show tonight, make sure they're here tomorrow. I'm expecting the whole town, ya hear?"

"Be more than glad to help spread the word, Mayor!" Murphy called out and James couldn't help but smile at her.

A dozen senior citizens and several parents carrying young children called it a night, but the majority of the townspeople remained in the firehouse, eager to assist in Bennett's surprise celebration.

"I hope he survives his homecoming," James murmured as he and Milla joined the group in charge of refreshments. Lucy and Lindy decided to work with the decorating committee. "There's no chance of him hiding out at home now."

"I'm going to make Bennett a whole Sweet Tooth goodie basket, so it'll be worth his while to stand in the limelight for a spell," said Megan Flowers, who was sitting across from James. "And we know where Bennett will be at this time tomorrow, but the real question I want answered is will Gillian be here too?"

"She'd better," Dolly stated firmly. "I'm not gonna close the diner early and cook all afternoon long for nothin'! I need to know how this love story ends, because whether Gillian admits it or not, that's what this is." Dolly sighed dreamily. "A small town love story." She poked James in his side. "Isn't it romantic?"

Luckily for James, Milla's relatives were coming to Quincy's Gap via car service, so he didn't need to take off work to pick them up from the airport. As he was finishing up the morning's hold and transfer requests, Scott gestured at the phone behind the circulation desk.

"Ms. Hanover's on the line for you, Professor."

Lucy was too excited to waste time in returning James's greeting. "We're really going to pull one over on Bennett this afternoon! The mayor has asked Sheriff Huckabee to escort Bennett from the Amtrak station back here. He's riding the lead car and I'll be taking up the rear."

"That's going to ruin the whole element of surprise, wouldn't you say?"

"Not at all!" Lucy laughed. "Listen to this part! The sheriff's brother is a retired FBI agent. He still works for them every now and then on a consultant basis, so he's got an official ID. He's going to put on a dark suit and some of those mirrored glasses and tell Bennett that he's investigating a federal case of mail fraud. He's going to tell Bennett that someone on his route is suspected of being the ringleader and ask for his help in obtaining information about this person."

James couldn't help but chuckle. No doubt Bennett would be completely distracted by such a ruse. "Who's agreed to play the master criminal?"

"Mrs. Horner."

"Our old school nurse? Oh, that's perfect." James grinned at the image of the prim and proper Mrs. Horner committing mail fraud.

"*That's* today's good news," Lucy continued, her tone suddenly tight with hostility. "If I didn't have tonight's celebration to look forward to, I might have had to shoot somebody as a stress reliever. Prepare yourself, James. Murphy's book came out ahead of schedule. One of the deputies showed it to me this morning."

"Oh no!" James shouted in anguish. "Things were just looking up around here!"

When Lucy didn't respond in agreement to his sentiment, he asked, "Did you read any of it?"

"Most of the first chapter during my coffee break, and that was *enough!*" Lucy replied angrily. "The beginning is all about us, James. We're called the Cellulite Club! *Cellulite!* Murphy made us out to be a group of fat, bumbling nitwits. I'm this aggressive, man-hating secretary; Lindy's a giggly, flighty teacher desperate for love; Bennett's a total nerd — she even has him wearing thick glasses and a pocket protector — and Gillian's just plain nuts. Murphy made *her* an animal psychic!"

James felt his stomach clench. "And what about me? Ugh, I'm almost afraid to ask."

Lucy hesitated for a long moment, and James was unsure whether she was trying to be unnecessarily dramatic or was merely unwilling to be the deliverer of bad tidings. "You're kind of wishy-washy," she finally replied. "She uses the word 'weak' a lot to describe you. Everyone else makes decisions while you hide in the background. Murphy portrays you as someone who's been permanently destroyed by his ex-wife, so now you let women run all over you."

"Jane wasn't that bad," James stated in disbelief. "Our divorce hurt because I was still in love with her, but I'm not weak! And yes, she left me for another guy, so *that* didn't feel great, but she didn't *destroy* me! We had a lot of happy times together, and those help balance out the painful ending of our marriage."

"Do you ever talk to her? To Jane?" Lucy seemed genuinely curious though James suspected she was just trying to change the subject before he could work himself into a full state of indignation.

"We exchange Christmas and birthday cards and an occasional e-mail, but I don't really know much about her life now. The Christmas card she sent didn't have a return address on it and was postmarked from Charlottesville, so I'm not even sure if she's still living in Williamsburg." An image of Jane smiling up at him as he slipped a platinum band on her ring finger arose unbidden in his mind, but he pushed the memory aside. "Tell me more about the book."

"I only read the first chapter!" Lucy refused to play along. "Aren't you getting a copy?"

James snorted. "I ordered four copies for the library, though it killed me to spend the money! Still, I know my patrons will be standing in line to get their hands on Murphy's *novel* whether *I* like it or not, and it's contrary to the librarian's creed to censure reading choices."

"Too bad," Lucy grunted. "This seems like a great time to gather up a big pile of kindling and have us a good old fashioned book burning." She sighed mournfully. "See you tonight."

James hung up the phone and sank onto a nearby stool. For the rest of the morning, he did his best to be his solicitous self for the benefit of his patrons, but as lunchtime grew closer, his anxiety over Murphy's portrayal of him increased. Before he was even aware of what he was doing, he had purchased two packages of snack-sized cheese puffs from the vending machine in the lobby. He then sneaked into the men's room and locked himself in a stall. He practically inhaled the first bag and without even pausing to lick the salty, orange dust coating his fingertips, he tore into the second. He was halfway through that bag when he heard Francis's voice.

"Professor? You in here?" Francis asked apologetically.

James hurriedly swallowed a mouthful of cheese puffs. "Yes."

"Sorry to interrupt, but Milla's on the phone and she sounds . . . well, I think she's been crying."

"Be right there." James balled up the evidence of his frantic snacking and flushed the toilet for good measure. Francis was already gone when he emerged from the stall, shoved the cheese-puff bags in the trash can, and then hastily rinsed and dried off his hands.

"Everything okay?" James asked as he picked up the receiver.

"I'm sorry to bother you at work, dear. I'm just having a hard time dealing with Chase. He told me a few days ago that he didn't care about the funeral arrangements, but now he's criticizing all the choices I made, saying that I barely knew my own sister." Milla sniffed. "That hurts my feelings, James. I tried so hard to keep in touch with her, to be a part of her life."

"I know you did," he assured her. "And I'm confident that Chase is giving you plenty of *helpful* opinions without offering to write a check. Am I right?"

"Yes." Milla sighed. "Paulette's already been cremated. That's what she asked for in her will so I took care of it, but Chase wants to scatter her ashes off the mountain and I'd like to bury them in the churchyard. I know it's selfish, James, but if she's there I could go visit her. Talk to her." Milla's voice broke, but she quickly regained control and said, "Your father has been very gallant. Even though he still doesn't like to go out in public, I had to stop him from running over to the hotel. He said he was going to teach that young man a thing or two about manners, but I'm afraid I volunteered you to state my case for me. I'm afraid Jackson's temper might get the better of him."

James wished he were at home so he could wrap Milla in a comforting embrace. "I'll speak to Chase over my lunch hour, but if that punk is rude to you again, I'm going to let Pop at him!"

More stressed than before, James closed

his eyes and rubbed his temples. He had thirty minutes until he turned the library over to the care of the Fitzgerald twins, and he knew that the fruit salad and vegetable soup he had brought for his midday meal were not going to cut it. Visions of grabbing a double cheeseburger, large fries, and a chocolate shake seemed overwhelmingly appealing.

"You look like you're thinking happy thoughts," said a familiar female voice.

"Dr. Ruth!" James opened his eyes and glanced away guiltily. "Nice to see you."

Gesturing at the corner of her mouth, the nutritionist grinned. "I think you have some cheese-puff residue on your chin."

Ripping a tissue from the plastic holder next to the barcode scanner, James swiped at his mouth and chin. "You caught me, Dr. Ruth. Not only did I eat two bags of cheese puffs while hiding out in the men's room, but just then, when I looked happy, I was fantasizing about having Burger King for lunch."

"Oh?" Dr. Ruth placed a copy of Jodi Picoult's latest release on the counter and waited for James to continue.

"It's stress-related, I know that." James scanned her book and tucked the small receipt listing the due date inside the front cover. "I also know that we're not in your office right now, but can you give me a recommendation on how to stop myself from surrendering to cravings when I get like this?"

Dr. Ruth touched him on the sleeve. "Don't worry, this happens to all of us. Stress eating is a big obstacle when we're trying to maintain a balanced diet. But life throws us curves, James, and sometimes you just need a Happy Meal."

James felt himself relaxing in Dr. Ruth's calm presence. "Can't I overcome how powerful my urges are?"

"Absolutely. First, you could come up with an alternative for dealing with stress. Exercise is a wonderful solution, a drive through the mountains, or settling down to a jigsaw puzzle or some kind of craft project." She examined his face. "But if you get worked up here and can't escape to a more peaceful place, then try chewing gum, or taking a quick walk outside, or calling a friend to vent. Try *not* to reach for food. Make that choice very deliberately."

"That won't be easy," James mumbled.

"No, it won't. But you're aware of your behavior, James, and so you've already won half the battle." Dr. Ruth smiled as James held out her library book. "And I'm glad we had a chance to speak because I wanted to tell you that your next appointment with me will be at no charge. A little bird told me that you had a lot to do with the number of new clients I've had since the holidays. I'm very grateful, Mr. Henry. Thank you."

As Dr. Ruth walked away, James realized that he no longer craved a Burger King lunch. "I can face Chase Martin without a double cheeseburger!" he pronounced, and then marched into the break room to retrieve his low-calorie lunch.

Chase was seated in the hotel lobby with all the bored and haughty authority of a monarch awaiting a gesture of supplication from one of his subjects. Clenching his fists, James recalled Milla's wounded voice on the phone and felt a strong desire to slap Paulette's son on both cheeks until his demeanor was a bit more humble.

"I know why you're here," Chase said without preamble. "But my mother was not a religious person and she'd find it hypocritical to be buried in the churchyard."

"I understand," James answered, and he took a seat next to the irksome lawyer. "However, your mother is gone and Milla is here. It would be a comfort to her to visit Paulette's gravesite. I'm asking you to find some compassion for your mother's sister and grant her this request." He spoke as pleasantly as possible, which was very difficult since he really wanted to grab Chase's coffee cup and hurl its scalding contents into the man's smug face.

Chase eased deeper into the chair and placed his right ankle on his left knee. Licking his finger, he rubbed at a faint scuff in the walnut-colored leather of his costly loafer. "Even Chloe agrees with my decision to release Mother at some pretty place. 'Course, my little sis wouldn't care if I scattered the ashes in a landfill, but with the right *incentive,* she'll back me on this issue."

James couldn't keep his feelings of distaste inside. "Did you bribe your aunt too?"

"No need," Chase replied with a satisfied smirk. "She only came back to this hick town because Milla paid for the plane ticket. I suppose she'll do her best to leech off your folks until she's too infirm to go back to Natchez."

How could I have ever believed this man had a single decent bone in his body? James thought back to their family dinner at Mamma Mia's and how, when Chase was in a state of inebriation, he seemed almost likable.

"I'm sure the two sisters merely wish to

spend time with each other. Aren't you in a hurry to return to your own family?"

Chase snorted. "I can expect a big, fat check once my mother's estate is settled, so I can now afford to pay the ridiculous alimony my wife's demanding. The only thing I'm in a rush to do is divorce her, visit my spoiled, bratty daughters as little as possible, and spend a month in the Bahamas with that cute stewardess I met flying down here in December."

James stood. "I can see there's no reasoning with someone without a shred of empathy. Would you condescend to telling me where and when you plan on scattering the ashes? I'd like to accompany Milla to the . . . event."

"Tomorrow morning. Early." Chase inspected his fingernails. "After all, I've got places to be and things to buy. I found a nice little scenic spot in one of the hotel's brochures on the Blue Ridge Parkway. Bluff Mountain Overlook. Eight a.m. You bring your gal and I'll bring my charming relatives. You can inform that Willow creature about our little soirée as well. No one's speaking. There'll be no music. I'm walking to the edge of the cliff, opening the cardboard box that Mother's in, and tossing her out to the four winds. After that, you'll be rid of me for good."

"I can hardly wait," James muttered crossly.

Chase rose, clapped him roughly on the shoulder, and then strutted through the lobby and disappeared down a hallway leading to the guest rooms. James's lunch hour was running out, so he moved toward the display of wooden shelves containing dozens of area attractions and searched for the brochure on the Blue Ridge Parkway. He needed to determine the milepost marking their meeting place. He scanned the upper rows and, only seeing pamphlets highlighting the area's caves and caverns, squatted down to look at the lowest shelf. Just as he was reaching out to grab the brochure showing a photograph of a two-lane road winding through the Shenandoah Valley's beautiful, blue-hued mountains, he heard the murmur of familiar voices.

"She's always found us both wanting." James recognized Chloe's customary whine. "Why shouldn't we be compensated after living a life filled with suffering? You lost the man you loved, and I feel more comfortable with sea mammals than I do with people. Mom ruined us both."

"You're young, dear. Plenty of time left for a sunny day," Wheezie replied in a childish singsong, which James could only assume was simply an odd character trait. "Anyhow, I got what I wanted. Al and I are spendin' nearly every minute together. I wanna catch up with Milla and then go back home and try to be happy. You should try that too." She began to hum.

"What about you, Willow?" Chloe demanded petulantly. "How are you going to start over again without any money? Chase owes you too!"

"That's true. I'm still owed my salary for the month of December. Your brother promised to pay me and give me an extra month as a bonus for being so devoted Paulette, but now it seems as though he's forgotten how to sign a check," Willow remarked sourly.

Her voice was so close that James realized the three women had settled into the cluster of lobby chairs he and Chase had previously occupied. *How am I going to get out of here?* he thought as he glanced at his watch.

"We can't let him treat us like this!" Chloe hissed. "He doesn't deserve to be rewarded. He's a greedy, lying, cheating son of a bitch. I've lost my husband, my house, and any hope of security. If I had *half* of what Chase had, I could start the marine life tour business I've been dreaming about *and* pay off my bills."

"Everything's going to be just fine," Willow assured her coolly. "I'm going to get my money and you can look to your future without so much anxiety. Trust me. If I could handle Paulette Martine, I can handle her son."

James listened as the women moved away. As he drove back to the library, he couldn't quell a feeling of uneasiness. How did Willow plan to get the better of Chase Martin?

It's just Murphy's book that's bothering me, he told himself. *The supper club will get through this uncomfortable experience just like I'll get through this last family get-together tomorrow morning. After that, I can finally expect some peace in my life.*

The firehouse looked the same on the outside, but by the time James and a troop of other volunteers were done, the garage looked like a scene from a high school prom. Colorful streamers and glitter-encrusted gold and silver stars hung from the ceiling. Bunches of festive balloons were tied to the backs of folding chairs positioned around the room's perimeter and a huge banner reading *Congratulations Bennett* hung above a wooden podium.

"Luis had the risers and the podium brought over from school," Lindy proudly informed James. "He's also got the drama teacher rigging the sound system. We're going to have a dance after the mayor's speech. Look! They're putting up the disco ball!"

"And here comes the food!" Lucy announced as she carried in a commercial baking tray filled with cookies. "Aren't these awesome?"

James waited until she set down the tray and then moved alongside her. Confused, he asked, "Why are the cookies shaped like keys?"

"Because the mayor's giving Bennett the Key to Quincy's Gap," Lucy answered happily. "These are snickerdoodle cookies covered with golden icing. Megan and Amelia Flowers have made hundreds of them. I had to quit the decorating committee just to help ice them."

"I didn't realize our town had an official key," James said, reaching out to take a cookie.

Lucy slapped his hand away. "We didn't, but the mayor came up with one to present to Bennett as a prize."

"Did you bake cookies in your uniform?" Lindy teased.

"No. And I just put the frosting on,

though I stopped to lick my fingers at least twenty times." Lucy smiled. "Well, I've got to run. I'm part of the escort bringing Bennett back here. If I was in a cruiser without being in uniform, Bennett would be suspicious. See you soon!"

James straightened a wrinkle in the tablecloth as Lindy placed two flower arrangements in the centers of the longest buffet tables.

"Any word from Gillian?" he asked her.

"Just an e-mail. I've been calling her all day, but I guess she didn't feel like talking. She wrote back that she needed to take her time getting ready but that she'd be here tonight and we shouldn't be worried."

The two friends continued their preparations. By the time they were done decorating, dozens of women had arrived bearing dishes of food. There were side salads of every variety including green salad, Waldorf salad, ambrosia salad, three-bean salad, and three kinds of potato salad. There were huge aluminum trays filled with fried chicken, macaroni and cheese, lasagna, tuna casserole, baked beans, collard greens, and mini corn cobs. There were baskets of bread including French baguettes, Italian bread, garlic bread, onion rolls, pumpernickel rolls, and buttered white rolls.

The dessert table was so full of pies, cakes, cupcakes, and cookies that the yellow tablecloth was barely visible. James strolled along the table, examining the homemade treats with a lecherous eye. He wasn't alone. Most of the men in the room were discussing which sweets they'd be choosing once the women allowed them access to the food.

Bit by bit, the large garage filled up with revelers. Bottles of cold beer were handed out, glasses of cheap white wine were distributed, and the noise rose exponentially as more and more townsfolk arrived.

James surveyed the faces of his fellow community members. He said hello to teachers and beauticians, Mr. Goodbee the pharmacist, Doc Spratt, the Fitzgerald twins, the employees from the liquor and grocery stores, Sam and the other bartenders from Wilson's Tavern, the wait staff from Dolly's Diner, the excited postal workers, Dr. Ruth and her sons, Custard Cottage's Willy Kendrick, and even Joan, his ambitious real estate agent.

"The sheriff just called!" someone yelled. "Bennett's five minutes away!"

As James turned to identify the exuberant messenger, he was flabbergasted to see the last person he'd ever expected to find inside the Quincy's Gap firehouse. It was Jane, his ex-wife.

Blinking to clear his eyes of what clearly was a hallucination, James looked again. Without doubt, it was Jane. There was no way he wouldn't recognize her wavy brown hair, which she had cut short into a carefree bob, her angular jaw, or her luminous skin. Her figure had grown fuller since he'd seen her last, but the extra weight had made her softer. The areas of her body that had once been tight and sinewy with muscle were now curvy and alluringly feminine. The Jane he had known for over four years had always dressed to the nines in form-fitting skirts and glitzy accessories, but the woman smiling at him from the other side of the room wore jeans, a white blouse, and cowboy boots.

"She's beautiful," James spoke aloud and began to weave his way toward her.

When he finally stood in front of her, he didn't know what to do, but Jane took charge as she always had. She reached up, embraced him warmly, and said, "Sorry to give you such a shock."

"These days my life is full of them," James replied as he continued to stare at her. In the few years they had been apart, fine lines had sprung around the corners of Jane's eyes and around her mouth, but she was still one of the loveliest women in the room. "But it's good to see you, even though I can't begin to imagine how you ended up here."

Jane laughed. "It's good to see you too. And you're as handsome as ever. I thought I'd pick a public place to make my appearance. I wanted to make certain there'd to be a defibrillator around in case you needed a hasty revival."

"That's very considerate of you." James couldn't help but grin. Jane and he had always shared a similar sense of humor. "And are you here with someone?" he couldn't help but ask, with a trace of unkindness, for his wife had left him for a hotshot trial lawyer. And having seen the disagreeable Chase Martin Esquire only hours before, James wasn't particularly fond of those working in that profession.

"I'm alone. Kenneth is out of the picture," Jane replied flatly. "He has been for a while now." She shrugged and looked away. "I left a decent and devoted husband for a cruel playboy. I was afraid of becoming predictable and I longed for excitement and well, I got it."

The pain and fear in her voice stirred protective feelings in James. "He didn't hurt you, did he?"

She shook her head, her eyes blazing in anger. "No. Not me."

James was just about to ask what she meant by that remark when the sound of a bugle call caused him to whip his head around so that he faced the door. The startling noise was immediately followed by unified cheering from the townsfolk as Bennett was led into the room.

It was obvious that Bennett had not expected such a reception. His eyes darted wildly about the dozens and dozens of shouting, clapping figures, a smile frozen on his face.

"I'll be back!" James yelled to Jane over the roar of the crowd. "I think he could use a friend to lean on right about now."

Jane patted him on the back. "You always excelled at that," she said loudly. "I've never met a more loyal man than you. Go on! I'll catch up with you later."

For once, James was glad to possess some bulk, for his height and solid physique enabled him to barrel forcefully through tight clusters of well-wishers until he reached Bennett's side.

"I can't believe this." Bennett was clearly dumbfounded. "Can we escape out the back door?" He asked weakly, but the tide of townsfolk closed in behind them and the two men were gently prodded forward toward the temporary stage.

"It'll be over in a minute," James assured his friend and pushed him up the last step leading to the dais.

Bennett glanced over his shoulder and said, "That's what they say about executions, but that doesn't mean I wanna go to one!"

The mayor pumped Bennett's hand up and down heartily and then, throwing decorum aside, gave him a maternal hug. Leaning over the microphone, she recited a brief speech.

"Welcome home, Bennett Marshall!" She paused to allow for applause. "You have made us all very proud. The world is now aware that the community members of Quincy's Gap, Virginia, can be both smart and sincere. And darn good looking on that television screen too. Wouldn't you agree, ladies?" The majority of the women whistled and hooted. "Now, we didn't have much time to prepare you a formal celebration, so we did things Quincy's Gap style. Your friends and neighbors have fixed a mouth-watering feast and The Overlook Boys will be providing us with some down-home entertainment. But first, I'd like to present you with a very special award. Bennett Marshall, I give you the Key to Quincy's Gap."

The mayor stepped away from the mic in order to hand Bennett a shadow frame containing a brass key that had been engraved with the date and the town name. Kissing him on the cheek, the mayor gestured at the podium and waited expectantly for Bennett to address the crowd.

"Thank you," he spoke from too great a distance from the microphone and only the front row could hear him.

"Git closer, son!" A man hollered kindly.

"Um, thank you all for doing this," Bennett said. "I sure didn't expect it and I don't believe I deserve it." He cleared his throat nervously. "This would be too much even if I'd won, and I don't know if you were watchin' a rerun or something, but this mailman didn't bring home the trophy." He held out the key to the mayor. "I'm not worthy of this. I didn't win, ma'am."

But the mayor didn't raise her arms to reclaim the key to the town. Instead, she grinned widely and jerked her head toward the front door. Along with every person in the room, James swiveled around and watched as the crowd parted to allow Gillian passage to the podium

As his friend walked up the aisle like a bride, James gasped. Gillian looked absolutely stunning. She was dressed in a flowing silver dress that shimmered as she moved. Her neck was bare of her customary string of necklaces and she wore a single silver bangle on her right wrist. Her hair, usually so bright and wild, had been colored a dark auburn and was swept off her face using a narrow headband of light blue. Her aquamarine eyes were fastened on Bennett, and as she seemed to float to him, he appeared utterly stricken by a mixture of terror and adoration.

"She looks like a mermaid," someone whispered and James agreed. Beautiful and serene, Gillian could have just walked from the frothy surf like a modern-day Botticelli Venus.

Gillian walked up the stairs to the podium with deliberate grace and then stopped within inches of Bennett. Placing her hands over her left breast she said, "You *did* win, Bennett. You've earned the admiration of your fellow citizens and *stirred* the emotions of countless television viewers." Bennett remained frozen. Gillian's next words were whispered softly, but James was close enough to overhear her say, "And Bennett Marshall, you have won my *heart*."

Bennett released his pent-up breath and offered the woman before him a dazzling smile. With the entire town looking on breathlessly, he then pulled Gillian roughly toward him and commanded, "Kiss me, woman!"

The couple's lips met, tentatively at first, but then their arms wrapped around one another's backs and they seemed to melt together.

The audience erupted in ecstatic cheers.

THIRTEEN: ARTICHOKE AND SUN-DRIED TOMATO CHICKEN

The sound of his alarm, which could easily rival a nuclear-fallout siren, harshly forced James into wakefulness. Glancing at the clock numbers, he was certain there must be some mistake. He had just gone to sleep, hadn't he? Noting that his wool blanket was in a heap on the floor and that his pillow protruded halfway out of its wrinkled case, he realized that the little sleep he had captured had been very restless.

And no wonder, he thought as he wearily sat up and ran his hands through his hair, which was sticking straight out like a porcupine's quills. *All that excitement with Bennett and Gillian and Jane. Oh my Lord, JANE! My ex-wife was in Quincy's Gap. I looked for her everywhere in that firehouse, but she was gone! Was she a hallucination?* He considered the possibility. *Brought on by eating too many brownies?*

Sifting through his closet, James wondered what one was supposed to wear to an ash scattering ceremony. Except that it wasn't a ceremony. Chase clearly planned to toss out the ashes with no fanfare and had already forewarned his relatives that no words would be spoken.

"Paulette's memorial should take all of five minutes," James muttered as he selected a pair of espresso-brown corduroy pants and a forest green sweater and laid them across the foot of his bed.

Downstairs, Milla was standing behind Jackson's chair with a hot griddle. She piled pancakes directly onto his plate until she had formed a small tower of golden brown dough.

"I whipped up these pancakes just for you, James!" Milla handed Jackson a jug of pure maple syrup and kissed him on the top of the head. "Whole wheat banana pancakes. Marvelously tasty *and* low calorie. Dr. Ruth would approve. I even substituted apple sauce for the vegetable oil, so eat up, my dear!"

Jackson, who was just about to shovel a forkful of pancake into his mouth, dropped his eating utensil with a clank. "Whole wheat? Wheat's got no place in a man's pancake."

"Take a bite. I dare you," Milla taunted as she gazed at her future husband tenderly. "If you don't like them, I promise to put them right in the garbage disposal. Go on now."

Grudgingly, Jackson plunged his fork into his mouth and chewed without meeting Milla's eager eyes. When he merely grunted in response, she reached out to take his plate, but he lightly smacked her hand away. "I'd rather eat them than fix that damned disposal again. Bananas in pancakes. Hrmph!"

Milla exchanged a conspiratorial grin with James and the three of them quickly consumed the delicious breakfast.

James could hardly believe that such savory pancakes were low calorie. As he loaded the dishwasher, he begged Milla to come up with a few more recipes he could make for himself.

"Don't remind me that you're leaving us

soon!" She wailed and hid her face behind the dishtowel. "But don't you worry about food. I'm going to stock your freezer with dinners and when you're tired of defrosting those, you can drive right over here for a hot, home-cooked meal." She wiped her hands on her apron. "All right, men. Let's get a move on. James, you need your truck to get back to work, so Jackson and I will meet you at the overlook. It's not the ending I wanted for my sister, but it's an ending."

Milla glanced at the tidy kitchen and began to wrap a scarf around her neck. Jackson gulped down the rest of his coffee and pulled on his warmest parka. "If Paulette's boy sasses you once, I'm tossin' *him* off the cliff."

"With both of my men by my side, Chase wouldn't dare say a thing," Milla replied proudly and buttoned up her long wool coat. After adding gloves and hats to their ensemble, the couple left the house, confident that James wouldn't be far behind them.

The phone rang as James was in the middle of brushing his teeth. He quickly rinsed out his mouth and grabbed the portable phone. He said hello as he hurried down the stairs, preparing to tell the caller that he had no time to talk.

"Are you on your way to the overlook?" Lucy asked without preamble.

"Yes, and I've got to leave now. Jackson and Milla headed out five minutes ago."

Lucy sighed in what sounded like relief. "So you three have been in the house all morning?"

"Where else would we be?" James was puzzled. "It's seven thirty, Lucy." He immediately grew concerned. "What's going on?"

"The short version is that I looked up the regulations on scattering human remains at a Shenandoah National Park site. Without obtaining a special permit from the director of the National Park Service, it's an illegal act."

James put on his coat as they talked. "Why did you research that?"

"Because last night, at the firehouse, Milla told me how much she had wanted a place to visit Paulette and how Chase so rudely denied her request," Lucy quickly explained. "I figured if I showed up at the hotel this morning in uniform and threatened him with arrest, he might reconsider his plans."

"That was really kind of you, Lucy!" James gushed.

"Well, Chase had already left the hotel

when I got there, which I thought was odd. Stranger still, he didn't take Chloe or Wheezie with him."

James suddenly felt anxious. "I don't like the sound of this. Has Chase run off with the ashes? Is he trying to torture poor Milla?"

"Um, I know exactly where he is." She hesitated. "I'm calling you from the overlook, James. I had to call for backup first, but I wanted to stop all three of you from coming out here. Guess I'm too late."

"Would you please tell me what happened?" James's anxiety level had grown exponentially as he pictured Lucy sitting in her brown cruiser, frantically radioing for help.

"Chase is dead, James. His car is at the bottom of the ravine, and it's been crushed like a tin can. I can't get to him, but I've got binoculars in my car and I was able to see enough to know that he isn't going to be revived by the paramedics I called." She expelled a deep breath. "He was actually thrown free of the car, but his body — well, his arms and legs are at impossible angles."

His thoughts whirling, James asked, "Was it an accident? Do you think he was drunk or something?"

"No," Lucy answered. "This was murder,

plain and simple."

"You're sure?"

"Positive. I'll explain the details later."

James spluttered, "But if Chase was murdered —"

"Then maybe Paulette was too?" Lucy finished his thought. "I'll do my best to send your folks back home, but you might want to come out here in case they don't feel like listening to me. Milla's a sweet woman, but she's got a stubborn streak, just like the rest of the folks living under your roof, and I don't want her to see Chase like this. After all, he *was* her nephew."

"I'll be right there, Lucy," James promised and ran out to his truck. Slapping his dashboard, he revved the engine into life. "Come on, old friend. Time for one of our shortcuts."

The old Bronco didn't fail him. As though sensing its owner's need, the truck climbed the steep, curving mountain roads and dove into the valleys. James had never driven so recklessly over the winding roads. Normally, he followed the forty-five-mile-per-hour speed limit with care, because thick patches of fog could obscure the road at any time of the day. And even though there were fewer sightseers on the Parkway during the winter, one could never tell when an RV driver would suddenly decide to pull off at one of the scenic lookouts or when someone unaccustomed to the highway's sharp bends would slam on the brakes.

When James arrived at the overlook, Lucy was speaking to Milla through the driver's side window of her minivan. Steering well clear of the ambulance, park ranger vehicles, and Sheriff's Department cars, James parked his truck and then jogged toward the van.

"Tell them to go on home, James." Lucy's voice held both a command and a plea.

"It's not that I want to see anything," Milla assured Lucy. "I'm honestly just trying to get a grip on myself before I put this clunker into reverse. First Patty. And now Chase. I can't believe this. The size of my family is shrinking fast." She removed her trembling hands from the steering wheel and put them in her lap.

Reaching over to clasp her wrinkled hands in his, Jackson peered at Lucy. "That boy didn't drive himself over that cliff, did he?"

Lucy shook her head. "No sir. The ground is too hard to allow for defined footprints, but you can see where somebody *helped* Chase's rental car over the side. A nice little push, but it was enough." Behind her, the park rangers were setting up climbing gear and unwinding lengths of cable. Lucy turned, looked at the action occurring among the officials, and seemed impatient to join them. "I've got to get back there, but as soon as you're able, I'd like y'all to clear on out, go home, and sit by the fire with a hot cup of coffee. I promise to call you when I know more about this mess."

"You're a good girl," Jackson said, and James could see that Lucy was pleased to receive some of Jackson's rarely offered praise.

As the older couple drove off, Deputy Keith Donovan strutted over and stood squarely in front of James, invading his personal space in an attempt to be intimidating. Hands on his hips, as though he wore spurs and was about to draw a pair of revolvers and gun down an outlaw, Keith looked James over and made it clear that he was unimpressed by what he saw.

"You're always sniffing around my crime scenes, librarian," he growled. "And here I thought you only got turned on by books."

"Books are more enriching than you'd ever know," James answered, refusing to be baited by the red-haired deputy. "It's too bad you don't give one a try. You might widen your horizons, which are about as narrow as the space between my fingers." James held up his gloved hand and pressed his fingers together.

Scowling, Donovan turned to Lucy. "While you were having a cozy chitchat session with his folks, the rangers have rappelled down the cliff. In case you're interested, they're ready to send the body up. I can take over the lead on this case if you'd rather stand around and run your mouth. Even better, you could go fetch the men coffee and donuts and let us handle everything." He spat derisively on the ground. "That's the way things should be anyhow."

"Piss off, Donovan. You couldn't solve a Hardy Boys mystery, let alone a real one," Lucy hissed, and then walked away toward the ambulance.

Recognizing that his presence might compromise Lucy's authority, James pretended to return to the Bronco, but he made a wide arc as he walked in order to take a glimpse over the edge of the overlook. Glancing down, he saw Chase's rental car. It had fallen nose-down and the bumper had smashed right into the jagged, rock-strewn bottom. James had no talent for guessing distances, but the car had plummeted at least one hundred feet before impact. The front half had folded into itself like a paper fan, and James couldn't imagine what a human body would look like compared to this contorted wreckage of metal.

"You were an ass, Chase Martin, but I sure hope you were unconscious before that fall," James whispered into the frosty air. Having viewed the mangled car, he retreated from the lip of grass, feeling deeply cold both inside and out. Wanting nothing more than to be comforted by the presence of stacks and stacks of books, hushed voices, and the murmur of the library's ancient furnace, James got in his truck and headed back to Quincy's Gap.

It wasn't his intention to stop at the Sweet Tooth, but when he saw Megan Flowers sweeping the bakery's stoop, his impulses switched to autopilot, and he pulled into a parking space in front of the store.

"Good morning, Professor!" Megan welcomed him. "Staff meeting today?"

James nodded in surprise. "I almost forgot all about that! If I hadn't seen you, I would have driven right by."

"Lucky you, then. I've made some heavenly cinnamon buns," she said with a smile. "Fresh from the oven and just dripping warm maple-walnut frosting."

"Those will definitely work," James said, trying to retain enough control over his appetite to refrain from asking for an éclair, a Long John, or a jelly-filled donut to cram into his mouth in the privacy of his truck. "But don't let me order *anything* for myself," he begged. "I'm stressed right now and am trying to master my cravings when I feel like this."

Megan studied James with concern. "Here." She handed him a thin sliver of raisin bread. "You just need to chew on something, but it doesn't need to be an entire layer cake. A few plump raisins combined with a crisp, buttery crust should settle you down without ruining your diet."

She was right. Munching the fresh bread, with its ribbons of cinnamon and fresh, moist raisins, James felt himself relaxing. By the time he finished the snack, his intense desire to rapidly consume a pastry had passed.

"You are a wonderful woman." He kissed Megan on the cheek. "Can you slice a loaf of that bread for me to take home to Milla and Pop? I believe it has magical healing powers."

"Everything okay, James? You're not fretting over that silly book, are you?" Megan shouted over the noise of the bread slicer.

"Ugh," James groaned. "I'd forgotten all about that."

"Easy to do, what with everybody talking about Gillian and Bennett."

"People won't discuss the two lovebirds for long," James answered glumly. "Happy endings don't make for good gossip."

Megan handed him the cinnamon buns and bread. "I'm afraid that's true. And the ending of Murphy's book sure isn't happy, even though it's already been adding more dollars to my cash register. No complaints here about her writing about that poor boy who died here."

James wasn't interested in recalling the supper club's first murder case. "What happens at the end of the book?"

"It's too awful to say out loud, so you'll just have to read it for yourself." Megan patted him on the arm, wished him a lovely day, and then busied herself arranging a tray of black and white cookies.

James left the shop in a state of puzzlement, but he didn't have much time to think about Chase Martin or Murphy's books, because he reached the library within a few minutes. UPS had delivered boxes of books the day before, and Murphy's book must have been inside one of the boxes because when James reached the circulation desk, the twins were each poring over a copy.

"This is the only chance we're going to

get to look at this book," Francis explained apologetically. "We've got eighty-five requests for our three copies, and I heard Murphy's going to be on *The Today Show* next week."

"Why?" James asked crisply. "It's a run-of-the-mill thriller. Dozens of books just like hers were released this month, so why is *she* getting that kind of publicity?"

"The show's teaser mentioned the book in conjunction with the sudden death of the Diva of Dough," Scott answered after a moment's hesitation. "I think they're going to spin that event so that it looks like Murphy has an insider's perspective and a possible subject for her next mystery."

"The mystery angle may prove correct." James sighed heavily and told the Fitzgerald brothers about Chase's death.

"Are you sure you should be here, Professor?" Francis eyed his boss carefully. "We can handle things if you need to hang out with Milla."

The young man's caring nature touched James. "Thanks, Francis, but we're just a bit shocked. There's nothing we can do about what happened, so we might as well put our heads down and get on with our day."

Scott tapped on Murphy's book. "I don't

know what the *Cellulite Club* would do, but when this town's been in trouble before, we could always look to your supper club to straighten things out."

"You're right!" James stared at Scott and then clapped the twin fondly on the back. "I'll call a meeting for tonight. We can't allow people to be pushed off our mountains!" he exclaimed. "We need to act!"

Scott and Francis watched their boss hurry into this office where he switched on his computer. "Way to distract him," he heard Francis whisper. "He's going to get all kind of grief from that book as it is."

"I wasn't trying to distract him," Scott replied. "I meant what I said. Our boss is like a librarian superhero."

"Dude, that would make an awesome graphic novel!" Francis remarked enthusiastically and the pair moved off, exchanging character, plot, and costume ideas.

"I hope they don't make me wear a cape," James muttered with a grin.

The supper club members didn't have much time to prepare an elaborate meal for that evening, and since Bennett and James were interested in relatively low-calorie food, the five friends e-mailed one another until they agreed upon a simple, well-balanced meal. James assumed Lucy would be far too busy to cook, so he informed her via e-mail that she was exempt from having to bring anything but information to the Henry table. He then called Milla to forewarn her that she and Jackson should expect the supper club members to appear between six and six thirty.

"Thank the Lord!" she exclaimed happily. "Oh, please let me cook! It'll give me something to do! I just discovered the perfect recipe for a healthy main dish: artichoke and sun-dried tomato chicken breasts drizzled with a nice pesto sauce. A little garlic, a few onions, and some excellent olive oil . . ." James could hear her making a mental grocery list.

"Don't buy too much," he advised. "Gillian's making whole wheat spaetzle and Lindy's bringing steamed zucchini. And I should help with *something*."

"You can help me with the chocolate mousse. I know a sumptuous recipe that uses rich, dark chocolate instead of sugar, and brandy and coffee instead of heavy cream. It's been ages since I made it, but I still remember how good it is." She lowered her voice. "I have to confess, James, I am thrilled to have an excuse to get your father out of the house. There's nothing on TV about Chase's accident and he says he can't focus on work without knowing more about what happened, but *I* know he's really moping because he doesn't know who to paint next. No one's hands are inspiring him."

"Oh dear." James knew how ill-humored his father could be when he was between projects.

"I hope these awful events revolving around my family members aren't going to turn him back into a hermit," she added. "I wish I could think of something I could do to bring some sunshine back into our lives."

"Me too," James sympathized.

That evening, Bennett was the first to arrive. He handed James a thermos of hot spiced cider and fell into one of the kitchen chairs in exhaustion.

"My route has *never* taken as long as it did today. Every man, woman, and dog wanted to hash over my love life." He shook his head wearily. "Man, what was I thinking doing what I did how I did it? That is *so* not my style!"

"Too late now," James replied cheerily. He was enjoying Bennett's public romance. "Besides, now you've given Murphy fodder for her next book."

"Shoot, that's the *other* thing everybody's yapping about. What's the big shocker at the end?" Bennett inquired as someone rapped knuckles against the panes of the back window.

"No clue," James stated as he opened the door, letting in Lindy, Gillian, and a burst of cold air. "I haven't read it."

Lindy pulled the book out of her grocery bag, her face dark with anger. "I'm on chapter eleven, and every page I read makes me madder and madder. I spent my entire lunch hour plotting revenge against Murphy Alistair!"

"What's your opinion?" James asked Gillian nervously.

Gillian removed a hand-knit turquoise beret from her head and fluffed her hair. "I don't plan on reading it," she answered calmly. "Ever. I'm certain I wouldn't be pleased with Murphy's depiction of my spiritual beliefs, and I would prefer *not* to have a reason to feel any animosity toward a member of my community. I'd like to continue to treat her with *respect* and *fellowship.*"

"You wouldn't if you read the part about how the scented candles you burn while you're trying to communicate with a moody parrot actually cause the bird's death," Lindy grumbled.

Gillian's hands fluttered over her heart.

"What?"

"Yep," Lindy pursued ruthlessly. "His feathers catch fire and he burns up while screaming *'Help me! Help me!'* "

"That little witch!" Gillian snarled and ripped the book from Lindy's hands. "What page is that on?"

Lindy opened to a section she had marked using a paper clip. "You think *that's* bad? Read this! Here's where I strip down to my underwear and lay across the school principal's desk in hopes of seducing him. Luis, whose name is Carlos in this piece of trash, eventually enters his office and he has one of my art students with him! The boy takes a picture of me with his cell phone, and suddenly I'm all over YouTube!" She reddened. "I've never done anything remotely like this, but I'm terrified to show my face at school!" She snapped the book shut and tossed it on the table.

At that moment, Lucy let herself in the back door. Smiling at Lindy, she remarked, "And I thought *I* had a rough day." She brandished the six-packs she held in each hand. "I got Miller Lite in case anyone wanted to join me, because after looking at Chase Martin's battered body, a diet soda is *not* going to do it."

Everyone accepted a beverage and moved

into the dining room. James took a beer into the den, handed it to Jackson, and then said, "Everyone's here, Milla. I think we should eat first and then listen to Lucy's report."

"Should I bring you a tray?" Milla asked Jackson.

Jackson nodded. "I'd rather watch *Deal or No Deal* than listen to all that yammering." As Milla turned to leave the room, he grabbed the sleeve of her sweater. "But I'll come in and sit with you when they talk about the boy."

"You're simply the sweetest man underneath all that huff and puff." Milla kissed him on the forehead.

Over the next few minutes, James set the table as the supper club members carried in side dishes, a pitcher of water, and Milla's fragrant entrée. They ate hurriedly, exchanging banal small talk about their days. When the meal first started, James found himself wondering if the tone of their gatherings would change after Bennett and Gillian's public kiss, but the pair acted as they always had. Everyone laughed over Bennett's descriptions of being teased and playfully harassed by the individuals on his mail route.

"And don't tell me you've got some wacko tea that'll ease my humiliation, woman."

Bennett pointed a finger at Gillian.

She fluffed her hair and replied, "You were able to answer the second Daily Double correctly because of your knowledge of herbal teas. Now, I *wonder* who told you all about that subject."

As Milla served the chocolate mousse, to a chorus of appreciative *oohs* and *ahs,* Lucy could sense that it was time to turn to a more somber subject. After taking a reserved bite of her mousse, she nodded ever so slightly at James, signaling that he should collect Jackson from the den.

Milla scooted her chair closer to Jackson's as soon as he was seated and, gripping the handle of her coffee cup, announced that she was ready for Lucy to begin.

"Chase Martin was definitely murdered," Lucy stated flatly. "It would appear that he was hit on the back of the head with a blunt object — the ME thinks it might have been a shovel — and then positioned in the driver's seat of his rental car."

Lindy gasped. "That's horrible! Do you think he was unconscious before . . . before the crash?"

"Most likely. It was a hard blow, the kind that would render most of us senseless," Lucy said.

"That's a *small* blessing in the midst of

this *gargantuan* tragedy," Gillian declared theatrically.

Lucy ignored the comment and continued. "The killer seems pretty confident that he or she won't get caught. We don't have the shovel, but this person didn't bother with subtlety. We found blood evidence on the pavement where the car would have been parked before it went over the cliff, and there was a cinder block duct-taped to the gas pedal."

"Now all you need is a set of fingerprints," Bennett stated.

"Unfortunately, this guy wore gloves." Lucy said. "And I'm going to refer to the murderer as a 'he' because this crime feels very male to me, but I'm not ruling out the possibility that the killer is a woman."

James had listened quietly up to this point, but when the friends suddenly began exchanging ideas concerning motive, he cleared his throat and looked sadly at Milla. "Every suspect *I* come up with is female." He quickly repeated the conversation he had overheard between Willow, Chloe, and Aunt Wheezie when they were together in the hotel lobby.

"I've been spending a lot of time with Willow lately." Milla's eyes flashed defiantly. "I cannot see that girl hitting Chase with a shovel and pushing him off a cliff over a month's salary."

"Do you have alibis for the three ladies?" Lindy asked Lucy.

"Naturally," Lucy's tone was scornful. "They were all getting dressed for the ash scattering. Both the hotel maid and the front desk clerk saw Chloe and Wheezie heading out to Chloe's rental car, but no one in Willow's apartment complex noticed her or her car, which is a pretty nondescript compact."

Milla reached over and grabbed Lucy's hand. "Willow was in the bed-and-breakfast when Paulette died. She knew how much my sister liked eggnog. One of her jobs was to do errands for Paulette, including grocery shopping. And now you're saying that she can't prove where she was this morning?" Milla was clearly distraught. "Despite how things look, I just can't believe she's capable of violence . . ."

"There are many layers to a human being," Gillian replied softly.

"So what's her motive? Revenge?" Lindy asked. "Paulette dumped on her one time too many, so after murdering her, Willow gets a taste for it and bumps off Chase next?" She waved her hand dismissively. "Why would she risk her fresh start in

Quincy's Gap? She seemed to be really happy lately." She turned to James. "You saw her at the firehouse the other night. I noticed she and Francis are getting pretty cozy, and the girl's talked to everyone who'll listen about Quincy's Whimsies. Why would she kill Chase?"

"That's a good point. She's become very optimistic," Milla agreed. "Why, just yesterday she found out that one of the lawyer's offices downtown is coming up for lease. It's the perfect size and location for our store, and Willow scheduled a meeting with the building owner for a week from now. She's pretty sure that's where we'll open our doors in a month or two. Does that sound like a murderer?"

Bennett frowned. "It could be an example of that arrogant confidence Lucy talked about. She's planning her future because she doesn't think she'll get caught."

Lucy cradled her coffee cup between her palms as the rest of the group fell silent, each of them trying to imagine Willow as a murderer.

"Is Paulette's case officially being reopened?" James inquired.

"Just by me," Lucy answered tiredly. "There's no new evidence regarding her case, and this one will keep us all busy. If

Chase hadn't been thrown from the car, we wouldn't even know about the head wound, but the killer forgot to put his seatbelt on and that's the only lucky break we've had."

"Ain't like that shovel's gonna be easy to find," Jackson spoke for the first time. "Every Tom, Dick, and Harry's got at least one. Snow shovels, garden shovels, shovels to use for cleaning the crap out of animal stalls . . ."

Lucy nodded in agreement. "The park rangers will search the area surrounding the overlook, but the killer could have tossed it in a lake for all we know. No, finding the shovel won't be how we crack this case. I think the answer lies in the motive. Chase became an extremely wealthy man because of Paulette's death, but who stood to gain by his abrupt ending?"

"His wife?" Milla guessed.

"We won't know until we see his will, but I've had the opportunity to view Paulette's, and *hers* contained an interesting clause." Lucy paused dramatically. "If anything were to happen to Chase, then the profits from Paulette's estate would go to Chloe, not to Chase's wife and children."

"And Chloe's in desperate need of money!" James exclaimed, and then grew thoughtful. "But she has a solid alibi for this morning, so unless she was working with someone all along . . ."

Lindy's eyes widened. "Like Willow?"

"It's possible," Lucy conceded. "Still, there's no evidence against either woman. These ideas we're tossing out," she gestured around the table, "are all circumstantial."

James glanced at the grim faces of his friends. Noting the resigned slump of Milla's shoulders, he sighed. "What can we do?"

"We can outsmart the killer!" Lucy shouted, startling everyone. "Look at us! We've brought wicked people to justice before, and we're not going to back down now!" She lowered her voice. "I know this case is tough, but I will *not* have this person or persons get the better of us. I won't stand for it. *This* is *our* town."

Rephrasing his previous question so that it formed a statement, James said, "Tell us what to do."

"Go back to the days preceding Paulette's death," she commanded. "I want a timeline of everything she did, every place she went, every person she insulted." Lucy gave Milla an imploring look. "Can you do that?"

"Of course, dear," Milla answered without hesitation.

"The key to this riddle lies with Paulette's

death. I'm sure of it." Lucy put her palm over her heart. "I *feel* it. Once James, Jackson, and Milla finish that timeline, the rest of you are going to be my foot soldiers. You're going to get every ounce of gossip, hearsay, or eyewitness accounts regarding Paulette's movements before she was poisoned. Are you willing to be relentless in pursuing the truth?"

"Oh, yes! Your passion is *absolutely* inspiring!" Gillian seized Lucy's hand.

"This isn't passion. This is anger," Lucy answered heatedly. "I missed something the first time, and my mistake has cost Chase Martin his life. I didn't like him. I doubt that many people did, but did he *deserve* to have his head bashed in, to be pushed off a cliff?"

"No one deserves such an end," Milla whispered.

"Exactly!" Lucy raised her voice again. "And we're running out of time! We can only detain Chloe and Wheezie for so long. I believe Chase knew the person who killed him. I think he was mighty surprised to see a shovel in that person's hands. But who did he meet on that overlook? Why did he get there early? I need to know what we missed in Paulette's case that can answer those questions."

James and Milla exchanged determined looks. "We'll start right now," he vowed.

"And we'll clean up the kitchen!" Gillian offered and pulled on Bennett's arm. "Let's go, mister. You're on wash detail."

Spluttering, Bennett followed in her wake as Lindy collected dishes from the table.

James fetched a notebook from his work bag, poured himself a large mug of coffee, and prepared for a late night. "I'm ready," he told Lucy. "Let's find that piece of the puzzle and end this thing for good."

Fourteen: Honey Barbecue Sandwich

In spite of how late he, Milla, and Jackson had stayed up the night before, James was alert and animated at work the following day. His Realtor had called just as he was turning on the lights in his office, asking if the closing could be moved up to that evening. It seemed the sellers wanted to attend a friend's birthday party on the afternoon it had originally been scheduled and would be eternally grateful if James were willing to take ownership of the house a few days early.

"I've already contacted the attorney and he's available," Joan pressed when James didn't answer right away. "But if it's a financial issue, then we can certainly wait until next week. It's your call, Mr. Henry."

The check he planned to write to cover the down payment and the first month's mortgage would nearly wipe out his savings, yet James had never been so excited about spending such a large chunk of money at once. "It's no problem. I'm just digesting the thought that I can move in sooner than I thought. I can be at your office by six."

"Splendid. We can order Chinese takeout," Joan suggested and then reluctantly added, "My treat."

Throughout the morning, James dreamed about his little yellow house. Before the day was spent, he'd hold in his hand the keys to 27 Hickory Hill Lane. After all these years living in his boyhood room, the most charming home in all of the Shenandoah Valley would belong to him.

"You've got a sparkle in your eye this morning, Professor," Scott commented as he passed by James's office with the reshelving cart. "Francis and I figured that after what happened to Milla's nephew, you might be feeling kind of gloomy."

"I'm closing on my new house tonight," James explained, and he picked up the day's edition of the *Star.* He showed Scott the front-page photograph of the mangled rental car being hauled up the cliff edge by a mammoth crane. "It's not that we aren't all upset by the . . . *accident,*" he said, for lack of a better word. "But we've got a plan to help the Sheriff's Department find out who did this." James stared solemnly at the photograph. "You and Francis reminded me that we didn't need to stand around and wait to see if any clue emerged. We're on the hunt for whoever did this."

"We knew you would be," Scott answered faithfully, and he moved off to organize the disheveled children's section.

Lucy phoned a few minutes before noon and asked James if he was free for lunch. "I'm not offering anything fancy," she said. "Just sandwiches from KFC. We'll be eating in the car."

"That's fine." James was curious. "Does this outing have anything to do with the outline of events we made last night?"

"Yes. It might not lead anywhere, but I'm going to investigate every angle. See you in ten minutes."

James spent the small chunk of time trying to avoid a book club that met between eleven and twelve once a month. Its members were comprised of middle-aged women who took over the magazine section for the meeting and always held passionate discussions about every book pick.

For the month of January, they had chosen to read *The Body in the Bakery,* and every one of them had pre-ordered the novel from Amazon.com. Because he had no desire to hear more unpleasant details about himself or the rest of the supper club members as they were depicted in Murphy's book, James hid in his office, pretending to answer e-mails.

At 11:58, as he put his coat on and headed for the lobby, James found himself bombarded by questions from the book club members, who literally chased him out the front door in their quest to have their curiosity sated. James couldn't remember ever being so relieved by the sight of the dirty, cluttered passenger seat inside Lucy's blue Jeep.

"Is it true, Ms. Hanover?" One of the women shouted as James climbed into the car. "Did you and Professor Henry talk over the Brinkley Myers murder case *in bed?*"

Lucy gave the woman her fiercest scowl. "That *book* is *fiction,* Mrs. Wright. *Fiction* means that it's a made-up story, kind of like

'Cinderella' or *Pretty Woman.* If you have questions about what Ms. Alistair wrote, why don't you send *her* an e-mail? In fact, why don't you all send her a note? Maybe *you* can be in her next book!"

"What a great idea!" Mrs. Wright trilled, and she rushed back to the library steps to share Lucy's recommendation with her group.

James looked over at Lucy and smiled, visualizing the women stampeding to the group of computers in the Tech Corner. "Nicely done. I'll have to remember that one. After all, Murphy created this mess, so why shouldn't *she* be the one to deal with the readers?"

"Exactly. Now eat your honey barbecue chicken sandwich. It won't take us long to get to the goat farm."

After unwrapping his sandwich from its cocoon of aluminum foil and inspecting it with happy anticipation, James spread a napkin across his lap and took a hungry bite. "Hmm," he murmured appreciatively. "Is this the farm where Milla was going to buy her wedding favors?"

Lucy nodded and began to eat her sandwich, holding it in her right hand as she drove with her left. James was impressed that she didn't allow any pieces of barbecued chicken to dribble out of the sandwich. His napkin was already littered with a dozen bits of red-tinged meat.

By the time they drove out of town, she had finished her lunch. It was a good thing too, because Lucy needed both hands to maneuver the Jeep over the winding, mountainous roads. Consulting a few lines of directions she had written on a piece of scrap paper, Lucy turned off the two-lane highway onto a dirt road. The Jeep made its way up an unpaved, rambling drive until James felt as though they were either lost or had driven right into West Virginia. Finally, the ground leveled off and a rusty tin sign that hung from an equally rusty mailbox indicated that they had reached the Cornflower Goat Farm.

"Cornflower. Like your eyes," James remarked as he gestured at the sign.

Lucy blushed and seemed on the verge of speaking when they saw a man appear around the corner of the main house, which was a two-story log cabin with a picturesque front porch. A pair of dogs trailed after him, barking defensively at the sight of the Jeep. The canines had cream-colored coats and tan markings as well as dark muzzles and flashes of white teeth. The man put a reassuring hand on the back of the closest dog and waved at James and Lucy.

"What beautiful dogs!" Lucy exclaimed as she slammed her door shut. "Are they shepherds?"

The man nodded. "Anatolian shepherds. Best livestock guard dogs in the world. This here's Knight and the smaller gal is Lady. My daughter named 'em." He held out a weathered, calloused hand. "I'm Kyle Mills. How can I help you folks?"

Lucy began by praising the goat's milk soap and lotion Milla had purchased in December and then casually asked Kyle if he remembered Milla and Paulette's visit to the farm.

"Sure don't, ma'am." Kyle scratched Knight between the ears until the dog's pink tongue unrolled sideways out of his smiling mouth. "I've owed the missus a vacation for nigh on ten years now, and she said if I didn't get her someplace warm for Christmas, I could go huntin' for a new wife." He gestured behind him at the rustic barn, the rectangular cement building James assumed was used to create and package the goat's milk products, and the vast stretch of pastureland. "Farmers don't get much time off. I got one kid, but she's at college and has got her sights set on bein' a nurse," he added with pride. "I hire some local boys to lend a hand now and then, but I couldn't leave for a month without some real help 'round here."

"Sounds like you found someone suitable," Lucy prodded.

Kyle grinned. "Seems like the answer to my prayers dropped right out of the sky. That boy we got could take care of animals and customers. He even showed me how to get my wares on the computer. Made back every dollar I spent takin' the missus 'round the state of Texas. Anyhow, Russ'd be the one who helped your lady friends."

"Could we speak to him about maybe ordering more favors?" Lucy inquired. "We'll only need a few minutes of his time."

Lady walked over to James and sniffed his shoes. Obviously deciding that he was not a threat to her or to Kyle, she stuck her wet nose against the palm of his hand and gazed up at him with a twinkle in her eyes. James rewarded her friendliness by stroking the soft fur on the back of her neck.

"I wouldn't mind, ma'am, but Russ ain't here." Kyle looked sorry to disappoint them. "He needed to run on back home for a week or so."

"He's not from these parts, I take it," James stated.

"No sir. He's got one heck of a long ride

back to Natchez."

James did his best not to lean over and nudge Lucy. Natchez! This couldn't be a coincidence. Wheezie, Paulette, and Milla had grown up in Natchez. Now this young man, Russ, who possessed both the physical hardiness to run a goat farm and the mental acuity to create an online business for his employer, had suddenly disappeared.

Lucy shot James the briefest glance, but in her eyes he saw a familiar, predatory glimmer. "Milla was so thrilled with the goat's milk products she bought from your farm that I believe she'd like to stock your products in her new gift store, Quincy's Whimsies."

"That'd be just swell." Kyle beamed, his weathered face crinkling in pleasure.

"She may also want to carry local food products, like homegrown eggs. Do you have chickens here too?"

Kyle seemed surprised by the question. "Funny you should mention that, ma'am. Russ wanted to experiment with raising some layin' hens, so he built a coop and bought the birds and feed outta his own pocket." The farmer ruffled the fur on Knight's back as he spoke. "Guess it didn't work so well, though. Them chickens all got sick and Russ scrapped the whole notion.

Whole pen was gone 'fore I even got home. I don't mind though," he confessed. "Young man's got a right to flex his muscles, but I'm relieved he's back to focusin' on the goats. He's real good with them, and I'm not overly fond of chickens myself. Damn birds stink in the summertime."

Acting as natural as possible, Lucy checked her watch. "Well, our lunch break is nearly done. We'd best be getting back to work. James, why don't you take down contact information for Mr. Mills and his assistant, Russ . . . ?" She turned to Kyle. "What is the young man's last name?"

"DuPont," the farmer answered. "Russ DuPont."

James pulled out Dr. Ruth's business card from his wallet, flipped it over, and wrote down the phone number for the Cornflower Goat Farm. Handing the farmer one of his own cards, he shook the calloused hand once again. "Please call as soon as Russ has returned, and we'll talk about placing regular orders for the shop."

"Will do." Kyle whistled softly out of the side of his mouth and Lady sprang from James's side and crashed against Knight in excitement. "Walk up!" he commanded, and the shepherds bounded away toward a fenced pasture behind the barn.

As James and Lucy headed back to the Jeep, Lucy paused to gaze around the farm. James followed her lead, assuming she was looking for where Russ lived. There was a sprawling pasture behind the barn, but the area surrounding the main house was embraced by trees.

"Maybe he stayed in their guest room," James suggested. Squinting, he thought he saw a break in the trees. "Is that a path?" He pointed to the right of the house.

Shielding her eyes from the winter sunlight, Lucy nodded. "Come on. We've got to check this out while we're here."

Because Kyle Mills was headed in the opposite direction with both dogs, James agreed. "But let's hurry. We don't need to make Mr. Mills suspicious, or we might never hear from him again."

He and Lucy trotted over the rough path, which wound through the pines and sloped gently downhill. Irritated at how quickly he became winded as he jogged behind Lucy's fleeter form, James vowed to be more disciplined about hitting the gym after work.

Now that Bennett's done with his studying, we can work out together again, he thought and decided to e-mail his friend as soon as he got back to the library so that they could schedule some cardio and weightlifting sessions.

"Look!" Lucy stopped abruptly as a small cabin came into view. "This has *got* to be where Russ stayed." With a burst of speed, she ran down the remainder of the path. By the time James joined her, she had knocked on the front door, tried the knob, and peered in all four windows.

"I can't see a thing!" She sighed in frustration. "Dark curtains, a locked door. Damnation! I don't dare force my way in. I'll have to do things the right way and come back with a warrant to search this cabin."

Relieved that Lucy was refraining from hurling a rock through the nearest window, James also tried to see inside, but the navy curtains were tightly closed, leaving no line of sight into the one-room cabin. He and Lucy walked around the perimeter once more, looking everywhere for clues. Aside from a stack of firewood, there was nothing of note near the cabin.

"It would have been nice to find a bloodied shovel right here." Lucy frowned as she gestured at the wood pile.

James noticed an object resting on the top of a stack of kindling. "Turtle shell," he said, passing the tawny hull to Lucy. "And here's another one."

Accepting the shells, Lucy inspected them

carefully and then returned them to the wood pile. Grabbing James by the elbow, she said, "We're done here, but we're not leaving empty handed. We've got a lead, James! *A lead!* I need to get back to my computer right away!" She winked at James, her face flushed with excitement and hope. "Good work, my friend. I'm going to run to the Jeep now. See if you can keep up."

Back at the library, James had trouble focusing on his regular tasks. As he assisted patrons in finding books or directed students to helpful periodicals and Internet sites so they might effectively research their latest school project, part of his mind kept trying to conjure an image of Russ DuPont.

What did this mysterious young man look like? Did he have a bulky, muscular body and an angry face with a pair of black, hate-filled eyes? Was he quiet to the point of brooding while he spent hours plotting acts of violence as he went about his tasks on the Cornflower Goat Farm? How did he tie into the murders? He couldn't have known Paulette when she was a child in Natchez. He wouldn't even have been born by the time she left the town for good, destined for Paris and a future of fame and wealth.

Yet he tried to raise laying hens, James

thought.

During a lull in activity shortly after four in the afternoon, James settled down at one of the computers in the Tech Corner and began to search for articles on salmonella. Several of the resources he found concentrated on how to avoid being exposed to the harmful bacteria, while others described the physical symptoms one experienced once one was infected.

"Ugh," James grimaced as he read. "What a messy illness. You're going to experience vomiting, diarrhea, cramps, or all three if you ingest that nasty bug. You'd better come down with salmonella in the privacy of your own home."

"Excuse me, Professor," Scott interrupted apologetically as he peered over his boss's shoulder. "I've gotta know what you're investigating over here. You're making all sorts of funny faces and you're talking to yourself."

Tapping the computer screen, James replied, "I'm wondering how eggs get tainted by salmonella. I know that the bacteria can be found in eggs and poultry, meat products, unprocessed milk, and even in water, but *why* are some eggs more susceptible than others?"

Fascinated, Scott's fingers flew over the

keyboard. "Unhealthy chickens can lay eggs with thin shell walls," he read from an online medical encyclopedia. "If the chickens live in an unclean environment, such as, um, sitting around in their own feces, they lay eggs with thinner-than-normal shell walls. That makes it easier for the bacteria to pass through the shell and into the egg." He grimaced. "Gross."

"So if someone bought sick laying hens, and *deliberately* kept them in a polluted environment, the chickens would produce infected eggs," James mused to himself.

Scott was completely absorbed by a microscopic image of the bacteria. "Man, I'll have to remember not to eat raw turtle or lizard eggs if I end up stranded on a deserted island." He turned to whisper to Francis, who was wiping off the computer screens using a specialized cleanser. "Do you think any of those *Survivor* contestants ever got salmonella? They eat wacko stuff on that show. I'm sure at least one of them has eaten undercooked lizard."

Intrigued by the subject, Francis paused in his cleaning and told his brother to search for exotic foods eaten by the reality show's contestants. As the twins groaned in distaste over the idea of consuming crickets, beetles, and maggots, James decided someone should return to man the vacant chair at the information desk.

"But I'd never eat a grasshopper!" Scott whispered in horror. "Way too crunchy."

"Crunchy's better than gooey," Francis argued. "You could pretend a grasshopper was a potato chip with legs or a granola cluster, perhaps. I don't think you could talk yourself into believing larvae were anything *but* larvae. Totally revolting."

"Totally," Scott said in agreement.

James filled the copier and sundry printers with fresh supplies of paper, took care of a few transfer requests, and tidied up the bookmark displays and a stack of schedules detailing the library events for the month of January. That done, he spent a few minutes assisting a young mother track down several cookbooks featuring meals that could be made in thirty minutes or less.

"Now, if only there were a book that could teach me to put my kids in a harmless trance for half an hour," she joked, and James pretended to take her request seriously.

"I'm sure we have a book or two on hypnotism," he said with a grin. He patiently listened to her describe how chaotic her household was between the hours of four and eight. She then declared that by the next time he saw her again she might need a reference book on battling fatigue *and* insanity.

James recalled hearing this complaint from other patrons raising small children. Rushing to the stacks, he grabbed the book he had heard several moms praise and hurried back to the checkout computer with a copy of *Time Out for Mom.* "I think you need this one too."

"Oh, I sure do!" The woman looked delighted. Thanking him, she left the library with a lightness to her step.

Feeling pleased with himself, James surveyed his peaceful kingdom and was once again shocked to recognize the face and figure of his ex-wife standing near the Children's Corner. As though sensing he was watching her, Jane looked up from the book she held, smiled, and walked over to him.

"Sorry to pop up like this again," she whispered. "It was so great to talk to you the other night, but I felt like I had really picked a bad time to seek you out."

"Yes, there were quite a few things going on," James admitted. "But for you to just disappear . . . ," he trailed off, no longer feeling angry about her behavior, merely puzzled.

She reached across the desk and covered his hand with hers. "I wasn't trying be dramatic, I assure you. I have some things to tell you, but it's a conversation that requires a bit of quiet and privacy. And it so happens, this is the perfect setting."

More mystified than ever, James could merely nod.

"First of all, I wanted you to know that I'm no longer teaching at William & Mary. I'm at James Madison now." She smiled. "I love it. What a gorgeous campus!"

"Wow. You're so close," he replied dumbly. "Did you change colleges because you and Kenneth broke up?"

"Partially," she replied enigmatically. "But like I told you before, Kenneth's been out of the picture for quite a while. I moved to Harrisonburg to start a new life. Getting rid of Kenneth was just the first step toward that goal."

James stared at Jane as she talked, noting how she spoke with so much more calm than when they were married. There was a serenity and contentedness to her expression, as though she had discovered the secret to happiness and now guarded it with careful devotion. He couldn't believe she was the same woman he had once known. She seemed so approachable, so comfortable in her own skin, and so incredibly lovely.

Stop it! He chided himself. *You've got enough going on without falling for your ex-wife all over again!*

Still smiling, Jane squeezed his hand and said, "Follow me for a moment, would you?"

James came around the desk and gazed at her searchingly, but she said nothing. She led him toward the Children's Corner, where a young boy who looked to be about four years old was slowly turning the pages of an oversized picture book about animals in the zoo. Jane took James by the hand and nudged him toward a wooden chair.

"Hold on to the back of that chair," she commanded in a friendly tone.

Utterly confused, James glanced at the boy again. He had light brown hair and was dressed in jeans and a gray sweater. His scarf was covered with racecars and his bright green rubber boots were shaped like frogs. Suddenly, he looked up from the book and looked right at James.

"My God," James breathed as he stared at the child. From the warm, brown eyes to the slight smattering of freckles across the nose, to the kind, rather serious face — he was the spitting image of James as a four-year-old boy.

"This is Eliot Henry," Jane whispered so softly that James could barely hear her. "I named him after my favorite poet. He's your son."

At those words, James felt as though his world had instantaneously turned upside down. His heart began to beat in hummingbird time and a buzzing sound rang in his ears, as though hundreds of bees had swarmed around his head. Somehow, he sank into the chair. Reaching down, he gripped the wooden seat in an effort to keep himself from floating away, his knuckles white with shock.

"James?" Jane grasped his shoulder. "Are you breathing?"

Blinking, James could not take his eyes off the boy. Even as his mind started to question the validity of Jane's statement, his heart stopped the thought from fully developing, for it knew she spoke the truth. His eyes confirmed what his heart felt. The boy was a Henry through and through.

"Eliot," James murmured, spellbound by the name, by the sweet, young face, by the sheer joy that coursed through his body and threatened to cause him to violently explode like a balloon filled with too much air.

"I found out I was pregnant soon after I left you," Jane whispered into his ear, careful to make sure that the boy couldn't overhear. "I didn't know if the baby was yours or Kenneth's. You and I had had that one night together a week or so before I left you, so I couldn't be sure. I'm sorry James. I handled *so* many things badly. It wasn't until Kenneth and I were on the rocks that I finally had a DNA test done. A part of me had always known that Eliot was yours, but I was a fool and I wanted things to work out with Kenneth. I thought having his baby would instantly make us a happy little family." She shook her head regretfully. "Like I said, I was a fool."

She paused, her voice trembling. "It wasn't until Eliot was two that I realized you must be his real father. Kenneth became aware of it too. It wasn't just that they looked nothing alike, but they never formed a bond either. That's when things really changed between us. He . . . ," she struggled to speak the words, "began to be cruel to Eliot. At first, the attacks were all verbal, usually occurring after Kenneth had been out drinking with his law partners. But one day . . ."

James tore his eyes away from the little boy and looked at Jane in horror. "He didn't!" His fists clenched in wrath. "He couldn't have!"

Swallowing hard, Jane continued. "Kenneth slapped him for spilling a glass of red wine. It was a simple accident. Eliot has always been a polite and well-behaved child. Always kind and sympathetic and affectionate." Jane's face twisted in anguish. "Kenneth said that Eliot had done it on purpose and smacked him so hard across the face that I thought Eliot lost all his baby teeth then and there. That's what it took for me to wake up. Eliot paid the price for my insecurity and stupidity, but he'll never suffer because of me again." She wiped tears from her cheeks. "We moved out that night when Kenneth went out for drinks with the guys. Since we weren't married and had separate bank accounts, it was a quick and final break. And we've never looked back. Eliot doesn't even remember Kenneth."

As though fearing the boy might disappear if he looked away from him for too long, James returned his focus to his son. He couldn't stop drinking in the sight of the sweet face, the small hands, the relaxed limbs, the curious eyes darting over the images in the book.

"My son," he whispered again. His heartbeat had slowed, but he couldn't wipe the jubilant grin from his face. Grabbing Jane's hand in both of his, he kissed her palm several times, quickly. "Thank you, Jane. Thank you! You may have made mistakes, but you have made me the happiest man in the world! You brought me . . . ," he stared at his son again, "the greatest gift. A miracle."

Fresh tears fell onto her cheeks. "I hoped and prayed you'd feel this way," she sniffed. "But I never doubted that you'd want to know or that you'd want to be a part of his life."

James stood up, pulling Jane close to him. He stared deeply into her eyes. "Of course I want to be a part of his life. I've already missed too many years, too many moments!" He knew he had a right to feel rage or scorn toward Jane for the poor decisions she'd made, but nothing could eclipse the pure measure of joy flooding his heart. There was no room for any emotion other than absolute bliss. "Where do I start?" His question came out as a plea. "How do I *become* his dad?"

"Let's start off with introductions." Jane's smile was blinding.

The parents knelt down in front of the little boy. Jane held on to one of the small hands. "Eliot. Remember I told you that you were going to meet your daddy today? Well, here he is. This is James Henry, but you can call him Daddy."

The boy studied James for a moment. "Do you like books?" he inquired seriously.

"Oh, yes!" James declared, thrilling in the sound of his son's high, slightly slurred voice. "That's why I work here. I love books."

"Cool." Eliot glanced around the room appreciatively. "Can I come here again?" He directed his question at James.

"As often as you like," he responded warmly. "Whenever your mom can bring you, you can come here. We can read lots of stories together."

Without any indication that he was about to do so, the boy stood up, handed his mother his book on zoo animals, and gave James a brief hug. "Okay! See you tomorrow, Daddy!" Eliot said in an exaggerated whisper, and then giggled as his scarf dropped onto the floor.

James drank in his son's aroma of chocolate milk, apple-scented shampoo, and dirt. It was the most beautiful perfume he had ever inhaled. With the greatest effort, he pivoted away from Eliot and gripped Jane's arm harshly. "Don't leave! I don't even know where you live! I can't lose him again!"

Nodding in comprehension, she pried his

desperate fingers off her arm and retrieved a sheet of paper from her purse. "Here's our address, phone number, and my contact numbers at work." She pointed at the paper. "This is where Eliot goes to preschool. I put you down as an emergency contact, just so you know. Now, I've got to give a lecture tonight, so we've got to get going, but I'd love to bring him back here tomorrow if you're free. Maybe we could all have pizza."

"Pizza. Yes." Feeling less anxious, James clung to the contact information.

Jane then handed him a photo album with a blue leather cover. "I made you a scrapbook too. I thought it might help you make it through the next twenty-four hours. But he's not far away, James, and when we get together tomorrow, we can talk about setting up a schedule. Eliot's as much yours as he is mine, and I'll never keep you apart again. That's a promise."

Jane laid the book on a nearby table and took Eliot's hand, and the pair waved goodbye and headed out the door to the parking lot. Starting, James raced to his office window and watched Jane buckle Eliot into a booster seat in the back of a Volvo station wagon.

"That's my son," James said, his voice filled with awe. "*My* son, Eliot. My son." He repeated the joyful mantra over and over again, long after the Volvo was out of sight. He wasn't even aware that he was crying.

FIFTEEN: BEEF AND BROCCOLI

James didn't remember driving to the Realtor's office. It seemed in one moment he was in the library, and then he blinked and found himself seated at Joan's conference table with a pen in his hand and a glass of water by his elbow. She prattled on and on, pointing to the highlighted sections of the thick stacks of legal-sized paper so that he'd apply his signature to dozens of pages of unfathomable documents.

Though James followed her directions, Joan's voice failed to penetrate his bubble of happiness. It was as though he was listening to her talk underwater. Occasionally, phrases like "inspection" or "home warranty" or "escrow account" would make their way into his psyche, but it wasn't until Joan pointed at a line in the contract and mentioned "removal of adhesive stars," that he finally paid attention.

"Can you repeat that, please?" he asked her.

She smirked. "I thought you'd fallen into a coma! It's pretty normal for first-time home buyers to feel overwhelmed by all of these terms. Why don't we take a break and eat supper. It'll give you a chance to ask me any questions you might have."

James noticed the cardboard takeout containers from the Dim Sum Kitchen. His stomach gurgled in anticipation. "When did this arrive?"

"You really *were* in a trance!" Joan laughed. "My assistant brought our dinner in while I was reviewing the guarantee of title insurance." Noting the blank look on her client's face, she handed James three containers. "I took the liberty of ordering you the healthiest things I could from the menu. I remembered some mention of you seeing a nutritionist, and I didn't want to get you in trouble by ordering General Tso's chicken." James searched her face for an indication of mockery, but Joan seemed sincere. "Here's your miso soup, steamed rice, and beef and broccoli. Enjoy!"

"This is really nice of you," James said gratefully as he popped off lids and pulled open white cartons, allowing steam to burst out of the apertures.

She waved aside his thanks. "I owe you one. Not only did I get a commission from the sale of the Hickory Hill Lane house, but I got a delightful finder's fee for placing your friend in a Mountain Valley Woods apartment."

"Right. Willow." James hungrily slurped down his soup. "What did you think of her?"

Joan poured reduced-salt soy sauce on her rice and shrugged. "She told me what it was like to work for Paulette Martine. I knew exactly what that poor girl went through. *I* used to work for a horrible woman when I first got into the real estate business. She was the tyrant of Northern Virginia, I tell you!"

"Willow seems much happier now than when I first met her," James said as he followed suit with the soy sauce. "I just hope she can make some friends her own age."

"Seems keen on one of your library twins,"

Joan replied, animated by the idea of exchanging gossip. "Doesn't he like her?" James didn't expect the name Russ DuPont to pass across Joan's lips, but he had to create the opportunity for his real estate agent to discuss Willow's personal life in as much detail as possible.

"I believe he does. But she needs more than one friend. Did she mention anything to you about her social life?"

"Let me think." Using her chopsticks, Joan expertly lifted a clump of soy sauce–saturated rice into her mouth. "She talked a lot about Quincy's Whimsies. I think the space they want to lease downtown will be perfect, by the way. And she adores Milla. Apparently, Milla is a lot like her own mother. Other than that, the only other people she mentioned were you and your supper club friends. She's very obliged to you for giving her a fresh start."

James decided to change direction. "I thought the apartment complex she chose was kind of pricey. I guess she must have gotten a decent security deposit back from her New York studio, because she doesn't exactly have an income right now."

"She must have more than the security deposit by now," Joan stated with conviction. "My friend who handles all the leases for that complex told me that Willow marched into her office two days ago and paid for six months rent in advance."

The large piece of broccoli James was about to swallow stuck in his throat. He took a large swig of diet soda and tried not to allow his surprise to register.

Where did Willow get all that money?

"Maybe her folks are helping her out," he said aloud, and then quickly gestured at his paperwork. "What was that you were saying about the star stickers?"

Taking the bait, Joan pointed at the contract. "The sellers took off $300 of the final price because they didn't have time to remove all those glow-in-the-dark things from the ceiling of the second bedroom."

As James recalled the dozens of stickers affixed to the white ceiling, he was struck by a delightful vision. He saw Eliot lying in a twin-sized bed, staring up at the illuminated planets and shooting stars with a sleepy but contented smile on his sweet face. "Oh, I don't mind them being there."

"Either way, I'm sure you could use the extra money," Joan remarked. "You've got a whole house to furnish after all."

Including a room for my son, James thought, and he was instantly too overwhelmed to speak. He was dying to shout out news for the entire world to hear, and even though Joan had been especially pleasant to him, she was not the person he most wanted to tell.

After dinner, James signed the rest of the documents in a state of polite impatience. It wasn't until Joan placed an envelope containing the house keys in his hands that he allowed himself a moment's pause. He dumped the two sets of keys onto his palm and was satisfied by the weight of their cool metal against his skin. He jiggled them in awe.

"Feels good to hold something solid, doesn't it?" Joan smiled at him. "I never get tired of watching people receive their keys. That's why I'm a top seller. I just *love* what I do!"

After gathering up the folder containing his paperwork, James gave Joan a brief hug. He thanked her, rushed out to his truck, and headed for home, practicing what he would say when he got there as he drove through the blue-black evening.

The words of his well-plotted speech deserted him the moment he entered the house, however. He hung up his coat, cast his eyes around the clean kitchen, and spent a moment listening to the peaceful gurgles of the dishwasher.

Jackson and Milla were in the den watching television. Orange-tinged light from a floor lamp gave the room a feeling of quiet, which was only interrupted by the voice on the television and the rhythmic clicking of Milla's knitting needles. James nearly tiptoed in, gripping the photo album under his arm. He waited in the threshold for a commercial break and then bounded forward and switched the TV off.

"What do you think you're doin', boy?" Jackson grumbled. "Ain't no one tells me when I should go to bed!"

"Pop." James ignored his father's gruffness and knelt down in front of him.

Jackson was taken aback by his son's abrupt proximity and shifted uncomfortably in his seat. "If you're thinkin' of proposin', I'm already taken."

Knowing that his father preferred plain talk over embellishment and theatrics, James tried to get straight to the point. "Something happened to me today, Pop. Jane, my ex-wife, came to see me at the library."

"What the hell for?" Jackson snarled. "Didn't she do enough to you? She back to drum up more misery?"

"No." James shook his head. "Jane's really changed. I know that sounds like a cliché, but I think she's truly different now. She has a strong motivation to be a better person."

"And why are you yammering to *me* about this?" Jackson raised his furry eyebrows in an impatient arch. "I'm watching *Law & Order.*"

Glancing at Milla, James pictured her in the kitchen teaching Eliot how to bake the perfect chocolate chip cookie. She looked up from her knitting and smiled at him, and her warmth made him grin in return. He turned back to his father. "Pop, Jane's moved to Harrisonburg. She's started a whole new life, but I'm going to be a part of it again." He raised his hand to indicate that he was not to be interrupted. Amazingly, Jackson remained silent. "Jane was pregnant when she left me, Pop. She thought the baby's father was her boyfriend Kenneth. That's that guy she left me for. But Kenneth wasn't the baby's father. I was. I mean, I am."

"What did you say?" Milla leaned forward in her chair, her needles still in her lap.

Without looking away from Jackson, James continued, "I have a son, Pop. He's four years old, and his name is Eliot. I met him today."

Jackson blinked and stared, blinked and stared. "You've got a kid?"

Instead of answering, James placed the scrapbook on his father's lap and opened it to the last page. "This must be a pretty recent picture of him, because this is how he looked today, except for the racecar scarf and the green frog boots."

"He sure looks like a Henry," Jackson stated with pride. "Strong hands, even for a little tyke. Look at 'em! Bet he's smart too. Like his daddy." He gazed at James briefly. "Lord, I think he's got my chin."

James examined the photograph closely. "I believe you're right, but let's hope he didn't get your eyebrows."

"Or your back-talking tongue," Jackson shot back cheerily. "Milla! There's another Henry loose in the world. Come on, come on! We gotta pour us a glass!" He tapped rapidly on the scrapbook page, a brilliant grin lighting his wrinkled face. "I'm a granddaddy. I'm gonna tell the boy to call me Pop-Pop."

"Oh my goodness gracious! You have a son!" Milla was openly crying, her kind face flushed with pleasure. "When do we get to meet this child of yours?" She asked, jumping out of her chair to embrace James. "I can't wait to get my hands on him. I bet he's cute as a button."

"He's perfect. You'll meet him soon."

James released her and poured three glasses of Cutty Sark. His hands were shaking as he passed out the drinks.

The three toasted the arrival of Eliot Henry into their lives. After another hour of speculation about the little boy's family resemblance, mannerisms, and likes and dislikes, they all went to bed with smiles on their faces. James lay awake for several moments making mental lists of the books he needed to buy for Eliot's room at 27 Hickory Hill Lane.

Somewhere between the titles *Goodnight Moon* and *Caps for Sale,* he fell asleep.

The next morning, James was showered, dressed, and in his truck before seven. He didn't notice the biting coldness of the air or the old Bronco's reluctance to rumble into life and travel at a brisk pace through the slumbering town.

"This is your new driveway," he told his beloved truck, patting it affectionately on the steering wheel as he turned off the engine in front of his little yellow house.

Practically skipping to the front door, James fit the key in the lock and stepped into his new home.

The first thing he did was switch on all the lights. He then inspected the empty rooms one by one. The previous owners had hired a cleaning service to give the place a thorough once-over and the aroma of Pine Sol and Clorox clung to the floorboards and bathroom tile. Digging a color palette from his coat pocket, James held the cheerful hue he had chosen for the kitchen against one of the walls.

"You get painted first," he informed the room and pointed at the paint square. "Honeydew for the kitchen and Desert Dune for the living room. Milla thinks that'll look good with the red sofa I ordered."

He swiveled around in the empty space.

Suddenly, there were so many things to do. Paint supplies had to be purchased, new carpet for the bedrooms ordered, furniture delivery scheduled, and a pizza dinner with Jane and Eliot arranged.

"I think I'll bring them here," James said, tapping on the kitchen counter. As he glanced out the window at the dormant grass and leafless trees, he saw two squirrels chasing one another across the boughs. Watching their antics, he was struck by an inspirational idea of how to make his first meal with his son memorable.

Whistling, James locked up his house and drove to the hardware store to pick up his paint, drop cloths, rollers, and brushes. He also bought a few cans of spray paint, some rope, and some pliable wire.

When he arrived at the library a full thirty minutes before opening, he saw two young women chatting together on the front steps. When Lottie noticed James, she waved goodbye to Willow, walked over to the book bin, and slid two novels through its slot. They fell into the metal cavity with a clank.

"Good morning!" James called out to her and was rewarded by a hesitant smile. He then turned his attention to Willow. "Are you really *this* excited about checking out a book or are you here to see me?"

"I need to talk to someone," Willow murmured, displaying traces of her former downtrodden body language. "I've already smoked half a pack of cigarettes, and I haven't had one since Paulette died."

Unlocking the front door, James beckoned her inside. "Let me pump up the heat and put on some coffee. We can talk in my office. While I'm doing those things, would you mind switching on all the lights and computers? It'll keep you from smoking the rest of that pack."

Moments later, James took a grateful sip from his new favorite coffee mug, which was embellished with a black shelving cart and the words *That's How I Roll.* He watched Willow cradle her warm cup in her hands and softly invited her to share what was on her mind.

"I know it's only a matter of time before Lucy comes knocking on my door, so I thought I'd practice my confession on you." She spoke with a catch in her voice. "She's bound to arrest me and the life I wanted to begin here will be over before it really started."

Observing the young woman carefully, James asked, "Why would she arrest you?"

Willow didn't answer immediately. She looked at the window, drank from her cup, and then ran her pale blue eyes over the items on James's desk. "With Chase's murder, the police are bound to review Paulette's death too. I didn't kill her, Mr. Henry, I swear. But if she was murdered, and I think she was now that Chase is dead, I'm in for it. I was with her at the bed-and-breakfast and I hated her."

"And Chase? Did you hate him too?"

Distracted by the sounds of the twin's laughter in the parking lot, Willow glanced in their direction and smiled. Then the happiness on her face melted quickly away. "I didn't hurt Paulette, but Chase may have."

Suddenly, James had a theory as to how

Willow received her influx of cash. "You were blackmailing him," he stated.

She didn't bother to deny it. "He and Paulette got into a huge argument the night before she died. He came to the Widow's Peak to ask her for a loan, but she told him he had enough money and that she wasn't going to give away her hard-earned money so Chase could jet off to Europe with one of his mistresses."

"Ouch!" James let out a little laugh. "I bet Chase didn't take being turned down too well. After all, he was Paulette's *favorite.*"

"Not that night, he wasn't," Willow remarked solemnly. "He actually replied, 'Isn't that how *you* got *your* start, Mother? As someone's mistress in Europe? And then a TV producer's mistress in New York? And so on?' "

James was shocked. "He said that to his own mother?"

"They really were two of a kind." Willow didn't seem surprised at all. "Anyway, at the end of their conversation, Chase promised that he'd get the money from her one way or another. He was very calm. It didn't sound like a threat, but after she died, I had to wonder."

"Why didn't you tell Lucy about this right away?" James demanded.

"I honestly didn't think he killed her! He respected her," she argued. "Besides, her death was ruled an accident."

"In your opinion, did Chase love his mother?"

Shrugging, Willow examined her nails. "I don't think Chase or Paulette loved anybody but themselves. They lived for money and recognition and the freedom to treat regular people like dirt." She sighed. "When Chase came back to town for the ash scattering, I told him that I'd heard his last conversation with his mother. At first, I was just trying to scare him into giving me my final paycheck, but he offered me a lot more. After all I'd been through with the Diva, I figured I'd earned it and . . . I took the money."

Suddenly, the promise Willow had made to Chloe and Wheezie in the hotel lobby that she would take care of Chase made perfect sense. James had eavesdropped on the three women right before Willow decided to blackmail Chase. She had been successful and he had given her a generous payoff. Though she'd made an error in judgment, James doubted Willow was a killer. If she was, then why confess to blackmail?

"I'm certain you earned every penny," James told the fraught young woman kindly. "Paulette underpaid you for years."

Willow seemed surprised to discover that James wasn't angry. "As much as I've tried to justify my behavior, I know it was wrong. When I heard about Chase's death, I knew I had to tell someone, but I was afraid to go to the sheriff by myself." Her face crumpled. "What will Milla think of me now? And Francis?"

"They'll think you're human, just like the rest of us." He walked around the desk and raised her from her chair. "I'll ask Lucy to come over and listen to your story. While we're waiting for her, why don't you ask Francis for a book recommendation? That would make his day. And might I suggest you also tell him about your 'mistake'? If you two are going to be a couple, you don't want secrets between you."

James waited for Willow to leave the office before phoning Lucy.

"I'm with Wheezie right now trying to figure out if she knows Russ DuPont," Lucy whispered into her cell phone. "I'll be over as soon as I'm done."

By the time the library officially opened, Francis and Willow had their heads bent together behind a spinner rack of science fiction paperbacks. Scott was near the checkout desk, placing books onto the shelving cart with unusual roughness. He looked completely dejected.

"What's wrong, Scott?"

"I went outside to empty the book bin, Professor," Scott answered as he gripped a book called *Women in American Journalism: A New History.* "And I saw boot prints in that muddy spot that never dries up between the sidewalk and the book drop. They were the same boot prints Francis and I noticed during our Christmas Eve stakeout."

"Uh-oh," James whispered.

"It didn't take much brainpower to figure out who checked out the books in the bin because there were only four in there. Two were borrowed by Lottie and two by Mrs. Finke. I've seen Mrs. Finke in here for years and there's no way she wears high-heeled boots. That means those boots are Lottie's." He put his head in his hands. "My *girlfriend* is Glowstar's kidnapper!"

James frowned. He couldn't argue with Scott's logic, and he didn't have the faintest idea what had motivated Lottie to inflict such a cruel prank on her own boyfriend. Feeling angry on Scott's behalf, James reflected on the fact that neither of the twins possessed an ounce of real meanness and yet, someone had deliberately tried to cause them anguish.

"I'm sorry, Scott." James put his arm

around the lanky young man's shoulders. "I don't know what to say."

"That's okay, Professor. This is no time for words!" Scott said heatedly. "I'm already planning what to do. First, I'm going to send a certain reporter on a little goose chase. Next, I'm going to get Glowstar back, and *then* I'm going to drink Red Bull and play video games until I go blind!"

"Before you lose your sight, I wanted to talk to you about something." Doing his best to contain his happiness in the face of Scott's misery, James told Scott about Eliot. He then explained what he wanted to create before he saw his son again that evening and begged for Scott's assistance.

"You are going to be *such* a cool dad!" Scott exclaimed when James was done, momentarily forgetting about revenge.

The two men returned to their librarian duties, leaving Francis free to sit with Willow until Lucy arrived.

"Can you ask Milla to meet me here too?" Lucy paused on her way into James's office. "The name Russ DuPont meant nothing to Wheezie. Everything rests on Milla's memory now. There has to be *some* connection between their past in Natchez and the two deaths. Milla may be the key to solving this entire puzzle, whether she realizes it or not."

James hurriedly complied and phoned his father's house, but there was no answer. He left a message and then turned his attention to an elderly patron who needed help searching the Internet for the best airfare to Fort Lauderdale. James then took care of the monthly budget, and by the time he was done paying bills, Willow, Francis, and Lucy had vacated his office.

Willow shot James a look of gratitude and left the library with Francis glued to her side. Assuming his employee was merely walking his girlfriend to her car, James settled at his desk and checked his e-mail. His face glowed as he read a message from Jane.

> Eliot is so excited to see you again. Where would you like to meet us? We have supper at six and he only likes cheese on his pizza.

Those few words were enough to light up his morning. He quickly typed his answer.

> I'd like you to be the first guests in my new house! #27 Hickory Hill Lane. 5:30. I'll have dinner waiting. I can't wait.

Lucy tapped lightly on his office door. "Were you able to reach Milla?"

"No." A flash of lavender passed by his window. "Hold on. She's here."

While James handled a telephone query, Lucy shepherded Milla and Jackson into his office. It took every ounce of James's concentration to complete his phone call and gently hang up the phone. In all his time as head librarian of the Shenandoah County Library, his father had never stepped foot inside the building where his son worked. Milla was slowly changing Jackson back into a social creature.

"It's nice to see you, Pop."

Jackson raised an eyebrow and then scowled at Lucy. "Let's get this over with, girl. Milla here's got a list a mile long, and I wanna get back home by suppertime."

Ignoring Jackson's grumbling, Lucy led Milla to a chair and sat down next to her. "I'm going to ask you to try really hard to remember something about your childhood. Take your time to think through my question. Try to recall families from school, your neighbors, church members, store clerks, anyone and everyone."

"I'll try," Milla promised.

Satisfied, Lucy leaned forward a fraction. "Did you ever know a family named the

DuPonts?"

Three pairs of eyes focused on Milla as her gaze drifted around the room, finally settling upon James's coffee mug. She grinned as she read the slogan and then her eyes grew distant. Her observers could almost sense her journeying back in time, shuffling faces and names through her mind, discarding one and then searching for another.

After two full minutes of silence, she shook her head. "No ringing bells. I'm sorry."

Something Milla had told him back in December suddenly came back to James. "Milla? Do you remember when you were telling Pop and me about Paulette's girlhood? You said she was called Patty then and there was a woman who taught her how to bake. What was that woman's name?"

Milla sat erect in her chair. "Mrs. D.!" Her shoulders instantly slumped again. "But that's all I know. Just the initial. I don't know if that stands for DuPont or not."

"What about the street address?" Lucy's predatory look flared in her eyes. "I could call some neighbors. I could ask Wheezie who the old-timers are in your former neighborhood and talk to them. I'm reaching here, but I'm getting a strong feeling that we're on the right track."

Closing her eyes, Milla murmured. "We lived on Idle Day Drive. To get to Mrs. D.'s I'd walk down our street, turn right onto the main road, and then a left onto . . . oh! I can *almost* see the street sign. That big live oak always blocked the first half of the word . . . Cobble something! Cobblestone Court!" She smiled triumphantly. "The house number was one. I remember that because she had one dog, one cat, and one child. I don't think she had a husband either. Seems to me she lived on a wing and a prayer and by selling her baked goods."

Scribbling the information into her notebook, Lucy asked James if she could use his phone. He led his parents back to the checkout desk and spoke to them in between accepting late fees and handing patrons their scanned books and receipts.

"Your materials are due back February twenty-third," he told a little girl who had checked out five books from the Baby-sitters Club series.

Milla watched the child walk away — her pigtails swinging back and forth like a metronome's needle. "Wait until Eliot learns he can bring home piles of books from his daddy's library." She moved closer to James. "I'm sorry you couldn't get me on the phone, dear, but me and Jackson were busy. We got married this morning."

"You did?" James looked from her beaming face to Jackson's. He noted that his father's expression showed a mixture of both pride and relief. "That's wonderful! You just went ahead and did it! Congratulations!" He hugged Milla tightly.

"You're not angry?" Milla sighed in relief. "I worried you might feel excluded, but my dear, I was in *such* a rush to make things official. When I meet your boy I want to be his grandma, not just Pop-Pop's girlfriend!"

Jackson tapped the face of his wrist watch. "My *wife's* been on the run all mornin'. The van's loaded to the roof with crap. Toys, pictures, lamps, curtains, a rug. I think she bought out the damn toy store. I haven't even had my third cup of coffee yet," he growled.

Milla linked her arm in Jackson's. "I couldn't help myself! I've wanted to be a grandma so badly and now I *am* one! James, get ready, because I plan to spoil your son rotten!"

"Your *son?*" Lucy's voice came out as a croak. She stared at James in disbelief. "Did I hear that right?"

James hadn't stopped to consider how this news might affect others, like his supper club friends. He'd simply assumed that everyone he knew would share his joy and would congratulate him on his happy reunion with his son. But there was an ashen appearance to Lucy's face that made him realize that the revelation he had a child with his ex-wife might not be welcome news to some people. As he struggled to speak, James suspected that, if Lucy still harbored any romantic feelings for him, they were about to be irrevocably destroyed.

As his parents sidled quietly away, James opened the scrapbook he kept close at hand. He opened to the last page and showed the photograph to Lucy. "It's true, Lucy. I only found out yesterday. This is Eliot Henry. My son."

Without making a sound, Lucy glanced at the picture, looked up at James with wounded eyes, and fled.

Sixteen:
Thin Crust Cheese Pizza

James gave the gum-chewing, iPod-wearing pizza delivery teen such a generous tip that the young man actually paused his music in order to say thanks. Smiling, James shooed him from his doorstep, slid the pie into his warmed oven, and then put the finishing touches to the makeshift dining table.

The doorbell sounded at exactly five-thirty, sending a shiver of pleasure up his spine. Here he was, James Henry, answering the door of *his* house for the second time that evening. And on the other side of that solid piece of wood was not a pimply-faced, skinny teenager wearing a backwards baseball cap, but his four-year-old son.

"I love this house!" Jane exclaimed as soon as she stepped inside. "You have such a huge yard! And a front porch too! It's just perfect for sipping lemonade in the summer and setting out jack-o'-lanterns in October, right Eliot?"

"Can we make a scary one?" Eliot asked James, his golden brown eyes wide with excitement. "Like a monster from *Where The Wild Things Are*?"

"When Halloween comes, we can carve whatever face you'd like." James was dying to scoop the little boy into his arms and cover his face with kisses, but he settled for ruffling Eliot's wavy soft brown hair. "I know the best pumpkin patch too! We can have a hayride and jump in a giant bin of corn kernels and you can go on a pony ride."

Eliot nodded. "I like ponies. 'Specially the ones with spots."

"Me too. And I'm glad to hear you're an animal lover," James said warmly. "Because we're having supper at the Hickory Hill Zoo tonight."

Cocking her head quizzically, Jane unzipped Eliot's coat and, after removing her own, looked around for a place to put them. "I'll just toss these on the kitchen counter. Eliot, you go with Daddy and find out what this zoo is all about."

Eliot reached out his hand and James enfolded it with his own. *Daddy!* He thought. *I'll never get tired of hearing that word.*

Wondering how long it would take for Eliot to start calling him by that title, James led his son into the living room, which was lit by battery-powered hurricane lanterns. James had spent his lunch hour in a bout of frenzied painting and had managed to transform the largest of his cardboard moving boxes into zoo animal chairs. There was a zebra, a lion, a giraffe, and an elephant. The heads were made out of shoe boxes and the giraffe's neck and elephant's trunk had been formed using part of a dryer vent. Scott and Francis, who had built the cardboard furniture while wolfing down bacon double cheeseburgers during their lunch break, had rigged all the heads with wire so they bobbed gently when touched. Given their uncanny technical skills, the twins weren't happy until the animals were given added features. James was delighted when they showed him how to attach a battery to some narrow wires in order to turn on the small light bulbs that would create a pair of illuminated eyes inside each animal head.

"They're not real, right?" Eliot asked, his high voice growing shriller in amazement.

"No, they're not. And that's probably a good thing considering our dining room table is a crocodile," James teased.

Scott and Francis had taken a rectangular box made for storing an oversized painting from their landlady's garage and transformed it into a green reptile with a long, spiked tail (another dryer vent cut in half) and jagged, Styrofoam cup teeth. To make the beast less threatening, the twins had painted the croc with neon pink polka-dots and a Cheshire Cat grin. James had set their plates, napkins, and cups on the table and had added another hurricane lantern in the center to enhance the safari-like atmosphere.

"Mommy!" Eliot screeched. "We're eating pizza on a crocodile!" He swiveled around the room. "I'm going to sit on the lion's chair!"

James served Jane and Eliot pizza on animal-shaped plates and filled paper cups covered by tiger stripes with cold chocolate milk. When Eliot asked to have his pizza cut up, James smacked himself in the forehead for not considering that a four-year-old might not want to eat pizza with his hands. Jane seemed completely unfazed, however.

"You're supposed to be a young lion," she admonished their son playfully. "So act like one! Rip that pizza apart with your giant lion teeth! Like this!" She tore at her slice and chewed with a satisfied growl. Giggling, Eliot copied her.

"How does a giraffe eat?" he asked James.

James sat very straight in his chair, stretched his neck out, bit off a mouthful of pizza, and did his best to chew it using only his molars, thus exaggerating the side-to-side motion of his jaw. Jane agreed that zebras chewed much like giraffes, and copied James's absurd style of pizza eating. Soon, all three of them were laughing.

After dinner, while savoring raspberry frozen custard pops from the Custard Cottage, Eliot told his parents what he had done at preschool. He went into great detail over which kids were his best friends and which ones made him grumpy because they repeatedly knocked down his block tower. As he licked his custard, Eliot listed all the words he knew that began with the letter *G* and confessed to the number of marshmallows he'd consumed on the sly while supposedly pasting a marshmallow snowman onto a sheet of blue construction paper. By the time his ramble was done, everyone had finished dessert and Eliot began to yawn and rub his eyes.

"I think we'd better head home," Jane suggested.

James nodded reluctantly. He didn't want the evening to end. "Can I show him something first? I'll be quick. I can see that our young zookeeper is getting tired."

"Go ahead. I'll clean up our plates and bring your trash bag out to my car. It's pickup day at our place tomorrow, and since you haven't officially moved in yet, I'm going to assume you don't have a garbage can." She smiled as James realized that he didn't even know what day to put a can out — not that he had one. "It's okay. Everyone goes through this when they move. It's going to take a while for you to figure out the rhythm of this place."

"At least I know who my mailman is," he said and felt comforted by knowing that Bennett would be passing by his house five out of seven days a week.

Beckoning Eliot to follow him, James led his son into the small bedroom whose window faced the backyard. "Okay, you've got to lie down on the floor for the magic to happen. No, roll over. You've got to be on your back for this trick. Good. Now close your eyes. Ready?" James waited until Eliot nodded. He turned off the lights and settled next to his son. "You can open your eyes now."

"Wow!" Eliot's voice came out as a whisper. "Magic stars! How'd you do that?"

"The house just came that way," James answered enigmatically. "Do you think you'd like to hang out in this room? I mean, would you like this to be your room?"

Eliot leaned back on his elbows and surveyed the space. Solemnly, he replied. "Yes. I like it." He then asked, "Am I moving here, Mom?"

Jane stood in the doorway, surveying the stars. "You're going to have two homes, Eliot. Isn't that cool? Sometimes you'll sleep at my house and sometimes at Daddy's." She glanced quickly at James. "But you and Daddy need to spend more time together before you start having sleepovers, okay?"

Her eyes met James's and he nodded in recognition that what she was saying was both wise and true. He did need to become more familiar with his son's habits before taking charge of him without Jane present as a chaperone. "Listen, buddy," he touched Eliot lightly on the hand. "I'm moving into this house over the next few days, but I haven't picked out stuff for your room yet. I don't really know how to decorate it. Maybe if you told me the name of your favorite book, I could make this room really special for you."

Yawning again, Eliot replied. "That's easy. I like *Curious George* the best. He's always getting in trouble."

"Come on, my little monkey. Time to go," Jane commanded.

Eliot gave James another of his rapid hugs and then submitted to being tightly enveloped in a coat, hat, scarf, and mittens.

"Are you free Sunday afternoon?" James asked Jane as she took Eliot's mittened hand.

"We sure are. Let's spend some time going over our calendars then. I figure Eliot's going to need to stay with me during the weekdays so he can get to school on time, but you could come to our place in the evening and he can come here on weekends. You know, not overnight at first, but for the day anyway." She drew Eliot close to her. "Why don't I take care of supper Sunday night? I've actually learned how to make a few dishes, believe it or not."

Recalling what an atrocious cook Jane had been during their marriage, James shook his head. "Pop's wife will never speak to me again if she isn't allowed to stock my fridge.

I know it's early on in this whole getting-to-know-each-other thing, but could Eliot's grandparents stop by for a bit Sunday? Maybe just for dessert? They want to meet him so badly."

"Of course!" she responded, and then instantly lowered her voice. "But I remember your father all too well. Is he going to hurt me after . . . how I treated you?"

James shrugged nonchalantly. "If Pop comes at you with his fists clenched, just use Eliot as a human shield. He'd never hit his only grandchild."

Giving him a playful punch in the arm, Jane waved goodbye and then gave their weary son a piggyback ride to the car. James watched as she buckled Eliot into his booster seat and then fired up the Volvo's engine. Eliot placed his small hand against the glass of his window and wiggled them in farewell. The car rolled slowly down the driveway and turned onto Hickory Hill Lane.

James stood on the front porch until the bright red taillights grew as small and distant as the winter stars.

Saturday was painting day. James dressed in a ratty sweatshirt and jeans and loaded a thermos with vanilla hazelnut coffee. Carrying a portable CD player and a copy of *Curious George* under his arm, he used his free hand to unlock the front door to his new house. He paused for a brief moment, allowing images from his pizza dinner with Jane and Eliot to bring a smile to his face, and then made preparations to paint the kitchen. As he listened to Sugarland's new CD and sipped coffee, he removed switch plates, filled in nail holes, and applied tape around the windows and woodwork trim. Dipping his brush into a can of white primer paint, James wondered what his friends were doing at the moment and when they'd get together in order to talk about the case. He wanted to tell them about Eliot too, but that kind of news had to be delivered in person.

He had just finished the primer coat when the doorbell rang.

"Surprise!" The supper club members shouted in greeting and filed into his house, rubbing cold hands together as they immediately began to inspect their surroundings.

Gillian strode into the center of the living room and plunked down a green hemp purse embroidered with lavender dragonflies. "Everyone stop right there! I'm going to perform a cleansing ritual called smudging that is practiced by the Native Americans of the Northwest." She dug out an apparatus resembling a torch from her bag and lit it with a purple Bic lighter. "I'm going to allow the smoke from this cluster of sage, cedar, and sweetgrass to *graze* the walls in every room. I'd like the rest of you to quietly *visualize* James living a life of peace and happiness in this house while I *purify* the air."

Murmuring to herself, Gillian spun around the room, directing a waft of torch into each corner. Bennett stared at her, in a state of bemused mystification, but Lindy stood with her eyes closed and her hands clasped, inhaling the pleasant scent of the burning herbs. James decided this might not be the best time to ask where Lucy was or if she had spilled the beans about Eliot.

Once Gillian was safely out of sight purifying the master bedroom, Bennett strolled into the kitchen and picked up a paint roller. "In addition to burnin' bushes in your new house, we're here to work. What color should I paint these walls, my man?"

"I can't believe you guys!" James was touched by the offer. "It's good enough just to see you. You don't need to spend your day off slaving over cans of paint."

Lindy threw her coat on the hall floor and

pushed up the sleeves of her paint-speckled artist's smock. "Many hands make light work. Lucy'll be here by lunchtime, so let's get something done before then. Where do you want me, James? Should I start priming the living room? Oh! Look at these adorable animals!" She pointed at the crocodile table. "Those look like the twins' handiwork."

Picking up his copy of *Curious George,* he said, "Scott and Francis are the marvelous animal creators, yes, but I'm also in need of *your* particular artistic talents, Lindy. I'll tell you why in a second."

James waited for Gillian to reappear in the living room. She had him extinguish the torch and asked him to inhale its revitalizing fragrance. Only after she'd waved the smoke over every inch of his body was he permitted to gather his three friends around his scrapbook.

They received his announcement exactly as he had expected them to: with shouts of joy, warm embraces, and dozens of questions.

"And you want *me* to paint his room?" Lindy exclaimed with misty eyes. "I am so honored!"

Bennett clapped James on the back. "Man oh man, you sure know how to throw one in from left field. I can't wait to see your

Mini Me. Eliot Henry. Congrats, my friend. Congrats."

"Oh, I just *adore* the auras possessed by young children," Gillian sighed rapturously. "And to know that your blood and a part of your essence is encapsulated in *this* child . . . James, I can't wait to lay my eyes on this boy!" She looped her arm through Bennett's. "I feel jittery already."

"That's it, woman," Bennett teased her fondly. "No more tree-bark tea for you."

"I'll introduce all of you, I promise. But I don't want to overwhelm the poor kid. He's going to meet his grandparents tomorrow night. I have another reason to be happy, because Milla and my father are now officially man and wife. They had a quick wedding down at the church." James tapped the scrapbook and then drew in his breath. "Oh no! I've been so wrapped up in my own affairs that I haven't done a thing to celebrate their nuptials. I haven't even bought them a gift! I was going to send them on a nice little honeymoon, but I don't have the time or the money to do that now. What am I going to do?"

"I imagine your coffers are a bit bare right now," Bennett remarked.

James nodded. "You can say that again. New carpet on Monday, furniture delivery on Tuesday, and flat broke by Wednesday."

"We'll brainstorm while we paint," Gillian suggested. "The cadence of our bodies moving our brushes and rollers up and down, up and down, might just stimulate the creative centers of our minds."

"Don't let that woman near your CD player," Bennett warned. "She'll put on some yoga mumbo jumbo and we'll all be chanting like Gregorian monks."

The four friends finished looking through Eliot's scrapbook and then got to work. They bantered, painted, and chatted all morning long. By noon, the kitchen and living room looked clean, fresh, and bright, and Eliot's room had been primed and was ready for Lindy's hand-painted designs.

"This is very cathartic," Gillian stated as she set down her paintbrush. "Do you have a nice, serene color chosen for your bedroom? I'm certain we could get that finished today."

James shook his head. "I hadn't expected this painting party, but I could go buy some. I think Lindy's going to need a few more colors for Eliot's room. And I'd love to treat for lunch. It's the least I can do."

"Hello!" Lucy called out as she let herself into the house. "Lunch is served!"

Bennett moved forward to remove one of

the two plastic bags from Lucy's hands. "What have we here?"

"Meatball subs. Except for Gillian's, of course. She's having provolone, mozzarella, tomato, and a pesto spread on herb focaccia."

James pushed a twenty dollar bill into Lucy's hand. "Hi," he said shyly as she looked down at the money.

"I'm not taking this." She breezed past him into the kitchen and laid the bill on his counter. "I missed half of my painting shift, so the least I could do was pick up lunch." Gazing into the living room, she smiled. "I call the zebra chair!"

"I thought you might be angry with me," James whispered to Lucy once the food had been handed out and the rest of the supper club members were making themselves comfortable in the living room.

Lucy feigned great interest in a Benjamin Moore paint chart. "I was just shocked, that's all. I . . . I've got to get used to thinking of you totally as a friend. And you are my friend, so don't worry. Come in here and eat your sub. I've got an update on our investigation."

After settling in the lion chair, she spread a napkin on her lap. "I ate half of my sub in the car, so let me take a few bites while it's still warm, and then I'll tell you about the phone calls I made to Natchez."

James couldn't believe how famished he felt. *Is there a chemical in the paint that induces hunger or is painting more of an aerobic workout than I thought?* he wondered.

Without bothering to consider that the contents of his hero might be too warm to chew, he released his sandwich from its tight package of aluminum foil and bit into the end of the sub, inviting molten marinara sauce and a large piece of scalding meatball into his mouth.

"Ahhh!" He felt as though he might breathe fire. "Hot!" Lindy shoved a water bottle into his hand, and he washed down the burning food as his friends looked on in amusement.

Bennett tossed him a snack-sized bag of baked potato chips. "Better start with those, my man. Okay, Lucy, whatchya got for us?"

"Russ DuPont is Mrs. D.'s grandson," Lucy began as she placed the remnants of her sub on the crocodile table to cool. "Russell DuPont's mother never married. She also died at a young age from alcohol poisoning. According to the neighbors, she'd always been a wild girl. Russ often went without meals or electricity, and he missed more days of school than he attended." She pried open her bag of potato chips and halted her narrative in order to eat one.

"That poor boy," Gillian sighed.

Lucy agreed. "I think he's lived a hard life. His grandmother ran out of money and was sent to a state-run home when Russ was ten years old. After his mother's death a year later, he was placed into foster care and, if I can believe what these Natchez ladies told me, was one angry boy. He got in trouble all the time." She raised her sub to her lips. "He's got an extensive juvenile record. From vandalism to petty theft to selling his grandma's prescription drugs on the street, this kid's done it all."

"The neighbors told you all that?" Lindy asked in disbelief. "Must be a smaller town than I thought."

Once she'd swallowed Lucy replied, "No. I called the Sheriff's Department and told them all about our case. They were very interested in helping me get a full picture on Russ. I guess he's got them out of bed more than once with his criminal activities. They're faxing me copies of his records."

"So we've got a hostile young man who drove to the Shenandoah Valley and got a job on a goat farm where he produced bacteria-infested eggs that he somehow gave to Paulette." James poked a meatball with his fingertip. "Sounds like a complicated and deliberate plan. Russ is no dummy."

Gillian's expression was sorrowful. "It *sounds* like that young man was *consumed* by a desire for revenge. Instead of trying to live a life based on higher principals, it seems like he's chosen to live one based on *blame* and the *baser* of our human emotions."

Lindy looked perplexed. "Am I missing something here? Why would this boy hate Paulette? Did she do something to his mother or to his grandma?"

All eyes turned to James. "That's an integral question and I'm hoping *you* can answer it." Lucy's voice held a plea. "If not you, then Milla."

A thought had been forming in James's mind while Lucy had been speaking, and now he spoke it aloud. "Milla told me about their neighbor, a Mrs. D. She was an older woman who had hundreds and hundreds of recipes in her possession. She had shoeboxes filled with them. All the recipes were created by Mrs. D. from scratch. What if — ?"

"The Diva stole her recipes!" Lindy shouted. "And published them as her own!"

"And don't forget got rich and famous off

’em too,” Bennett added. “While the DuPonts stayed poor and downright miserable, Paulette was autographin’ cookbooks and hostin’ television shows.”

They all chewed thoughtfully on their sandwiches as they tried to imagine Russ DuPont somehow discovering that his grandmother’s recipes had made another woman extremely wealthy.

“Our hypothesis makes sense,” Lucy determined. “If Paulette did make off with the recipes, it would certainly explain why she never returned to Natchez. Still, without a confession from Russ, our theories are circumstantial.”

“And there’s no sign of Russ right now,” James pointed out. “Do you think he’ll go back to the goat farm, or is he done exacting his revenge and is now on the run?”

Gillian drew in a frightened breath. “Is Chloe in danger?”

Lucy considered the question. “As the next beneficiary of Paulette’s estate, she may be.” Her blue eyes gleamed. “But if Russ is following the Diva’s money trail, it would mean that he won’t leave town — that he’s merely lying low someplace until he can get at Chloe. We’ve called dozens of hotels, but none of them have Russ DuPont registered as a guest. Still, he could be checked in anywhere under a false name."

"I'll tell you one thing." Bennett balled up his trash and scrutinized the crushed foil in his hand. "Aunt Wheezie ain't gonna be much help fending off an angry boy bent on murder."

"Don't worry," Lucy assured them. "Chase's death lit a fire under Sheriff Huckabee. With all the media attention zeroing in on Quincy's Gap because of Murphy's damn book, he doesn't want to look inept. He's got two deputies keeping an eye on Wheezie and Chloe. Someone's watching them round the clock."

"Uh, that *book!*" Lindy spat out the word.

"Would someone please tell me what happens at the end?" James pleaded. "I know it's off subject, but everywhere I go someone mentions the 'shocking ending.' Would someone just put me out of my misery?"

Lindy shook her head in refusal, but Lucy gave her friend a crooked smile. "Don't worry, Lind. I know Murphy's written it so that I get shot in the face in the final chapter. Donovan's read the section aloud in the station at least six times by now."

"She kills your character?" James was aghast. Only the danger of his last meatball falling from its cushion of bread was able to distract him from such a shocking announcement. "That's so —"

"Nasty, cruel, vindictive, abusive, and childish!" Gillian supplied him with several apt adjectives. "I've pretty much summed up all our characters right there!"

"I thought you weren't going to read it?" James remarked in accusation.

Gillian toyed with a tendril of hair. "I gave in to the temptation presented by my ego. And I regret it too. We should always be wary of giving in to our desire to see ourselves painted in a flattering light."

"My *character* doesn't die!" Lucy shouted. "I'm just a bit disfigured, that's all," she added caustically. When James and Gillian again began to splutter in indignation, she crossly gesticulated at the pair of them. "Hello! We've got a murder case to talk about! Can we just forget about that dumb book and . . . ," she trailed off, but James noticed that her eyes had darted toward Eliot's scrapbook at that moment.

"What are our options?" Lindy inquired innocently. "If Chloe's being guarded until she returns to Florida, there's nothing we can do. Short of sneakin' her away from her surveillance crew and leavin' her in a place where Russ is sure to come for her, our hands are tied."

James imagined Chloe standing on the

edge of the cliff from which her brother had been pushed, and he shivered. "Russ must've written Chase a note to entice him to the overlook earlier than everyone else. You didn't find any evidence of that?" When Lucy shook her head, he sighed. "Then this guy has to be caught in the act. We need to have some kind of private affair — a reason to keep Chloe and Wheezie around a little longer."

Bennett stroked his mustache. "Yeah man, some kind of get-together? If there's a bunch of folks around, Russ might feel like he can slip in and try to get to Chloe. And if Milla bought goat's milk goodies from this guy, she'd be able to recognize him in a pinch. She could whisper in Lucy's ear, and our favorite deputy would take him down!" He smacked his fist against his palm and then turned to James. "Got it! Is there gonna be a funeral for Chase?"

"Not here," James answered. "The 'merry' widow phoned Milla and said that she felt that the father of her children should be buried near where they live. Personally, I think she wants to dance on Chase's grave, but Milla wanted the girls to be able to visit Chase, much like she wanted to visit Paulette."

"If there's no need for a mourning ceremony," Gillian grinned, "why not host a surprise party instead? I believe *you* are quite close to a couple who have recently exchanged commitment vows. Right, James?"

"A party for my parents!" he exclaimed. "To celebrate their wedding! That's a brilliant idea, Gillian!" His face fell. "Except for the fact that I'm totally penniless."

Lindy made a dismissive sound over his despair. "This is Quincy's Gap, James!" She leapt up, grabbed her purse from the hallway, and pulled a pocket calendar from within. "Yes. I believe Wednesday would be a lovely evening for the supper club to host a surprise wedding reception in honor of Jackson and Camilla Henry. Does everyone agree?"

"We do!" James's friends shouted in unison and, still laughing at their response, they returned to their painting duties. Ideas and party plans were batted about as brushes and rollers covered the walls with warm hues.

At one point, Lindy came into the kitchen for more paint. Brandishing her cell phone at James, she said, "You stay out of your son's room until I'm done. I'm going to create the ultimate Curious George bedroom for him *and* call in a few favors from our friends and neighbors. We teachers are all blessed with the ability to multitask."

As she disappeared down the hall, James slung his arm around Bennett. "If Luis doesn't get down on one knee pretty soon, I'm going to have to take a baseball bat to his leg."

"Well," Bennett mumbled pensively, "that *would* get him down on his knees. But Lindy didn't say she was lookin' for a proposal. What she wants is for him to show the rest of the world he's her man. In public."

"Like *you* did on national television?" James teased.

"I'm gonna pretend you didn't say that," Bennett growled. "And no, that's not what I'm sayin'. I do believe a good old-fashioned kiss would do the trick."

"In front of a group of people, such as the throng we're going to gather together for our surprise party?" James inquired.

Bennett winked at him. "I couldn't think of a better time for that man to lay one on Lindy. We'll just have to help that happen, now, won't we?"

"Yes, we will." James dipped his brush into a bucket of primer. "But I'll bring my baseball bat. Just in case."

Seventeen: The Diva's Praline Pecan Cake

James and his parents attended church the next morning and, after a quick lunch of chicken tortilla soup and a salad of mixed greens, went their separate ways until suppertime. James wanted to stock his kitchen at 27 Hickory Hill Lane with food. He also wanted to arrange his new pots and pans, dishes, and eating utensils so that his family wouldn't be forced to eat off the remainder of his animal-shaped paper plates.

Having borrowed the Diva's latest cookbook from the library, James had ambitious plans to bake a stunning cake to serve his loved ones that evening. Despite these lofty intentions, he found himself standing in the middle in the baking aisle at Food Lion staring dumbly at the ingredient list for the Diva's Perfect Praline Pecan Bundt Cake.

"You look lost," a young woman's voice teased. Willow pulled her cart alongside James's and peered at the open cookbook. "She made that one for the TV show in December, remember? It's really a delicious cake."

"It sounds like a perfect wintertime cake," James replied with a sigh. "Too perfect. I'm not an experienced cook by any means, and I'm feeling daunted by these instructions."

Willow began scanning the shelves. She grabbed a box of cake mix and put it in his cart. "This situation calls for a shortcut. That cake mix is *almost* as good as the made-from-scratch batter, but it takes half the time and only three ingredients. Just concentrate on the icing and the candied pralines. Since you're making those two by hand, no one will suspect that every ounce of your cake isn't homemade."

Relieved, James scanned the directions for the frosting and pecans and decided they didn't seem so challenging. "Thanks, Willow. You're a lifesaver."

"No problem. I'm going to be using a few shortcuts too since I'm in charge of the wedding cake for Wednesday night's party." She looked pleased to have been asked. "I told Lindy that I plan to make cupcakes instead of a multi-tiered cake. Since we don't have an army of waiters, cupcakes are better for a buffet. Your parents will get a miniature cake, of course, but I thought they might prefer a pair of white doves instead of the traditional bride and groom toppers."

James laughed. "I suppose there aren't too many toppers of gray-haired couples. Thanks for being so thoughtful, Willow, and for taking care of all the sweets." James placed a bag of pecans in his cart.

"And don't worry that I might be offending Megan Flowers by baking the wedding cake. The Sweet Tooth is supplying rolls for the dinner and a tray of wedding-bell cookies. It was really important to me to make Milla's cake. She's been so good to me, so different from Paulette."

A thought occurred to James. "I wonder how I'm going to get those goat's milk products out of the house and packaged up before Wednesday. They're in Pop's shed and he *never* lets anybody in there when he's not around."

"Your friend Lindy's got that covered. She's going to visit your father this afternoon as a representative of her mother's art gallery and is planning to find a way to squirrel the party favors out."

James grinned at Willow. " 'Squirrel them out,' huh? I do believe you're turning Southern on us, my dear." His smiled evaporated. "Poor Lindy. She might not get the warmest reception. Pop's been in a bit of a painting drought lately."

"That happens to all creative types. Something or someone will get him back on track. Besides, two people who were supposed to be at his wedding are dead now," she pointed out. "That's got to have affected your father. Throwing him a surprise party ought to cheer him right up."

"You're only saying that because you don't know Pop. He's going to *hate* being the center of attention," James replied. Then he thought, *But to catch a killer, it's worth a little discomfort on his part.*

Quickly adding the rest of the cake ingredients to his cart, James also stocked up on toilet paper, paper towels, garbage bags, and cleaning supplies for his house. He nearly passed out when the total appeared in neon green digits on the cash register. Digging his credit card from his wallet, he sang wryly under his breath, "Hi ho, hi ho, into debt I go."

It was impossible to remain cross while filling the refrigerator and pantry in his newly painted kitchen. The room was too warm and welcoming to accommodate grumpiness. Switching on the radio, James sang along to a series of upbeat oldies, and he prepared the box of butter pecan cake mix. He was thrilled to be able to use the steel bowls, rubber spatula, measuring cups, and hand mixer Milla had bought him, and when he slid the bundt pan into the oven, he decided to make it a point to become an accomplished cook.

"After all, I'll be feeding my son on a regular basis," he informed the oven proudly. Musing over what foods were preferred by a typical four-year-old, James found himself heading down the hall to examine Eliot's room for the third time that afternoon.

The supper club members had painted until well after dark the day before, and when Lindy finally exited Eliot's room, she had looked tired but immensely pleased.

"It's got to dry overnight," she had warned James before she would let him enter. "And you should tell the carpet guys to be really careful on Monday. After that, try to keep in mind that this is a boy's room and every inch of it is gonna get dirty at some point."

"Stop stalling, woman!" Bennett had grabbed her by the arm. "Show us your masterpiece."

James, Gillian, Bennett, and Lucy had filed into Eliot's room. Glancing around, they had exclaimed in delight and congratulated Lindy on a job well done. Their artistic friend had gone all out in order to create a room that any monkey-lover would appreciate. First, she had divided the wall in half, so that the upper walls became a cobalt blue sky and the lower half was a tropical forest floor. Trees, exotic plants, and flowers bloomed everywhere and several monkeys resembling Curious George swung from jungle vines. Butterflies, dragonflies, hummingbirds, and macaws also populated the forest canopy. On the wall where James planned to place Eliot's bed, Lindy had painted George flying through the air as he clung to a bunch of balloons. The monkey wore his trademark grin of mischief and the shiny, plump balloons looked so realistic that James believed that if he stuck a pin into one it might actually pop.

"Girl, you've got mad skills," Bennett had praised Lindy.

Lucy had nodded in agreement and then,

a trifle sourly, asked, "What happens when he gets tired of Curious George?"

"Then his Aunt Lindy will paint him something else," Lindy had quickly responded, smiling at James. "I haven't had this much fun in ages. Thank you for letting me do this."

Now, standing in the charming room, James felt as though there were too many hours between now and three o'clock, but in truth, he didn't have that much time to finish his cake and assemble the kitchen table he'd hastily purchased from the local furniture store. The store owner attended the same church as the Henrys, and when James explained how desperately he needed his table and an extra two chairs delivered that very afternoon, the man promised to drive the items over himself.

The tile-top table and six ladder-back chairs arrived by two. And though James only had to screw the legs to the table base, he also had to bake the candied pecans, which would serve as the cake garnish, mix the frosting, and move the bouquet of yellow carnations he had sitting in the sink to a glass vase.

By the time the cake was cool, the kitchen table was set up and the flowers arranged. James was quite pleased with himself when he overturned the Bundt pan and the golden cake dropped effortlessly onto a cranberry-colored cake plate. James spooned the frosting over the top and sides, enjoying how it slowly dripped down the lines and crevices in the cake. Frowning at the puddle of icing pooling in the middle, he realized he'd probably poured on too much at once.

"Ah well. I'm not exactly the Diva of Dough," he remarked to his creation, and then he meticulously placed the candied pralines in a ring around the top of the cake. He ate half a dozen during this exercise, wondering how Paulette had stayed so slim working with such tempting ingredients. "It's a good thing library books aren't edible," he said, laughing at his weakness for sweets.

When Jane and Eliot arrived, James covered his son's eyes with a dishtowel blindfold and led him down to his bedroom. "Something smells delicious!" Jane exclaimed as she walked behind them. "And it's not the new paint either."

"That's the aroma of my homemade dessert wafting through the house. And as I mentioned on the phone this morning, Milla's taking care of the rest of our dinner, so prepare yourself for a host of sumptuous scents. I thought we'd play with Eliot's Legos until they get here. Milla bought enough blocks to add another room on to my house!"

Eliot stopped in his tracks, almost causing James to collide into his small figure. "What are Legos?" he inquired, tilting his face toward James's voice.

James directed a *tsk tsk* at Jane. "Has this child been raised by wolves?" He laid his hands lightly on Eliot's shoulders and prodded him forward. "Come on, son. I believe a few monkeys are waiting to meet you."

"Wow!" Eliot yelled when the blindfold was removed. "This is the best room ever!" After spinning around and around, he performed two somersaults in the center of the floor.

"Thanks a lot," Jane murmured and poked James in the ribs. "Now his room at my house is going to be unlivable in comparison."

"I wasn't trying to make this a competition," James apologized sincerely.

Jane poked him again, and he let loose an involuntary giggle. "I'm kidding, you big orangutan. I think this room is awesome! One of your supper club friends is the artist, right? Tell us more about her."

As the three of them settled on the floor

and began to build fantastical houses, pirate forts, and castles out of large-sized Legos, James fondly reminisced about how he and the supper club members had first met. Naturally, this led to the subject of how the five of them got involved in their first murder investigation, and before he knew it, James was confiding to his ex-wife how hurt and angry he felt about Murphy's book.

"I'd say this writer took poetic license to the extreme," Jane said sympathetically. "Why would she do something so cruel to Lucy's character? Did the women dislike one another?" She handed Eliot a red square. The boy was so intent in his building that he paid no attention to his parents, humming songs under his breath as he erected a colorful tower of blocks.

James spun the wheels of one of the Lego cars. "Murphy was always jealous of Lucy. You see, I, ah. I —"

"Let me guess. You dated them both!"

When his face flushed pink, Jane laughed. "Oh goodness, James Henry! The Casanova of Quincy's Gap is right in front of me! And now?" Her voice turned serious, but her eyes still twinkled with mirth. "Who holds the key to your heart, you rogue of a librarian?"

"He does," James answered and pointed at their son. At that moment, the doorbell sounded. "Ready to meet your grandparents, Lego Master?" he asked Eliot and the boy mumbled "Sure," without bothering to halt construction.

James fully expected his father to exude a chilly attitude toward Jane and at first, the reception she got was definitely frosty. But as the evening progressed and Jackson was able to witness what a fine mother she was, he eventually thawed. He and Eliot liked one another right away. When Eliot shyly asked Jackson if he should call him "Grandpa," Jackson leaned down and whispered something in the little boy's ear. Jackson winked and Eliot rewarded him with a smile before returning to his room. Eliot stayed there while his grandparents toured the house, but as soon as the adults were settled in the kitchen, the boy sidled up to Jackson and tugged on his shirt sleeve.

"My tower keeps falling over," he complained. "Can you help me, Pop-Pop?"

That simple utterance was all it took. Jackson smiled, showing more teeth than James knew he possessed, and marched off to his grandson's room to show him how to create solid building foundations.

Milla wasn't out of the loop for long.

Eventually, Eliot wandered back to the kitchen in search of a glass of water and before he knew it, he was standing on a kitchen chair using the hand blender to whip the potatoes. James cringed when he saw the white splatters peppering his clean countertops, but when Milla noticed his expression, she flicked him with a potholder and informed him that all good cooks made a mess in the kitchen.

"Am I cooking, Grandma?" Eliot shouted over the whir of the mixer.

"You are, darling! And you're a natural too!" Milla replied effusively, her eyes shining.

The dinner was a success. Milla made a roast chicken with stuffing, green beans, mashed potatoes, and biscuits. Everything that wasn't slathered in butter was drenched in brown gravy, and James knew there'd be hell to pay when he got on the scale the next day, but he didn't care. He served his praline pecan cake with decaf coffee for the adults and a cold glass of milk for his son, and he blushed at the compliments lavished upon him by the two women.

"It's fair passable," Jackson grumbled when Milla demanded that he open his mouth and comment on his son's culinary skills.

Eliot turned to James and repeated his grandfather's statement word for word in the same grouchy, reluctant tone. Everyone laughed.

"Seems we've got a smart aleck at our table, huh?" Jackson was obviously pleased.

All too soon, it was time for Jane and Eliot to leave. He gave his grandparents lightning-quick kisses on the cheek and then approached James for his customary hug.

"You're a good cake maker," he whispered into James's ear and, unable to help himself, James clung to his son tightly. Eliot snuggled against his chest for a moment and then broke away. He took his mother's hand and was once more carried off into the night.

"Is this part going to get any easier?" James asked Milla once the Volvo disappeared from view.

"Probably not," she answered with a compassionate smile. "After all, I'm gonna cry every time you leave our house."

"You cry over toothpaste commercials, Mrs. Henry," Jackson remarked. "Come on, climb into your coat. It's gonna snow. That damned dog next door's been howling his head off since lunchtime." He turned to James. "This is a good house, son. Well built." He nodded in approval. "And he's a fine boy. I'm gonna paint him tomorrow.

My head's right stuffed with pictures."

"That's great, Pop!" James was thrilled to observe the eager twitch of his father's fingers.

As though embarrassed by his candidness, Jackson gestured toward the kitchen. "You gonna bring the rest of that cake home for us to eat, right? I'll find a place to hide it 'cause you wouldn't wanna mess up your diet or anythin'."

"So you *did* like it?" James teased. "Yeah. I'll bring it. But I may have another piece. After all, this is my last night sleeping in my old room. I might just need some comfort food."

"Oh, don't remind me!" Milla cried. "I feel like we'll never see you again!"

"You will." James embraced her fondly and thought, *Next time we have dinner, it won't just be with me, it'll be with half of Quincy's Gap!*

Jackson, or rather the dog living next door to the Henrys, had been right about the snow. It fell all night long, but in timid flakes that appeared to lack direction. All signs of precipitation had disappeared by the next morning, but on Tuesday afternoon, a much more determined front had descended upon the Shenandoah Valley. A surreal pink sky welcomed a nearly stationary cloud bank and a cascade of vigorous flakes. When Wednesday dawned, the world was magically cleansed and completely muffled in white.

"The weather seems like nice complement to your parents' party," Mrs. Waxman remarked as she arrived for the evening shift two hours early. "The way those drifts have formed on the lawn outside — they almost look like piped icing, and the snow is so soft, like a veil covering one's hair." She patted James on the arm. "Enough of my metaphors. You'd better get a move on. And save me a cupcake or I'll be quite displeased."

James knew his former middle school teacher was teasing, but he stood a fraction taller out of habit and said, "Yes ma'am!"

He was careful navigating the snow-covered roads leading to the church and was delighted to note that Lindy, Bennett, and Gillian's cars were already in the parking lot. His friends were busy stomping their boots on the door mat in front of the fellowship hall when he entered. They each relieved him of his dual armload of bags containing decorations.

"What have we here?" Lindy inquired.

James poured out the contents of two bags

onto a buffet table. "I pretty much bought out anything the store had that was white or seemed to be remotely connected to weddings."

Bennett held up a hundred-count bag of white balloons. "And who's gonna blow these suckers up?"

"I bought a little hand pump." James clapped Bennett on the back. "Do you think you could make an arch over the far end of the hall? That's where the wedding cupcakes will be. I figured three hundred balloons ought to do it."

Spluttering, Bennett requested another job, but Gillian grabbed the hand pump from him and smiled. "You pump, I'll tie. I have *very* nimble fingers."

"Don't I know it." Bennett smiled at her affectionately.

James left them to their project and began to thumbtack glittering snowflakes, silver wedding bells, and cutouts of white doves hanging from curly white ribbon onto the ceiling tiles. His hands shook a little as he worked, and a feeling of anxiety began to swell inside his chest. Would the killer attend their celebration? Would the supper club members be able to conceal the fact that their eyes would be scanning each and every face in the crowd in search of the dangerous stranger? Would Russ DuPont wear a disguise or wait in the janitor's closet for a chance to ambush Chloe?

Perhaps this entire affair is a grave mistake, James thought worriedly as he moved his ladder a few feet to the right. *We're being so arrogant — playing with Chloe's life this way.*

James was just hanging the last pair of doves when the Fitzgerald twins breezed in carrying a stereo system and two sets of speakers. After renting the hall and paying for a weekend getaway to Asheville, James didn't have enough funds to hire a disc jockey, but Francis and Scott assured him they owned enough CDs to keep the party going all night.

"Let's hope it's not *that* much fun. We all have to work tomorrow," James had told them earlier that day. He had then showed them the printout of Russ DuPont's photograph, which Lucy had acquired from the Sheriff's Department in Natchez. "Be on the lookout for this guy. He probably murdered Paulette and Chase, and he may try to harm Chloe tonight. We're going to need every pair of eyes, so memorize this face."

The twins had studied the photograph for a long time. "Man, he totally doesn't look like a killer," Scott had remarked.

"That makes them the most treacherous.

Dark blond hair, blue eyes, about six feet tall," Francis read from Lucy's notes. "Sure wouldn't stand out in a crowd."

James stared at the young man's face for the hundredth time. "He'd better stand out tonight. Someone's life may depend on it."

As the twins got busy hooking up the stereo, Lucy arrived with Deputy Truett in tow. He was to come to the party as a guest, but a guest carrying a concealed gun. Lucy was armed and told her supper club friends that she was carrying a radio in her purse, just in case she needed to alert Sheriff Huckabee or Deputy Donovan. Huckabee was already camped out in the church office, which would serve as the law enforcement command center for the duration of the party. Donovan was in charge of outdoor surveillance. James relished the idea of Keith Donovan, his nemesis since junior high, sitting on the cold, gray leather of his black Camaro, drinking cupfuls of noodle soup and coffee in an effort to keep warm while the rest of them congregated in a heated room, enjoying a bountiful feast.

Surveying the room, James felt his anxiety ebb a little. It looked like a winter wonderland. With the glossy white balloon arch, the glittering silver and white cutouts twirling from the ceiling on satin strings, the ivory tablecloths, and the floral bouquets made from white amaryllis, the room glowed with enchantment. For a moment, James wished Jane and Eliot were attending, but he didn't want his ex-wife and son within miles of Russ DuPont, and though Jane's voice had been fraught with worry when he explained the situation to her on the phone, he promised he wouldn't do anything foolish in order to apprehend the young man suspected of murder.

"I'm a father now," he'd said to Jane. "Eliot is the number one priority in my life. Trust me. I want nothing more than to be with my son. And with you too, of course." Though he wasn't sure what he'd meant by that statement, James had to admit that he was both comfortable and content in Jane's presence and was genuinely looking forward to spending more time with her.

"Helloooo!" Lindy snapped her fingers in front of his face. "You're daydreaming, James!"

Gillian opened her arms wide and twirled around, her batik skirt opening outward like a flower with rainbow petals. "And why not? This place looks like a dream! And those cupcakes Willow made! Divine! Come see."

The trio walked over to the dessert table and gazed licentiously at row after row of luscious cupcakes. Each confection had been frosted with an inch of creamy vanilla hazelnut icing topped by a white chocolate heart.

"Try one of the hearts," Willow said as she placed a petite wedding cake in the center of the cupcakes. She gestured at a bowl of white chocolate hearts. "I thought we might sell them at Quincy's Whimsies."

James plucked a candy from the bowl and popped it in his mouth. The buttery chocolate melted on his tongue and he closed his eyes in bliss. "Ah, heaven!"

All of the supper club members helped themselves to candy hearts. As they showered Willow with compliments, the first guests began to filter into the room. No one came empty handed. People either carried a wedding gift or a tray of food, and it didn't take long for James to experience a bout of nervousness.

"Who *are* these people?" he asked his friends in an agitated whisper.

"Students from Milla's Fix 'n Freeze classes," Lindy answered calmly. "Lucy was in charge of drumming up volunteers to supply food, and she had the brilliant idea of inviting a bunch of guests who also happened to be darned good cooks."

"You're amazing!" James told Lucy and

she flushed with pleasure.

He then walked over to the far side of the room in order to introduce himself to the dozen people arranging entrées on the buffet table. Reading the placards standing in front of each warming tray, James was astonished by the assortment of gourmet food Milla's students had created. There was apple- and cranberry-stuffed pork loin, maple-glazed salmon, medallions of beef in a cognac cream sauce, lemon dill tilapia, cornbread-stuffed portobellos, spinach tortellini and roasted tomatoes in pesto, and chicken breasts in a white wine sauce.

As James moved down the line, making a mental checklist of which entrées to choose, more and more unfamiliar faces appeared at the table. Men and women of all ages unveiled platters of sides including risotto cakes, squash medley, wasabi whipped potatoes, wild rice pilaf, and glazed carrots.

It was with some relief that he recognized the trim forms of Megan and Amelia Flowers as mother and daughter set out bread baskets of Asiago cheese muffins in the center of each dining table and added an enormous platter of wedding-bell cookies to the dessert table.

All was ready.

James looked around the room and found

Chloe and Aunt Wheezie standing by the drinks area. Willy, the merry owner of the Custard Cottage, had volunteered to make virgin and champagne-spiked punch. Despite the chill in the evening air, folks were lined up to accept cold glasses of punch and Willy's jolly booming laugh echoed through the large room.

Suddenly, the lights blinked on and off three times — Bennett's signal that Milla and Jackson had pulled into the parking lot.

"Are you sure this is a good idea?" Lindy asked at the last moment. "Your folks aren't *exactly* young. What if we give them a heart attack?"

"If anyone's going to get hurt here, it'll be me," James joked, momentarily forgetting about Chloe. "Pop *detests* surprises. Here he comes, like any other dutiful new husband accompanying his wife to what he believes is her first choir practice. Instead of listening to the sweet melodies of a dozen robed figures, Pop's about to be set upon by seventy-five well-wishers. Considering he cast off his hermitlike existence fairly recently, I don't expect him to be thankful that I've propelled him to this level of socializing." He glanced at Lindy's clasped hands and at her pink face, which was aglow with excitement. "Luis is coming, right?"

She nodded. "He's gotta ditch the crazy PTA women first, but he'll be here."

As soon as she finished speaking, Bennett flicked the lights again and the murmurs of the crowd abruptly ceased. In the silence, the dual footsteps of Milla and Jackson proceeding down the tile-floor hallway caused James's heart to race. His eyes swept across the guests, but everyone's faces matched Lindy's. All the expressions were the same — that of jubilant anticipation. Even the undercover deputies, Lucy and Glenn, had their gazes fixed on the closed door leading from the fellowship hall to the corridor. And then, it eased open.

"SURPRISE!" Came the deafening, unified shout. Jackson's jaw dropped and Milla's hands flew to her heart.

James rushed forward to grab her by her free arm in case she fainted, but Milla merely repeated "oh my, oh my, oh my" while Jackson looked as though he might hurl himself through the closest window, regardless of the fact that it was a beautiful stained glass representation of the story of the loaves and the fishes.

"What have you done, James Henry?" Milla asked when she'd caught her breath.

"It wasn't me," James countered. "A few of your friends wanted to throw you a wedding reception." Avoiding his father's desiccating stare, James leaned toward Milla and whispered, "You sped up your wedding plans for Eliot's sake, the least *this* son could do was to ensure you celebrated properly."

Milla threw her arms around his neck and kissed him on the cheek with a wet smack. "And where's my darling grandson?"

James squirmed. "I didn't want him to come. He, ah . . ."

"Oh." Milla's eyes grew round. "You don't want him around Chloe and Wheezie in case that young man . . ." She too trailed off, and at that awkward moment, Scott and Francis hit a play button on their stereo and the Crystals belted out "Going to the Chapel." Most of the guests immediately began to sing along.

"I know this isn't your idea of fun, Pop, but it's just dinner and dessert, and then you can go back home."

Milla tugged on Jackson's earlobe. "Tell James something nice, dear. He went through so much trouble to put this party on for us. With the new house and Eliot and work and the other troubles we've been through . . . this is such a delightful surprise!"

"Yeah, what she said," Jackson grumbled, and James left his parents to mingle with their guests.

For the next thirty minutes, he circulated the room, smiling and small talking and never ceasing to look for the dark blond hair, the flat blue eyes, and the youthful face of Russ DuPont. All through dinner, as he sat on Milla's left and sampled the savory entrées her students had created, his eyes scanned and searched. He made certain he was never far from Chloe, and if she moved too far away from him or went out of the hall to use the restroom, Lucy was never far behind.

The Fitzgerald twins played Sinatra, Neil Diamond, and Pavarotti tracks throughout the meal, and when Willow led Milla and Jackson to the dessert table, they cued up "It's a Wonderful World." Hand over hand, the newlyweds cut their miniature wedding cake and gently fed one another a morsel of Willow's gift. When they were done, James saw his father reach out and snag a cupcake on the way back to his seat.

When James bit into his own treat, he was astonished to taste a creamy raspberry filling inside the sheet-white dough. He wondered if the cupcakes were Willow's recipe, Paulette's, or Mrs. DuPont's. "Did you taste Willow's chocolate hearts?" he asked Milla. "Your new shop is going to make a fortune."

Milla beamed. "I hope so, because we signed a lease this morning. I'm planning on a Valentine's Day grand opening. What do you think?"

A blast of music from the speakers behind his head prevented James from answering. He recognized the smooth and sonorous voice of Elvis, but couldn't understand why Scott and Francis were playing "Can't Help Falling in Love" at a decibel level that was sure to garner everyone's attention. And then he saw that it wasn't the twins who were looking for notice, but Principal Luis Chavez.

Standing behind Lindy's chair, Luis tapped her on the shoulder and when she turned, he got down on one knee and presented her with a single, long-stemmed red rose. He then grasped her arm softly and drew her to her feet. As she gazed around in astonishment, he led her to the front of the room and began to waltz with her.

The guests sipped their coffee and watched the couple move gracefully around a small section of the wooden floor. James met Bennett's eyes and they exchanged winks. It had been Bennett's idea to give Luis the red rose along with some friendly advice, and it seemed as though the dashing principal had heeded the mailman's counsel.

The song came to a gradual end and Luis dipped Lindy low to the ground. Holding her there, he gave her a lingering kiss on the lips. As he raised her up again, the guests clapped and whistled. Milla grabbed Jackson's hand and then took hold of James's.

"What a perfect party." She sighed with contentment.

Suddenly, James realized that Lindy's dance had distracted him from checking on Chloe's whereabouts. His stomach lurched as he saw the chair she had occupied during dinner was now vacant.

Slowly rising to his feet, he peered up and down the room, frantically searching for the familiar hue of Chloe's yellow dress. At that moment, Lucy must have been looking for Chloe too, for when her eyes met James's, they were bright with fear.

The party was over.

Chloe was gone.

The Diva's Praline Pecan Cake — Shortcut Version

For candied pecans

1 egg white
1 cup pecan halves
1/3 cup granulated sugar
1/3 cup brown sugar, firmly packed

For cake

One box Butter Pecan or Spice cake mix

For praline icing

1 cup brown sugar, firmly packed
1/2 cup butter
1/4 cup whole milk
1 cup confectioners' sugar, sifted
1 teaspoon vanilla extract

Preheat the oven to 350 degrees. Make the candied pecans first. Whisk the egg white until foamy; add the pecans, and stir until they are evenly coated. Stir together the granulated and brown sugar, and sprinkle it over the pecans. Again stir gently until the pecans are evenly coated. Spread the pecans in a single layer on a lightly greased baking sheet. Bake at 350 degrees for 18 to 20 minutes or until the pecans are toasted and dry, stirring once after 10 minutes. Remove the pecans from oven, and let them cool completely.

Make the cake as directed on the box. Spoon the batter into a greased and floured 12-cup bundt pan. (Willow prefers PAM Baking cooking spray.)

Prepare the praline icing: Bring the first three ingredients to a boil in a saucepan over medium heat, whisking constantly. Boil for 1 minute. Remove the mixture from the heat. Whisk in the confectioners' sugar and vanilla until smooth. Stir gently 3 to 5 minutes or until the mixture begins to cool and thicken. Spoon it immediately over the cake.

Top cake with Candied Pecans. If you have extra, put them in the freezer and snack on them for the next three weeks.

EIGHTEEN: CHAMPAGNE PUNCH

Lucy broke eye contact with James and flew for the door leading out of the fellowship hall. As she moved, James saw her reach into her purse for her radio. By the time she brought the device to her lips, Deputy Truett was already reacting. He had noticed her abrupt departure and was following closely on her heels.

Milla and Jackson had left their table in order to say goodnight to their guests. Several women, who were both Milla's friends and members of the church, were collecting the heavy-duty plastic dinner plates and taking them into the kitchen to be rinsed and placed in the recycling bin.

James found that he was frozen into a state of inaction. He had no idea what to do, and there was such a sudden flurry of movement in the room that he couldn't concentrate enough to come up with a plan. Between the guests making preparations to leave, the women cleaning up, the removal of the food trays, and the music pulsing in the background, the cacophony prevented him from having a single intelligent thought.

"Think! Think!" he muttered under his breath. "I'm sure the deputies have the outside covered, but what if Chloe's still somewhere in the building? We need to split up and search. Yes! Splitting up is key."

Hustling toward Chloe's seat, James noticed that her purse still hung from the back of her chair. Aunt Wheezie was standing by the punch table, ladling herself a serving of the spiked version. James noted that the old woman did not seem disturbed, but he'd need to ask her if she knew where Chloe went before he went running around the rest of the church. He picked up Chloe's bag and headed toward Wheezie, but Lindy and Luis jumped out of their chairs and blocked his path.

“This has been the best party ever!” Lindy beamed and took her man’s hand in her own. “Luis and I —”

“Listen!” James interrupted crisply. “Chloe’s gone. Can you check both restrooms? If she’s not there, try every closet, every door, every pew in this building.”

“Oh, Lord!” Lindy’s hands flew to her cheeks. “I completely forgot about her! When we were dancing I just . . .”

James touched her arm. “We were all distracted, but hurry up now.”

Gillian and Bennett were observant enough to know something was amiss. They intercepted James, and Gillian reached out and took Chloe’s purse from his hands. She inspected the contents and frowned.

“Her wallet’s in here and the keys to her rental car,” Gillian’s lips formed a thin line of worry. “What would have coaxed her from the room without her purse? Women rarely leave their valuables unattended, even in a place of worship.” Her eyes traveled toward the kitchen. “There’s a back door off the kitchen, right?”

“But Donovan can see that exit from his car,” James replied argumentatively. “She couldn’t have been taken that way. Keep Chloe’s bag for me. I’m going to talk to Wheezie. Maybe she knows something.”

"We'll check out that back exit," Bennett grabbed Gillian by the elbow. "With all this snow, Chloe would've left a trail of footprints even Dummy Donovan could follow."

People tried to stop James on his way to the punch table to congratulate him on a wonderful party, but he only cast brief smiles their way and did not pause to speak or shake hands with anyone. He left a wake of bewildered guests as he traversed the room.

Wheezie was placidly refilling her cup by the time he finally reached her. When she turned to look at James, he saw a mad glint to her eyes that sent a shiver up his neck. She knew about Chloe, he was certain of it. She knew and didn't seem to care.

"Aunt Wheezie. Are you okay?" he asked, studying her carefully.

" 'Course. Why wouldn't I be? It's such a nice party and I love balloons. And cupcakes. Yummy."

And punch, James thought ungraciously. "Have you seen Chloe?"

The old woman shrugged and used the ladle to push around the orange slices floating on the surface of the crimson punch. "Nope. I'm sure she's around and about."

"She left her purse on her chair and the party's breaking up," he pointed out impatiently. "We should find her so you two can head back to the hotel. You both have early flights tomorrow, right?"

Wheezie moved to take a sip of punch, but before her lips closed around the rim, James could have sworn he saw them form a grin. "Up with the rooster. Cock-a-doodle-do!"

"How are you going to get to the airport?" James inquired flatly, though anger was flaring within him. "Is Russ DuPont going to drive you? Or will the two of you forget about flying and just take his car back to Natchez?"

"Oh! Smart boy!" Wheezie replied with a crooked smile and poked him on the chest.

Repelled by her yellow teeth, which were partially stained pink by punch, James backed away from her a fraction. "You've been involved all along," he whispered in mounting horror. "You and Russ have worked together from day one, haven't you?"

Wheezie sipped her punch and hummed "Itsy Bitsy Spider."

James recalled the old woman's warped eulogy at Paulette's memorial service. "You weren't kidding about dancing on your sister's grave. You were never honestly interested in forgiveness. Your visit was all about revenge, and you got it." Wheezie's face was impassive. "And Russ DuPont got his too, didn't he? Did you know his grandmother?"

"Sure did. Delightful woman. Poor as a church mouse when she passed." She held out a glass of punch to James, and he reached for it without being aware that he did so. "Patty wrecked that whole family, same as she ruined ours. But it's all done now. All done!" She clinked her cup against James's and some punch sloshed onto her white blouse, blemishing the fabric with red.

Spurred by a righteous fury, James ripped the cup from her hand and tossed it on the table. "Where is Chloe, Wheezie?"

"In heaven maybe," the old woman answered. "Or maybe not. Don't really know the girl."

"And you?" he hissed at her. "People are never too old to go to prison. You could make things better for yourself if you help me save her! She did nothing to you, Wheezie," he pleaded. "She's an innocent."

"That dirty money would've turned her into Patty sooner or later. Look at that miserable son of hers. Breakin' the hearts of his wife and kids. Patty's bad blood flowed in him and in the daughter. Now the girl'll go to the Lord without bein' tainted."

"And how will *you* and *Russ* go to Him?" James snarled, pointing at the cross in the nearest stained glass window.

"I reckon we've suffered enough and the wrongs done against us will show up in heaven's book. There's bound to be a scale to measure such things." Wheezie picked up her glass again. "Reckon I'll know soon enough anyhow. See, dear boy, that nasty, nasty cancer runs in our family. Daddy had it in his lungs, Mama had it in her womb, and I've got it up here." She tapped the side of her head and issued another twisted smile. "Not much longer left for me now. They can put me in a cell, a hospital bed, down a hole . . . it don't matter. My hourglass is runnin' dry."

"What about . . . ?" James searched his memory for a name, desperate to find something, *anything* that would convict Wheezie to tell him where Russ had taken Chloe. "Alberto!" He shouted. "Won't Alberto be upset when he learns you let an innocent young woman die!"

Wheezie's mask slipped and all traces of her joker smile vanished. "Al's gone."

"So you were never together? That was all a lie?"

The old woman's face crumpled. "He got married when I was about twenty-two. Had a bunch of kids and lived right down the street and I loved him the whole time. Once I gave him my heart, it was his." Her eyes were filled with pain. "Not long ago, he moved away. I had nothin' left to live for. Not even the sight of him walkin' outside to collect his mail."

Her suffering was palpable. Even though he struggled against the feelings of pity that rose within him, he couldn't help but wish Wheezie's life had turned out differently. Betrayed by her own sister, she had lived out the rest of her days as a lonely, bitter woman, and during her time in Natchez, she had somehow made a connection with another victim of Paulette Martin's duplicity. Perhaps Wheezie's discovery that she had a terminal form of brain cancer came at the same time as Milla's invitation to join her in Quincy's Gap to celebrate her wedding. The old woman probably viewed the situation as providential, and she and Russ had acted immediately, obtaining him a position at the goat farm so that he might create bacteria-laden chicken eggs.

"How did you make sure Russ and Milla would cross paths?" he asked.

"Russ talked to her outside the grocery store. He'd worked on a bunch of farms in Mississippi and knew his stuff. Made some goat's milk samples and handed 'em out when Milla went shoppin'. He knew she'd be there 'cause he followed her." Wheezie snorted. "I just love her purple van. So, so pretty. And makin' bad eggs is easy. Start with bad hens, let the eggs sit in poop, and smear on some turtle dung for extra measure."

James recalled the website's warning about reptiles carrying the salmonella bacteria. The image of the pair of turtle shells resting on the wood pile outside the cabin at the Cornflower Goat Farm made him shiver.

Yet Wheezie's mention of her youngest sister gave James an idea, a definitive line of attack. "What about Milla? Your sweet, lovable sister, who has done *nothing* to harm you or Russ, is bearing the brunt of your selfish actions. Sure, Paulette hurt you. No one could argue that she did you a great wrong, but you're destroying Milla's happiness because you're hell-bent on revenge." Pointing at Milla as she hugged one of her students, James growled, "Does *she* deserve this misery?"

Wheezie waved decisively in her sister's direction. "Milla was always sugar and spice and everything *nice.* I can't help that she wanted to be friends with Patty or that these things had to be tidied up durin' her weddin'." She sighed heavily. "I'm wore out, boy. No more talkin' now. I'm gonna sit back in my chair until they come for me."

And with that, she shuffled back to her seat, looking older than she had at the beginning of the party. There was a sickly, almost greenish tinge to her skin, and the loose skin below her eyes seemed almost bruised.

Once again, James's feet seemed glued to the floor.

"James!" Lucy yelled as she rushed back into the hall. "We've got Chloe! She's all right!"

Running toward his friend, James gripped her by the hand. "What happened?"

Lucy breathed in a deep draught of air and then expelled it. "Russ was hiding in Milla's van. Someone must have taken the keys from her purse and hid them somewhere where he could get them. Chloe believed she was needed to carry a wedding gift to the van, but when she opened the rear doors, Russ pulled her inside, tied her up, and drove off."

"What was Donovan doing?" James spluttered. "Taking a nap?"

"Chasing a red herring," Lucy answered. "Russ gave a teenage boy fifty bucks to wear a hooded sweatshirt and slink around the perimeter of the church. Donovan was on him like sugar on a donut."

Cocking his head at the odd expression, James momentarily lost his train of thought.

"So Russ made his getaway, but he didn't get far." Lucy seemed reluctant to deliver a more explicit explanation.

"Why not?" James demanded.

"Lottie heard Donovan screaming into his radio and, thinking she'd heard a future headline coming across her scanner, jumped in her car and headed over here like an Indy driver on uppers." Lucy edged her way to the punch bowl. "We got lucky, because her maniacal driving caused her to crash into the van. Not hard, mind you, but with enough force to send Russ into a ditch. The sheriff heard the noise, radioed us, and we got there in time to apprehend our murderer. Donovan actually got to perform a piledriver on the guy."

Absurdly, James looked out the nearest window, but couldn't see a thing through the tinted glass. "Where is Russ now?"

Lucy scowled. "With Huckabee. The sheriff wants to play the hero this time. It's an election year, after all." Serving herself some virgin punch, she drank down a cupful in several thirsty swallows. "Of course

Donovan's there too."

James pulled a chair over to the table, sank into it, and served himself a full glass of spiked punch. "You've still got a major role to perform, Lucy. Huckabee's only got one of two guilty parties down at the station." He quickly explained Wheezie's role in the killings.

"Some dying wish," Lucy mumbled when he was through. "Her sister invited her to a wedding and she came to seek out revenge? Aren't people supposed to live their last days giving to charities, jumping out of airplanes, and making peace with enemies?"

"In a perfect world, yes." James slurped more punch, welcoming the warmth the champagne and brandy were creating in his stomach. *A third glass should knock out the jitters,* he thought and poured again.

Lucy placed her hand on James's shoulder. "This will be the hardest arrest I've ever made."

James was surprised by this statement. "Why? She's expecting it. I doubt she's going to struggle or make a dash for the back door."

"That's not what I meant." Lucy's blue eyes were sorrowful. "I've got to bring an old, dying woman to jail. A woman who's wasted her life because of some *man.*" She removed her hand from James's arm. "That'll never be me, I tell you. My life belongs to nobody else *but* me."

James watched her walk away. He reflected that he couldn't agree with Lucy's sentiment, as he wanted nothing more than to belong with someone and to have that person belong with him. He *wanted* to need someone, to love someone so completely that he wasn't fulfilled without that person nearby.

Eliot's sweet face rose in his mind, and James felt revitalized by the mere thought of him.

Searching for Jackson and Milla, James saw them standing near the doorway, speaking to Lindy, Gillian, and Bennett.

"My family," he whispered. "I'd be nothing without them. Nothing at all."

As he didn't want Milla to see Lucy take Wheezie away, James slapped his cup on the table and hurried over to his parents. Handing his father the keys to the Bronco, he ordered them to go straight home.

"Russ has been caught and Chloe's just fine," he told Milla when she began to protest. "I'll check on her right away, and then I'll call and tell you what I know."

"All I know is my darling van's been in an accident! But your friends are telling me that reporter girl actually saved my niece's life by crashing into it." She rubbed her eyes wearily. "Jackson, honey. I had no idea that living in Quincy's Gap was going to be so . . . so exhausting!"

"Take Milla home, Pop. I'll take care of everything here."

With his parents gone, James relaxed a little. Lucy had thoughtfully waited for them to drive off before helping Wheezie into her coat and leading her by the arm to the Jeep. Anyone observing the two of them would simply believe Lucy was kindly chauffeuring an old and rather inebriated woman back to her hotel. In fact, most of the guests left the party without having the slightest clue that something other than the celebration of wedding nuptials had occurred.

"Is there anything we can do?" Lindy asked James once all the guests were gone. "The twins left to look after Lottie, and we can take down the decorations tomorrow . . ."

"You should all get some rest." James embraced Lindy and Gillian and slapped Bennett on the back. "I'll go down to the station because Wheezie confessed to me, and if she's gone quiet all of a sudden, I'll be able to fill them in on how she and Russ DuPont killed Paulette and Chase." He rubbed his tired eyes. "Besides, I think I'll bring Chloe to my parent's house to sleep. My old room still has a bed in it and she might not want to be alone tonight."

"The poor girl must have been terrified!" Gillian exclaimed. "She'll need to be completely cleansed of this experience. Perhaps I should drop by early in the morning with some incense and tea."

"Pop wouldn't let you in bearing those items," James said with a smile, and he then felt a wave of affection for his friends sweep over him. "Before you all go, I want to say thank you. Not just for throwing this party, but for always being there for me. You're the best friends a guy could have."

Lindy's eyes grew wet with tears. "And this is what friends do, James! We support each other, protect one another, and stick together no matter what." She put her arm around his waist. "This investigation's had an ugly ending, but we'll get through it. If you or Milla or Chloe need anything, remember that we're just a phone call away."

On their way out the door, James saw Gillian walk over and lay a hand on the cold glass of the stained window depicting a lion and a lamb. The animals were resting on their bellies with their heads bent toward one another.

"What a tragedy," he heard her say. "Revenge could never have brought them peace. Only forgiveness can do that. And now the *ripples* of violence have spread out across the surface of our little pond."

"Woman, there ain't gonna be no more ripples," Bennett declared firmly. "What there's gonna be is more snow. Come on, I'll take you home."

Home is all James wanted too. The only furniture he could afford in his new bedroom was a bed and a single nightstand, but he had slept soundly for the past two nights and would like nothing more than to crawl between his soft sheets and roll himself like an enchilada inside his down comforter. Instead, he took the stuffed trash bags out of the kitchen and placed them in cans outside the back door, turned the lights off, and headed to the jail.

Deputy Glenn Truett directed him to a small office, recorded his statement, and gave him a few papers to sign. Knowing that James would ask, Glenn told him that Lucy, Donovan, and Huckabee were busy interviewing Wheezie and Russ DuPont.

"I've never even seen this guy," James muttered darkly as he handed Glenn the forms. "That makes everything that's happened to us since before Christmas feel unresolved. I mean, Russ DuPont's murdered two members of Milla's family, yet he's still a total stranger to me. To all of us."

Glenn stood and escorted James toward the station's front door. "You're not gonna see him now either." His mouth formed a conspiratorial smile. "I *will* tell you that he's a nasty piece of work. He's back there rantin' away with Donovan and Huckabee. Shoutin' and carryin' on somethin' fierce." He opened the door for James and gestured for him to leave. "So you can see him all you want at the trial, though it's gonna be a short one. Twelve kindergartners could pronounce that boy guilty in about five minutes."

"And Wheezie?" James couldn't help himself, but he hated to think of the old woman lying in a jail cell, her body aching and her mind addled.

"I imagine she'll be in some kind of hospital by tomorrow. She ain't well, and we can't give her any of the drugs she says she needs." Glenn held out his hand, allowing a cluster of snowflakes to fall like confetti on his palm. "It's right hard to see the state the old lady's in, but if you take up a sword against justice, you gotta pay the price."

Eyeing Glenn with interest, James also

reached out into the snow. "I'd like to take Chloe to my parents' house. Can't I at least wait for her?"

Glenn shook his head. "She's gonna be a while, but I'll run her over there myself. You have my word on that. Goodnight, Professor."

James drove home through empty, slick streets. His body was beyond tired and it felt good to slip off his clothes and put on a pair of flannel pajamas, but his mind was too unsettled for sleep. Knowing what Gillian would recommend, he boiled some water and, after fixing himself a cup of chamomile tea, sat down at the kitchen table. He turned off all the lights and sipped his tea while gazing out the window at the snow.

"Tomorrow, everything will look fresh again," he whispered, knowing that the picturesque scene he and his friends and family would wake to might serve as a slight restorative, but the days and weeks ahead would be filled with pushy reporters, questioning neighbors, and court dates.

Normally, James would have trudged to bed feeling gloomy at the thought of such challenges, but the clouds on the horizon were silver-lined. Milla would hurt, but she had Jackson to comfort her. Lindy had Luis, and Bennett, Gillian. Lucy claimed to be completely fulfilled by her job and if that were truly the case, then her February would be both busy and rewarding.

And I have a new mother, four best friends, and Jane and Eliot to see me through, he thought, wrapping himself in the knowledge that he was loved by such a remarkable group of individuals.

As their precious faces floated through his mind, sleep sneaked into James's room and carried him away.

EPILOGUE:
CONVERSATION HEARTS

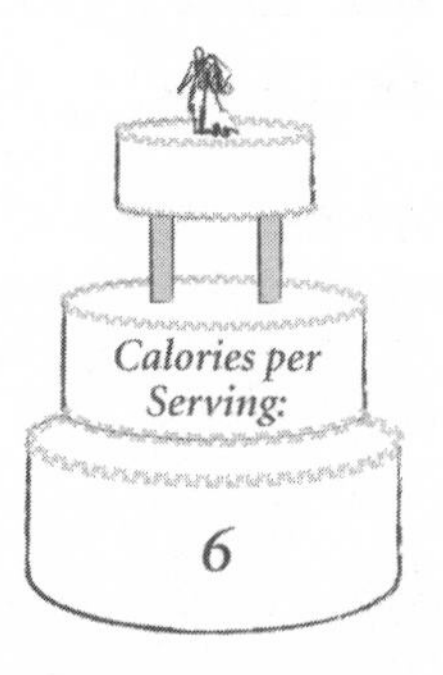

James checked his watch again. It was almost five in the afternoon, and he was itching to leave the library. However much he loved his job, he was much more excited by the prospect of being the first person to step inside Quincy's Whimsies before tomorrow's Valentine's Day grand opening.

He was just about to head back to his office in order to collect his coat and lunch box when Lottie walked through the front door. James had only spoken the words "no comment" to Scott's former flame as she'd been relentlessly harassing the Henry clan in an attempt to obtain a statement about Russ and Wheezie's arrests. After calling James at home and at work, staking out the library, and even accosting him in the grocery store, the pushy reporter was one of the last people James wanted to see.

"Don't you dare come in here and start pestering me. I've told you before that if you want the story on Russ and Wheezie to go ask them yourself. I won't set eyes on Russ until our court date, so just drop it," he growled as soon as she approached the desk. "You're a pariah, you know."

Lottie held up a red gift bag in one hand and made a peace sign with the other. "I'm not going to ask you about the murders anymore. Murphy's back in town, and she's taken over the story and everything else." Her tone belied a hint of resentment. "I'm back to covering dog shows and farm auctions, even though I ran the whole paper while she was off on her book tour."

"I guess journalism is a cutthroat business, even in a small town," James replied without sympathy.

To his surprise Lottie declared, "Well, *this* reporter is moving to a new small town. I still want to work at a newspaper, but not if I lose everyone I care about in the process."

"Where are you going?"

Lottie smiled. "To Warren County. It's far enough away that I won't offend people in this town anymore, but close enough for me to see Scott. That is, *if* he'll see me."

"You moved for Scott's sake?" James was impressed. Maybe there was more to Lottie than he thought.

"Is he here?" She looked around nervously. "I've got something for him before I go."

James pointed to the section of audiobooks. "He's putting some new materials on the shelves. You can't see him from here because he's deep in the stacks, probably busy in the nonfiction section."

As Lottie moved off, James saw Mrs. Waxman removing a pair of galoshes in the lobby. "All that melting snow! It makes such a mess," she said as she breezed past the security gate. "And it's supposed to drop below the freezing mark tonight. I certainly hope the sun comes out for Milla's big day tomorrow."

"Me too. I'm going to check weather.com before I leave." James darted back to his office and examined the local forecast for the upcoming weekend. He *was* interested in the freeze warnings, but he was also reticent to leave Scott without knowing whether the young man would need someone to talk to. Francis was off on an office-supply run and probably wouldn't return for another half an hour, so if Scott required a sympathetic listener, James was it.

Relieved to discover the sun was supposed to make an early appearance the next day, James read some uninteresting e-mails and was just about to shut down his computer when Scott entered the room. Smiling, he pointed at the red gift bag.

"Look who came back to us, Professor!" He whipped Glowstar out of the bag with a flourish. "He's had quite an adventure! Hey, *that* could be a cool video game. *Where's the Elf? A Holiday Scavenger Hunt.* I'll have to bat the idea around with Francis."

"I'm very glad to lay eyes on our resident elf again," James answered, searching Scott's face. "But I'm more pleased to see *you* happy. It hasn't been the easiest winter for you."

Scott collapsed into one of the chairs facing James's desk. "You and me both." He dug around inside the bag again. "Lottie asked for a second chance, Professor. And you know, I'm going to give it to her. I really, really like her, despite how she's acted." He shrugged. "We're in our twenties. That's when people are supposed to make big mistakes while they're figuring out what kind of lives they want to lead, right?"

James laughed. "I don't think there's an age cap on mistakes, Scott. But if you truly care about her, then you've made a good decision."

"Thanks, Professor. I knew I'd have your support." He pried the lid off a box of chocolates and offered them to James. "Lottie and Willow have been hanging out lately. Willow taught her how to make truffles. Awesome, huh? Want one?"

It took a masterful effort for James to shake his head. "I'd better not. When I saw Dr. Ruth yesterday, I was two pounds heavier than when I first met with her."

"Well, you *have* been through the wringer, Professor. So you ate a pizza or a piece of cake here and there. It's not like you did drugs or turned to liquor when things got tough."

Smiling, James said, "That's pretty much what Dr. Ruth said. Besides, I plan to get back on track. I *am* totally motivated. I want to be able to chase Eliot around the yard in the spring, dash through the sprinkler in the summer, and dive into big piles of leaves in the fall."

"Ah, speaking of time flying." Scott gestured at his watch. "I know you've got someplace to be and that you were just waiting to see if I was all right. Thank you for that, Professor."

"You can make it up to me tomorrow. Buy Lottie's Valentine's gift from Quincy's Whimsies!" James said, threw on his coat, and drove half a mile to Milla's new store. He parked right in front and knocked on the locked door.

Willow opened it a crack and whispered, "Milla just got here. She went to visit her sister in the prison hospice again."

"She's a saint," James murmured. "Did she read to her again?"

"Yes. Walt Whitman and the Bible. Wheezie's been speaking to Reverend Emerson too. There's been a lot of talk between the three of them about forgiveness. So there you have it. Milla's a saint *and* a magician. Wait until I turn on all the lights and then you can see for yourself."

James turned his back to allow Willow to make her preparations. "Come in, darling!" Milla's voice called out and James stepped into a fantasy land.

His first impression was of rainbows. The entire ceiling had been covered by lengths of gauzy fabric in vibrant colors and the carpet below was awash in pools of colored light. Plain white shelves were stocked with beautiful handmade pottery, candles, and luxurious bath products. A picnic table to the left of the entrance was covered with Valentine's Day–themed gift baskets for men, women, and children. As James moved deeper into the store, he noticed that Milla had decided to incorporate a section of locally crafted toys. He ran his palm over a hand-carved wooden train, a checkerboard, and a display of puzzles featuring several popular children's names.

On a wall above the toys hung darling artist smocks, bibs, and burp cloths. The children's apparel merged into a beautiful assortment of aprons, tea towels, and embroidered hand towels. Floral and toile oven mitts and potholders came next, and it wasn't until James wove his way back to the center of the store that he noticed the lengthy glass case stuffed with candy, jams, and sauces.

"I knew I smelled chocolate!" he said, inhaling the divine scent.

"Free samples for our first fifty customers!" Milla trilled and handed James a plastic bag tied with a pink ribbon containing several chocolate hearts.

James embraced his stepmother. "This place *is* magical! You did it, Milla! No one will be able to resist this store!"

"I hope not," Milla replied with a twinkle in her eye. "Because my life's savings is invested in this place. But it'll be worth every cent when I see my grandson's face when he comes through that door."

"Then you'd better look sharp," Willow warned. "I see the Volvo pulling into a parking space."

"Oh my stars!" Milla patted her puffy hair, touched her pink-flushed cheeks, and smoothed her apron, which was covered by red hearts on a field of chocolate brown.

Jane and Eliot slowly opened the front door and craned their necks as they tried to absorb all the colors and products around them. Eliot bypassed the gifts and toys and headed right for the candy counter.

"Grandma!" he yelled. "Is all this candy yours?"

Milla chuckled as she gathered the boy in her arms. "No, dear. Grandma's selling it. But you can have a *small* bag of *whatever* candy you want." She looked over Eliot's head at Jane. "I'll let your mama decide how much you can eat before dinner."

Eliot jumped up and down in excitement and then instantly grew still as he examined the selection of truffles, heart-shaped chocolates, rock-candy lollipops, toffee bites, chocolate-dipped strawberries and apricots, and oversized conversation hearts. "I like the hearts with the words, Grandma."

"One order of hearts with words coming right up!" Milla buried a silver scoop into the tray of hearts and dropped the pastel candies into a bag. As she prepared to tie the sack with the store's signature pink ribbon, Eliot ran behind the counter and cried, "Wait!"

Concerned, Milla bent down and said, "What's wrong?"

Eliot gestured for her to come closer, and then he leaned forward and whispered in her ear. Milla nodded in understanding, grinning at being in on a secret. "Got it." She rummaged through Eliot's bag and then placed a single green heart into the boy's hand.

Walking purposefully to the front of the counter, Eliot marched up to James and beckoned for him to come down to his level. James immediately acquiesced and then followed Eliot's command to hold out one of his hands.

Eliot placed the green heart, which read *Love Ya,* in the center of James's palm and said, "This is for you, Daddy."

A bolt of joy shot through James. Daddy! It was the first time Eliot had called him that. Tears sprang into his eyes and blurred the image of the green heart.

"Is it okay if I keep this instead of eating it?" he asked his son when he could speak.

"Sure, Daddy." Unaware of the happiness he had given his father, Eliot then ran over to his mother and gave her a white heart. She kissed him on the cheek and popped the heart in her mouth. While Milla showed him the wooden toys, Jane took James's trembling hand.

"I will *never* grow tired of hearing him say that," James whispered to Jane and wiped his eyes.

Jane smiled. "I do believe it's time to host a sleepover. Is tomorrow too soon?"

"No," James answered. "Tomorrow is perfect."

The next day, there was a line of people waiting to be let inside Quincy's Whimsies. Whether it was the ad in the *Star* announcing free samples of chocolate or the bright winter sunshine that caused people to show up en masse by ten o'clock in the morning, James drove by a sidewalk crowded with potential customers and honked his horn at his friends and neighbors.

He spent the day assembling a wooden bookshelf to hold Eliot's books, which he then covered with two coats of forest green paint. When Eliot arrived, James led him into the kitchen and the two of them cooked up some herb chicken nuggets and heart-shaped sugar cookies. After a dinner of nuggets dipped in honey mustard and a side of peas, James allowed Eliot to frost a heart cookie and cover the icing with red, pink, and white sprinkles.

"Can I play Legos before bed?" Eliot asked once all that remained of his cookie was a pile of crumbs.

"Let's get teeth brushed and pajamas on first. Then you can play while I clean up the kitchen."

Ten minutes later, while James sang "Five Little Monkeys Jumping on the Bed," Eliot had brushed his teeth and changed into his stegosaurus pajamas. In his room, Eliot removed *Curious George Goes to the Library* from his overnight bag and tossed it on the bed. "That's for later. Right now I'm gonna build a store like Grandma's."

"And I'm going to clean up. Later gator." James returned to the kitchen and hummed to himself as he loaded the dishwasher and sorted through a pile of mail. He picked up Friday's paper, which featured a mug shot of Russ DuPont on the cover and a headline reading "The Diva's Killer Gets Life." The article rehashed previous stories detailing how Paulette and Chase had died, profiles of Russ and Wheezie, and statements from guests at Milla and Jackson's party as well as those from the Sheriff's Department.

Lucy was quoted frequently, and she had told James she enjoyed being the official spokesperson for her department. Lucy wasn't the only one who was doing well. In fact, all the supper club members appeared to have recovered from their latest investigation and were looking forward to an uneventful February.

"This case was weird," Lindy had remarked at the last dinner meeting. "We didn't have a moment's contact with the murderer. It almost makes it harder to close the book on the whole thing."

"Well, Chloe had contact with him and *she* doesn't seem the worse for wear," Bennett had added. "What's a little car crash in exchange for your life and a bank account stuffed with a million dollars?"

Indeed, when Milla and James had driven Chloe to the airport, the young woman had seemed absolutely fine. Her whiny tone had completely evaporated, and she was filled with a renewed sense of hope and energy. She assured them that Paulette's money would be put to good use and that hundreds of Florida's marine animals would benefit from Chloe's newfound wealth.

Milla had watched Chloe walk resolutely inside the terminal and then had turned to James and said, "I'm ready to start over too, dear. Let's get back to Quincy's Gap and do just that."

Recalling her words, James folded the paper in two and threw it in the recycling bin. The paper landed on top of an invitation to listen to Murphy Alistair read from her novel and to hear a teaser from her upcoming work, *The Body in the Diet Center.*

James started the dishwasher and put the heart cookies in the monkey-shaped cookie jar Jane had given him for Valentine's Day. He took one last glance around the warm, clean room and then went down the hall to read a bedtime story to the love of his life.

ACKNOWLEDGMENTS

The author would like to thank, in no particular order, the following friends: Mary Shirley Harrison, Anne Briggs, Holly Hudson, Jessica Faust, Diane Williamson, Bill Krause, Karl Anderson, Marissa Pederson, the Cozy Chicks, and the lovely folks of the Yahoo! Groups: Cozy Discussion, Cozy Mystery Korner, and Cozy Armchair Group.

ABOUT THE AUTHOR

J. B. Stanley has a BA in English from Franklin & Marshall College, an MA in English Literature from West Chester University, and an MLIS from North Carolina Central University. She taught sixth grade language arts in Cary, North Carolina, for the majority of her eight-year teaching career. Raised an antique lover by her grandparents and parents, Stanley also worked part-time in an auction gallery. An eBay junkie and food lover, Stanley now lives in Richmond, Virginia, with her husband, two young children, and three cats. Visit her website at www.jbstanley.com.

We hope you have enjoyed this Large Print book. Other Thorndike, Wheeler, Kennebec, and Chivers Press Large Print books are available at your library or directly from the publishers.

For information about current and upcoming titles, please call or write, without obligation, to:

Publisher
Thorndike Press
295 Kennedy Memorial Drive
Waterville, ME 04901
Tel. (800) 223-1244

or visit our Web site at:

http://gale.cengage.com/thorndike

OR

Chivers Large Print
published by BBC Audiobooks Ltd
St James House, The Square
Lower Bristol Road
Bath BA2 3SB
England
Tel. +44(0) 800 136919
email: bbcaudiobooks@bbc.co.uk
www.bbcaudiobooks.co.uk

All our Large Print titles are designed for easy reading, and all our books are made to last.